THE KING'S RETRIBUTION

Book Two of
The Plantagenet Legacy

BOOKS BY MERCEDES ROCHELLE

Heir to a Prophecy

The Last Great Saxon Earls Series
Godwine Kingmaker
The Sons of Godwine
Fatal Rivalry

The Plantagenet Legacy Series
A King Under Siege
The King's Retribution

THE KING'S RETRIBUTION

Book Two of
The Plantagenet Legacy

Mercedes Rochelle

Cover art: King Richard II is taken into the Tower of London as a
prisoner. Jean Froissart, Chroniques (the 'Harley Froissart') (Frossart's
chronicles). Volume IV, part 2. S. Netherlands (Bruges), 1470-1475.
Source: Harley 4380, f.181v (detail). Reproduced by courtesy of The
British Library Board

CAST OF CHARACTERS

ANNE OF BOHEMIA, QUEEN OF ENGLAND, First wife of Richard II

ARUNDEL, RICHARD FITZALAN, 4th EARL OF, 9th Earl of Surrey, Brother of Thomas Arundel, One of the Appellants in 1387-88

ARUNDEL, THOMAS, BISHOP OF ELY, later Archbishop of Canterbury and Lord Chancellor of England, Brother of Richard Arundel

ARUNDEL, THOMAS FITZALAN, 5th EARL OF, 10th Earl of Surrey, son of Richard Arundel

AUMALE, EDWARD DUKE OF: See Rutland, Edward

BEAUFORT, JOHN, EARL OF SOMERSET, Eldest son of John of Gaunt and Katherine Swynford, one of the Counter-Appellants of 1397, created Marquis of Dorset in 1397* (reverts to earl 1399)

BOLINGBROKE, HENRY, DUKE OF HEREFORD, Earl of Derby, future King of England (Henry IV). Son of John of Gaunt, One of the Appellants in 1387-88

DESPENSER, THOMAS, one of the Counter-Appellants of 1397, earl of Gloucester 1397* (deprived 1399)

GAUNT, JOHN OF, 1st DUKE OF LANCASTER, Third surviving son of Edward III and uncle of King Richard

GLOUCESTER, THOMAS OF WOODSTOCK, 1st DUKE OF, 1st Earl of Buckingham, 1st Earl of Essex, youngest son of Edward III and uncle of King Richard, One of the Appellants in 1387-88

HENRY IV: See Bolingbroke

HOLLAND, JOHN, EARL OF HUNTINGDON, younger brother of Thomas and half-brother of King Richard II through his mother Joan of Kent, one of the Counter-Appellants of 1397, Duke of Exeter 1397* (reverts to earl, 1399), Chamberlain of England 1389

HOLLAND, THOMAS, 2nd EARL OF KENT, 3rd Baron Holand, half-brother of Richard II through his mother Joan of Kent

HOLLAND, THOMAS the YOUNGER, 3rd EARL OF KENT, one of the Counter-Appellants of 1397, 1st Duke of Surrey 1397* (reverts to earl, 1399), 4th Baron Holand, eldest son of Thomas Holland

HOTSPUR: See Percy, Sir Henry

HUMPHREY, 2nd EARL OF BUCKINGHAM, son of Thomas of Woodstock Duke of Gloucester

ISABELLA OF VALOIS, Queen of England (married 1396 aged 7), daughter of Charles VI of France

KENT, EARL OF: See Holland, Thomas

LeSCROPE, WILLIAM, one of the Counter-Appellants of 1397, Earl of Wiltshire 1397*, Lord High Treasurer 1398

MARCH, EARL OF, see Mortimer, Roger

MORTIMER, ROGER, 4th Earl of March and 6th Earl of Ulster, grandson of Lionel of Antwerp (3rd son of Edward III) through his mother Philippa. Thought by many to be the heir presumptive to the throne after Richard.

MORTIMER, THOMAS, illegitimate son of Roger Mortimer, 2nd Earl of March, associated with the Lords Appellant. Uncle to Roger Mortimer.

MOWBRAY, THOMAS DE, 1st DUKE OF NORFOLK, 1st Earl of Nottingham, 3rd Earl of Norfolk, 6th Baron Mowbray, 7th Baron Segrave, Earl Marshal, One of the Counter-Appellants in 1387-88

NORTHUMBERLAND, HENRY PERCY, 1st EARL OF, 4th Baron Percy

PERCY, SIR HENRY a.k.a. HOTSPUR: Son of the Earl of Northumberland

PERCY, THOMAS, 1st EARL OF WORCESTER, younger brother of the Earl of Northumberland, later Vice-Chamberlain to Richard II

RICHARD II, KING OF ENGLAND, son of Edward Plantagenet the Black Prince and Joan of Kent

RICHARD ARUNDEL: see Arundel

RUTLAND, EDWARD, Earl of, eldest son of Edmund Langley, Duke of York. One of the Counter-Appellants of 1397, Duke of Aumale (or Aumerle or Albemarle) in 1397* (reverts to earl, 1399), later Earl of Cambridge 1402, 2nd Duke of York 1402

SALISBURY, JOHN DE MONTACUTE or MONTAGU, 3rd Earl, one of the Counter-Appellants of 1397, accompanied Richard to Ireland in 1395

SCROPE, WILLIAM, see LeScrope, William

SOMERSET: see Beaufort, John

THOMAS OF WOODSTOCK: see Gloucester

WARWICK, THOMAS DE BEAUCHAMP, 12TH EARL OF, One of the Appellants in 1387-88

WESTMORLAND, RALPH NEVILLE, 1st EARL OF, created in 1397, rival northern earl to the Percies, brother in-law to Henry IV

WOODSTOCK, THOMAS OF: see Gloucester

YORK, EDMUND OF LANGLEY, 1st DUKE OF, Fourth surviving son of Edward III and uncle of King Richard

*To save the reader the confusion I experienced trying to keep these dukes and earls created in 1397 (then deprived in 1399) straight, I have decided to refer to them throughout by their original titles, with rare exceptions.

Map of
England

Map by Gregg Sollisch

*Sage and elegant, lawfully Richard II,
conquered by fate he lies here depicted beneath
this marble. He was truthful in discourse and
full of reason: Tall in body, he was prudent in
his mind as Homer. He showed favour to the
Church, he overthrew the proud and threw
down anybody who violated the royal
prerogative. He crushed heretics and laid low
their friends. O merciful Christ, to whom he
was devoted, may you save [Richard], through
the prayers of the Baptist, whom he esteemed.*

*(Inscription around the ledge of Richard's tomb
in Westminster Abbey, commissioned by himself
1396-99)*

CHAPTER 1

It was early June. The roses were in full bloom and the air was heavy with the scent of honeysuckle. Richard and Anne were walking in the garden of their private royal pavilion called La Neyt, on an island across from Sheen Palace. Anne bent over to sniff one of the blossoms when suddenly she tripped to the side, falling against her husband. He was quick to catch her, but as he tried to straighten she had already lost consciousness.

Scooping the queen into his arms, Richard strode into the building. "Help me," he cried, placing Anne carefully on the bed. "Help, the queen has fainted." Her lady's maids ran into the room as he stepped aside. They did their best to loosen her garments, though her head lolled and her arms were heavy. "Careful," Richard murmured, bending over the bed and trying to support her. As another servant came up the king looked at him frantically. "Send for Master Pol. Hurry."

The man turned and rushed from the room as Richard took hold of Anne's shoulders, pulling her toward him so the laces could be loosened. He buried his face in her hair. "What ails you, my love? What has happened?" More women came forward and he left them to their work, getting up and standing helplessly against the wall. They finally succeeded in pulling off her outer dress and tucking the queen into the bed. The physician came into the room and passed by the king without seeing him. Satisfied for the moment, Anne's ladies moved aside while he put a hand to her forehead, then an ear to her chest, listening.

"She's feverish," he muttered.

"It happened so suddenly," Richard said and the doctor swung around, startled.

"Oh, sire. I'm sorry. I didn't see you."

Richard moved toward the bed. "What could it be?"

The physician moved her head and she let out a little groan. "My dear," Richard said, sitting next to her. "Can you hear me?"

Anne blinked. "Richard. I feel so faint. I am so tired."

"Shh. Don't push yourself. I'm here." He looked at the physician.

The man shrugged. "I would have to say there's an imbalance of humors in her body. We must check her urine. Then we should let some blood."

Richard knew nothing about medical procedures; he nodded in agreement. "Come," he gestured to the maids. "The physician needs her water."

As Master Pol went off to prepare his tools, together they coaxed the queen out of bed. The physician came back shortly with a specially shaped glass to collect a sample, then left the room to give Anne privacy. Taking the queen behind a screen, the maids did what was necessary, but they soon called the king for help. They were having difficulty holding Anne up and she moaned as he put her arm around his neck. Picking her up again, he laid her gently on the feather mattress. He removed his outer garments and crawled into bed, taking Anne into his arms. She laid her head on his shoulder but couldn't stay in that position for long; her breathing was too labored.

When the physician returned, he shook his head. "Sire, she might be contagious. You could get ill."

"It is no matter. She needs me."

The other sighed, knowing that if the king died, he would probably follow in short order—not by natural causes. Resignedly, he laid out a cloth on the bed and lined up his blades before taking the flask, holding it before a candle and studying its color. Tilting the glass, he sniffed before dipping his finger into the urine and tasting it.

"You see it is reddish," he said to Richard. He glanced at the maids. "Is she having her monthly course?" The women shook their heads. "Then we must conclude there is too much heat in the liver. I recommend bloodletting to help balance the humors."

"Do what you must." The king paid little attention to the procedure, concentrating instead on Anne's comfort. The doctor performed his ministrations quickly and efficiently. He tied her

2

arm above the elbow, then straightened it over a bowl and made a slight cut into her vein. A small red stream ran into the dish. When he felt enough blood had been shed, he loosened the tie and bound the small wound.

"I will examine the urine after it has cured overnight," Master Pol said. "I will return in the morning."

Richard nodded, kissing Anne on the forehead. "You must get well," he whispered.

Her eyes fluttered open. "Richard," she said faintly. "Something is very wrong with me. I think I'm dying."

"Shh. Don't speak so."

She took an uneven breath. "Call a priest, my dear. Don't let me die unshriven."

"That won't be necessary. But don't fret. As you wish." He turned, beckoning to one of the ladies. "Summon the queen's confessor."

The maid ran from the room and he put an arm around her shoulders. "Now tell me, are you in pain?"

She nodded. "Down here." She put a hand on her lower belly. "I don't know what it is. Oh." A quick intake of breath alarmed Richard more than anything else. He stroked her hair. "Your priest is coming. He will pray for you."

"Listen to me," she gasped. "If I am gone, you mustn't lose your faith. I will be watching over you. Remember, you must be strong. Don't let your enemies find any reason to rebel against you. Be kind..."

"Shh. You are not going anywhere."

The priest hastened into the room and knelt beside the bed. "Your Grace, I'm here."

Anne turned toward Richard. "I won't need much time. Stay with me."

The king watched in disbelief while the last rites were given to his wife. As the minutes dragged on, her eyes got heavier and heavier, her breath even more labored; her voice shrunk to a whisper. The priest crossed himself, then kissed a crucifix, handing it to her. She placed it against her chest and closed her eyes.

"I thank you," Richard said. "I don't know why she thought she needed you. I will watch over her this night."

"God will watch over her, too, sire. I will pray for her."

Anne's breathing was even, so Richard leaned against the wall, prepared for a long night. She slept for a while then woke with a moan. Startled awake, Richard leaned over her.

"Hold me," she whispered.

Taking her into his arms, he murmured endearments. She put her hand on his cheek and sighed. But she didn't breathe in again.

Richard waited, terrified. He gave her a little shake and her hand fell to the pillow.

"Anne. Anne. Wake up." He shook her again and her head dropped to the side. "Anne. Don't leave me. Don't go." His voice was more insistent, but there was no response. "You can't leave me. You can't. I can't live without you." He held her tight, to no avail. Sobbing, he laid her back against the pillows.

Concerned by the king's voice, Anne's maids slipped into the room. He didn't notice them. Patting her on the face, Richard kept trying to revive her. "Wake up. Come back to me."

One of the ladies ran for the physician while the others gathered around the bed. Richard finally raised his head, tears streaming down his face. "It can't be. She can't be dead."

Master Pol stood in the doorway, unwilling to enter. "Come in, man," Richard growled. "You couldn't save her but at least you can determine whether she has fainted or has truly passed on."

The doctor knelt at the bedside and pulled a feather from his pouch, holding it in front of her nose. No movement. He lifted her eyelids, felt for her pulse, and turned to Richard with professional restraint. "God has taken her from us," he said sadly.

"It can't be true. You must bring her back. She can't be dead. We were just walking together in the garden."

By now, others had gathered inside the room. "Did she have the plague?" someone whispered.

"Who said that!" the king cried, whirling around. "Who dares speak so?"

The witnesses took a step back. *Why else would she have died so suddenly?*

4

"There is no one here with the plague!" Richard insisted. "No one!" Turning back to his wife, he took her hand in his. He could no longer deny what was obvious to everyone else. Throwing his head back, Richard let out a wail so chilling, that for a moment the others doubted his sanity. Then he threw himself on her body, taking her back into his arms and lifting her against his chest. "No! No!" he kept crying, over and over.

Nobody knew what to do. Richard had no one to console him. Everyone who had once been close to him had died, leaving the queen as his only companion. Even his beloved Robert de Vere had been dead for two years, killed on a boar hunt while still in exile. Queen Anne was his friend, his love, and his partner. She alone knew how to calm him when he was angry, to comfort him when he was sad, to laugh at his jokes and cry at his pain. And now she was no more and he was devastated.

Still weeping, he laid her back down. He knelt on the floor and leaned on the bed, burying his face in her hair. "My life is over," he sobbed. "What am I going to do?" The others watched him in silence.

Finally Thomas Percy, his steward, came into the chamber. He slipped over to the king and put both arms around his shoulders, whispering into his ear. Richard nodded, allowing himself to be pulled away. The growing crowd parted for the two of them.

Thomas rowed Richard back to the palace. The king was mostly unresponsive, and Thomas knew the best thing would be to give him a quiet place to grieve. He attended Richard by himself, helping him undress and ordering a sleeping draught, which the king took unresistingly. Lying down, Richard put his hands over his face.

"Let this all be a bad dream," he said, his voice muffled. "Or let me never wake up."

Pausing at the door, Thomas looked into the darkened room. His heart went out to this unhappy king. Richard was only twenty-seven years old, and once again he was alone. Anne was unable to give him children. His father died when Richard was only nine. His grandfather was feeble at the end of his life and barely recognized him. His mother was gone these last ten years.

Before Richard was even twenty the Lords Appellant destroyed what friendships he was able to cobble together. How does a man find consolation when he has no peers?

Richard might have been consoled had he known the extent of the mourning experienced by his whole household. But he could spare no emotion for anyone else. Queen Anne's embalmed body was brought over to the palace and for two months Richard kept watch whenever he could, speaking to her when he thought they were alone, lighting candles at night to keep the shadows away.

There was much to do. Richard sent out letters addressed to his barons and leading officials in London, requiring their attendance at her funeral: *"Our beloved companion the queen (whom God has hence commanded) will be buried at Westminster on Monday the third of August. We earnestly entreat that you (setting aside all excuses) will repair to our city of London the Wednesday previous. Bring with you our very dear kinswoman, your consort at the same time. We desire that you will, the preceding day, accompany the corpse of our dear queen from our manor of Shene to Westminster... Given under our privy seal, June 9, 1394..."*

The king spared no expense while planning the elaborate funeral. He ordered huge quantities of wax from Flanders for candles. Black robes and hoods were commissioned for all the nobles who would accompany the processional train. Elegant black horses were purchased to draw the funeral coach.

On Tuesday before the ceremony, Richard's uncles and barons arrived at Shene so they could accompany the queen to St. Paul's Cathedral; there she would lay in state. As expected, the barons brought their wives and households—many of whom had to be assigned lodging elsewhere. Richard made it a point to greet every one of them, graciously accepting their condolences. This was the time to bury old antagonisms—at least for a while.

Fortunately, the next day dawned warm and sunny and once they had broken their fast the attendees lined up for the procession. The men were to ride on horseback and the women in covered wagons behind the vehicle carrying Anne's coffin with its black canopy. The meticulously carved wooden effigy, draped in velvet robes, looked so realistic you could almost see it breathing. Every time Richard passed it, he looked aside, blinking back his tears.

On his way to the front of the cortège, the king paused next to John of Gaunt. "Where is the Earl of Arundel?" he asked angrily, looking around. He hated the man, but that didn't excuse the earl from attending. It was a matter of respect.

"Perhaps my brother knows," said John, gesturing to Gloucester. "They are friends."

Richard grimaced. He had no love for Thomas, Duke of Gloucester either. Although six years had passed since the terrible Merciless Parliament—six years while he pretended to forgive and forget in an effort to disarm his mortal enemies—the rancor he felt had not diminished. Gloucester was as arrogant as ever, and just as antagonistic. Kicking his horse forward, Richard decided to wait; Arundel might still join them en route.

Londoners lined the roads as the somber cavalcade walked the fourteen miles to St. Paul's. The king rode by himself, looking neither to the right nor the left. His priests, walking behind the funeral wagon, handed out alms, a customary safeguard to protect the dead against eternal unrest.

It was a tradition for medieval royalty to lay in state at St. Paul's Cathedral before moving on to their funeral at Westminster. This cathedral was the pride of England—one of the longest in Europe, famous for its impressive spire. The soaring nave was so huge it was named Paul's Walk and became a favorite meeting place to discuss business or catch up on the most recent news. Walking up and down, up and down, people strutted their latest fashions, gossiped, and even sought out prostitutes while pickpockets and petty thieves practiced their trade. Booksellers set up shop in the cathedral and outside in the churchyard, using St. Paul's as their permanent address.

But all this came to a temporary stop while the king's men cleared the space for Queen Anne's vigil. Once the funeral party reached the cathedral, Richard watched as six of his knights carried the queen inside. Placing her casket into the center of the nave, they stood guard for five days while large crowds of grieving subjects paid their last respects.

On the last day, Thomas Arundel, the Archbishop of York waited for the king to finish his prayers before the altar. He was preparing to preach the funeral sermon and wanted to discuss his choice of biblical passages. Richard had been kneeling for more than an hour, and when he finally rose to his feet, the tears were still running down his face. The archbishop felt a rare pang of sympathy for the king, but it didn't last. As soon as Richard saw him, he strode over in anger.

"Where is he? Where is your brother?"

Taken aback, Thomas almost put up his hands to ward off the king's temper.

"Sire, I haven't heard from him."

"How can he be so disrespectful?" Frowning, Richard waited for an answer.

"I can only assume he was delayed by urgent matters."

"This is unforgivable. He must be found."

Thomas bowed his head, forgetting about his mission. It was more important to get away from the king until he recovered his composure. For now, Richard must be forgiven his immoderate grief. Hopefully, it wouldn't last too long.

On Monday the third of August, the same cortège of important mourners made its way to Westminster. The monks and abbot met them halfway and led the procession to the abbey. Draped with the queen's coat of arms, Anne's coffin was brought through the great west door and placed before the altar. It seemed so tiny under the vaulted ceiling, flanked by huge pillars and gothic arches reaching to the heavens. The vast nave was soon crowded with standing attendees, and the roof echoed with *De Profundis*, chanted by a choir of young boys.

Halfway through the ceremony, Richard of Arundel entered with his immediate retinue, jostling their way through the congregation. At first, the king tried to ignore him, but couldn't concentrate on the services. He kept looking at Arundel, who spent much of his time whispering into his wife's ear.

After the sermon was over, there was a pause while the monks prepared the body for burial in Edward the Confessor's chapel behind the high altar. Richard was watching their efforts, dabbing his eyes with his handkerchief, when the Earl of Arundel stepped up beside him. The king turned, annoyed. Arundel didn't take notice. "Sire," he said, "I have urgent private business to attend and request that you excuse me from the rest of the ceremony."

For a moment the king stared at the earl in disbelief, his hand still. Even Arundel's stance was disrespectful, his arms crossed while those bulging pale blue eyes looked around the crowd as if searching for someone. Richard's handkerchief fell to the floor and he turned around, snatching a rod from one of the vergers who was trying to direct the participants. "How dare you!" Richard cried, and dealt the earl such a blow he fell to the floor, stunned. Blood flowed from his head spreading over the tiles like spilled red wine.

Gasps rent the air as people stepped back, startled by the king's rage. Trembling, Richard pointed at the prone earl. "Take this man to the Tower," he growled, and two of his knights stepped forward, dragging Arundel off the floor. Archbishop Thomas, drawn by the commotion, pursed his lips as he watched his brother get hauled away. He didn't dare object. Turning to the king, he said, "We will have to purify and reconsecrate the Abbey before we can continue."

Richard nodded. "Proceed at once."

This was a terrible inconvenience. The cathedral was crammed with people, the religious ceremony was finished and they had nothing more to do but entomb the body. Everyone was going to have to wait; there was nothing else to be done.

Edward of Rutland was one of the few who dared approach the king, who stood, for the moment, alone and haggard. If Robert de Vere had been here, he could have offered some comfort; but Robert's closeness to the king was the very reason he was driven into exile by the Lords Appellant. Over the last couple of years, Edward had slowly taken his place in Richard's affection—after all, he was the king's first cousin. Fortunately, he had not taken part in the Merciless Parliament, just six years before. He knew Richard had never forgiven his enemies for humiliating him. At least Rutland was blameless in that respect.

9

"Sire, perhaps you would like to sit," Edward said, pointing to the choir stalls built into the nearest wall. Nodding, Richard put an arm through his and together they walked across the floor as those who blocked their way parted, clearing a large path. For a few minutes Richard watched as the monks cleaned up the blood and washed the floor. Then he leaned back in the stall, closing his eyes.

"That man sets such a terrible example," he muttered. "He thinks he can show as much disrespect as he pleases, just because he was once my councilor in my youth."

Edward held his breath for a moment. Here was a perfect opportunity to strike a blow at this troublesome earl. Arundel was one of the wealthiest magnates in England—after Lancaster—and his power was almost unassailable. Except, of course, that he was one of the Lords Appellant, which put him forever at odds with the king. And here Arundel had just incurred his own self-inflicted wound. *Don't be too obvious*, he told himself. *Let the king come to his own conclusions.*

"There must be a way," Edward mused, "to raise you so high no one would dare offend against Your Majesty. I think we might enhance the vocabulary of kingship to distance you from your subjects—." He paused, daunted by his own words. Maybe he had gone too far.

Richard sat so long with his eyes closed that Edward wondered if he had even heard. But no, the king opened one eye and cocked his head. "Weighty words, cousin," he said. "In the days of Saint Edward the Confessor, when the king was closer to God, he was called Majesty. Did you know he was the first king of England to touch his poor subjects suffering from scrofula?"

"The king's evil? No, I did not."

"Because the king could cure that terrible skin disease by touch, it was proven that his right to rule was God-Given. Arundel would do well to remember that," he added bitterly. Then he fell into thought. "Majesty. Perhaps you are right." Edward watched as his mouth began to quiver. "I wonder what Anne would think."

Richard said no more, putting his hands in front of his face. When his shoulders began to shake, Edward got up and stood before him, trying to block everyone's view. At least he hoped so.

10

Richard's raw grief was painful to watch unless you were his enemy. And there were too many of those in the hall who didn't need to gloat.

The attendees waited until well after dark, while the extra wax ordered from Flanders was put to good use and greatly appreciated. Finally, shortly before midnight, the obsequies were finished and the exhausted mourners went home.

Accompanied by a small entourage, Richard walked from Westminster Abbey to the palace. En route, he summoned the captain of his guards. "Make sure the Earl of Arundel is comfortable, but he gets no visitors. Let him stew. He is permitted to send a messenger for his bond which I shall set at—" Richard made a wry glance at Rutland—"£40,000. That should teach him a lesson."

Even for Arundel, that was a small fortune. When he was finally released after an anxious week, he went home embittered, though no wiser for his experience. Although the king's behavior was remarked upon, it was generally believed Arundel deserved what he got.

CHAPTER 2

A stint in the Tower did nothing to curb Richard Arundel's behavior. As far as he was concerned, his rank carried certain privileges, and no one was going to tell him what to do—not that high-handed irresponsible sovereign, nor that overbearing John of Gaunt. The more Arundel thought about it, the more aggravated he became. Ever since Gaunt's aborted campaign in Castile—which had nothing to do with the French wars—Lancaster had switched his support to the king's senseless peace policy. It didn't matter to John that unemployed soldiers swarmed back to England—men without means of support and unsuited for gainful employment. The vast majority of disgruntled veterans went right back to Chester, bordering Arundel's territories. He had his hands full, dealing with the unrest.

No one really understood what Gaunt was planning next. As usual, rumors had a way of growing out of control, and the great Northern rising was no different from any other disturbances. Someone got the idea that John of Gaunt was taking the rule of France and Chester away from the king, and that he planned to do away with Chester's ancient liberties. Instigators nailed accusatory writings to parish church doors and sent them to adjacent counties, calling for help. And before long, thousands of armed men and archers gathered, terrorizing towns and wreaking havoc.

Arundel gathered together his own retinue of knights and squires and encamped with them at his castle of Holt on the Welsh march. He did not attempt to suppress the uprising, but merely lingered on its margins, waiting to see which way the winds would blow. Meanwhile, Gaunt was commissioned to pacify the rebels. It didn't take him long. Much to Arundel's disgust, through mild persuasion Lancaster offered employment to those who were willing to join his upcoming campaign in Aquitaine. The few remaining agitators were turned over to the king's justice, and no one sought to rescue them. The rebellion soon collapsed, though not before Gaunt was informed about Arundel's suspicious behavior.

The next Parliament brought their dispute into the open. John stood before all the great lords and archbishops and pointed a finger at the mulish earl, who sat with crossed arms and clenched teeth.

"I accuse this man of instigating the Cheshire uprising! I have proof that he summoned his knights to his castle of Holt in preparation for supporting the rebels."

Arundel leapt to his feet. "You lie! I gave no aid to the rebellion!"

"Then why did you not put it down? You were right there, yet I had to march west from Yorkshire!"

"By the time you put down the revolt, there was no need for my aid."

They went back and forth. It soon became clear that no evidence could be offered to support either side. The chancellor stood. "My lords, your objections have been duly noted."

Gaunt glared at the earl, but decided to sit.

Arundel, on the other hand, was just getting started. "My Lords, there are certain matters close to my heart that I cannot in good conscience conceal. I charge the Duke of Lancaster with usurping royal powers and oppressing both the king and the nobility!" He pointed at Gaunt, affecting concern and dismay. "My first charge is this: it is against the king's honor that the Duke of Lancaster should be seen so often in his company, even daring to walk arm-in-arm with him as if they were equals." His voice rose in scorn at that last word. "Secondly, it is unseemly that the king should be wearing Gaunt's livery-collar as though he was Lancaster's retainer. Thirdly, it is unsuitable that the king's retinue should also wear Lancaster's livery." Warming up, he took a couple of paces, still pointing at Gaunt. "Fourthly, the Duke of Lancaster uses such rough and bitter words in council and Parliament that no one else dare speak their minds fully. Fifthly, he is defrauding the king by grasping at the Duchy of Aquitaine.

And sixthly, he squandered public money in his private war against Castile."

Out of breath, Arundel ran out of objections. After glaring at his opponent, he turned and looked around the chamber, expecting a roar of outrage. But the earl had misjudged the temper of his audience. The years had mellowed the Duke of Lancaster, as well as attitudes against him. Now a respected elderly statesman, Lancaster had proven himself more than ever the bastion of Richard's throne. The bad old years of Edward III's dotage were long forgotten. The Lords bent toward each other, muttering their opinions. No one was shocked by the accusations. No voices were raised in agreement with Arundel. Lancaster sat silently, and the annoyance on his face signaled his disdain. This was a pathetic display of bile—not worth Parliament's time.

The king could barely contain his glee. This was the perfect opportunity to put Arundel in his place. Of course, long ago he had learned how to mask his emotions, and putting on a show of dignity, he rose from his throne and arranged his sleeves while everyone quieted down.

"My Lord, I have answers to your concerns," he said smoothly. "As for your first objection, it was I myself who requested my uncle stay by my side, just as I did with my other uncles in his absence. Also, it was I myself who took my uncle's collar from his neck and put it on my own, as a sign of my great love and unity between us." He turned to Gaunt, nodding slightly. "It was my choice and desire that the men of my retinue wear Lancaster's livery. As for your fourth complaint, I don't remember any time when you were refused the opportunity to speak without fear." He gestured to the room as if asking for confirmation. "And the duchy of Aquitaine was given with the assent of all the estates in full Parliament, as well as half the money for his expedition to Spain. For the rest, Parliament remitted his loan in thanks for his service en route to Spain when he relieved the castle of Brest and elsewhere."

By then, Arundel's face was red from frustration, and he was further obliged to sit and sweat while Parliament wasted even more time discussing his objections and the king's answer.

14

Finally, he was asked if he had any more to add, and a deflated Arundel answered to the negative.

The chancellor rose and pronounced the matters were of no substance or relevance, and the Duke of Lancaster's honor was entirely untainted. "Further, on the Lords' advice it is the decision of the king that you should give a public apology."

This was a bitter humiliation, and the Earl of Arundel did not obey graciously. But obey he did, and he stepped forward, addressing his words to the duke. "Since it seems to the king and the other lords that you have been greatly displeased by my words, I beseech your forgiveness."

Not waiting for an answer, the earl turned and left the chamber, nursing his grievances against both king and duke. Little did he realize his ploy had just made a mortal enemy of Lancaster, and in time, repercussions would prove his undoing.

There was a public Richard and a private Richard. He was still a man in mourning. It was all he could do to keep body and soul together during Parliament, but when alone the tears threatened to overwhelm him. By now, Richard's inordinate grief for Anne was known to all in his household. Outsiders were another matter.

A few months after Anne died, John Gedney, clerk of the king's works, was summoned to Westminster. While he was waiting to be announced, Gedney stood aside while Henry Yevele came out of the room, a set of drawings under his arm; he was London's foremost stonemason and well known in the trades. They nodded to each other before Gedney went inside.

The king sat at a table with Edward of Rutland, looking at a set of his own drawings. He gestured to a chair. "We are going to construct a tomb of pure marble for myself and my dear queen," Richard said, pointing at the parchment, "to be placed in Edward the Confessor's chapel. Here, I have commissioned two gilt bronze effigies of myself and the queen, lying side-by-side and holding hands." His lips tightened for a moment as he suppressed his sorrow. Then he looked at Gedney.

"I know you have been working on the renovations at Westminster Hall. But I have a job for you. I want you to

15

demolish the cottage and all the structures on La Neyt at Sheen. Raze them to the ground."

Gedney was taken aback. He had been part of the construction team that put so much love and care into building Richard's getaway. Shocked, he blinked back tears, at a loss for words. The king watched him, annoyed at the man's reluctance. *Didn't he just give a command?*

But after a moment his pique gave way to empathy. "I loved that place, too," Richard said softly. "So did my queen. But can't you see? La Neyt was built for her and her only. And now I can no longer bear the sight of it."

The king suddenly jumped to his feet and dashed from the room. Rutland sighed heavily, leaning back in his chair while Gedney stared at him in confusion. "He doesn't want us to see him weep," Edward said. "He tries to divert himself from...her death by staying busy. But it doesn't work."

Both men looked down at their hands when Richard finally came back and sat quietly. Gedney was appalled at his new assignment, yet the king was master and his word was law. He swallowed, looking up.

"When do you want this done, sire?"

"At once. Spare no expense."

An unwilling crew left the next day to do the king's bidding. Gedney would have been even more surprised to learn that King Richard declared he would not enter any chamber which Anne had used for a whole year, excepting churches. Then again, maybe he wouldn't have been that surprised after all. Obviously, the king was prone to grand gestures. It was an eccentricity only the highest lords could indulge in.

There was another matter weighing heavily on Richard's mind. Sparing no expense, the king had brought Robert de Vere's embalmed body back from Belgium. Exactly three years after his beloved friend had been killed in a boar hunt, Richard put him to rest in his family crypt at Colne Priory, in Essex. He staged an elaborate funeral, though many of the great lords were conspicuously absent. The Lords Appellant—with the exception of Mowbray—harbored rancor toward Robert de Vere that extended far beyond his death. Richard's uncles chose to ignore the king's eccentric loyalty toward a declared traitor. Even Thomas Arundel, his own chancellor, had sent his apologies. There was no mistaking the disrespect: the king noted the absence of every one of them.

On a late November evening, services began just at the cusp of twilight. Church bells tolled and swirling black clouds threatened rain. Two by two the funeral procession wended its way through the narrow streets of Earl's Colne, spaced perfectly in a seemingly endless column. Each man wore a black robe with a black hood drawn forward to cover his face. Every one of them carried a torch with a tiny shield bearing de Vere's arms below each flame. The torches cast a soft glow as the mourners walked past silent citizens lining the street. Finally the Archbishop of Canterbury and six other bishops brought up the end of the cavalcade, swinging incense burners that filled the air with sweet-smelling smoke. Their appearance signaled the presence of the king, also robed in black, though instead of a hood he wore a gold crown. He was followed by five knights: his nephew Thomas Holland, Earl of Kent, his cousin Edward Earl of Rutland, his half-brother John Holland, Earl of Huntingdon, Thomas de Mowbray Earl of Nottingham, and John de Montacute Earl of Salisbury. These five supporters of the king were worthy of note; they were destined to be among his closest advisors and friends, carefully marshaled to help support his throne. Never again would Richard be accused of elevating unworthy favorites; only earls and dukes would grace his inner chamber.

The silent participants filed into the church where the cypress coffin lay on its bier next to an open grave in the floor near the altar. A row of candles on tall iron stands threw a circle of light onto the deceased. An unseen choir, placed behind a curtain, filled the space with soft tones.

As the king entered the church the tolling ceased. He took his place in a stall topped by a crown and listened while Archbishop Courtney began the services, echoed by his bishops. The Matins for the Dead were followed by Nocturnes and Lauds.

17

Then there was the Prayer for Absolution and the Celebration of the Mass. The candles had burnt to a nub and the air of the church was cold before Richard was finally able to approach the funeral bier.

With an expression of tenderness, Richard looked down on his dear friend. The king had paid for the best embalmer in Brittany, and Robert seemed to be sleeping before him, his face betraying no evidence of his violent death. The king gazed at Robert for a long time, toying with a sapphire ring on his own hand. Blinking rapidly, Richard drew off the ring and lifted Robert's wrist, pushing the band gently onto his friend's finger. He bent over the coffin and whispered something for Robert's ears alone.

"Mine eyes have longed to see your face," he said. "I will never forget you, nor will I rest until we are avenged on those who drove you from my side. Fear not, dear Robert. My resolve is firm and I would have you rest in peace."

Although everyone nearby strained to hear what Richard said, no one—even his closest friends—could decipher the words. But it didn't take a great leap of faith to guess the meaning of his gestures. Richard's enemies would later dismiss the legend that had grown from Robert de Vere's funeral services, but those who witnessed it were never able to shake a sense of foreboding.

All the king lacked was a pair of wings to complete the picture of an avenging angel.

It was the first day of the month. Right on schedule, Thomas Percy carried in a pile of documents to review with the king. Balding, stocky, but physically fit, Percy's energy belied his fifty some-odd years. As steward he managed the day-to-day affairs of the royal household. There was always something that needed tending to, though when it came time to work with the king, all other considerations were secondary. He enjoyed their sessions; Richard gave him his full attention, and they were able to accomplish much.

As he entered Richard's favorite chamber at Windsor Castle, Thomas noted with satisfaction that the breeze from the open windows sweetened the room with that delicious after-rain fragrance. The wall hangings swayed ever so slightly and he could hear cows lowing in the distance.

The king walked over to the table and sat, holding out his hand for the first writ. But instead of reading it, he put the parchment down and cocked his head slightly, looking at Thomas curiously.

"I always wondered why you left Northumberland," he said. "Was it because you were the younger son?"

Thomas blinked in surprise. Ever since the queen's death, Richard had been morose—withdrawn. This sudden curiosity was encouraging. Perhaps his spirits rose because of this beautiful day.

"Well, sire, partly. I really wanted to serve with your father."

"Ah." Richard smiled. "The famous Black Prince. Did he truly deserve his reputation?"

"Every bit of it. He was a magnificent soldier and proved an inspiration to all. And after—" he paused, reluctant to refer to the prince's fatal illness. "I served with the Duke of Lancaster. Most of my knightly education was in France."

"And yet you have been an admiral, a diplomat, ambassador, chief justice, chamberlain... I dare say, you can do anything."

"Serving you gives me the most pleasure," Percy said, smiling.

Richard accepted his compliment. "You know, Thomas, I have few friends any more, since—" he sighed, remembering the Merciless Parliament. "To this day I miss Sir Simon Burley. He was like a father to me." He pulled the parchment closer but still didn't look at it. "Your presence gives me comfort, like his did."

Thomas was touched. Rarely did Richard let his guard down. "I am gladdened you feel that way."

"You know, I am a younger son, too. I was not supposed to be king." His eyes took on a contemplative look. "What would my life have been if my brother Edward had lived? Would I have been happier?"

"God's will." Thomas crossed himself.

"God's will. Not very comforting, is it? God willed that I be king at age ten. That was the beginning of my troubles."

So much for Richard's high spirits, Thomas thought. He leaned forward. "But look at the good you've done. Since your majority, this country has been more prosperous than ever in anyone's memory. We have no wars, no invasions. Your countrymen are well fed, your court is unrivalled throughout Europe. You have pacified Ireland and disarmed the Lollards. You have much to be proud of."

Nodding, Richard picked up the parchment. "Thank you, Thomas. You remind me that I am indeed fortunate. I'm glad you stayed in London. Your brother's loss is my gain."

Thomas nodded, pointing out something he wanted Richard to read. "I love my brother dearly, even when he is obstinate." He laughed.

"The Duke of Northumberland is a difficult man to know. He keeps his thoughts to himself."

"Oh, yes. But his son Harry makes up for his reticence."

"Hotspur? How did he acquire that byname, anyway?"

Thomas laughed. "That came from his impetuous behavior on the battlefield. He would rather attack than play it safe, as the Scots found out to their amazement."

"I would like to meet him someday."

"You would enjoy his company. Everybody loves him."

Richard flicked the corner of the parchment absent-mindedly. "What a blessing that would be! They said the same thing about my grandfather, at least in his younger days. When he was the conqueror of France."

"Hmm. As long as he was successful."

"And that didn't last! I see scant benefit to waging war. Why must I be reviled because I want peace?"

"Sire, sometimes I think mankind is terribly flawed. If we are made in God's image, why do we love conflict and bloodshed?"

"I wish more people saw it your way. Thomas, sometimes I am so tired." Sighing, Richard picked up a quill. "Without my dear Anne, life has been almost unendurable. You know, she understood me so well. She could see when I was upset, and she

20

could talk me out of my anger, even when I didn't realize it." He dipped the point into the ink and signed his name. "What's going to happen to me now that her influence is gone? Who is going to restrain my temper?"

CHAPTER 3

A childless king could spare little thought for his own bereavement. But there was more than one way to satisfy demands for Richard's remarriage. Charles VI of France offered him the perfect opportunity to renew their diplomatic relations by offering the hand of his seven year-old daughter Isabella. Richard jumped at the chance; not only would he have time to grieve for his dear Anne before entering into marital relations with another wife, but the two kings could also discuss a very real possibility for a long truce.

To make everything official, the king sent his cousin Rutland and Thomas Mowbray to France with a formal proposal—and to meet the princess. At Eltham, while waiting for their return, Richard sent for Jean Froissart who had been visiting at the King of France's behest. The chronicler entered the king's private chamber, surprised to see Richard still reclining in bed.

"Today I am at leisure," the king said cheerfully. "I understand you have prepared a book for me."

Jean pulled the volume from under his arm and laid it on the bed. Richard leaned forward, impressed. The book was bound in crimson velvet with ten silver-gilt studs on the cover and roses in the middle. Two large clasps of silver-gilt were engraved with more roses. The king ran his fingers gently over the velvet.

"It is gorgeous," he said. "What is it about?"

"It's about love."

"Ahh. Poetry." For a moment, Richard's eyes filled with tears. "My dear Anne couldn't get enough of it. She so loved French verse."

Putting the book carefully on his lap, Richard opened the clasps. The illumination on the title page was delicate and brilliant and he touched it lightly, looking at Jean. He turned a few pages and read out loud in perfect French,

> *Mon coeur s'ébat en respirant la rose*
> *Et se réjouit en regardant ma dame.*
> *Mieux vaut pour moi l'une que l'autre chose;*
> *Mon coeur s'ébat en respirant la rose.*

> *My heart flutters, breathing in the rose*
> *And rejoices looking at my lady.*
> *Better for me one than the other;*
> *My heart flutters, breathing in the rose.*

Froissart was always to remember the angelic look of happiness on Richard's face. He had heard that the king appreciated beautiful things, and it was gratifying to see that his present was greatly valued. Jean was even more gratified later on, when a finely chased silver goblet was presented to him, filled to the top with one hundred nobles. He was later to say that this gift was of infinite use to him.

By the end of 1396, all was arranged to meet the French king despite the objections of Richard's militant nobles. Gloucester and Arundel saw no benefit from Richard's peace policy, and they continued to criticize the whole concept of an alliance with their historic enemy. What was worse, the government had to borrow £10,000 to pay for the expedition so the King could impress his future father in-law. Transporting his distinguished entourage—dukes, earls, and their families—was going to be as elaborate as a small military campaign.

A small army of workers was sent two months in advance to set up the great encampment. Huge pavilions were designed to accommodate banquets and dancing for the royal entourages, and lists had to be constructed for jousting tournaments and other spectacles. The chosen site was in the Pale of Calais, a neutral territory between France and England. Richard's meeting with the King Charles VI would be held in the same location as the Field of the Cloth of Gold between Henry VIII and Francis I a hundred twenty-four years later.

The first day, a grand entrance was staged to please all the attendants. It was a beautiful October morning, and both kings entered the encampment from opposite sides. Four hundred French knights awaited their king, and just as many English knights stood on Richard's side. As Froissart said, "all were brilliantly armed, with swords in hand", drawn up in ranks with a wide passage in their midst through which the royals progressed. In an elaborate processional with minstrels playing and the crowd cheering, both kings met at their assigned place and joined hands. Already they had felt an affinity for each other. Both were close to the same age, and like Richard, Charles's father died when he was young. The French prince became king at eleven, and during his regency he, too, was bullied by his powerful uncles.

For a long moment, the kings looked at each other. "I am so happy to finally meet you," Richard said. "I have long desired peace between our people." He smiled. "Though I think of you more as a brother than a father!"

Charles laughed. "Especially since I'm one year younger than you! We will have to get used to that."

Charles led Richard to his pavilion, which was decorated with fleurs de lis on its valance. The inside was painted like a great hall, with faux stained-glass windows and arches on the roof. For a few minutes the kings spoke quietly together before the dukes entered, ready to serve them confectioneries and wine. All was very proper and ceremonial, and the other princes, magnates, and prelates came in as well, to be served by the knights of France and England. Gifts were exchanged to the applause of the guests.

All parties settled down for a long discussion. After much back and forth they resolved to resume peace talks and try to find a way to end the papal schism. While the kings did most of the talking, many of Charles's advisors noted the Duke of Gloucester's ungracious attitude. He often frowned and shook his head, and his every move was watched, to be discussed later on. Richard ignored him completely.

Finally, the monarchs took leave of each other. King Richard rode to Guines with his dukes, and the rest of the royal party went to Calais. King Charles took the other direction to

Ardres with his retinue. Thus the great lords and their hosts dispersed, their gay pavilions left standing empty for the night.

The following day, the King of France hosted the first dinner in his pavilion, and the monarchs were served by three French dukes. The tables were set with gold and silver plate, and a sideboard was heaped with elaborate dishes for the knights who would present the most delectable choices to the nobility. More gifts were exchanged, pleasantries bandied, and the duc de Bourbon, at his most amusing, remarked, "My lord king of England, you ought to make good cheer, for you have all your wishes gratified. You have a wife, or shall have one soon, for she will be speedily delivered to you."

"Bourbonnois," chuckled the French king, "we wish our daughter was older—though we would have had to double the dower," he added as an aside, "for then she would love our son of England that much more."

Richard nodded graciously. "Good father in-law, the age of our wife pleases us right well," he said. "We don't really pay heed to her age, as we value *your* love above all. We shall now be so strongly united that no king in Christendom can in any way hurt us." This was well received by the French—not so gladly by the Duke of Gloucester, who again caused eyebrows to rise among his counterparts.

After the meal had finished, everyone moved over to the English royal pavilion, embellished with Plantagenet lions. Minstrels had already gathered to play joyful tunes. Jugglers performed breathtaking tricks, tumblers ran forward and climbed on top of each other to create a human pyramid. Soon, the floor was cleared for dancing and caroling.

But their enjoyment was interrupted by a long rumble of thunder, and servants dashed from the pavilion, intent on securing the camp against the oncoming storm. The wind started to shake the sides of the tent, and soon the shaking turned into flapping as the sky opened up and the rain fell in torrents. Luckily, the English encampment was built in the shelter of a large hill, which broke the force of the wind. But it didn't stop the pavilion walls from shuddering, and the rain soon pooled on the roof, quickly streaming through the fabric at the edges near the sides. Crying

25

out in alarm, the ladies crowded into the center of the pavilion while the men did their best to shelter them. The thunder was deafening, the tent shook, and for a few minutes the crowd feared the pavilion might come crashing down on their heads. The storm raged violently, then it tapered off just as quickly as it started.

It was still raining slightly when the men ventured out of the pavilion and gasped at the destruction. Many of the tents had completely washed away; others were lying on the ground, held in place by their guy ropes. The French royal pavilion was still standing, though one of the sides had caved in. King Charles let out a groan.

"Oh, I fear this is all for today. Please accept my apologies for this unforeseen disaster. Our knights will have quite a job for this evening, putting things in order. We shall meet again on Monday, when I will hand over my beautiful Isabella to be your queen."

What else could they do? The grooms brought up the jittery horses who had endured the same scare in their own pavilions. Fortunately, after walking the horses back and forth, everyone calmed down and the royals were ready to return to their quarters and a warm bath.

On the road to Guines, Richard nudged his horse up to the Duke of Gloucester, waving the others back so they could talk alone. The last thing he wanted to do was confront his uncle—who still intimidated him—but his behavior was deplorable.

"Uncle, you have done everything in your power to hinder our peace policy. If you persist, you will undo everything I'm trying to accomplish."

Gloucester looked straight forward, clenching his jaw. "Sire, you know I am not in agreement."

Richard sighed heavily. "Even if we wanted to, we cannot afford a war."

"Hmm. Did you notice the rich plate of gold and silver, even for this informal setting? France is still a very wealthy country."

"And ripe for plunder. Can't you see past your own greed?"

Gloucester pursed his lips, refusing to answer.

26

Richard gripped his reins, suppressing his anger. "I see no reason to discuss this all over again. What must I do to ensure your cooperation?"

The duke was startled into looking at the king. Then he caught himself, resuming his arrogant posture. He cleared his throat. "Preparing for this event has emptied my coffers," he stated.

Richard doubted it; his exchequer had paid for most of the expenses. Nonetheless, this was an expedient solution. "I shall reimburse you 50,000 nobles when we return home, provided you refrain from interfering."

That was a huge sum. Gloucester wasn't above accepting a bribe. "On one condition, sire."

"What is it?"

"Do not lose Calais. We cannot have that."

Richard shrugged. He had no intention of giving away this most precious jewel in the royal crown. "Agreed. For the rest of our visit, I expect you to support me." Without waiting for an answer, Richard kicked his mount forward.

Relaxing, the duke reached for a water flask; he would never admit it, but the king made him uncomfortable. Archbishop Arundel moved up beside him.

"What was that all about?"

Gloucester grunted. "The king accuses me of interfering with his policy."

The other nodded. "There is a time and a place for everything."

"Indeed. We shall pick the right time."

On Monday, King Richard finally met his bride. Sunday had been taken up with religious observations, which gave the encampment time to dry out. Fortunately, this morning Richard couldn't have asked for better weather. The sun was shining and colorful banners fluttered in a gentle breeze. Rugs were laid on the ground to accommodate the royal feet and musicians played as once again the two parties approached from opposite directions and met in the middle.

Richard wore a long red gown bearing the white hart; his retinue's garments were embroidered with the late Queen Anne's

27

coat of arms. The King of France, accompanied by his four dukes, brought forward his daughter, dressed in a dark blue sideless surcoat sewn with gold fleurs de lis. A petit crown graced her head and her long blond hair hung loose to her waist. Putting his hand on the child's shoulder, King Charles blinked away a tear. "I give you my eldest daughter, whom I love most of anything in this world save my son, the dauphin, and the queen," he said.

Charmed, Richard knelt so he was eye-to-eye with the princess and slipped his arm around her in a light hug. She was a pretty child and smiled sweetly, captivated by her handsome king. Richard smiled back. "I thank you, King Charles, for your precious gift," he said, standing and taking Isabella's hand. After increasingly expensive gifts were exchanged, Richard turned Isabella over to the duchesses of Lancaster and Gloucester and the countesses of Huntingdon and Stafford. The princess climbed into a gorgeously bedecked litter, along with the lady de Coucy, who would be traveling to England as her governess. Other litters followed behind, carrying the duchesses and great ladies as King Richard and his nobles preceded them on horseback.

They entered Calais to great acclaim. Brilliant banners hung from balconies, pretty girls dressed in delicate white gowns threw rose petals before the king's horse. Princess Isabella leaned from her litter, waving to the crowd as she passed.

As long as she was surrounded by activity, Isabella was smiling and happy, but when Richard visited her that evening, he saw quite a different face. She was sitting in her bedchamber with the Duchess of Lancaster, surrounded by beautiful garments. Sadly, her cheeks were covered with tears and Katherine had gathered the girl into her arms, trying to comfort her. As soon as they saw the king, Isabella sat up straight, wiping her face with the back of her hand.

Richard couldn't help but notice that none of the other ladies were present. And no wonder: just that very year John of Gaunt had scandalized his nobles by marrying his mistress of twenty-five years, Katherine Swynford. All the other duchesses and countesses swore they would never set foot in the same room as this upstart who outranked them all, but Richard overrode their objections and insisted she attend the festivities. And here she was

28

now, the only one offering comfort to a child who was crying for her parents. Katherine knew exactly what to do, having practically raised all of Gaunt's children as well as her own. As he knelt beside them, Richard swore to himself that Katherine was worth more than all of the other duchesses put together.

"Oh," he said gently, picking up one of Isabella's hands and kissing it, "my poor child. I hope you are not afraid."

The princess shook her head. "My father told me I must be brave. I am trying very hard."

"It's so much for her," Katherine said, stroking her hair. "So many new names to learn, so many new faces. I think you're just tired, Isabella."

"But tomorrow will be such a wonderful day," Richard reassured her. "You have made me very happy."

Isabella's smile shone through her tears. She put her arms around Richard's neck and gave him a hug. When she pulled back, he reached into his sleeve and drew out a handkerchief. "Try this. It's embroidered with my white hart." He wiped her cheeks and put it into her hand.

Gratefully accepting the handkerchief, Isabella jumped down and picked up one of her dresses, holding it in front of her. "Do you like it?"

Sitting on the floor, the king put a finger against his lips. "I think...I think you are the most beautiful lady in my court. It's perfect."

All tears forgotten, Isabella proceeded to pull out all her favorite things which she showed her two companions. Katherine helped her try on her jewelry while Richard watched with a smile. It was a long time since he allowed himself to relax in the presence of ladies, and the ache in his heart receded somewhat. He knew dear Anne would understand. Tomorrow he would marry another, though his dearest wife would never be replaced in his soul.

King Richard and Isabella were married in the church of St. Nicholas, which stood near the castle. The Archbishop of Canterbury read the services. Historians tell us nothing more except there was great feasting, dancing, and music afterwards, and "the heralds and minstrels were so liberally paid that they were satisfied." That must have been great praise, indeed!

A few days later, King Richard and his new queen embarked for Dover, which they reached in an unprecedented three hours. Preparations for her coronation immediately went underway, and the child queen was crowned on January 7 in Westminster Abbey.

CHAPTER 4

The Duke of Gloucester was not one to give up his principles just because he was out of favor with the king—again. Regardless, as far as Gloucester was concerned, peace and prosperity in England mattered far less than the military glory that could be achieved on the fair fields of France. As he picked up his helm and rubbed away a smudge, the duke wished once again that he could have fought with his father, Edward III, at Crécy. Those were the days people cherished, when the English army stunned the world by trouncing a much larger French force. Though it was only fifty years ago, times had changed so much it felt like ancient history. And then ten years later, Gloucester's brother Edward the Black Prince achieved a similar victory at Poitiers, capturing the King of France in the process. The ransom was enormous and the benefit to the exchequer incalculable—even though it had never been completely paid off. What did it matter? The prestige was unrivaled.

The duke replaced his helm on its shelf, straightening the mantle hanging from its crest—a lion with its own crown. And what happened with the Black Prince's son? He grimaced like he always did when thinking of Richard. The best his nephew could manage was an unprofitable expedition to that backwater Ireland. And what came of that? Nothing. And then he bent his knee to the mad King of France who is totally unfit to sit on the throne. And what came of that? A seven year-old queen! And Richard was twenty-nine! Unheard of! The king's peace policy was a disgrace. Idle soldiers turned into brigands; armorers fled to the continent to practice their trade, for there was no work in England. And worst of all, instead of attaining glory the dukes and earls had to be satisfied with begging for crumbs dropped by their milksop king.

Something had to be done. Taking matters into his own hands, Gloucester sent a letter to the other Appellants of 1388, requesting them to gather at Arundel's Reigate castle, just south of London, to discuss an important matter. He also sent a letter to Thomas Arundel, recently promoted to the Archbishopric of Canterbury; he had proved himself greatly adept as an administrator. Younger brother to Earl Richard, Thomas was sophisticated and learned, whereas the earl was brusque and tactless. Tall and finely featured, Thomas was like a foundling compared to his brother. Not for the last time, Gloucester wished their roles had been reversed. Of course, the earl would have made a terrible chancellor! Unlike his sibling, he couldn't be bothered with diplomacy—that much was for certes.

Henry Bolingbroke declined the meeting, but Thomas de Mowbray agreed to come. Thomas was welcomed warmly, and he brought his cleric Thomas Haxey to act as secretary. Tall and robust from constant knightly training, Mowbray would best be called plain-featured, or at worst, ugly. Cursed with a hook nose and crooked teeth, he prided himself in his skill at arms. Good looks, he always said, were useless a fight.

As usual, the Earl of Warwick was late. They waited for him impatiently until he showed up with an apology. Then all sat down to an elaborate feast provided by their host.

"I thank you for coming," said Gloucester, gesturing with his goblet to the others. "Since the king is summoning a Parliament in January, I believe it is time we used our influence with the Commons to call him to task for his lack of good government."

The archbishop leaned to the side as a servant reached past him, pouring more wine. "I understand the king has responded to overtures to make him Holy Roman Emperor. Two of the Electors have been granted pensions of £1000 per annum for their support—"

"Which the exchequer can hardly afford," Gloucester spat.

"And how much did he spend on the wedding and coronation?" Arundel asked.

"Over £200,000, much more than the princess's dowry," said the archbishop. "The profusion of gifts and jewels was immoderate, to say the least. He and Charles competed with each other to see who could spend the most money."

"And all that so he could enlist the King of France to support him against his own nobles," Gloucester grumbled.

"Now, we don't actually know that," interrupted Warwick.

"It's as obvious as the nose on your face! He's threatened it enough times. Open your eyes, man!"

"Peace," said the archbishop. "This is getting us nowhere."

"And I say the truce with France is detrimental to our country's interest," Gloucester insisted. "Look at what he's done with the fortress of Brest. After all it took for my father to capture it, then King Richard just hands it over the Duke of Brittany without consulting anyone."

Warwick scratched his neck. "Now in all fairness, you know it was in exchange for a loan. That was part of the treaty—for a £20,000 loan to the duke—which he has paid off—we were granted the fortress for the duration of the war."

"And the war is not over!"

"A 28-year truce is as good as an end."

"And what about the cost of garrisoning the fortress all these years? What about all the English blood we spilt in its defense?" He hit the table with his fist. "I'm not the only one who is astonished that the king has no conception of what happened in the past. Worse than that, he pays so little attention to present hostilities that he allies himself with our enemies. What is the king going to give away next? Calais?"

"Peace! Move on, Thomas. Please."

Gloucester grunted, undeterred. "All right. Then there is the question of the king's Cheshire Archers. At last count, he's retained 600 archers just for his bodyguard."

"More than that, I believe," said Arundel. "And when they travel with the king, there is no stopping their depredations. They rape and plunder without restraint."

The table fell silent as each man contemplated his own personal grievances. As the servants began clearing the table, Mowbray stirred himself. "I brought my cleric Haxey here to help organize our petitions."

Archbishop Arundel looked at him approvingly. "Good. Let us get down to business."

Gloucester stood and started pacing. "I think it's very important for us to determine just how much influence the Commons retain over the king at this point. They are not as powerful as they once were."

Everyone knew he was referring to the Merciless Parliament, when he and the other Appellants took control of the government—in rare accord with the Commons. After King Richard formally declared his majority, the Appellants' authority had declined while Richard's sway over Parliament had increased.

Warwick cleared his throat. "And how do you plan to go about determining the Commons' influence?"

Gloucester bit back a sarcastic remark. After all, he wasn't entirely sure. "What do you say about feeding them the usual complaints, to start with? We can gauge Richard's humor by the tenor of his responses. We'll start with easy grievances, then over the days we can challenge his policies. At the rate he is going, England will lose all of its continental possessions and the king stands to find himself in thrall to Charles VI!"

"God forbid," said the archbishop. The others crossed themselves.

"He has beggared the exchequer with his extravagant court. Like a Persian, he possesses one robe covered with precious stones costing 30,000 marks. I saw it with my own eyes. He surrounds himself with a multitude of bishops and ladies whose only function is to amuse. There were never women at court in the past! His household has increased to twice what it was in his minority. What does he need 300 knights and squires for?"

No one answered, which was a good thing. He wasn't finished. "Now that we are at peace, the king should relieve this country of the outrageous war tax. But no, he needs the money for idleness, dancing, and feasting!" Crossing his arms, Gloucester sat down on a bench. Hard.

It was destined to be a long meeting; there were plenty of things to complain about. By the end, they had narrowed down their petitions to four items with which they would confront the king.

Mowbray rolled up Haxey's carefully drafted document and prepared to leave. "My retainer, John Bushy is certain to be elected Speaker of the House once again, and I shall make sure he presents our petition."

Tired, Gloucester waved him on. "Give my regards to my daughter," Arundel said before taking a drink of ale. Mowbray nodded and left.

Thomas de Mowbray and his entourage rode swiftly toward London. As soon as they were safely away, Haxey spoke up. "Forgive me, my lord. I am perplexed. I know you are the king's man, yet you participated in this seditious meeting."

Mowbray gave him a crooked smile. "You didn't see me participating much, did you?"

The other shook his head, still puzzled. Mowbray understood his confusion. It wasn't easy separating friends from enemies. Even after all these years, he was not comfortable, knowing his fortunes could change in a heartbeat. He doubted that the king ever forgave him for his former alliance with the Lords Appellant. Although Richard had shown no sign of reprisals to any of them, Thomas would almost have preferred that the king express a little hostility now and then, rather than his usual restrained civility. Nonetheless, if taken at face value, it would seem he was high in the king's favor. He was Marshal of England for life, he had been appointed Captain of Calais, and recently he was made Warden of the Scottish Marches. Yet still, he felt he needed to prove his loyalty.

"Listen," he said to Haxey, "there's no harm in letting the others think I share their opinions—especially my father-in-law." Marrying Arundel's daughter was the reason he originally fell out of favor with the king, though Richard eventually came to accept it. "However, you are right. I serve King Richard first. And this is why I am sending you to him."

"Me? Why would he see me?"

"Because you are going to show him these petitions. Never fear, I will send a letter with you, explaining it all. I dare not be seen entering his presence until this is over. But you, as cleric, have served him before, haven't you?"

35

Haxey nodded. Richard made use of many clerics; he had a preference for members of the Church. "On occasion. But I still don't understand."

"Once Richard has taken the time to consider these complaints, he will be able to control his temper. I will suggest he use this opportunity to test the disposition of the Commons. That's what the Appellants are doing, after all. Why shouldn't *he*? If the king uses his anger to chastise his enemies, he may well discover the Commons are more amenable than he thinks."

"You think he might frighten them into submission."

"Exactly."

"And I am to be sacrificed?"

"Good Lord, no. You are too valuable."

Mowbray kicked his horse forward, leaving Haxey with the uncomfortable feeling he was more valuable as a pawn than a secretary. However, if he was clever enough, he might go far in the royal service. Everyone knew that's where the best opportunities came from.

Stopping over at Mowbray's London residence, the earl wrote a letter to the king and sealed it while Haxey waited. "There is no time to waste," he said. "You must take this to the king at Westminster, first thing in the morning."

The next day, as he gained entrance to the king's inner chamber, Haxey was relieved Richard wasn't alone. This situation was delicate enough that he was glad to have witnesses. The king's steward Thomas Percy was in attendance, as well as John Holland, Richard's half-brother. Holland turned and studied Haxey with disconcerting deep blue eyes, sending a chill down the cleric's back. Although he had outgrown his violent tendencies, Holland was still known as a man to be cautious around. Percy, the younger brother of the Earl of Northumberland, was less intimidating; he was sorting through a pile of documents like someone who needed to get on with his business.

Richard leaned back in his chair, chewing on an apple. Even in the privacy of his cabinet, he was magnificently dressed, his dark blue robe sprinkled with gold stars. His red hair rested elegantly on a high collar lined with ermine, and gold buttons ran all the way from chin to hem. "I understand that Thomas de

36

Mowbray has sent you?" He held out a hand. "What is this all about?"

Haxey knelt, handing over the whole package. "Sire, Sir Thomas sends his greetings and begs you to read his letter before opening up the petitions."

"Petitions?" Richard took the letter and passed the rolled document to Percy. "What has Sir Thomas been up to?" He didn't expect an answer and his messenger offered none, watching the king read the letter. At first, his face clouded. Then he squinted at Haxey. "So, they are at it again, are they?"

"What's this?" Holland reached for the letter.

"Sire." Head lowered, Haxey felt short of breath. "Sir Thomas thought it best to attend this meeting between the former Appellants so he could be your ears. I am to approach the Speaker of the House with a petition for the Commons, but he wanted you to be prepared for it."

"A petition from my loving uncle Gloucester," growled Richard. "That man is never happy unless he is causing strife."

"We can beat him at his own game," Holland said. "He has lost much influence the last couple of years."

"Yet he is still London's favorite," the king said, taking back the letter. "As is Arundel, curse his black soul. So, Percy, what do the petitions say?"

The steward shrugged. "For the most part, they are the usual complaints. They object to your sheriffs serving more than one year, in violation of the statutes. They grumble about the abuses of livery. They complain about the violence in the Scottish marches." Percy paused, looking at the king. "The last petition concerns the costs of your household."

"What?" Richard's face grew redder.

"It says something about too many bishops and ladies, costing the exchequer needless expenses. It petitions to remedy and reduce the household's spending."

"The bastards! They dare attack my regality!"

Haxey barely controlled his trembling, and he was grateful the king wasn't paying attention to him. Richard was staring at Percy. "This cannot, will not happen again," he said, lowering his voice.

37

Not having witnessed the events of ten years ago, Haxey was puzzled. Holland, on the other hand, knew perfectly well what was bothering the king. He had never recovered from his humiliation at the hands of the Lords Appellant. "Now I understand why Mowbray sent you," he said. "He is clever, that man."

Richard was still angry, though at least he willing to listen. "Well, John, I suppose you are right. I would crush them under my foot, but I need a more permanent solution." He stared at Haxey. "What does your master Sir Thomas suggest?"

Ever since he was given this task, Haxey had been trying to compose the correct speech over and over again, but under the king's scrutiny his clever words escaped him. "Sire," he faltered, "Sir Thomas suggests this would be a good opportunity to test the resolve of the Commons. If you...if you were to pretend you were outraged—"

"Oh, there is no pretense!"

Haxey took a deep breath. Frowning, Richard gestured for him to continue.

"And if the Commons retract their petition—"

Holland sat up. "You will know that you can bend them to your will!" he finished. "It's the perfect opportunity to force them into submission."

Richard's flush receded. He put his hand to his mouth, considering. "The Judges."

Nonplussed, everyone looked at him. "They declared it was treason to violate the king's prerogative," he reminded them. "They were outlawed for their supposed insolence. But I agreed with them. It was treason in 1387 and it's still treason today. I lost that fight, but I've never changed my mind."

Everyone knew that, due to Richard's insistence, the Judges' redefinition of Treason precipitated the whole Merciless Parliament episode. Even Holland was dazzled by the king's daring.

Percy wasn't so sure. "Are you certain you want to reopen these old wounds?"

Richard let out a grunt. "I don't need to go that far. Just the reminder should prove a point. Especially if I bring the Judges back from Ireland." He looked at Percy. "It's past time, you know. They never deserved to be outlawed." He took another bite from his apple, thinking. "Thomas Haxey, I'm going to ask you to do something for me. You must be brave, but trust me. I intend to follow Mowbray's advice. I shall rely on you to help make it work."

Haxey bowed his head. "I am your loyal servant."

"Good. Present the petitions to the Commons as planned. I will...pretend to be angry—so angry I will accuse you of treason. They will take you away, for a short time. But never fear. You will be released once I have made my point."

The thought of being taken away, whatever that portended, wasn't encouraging. Still, there was no backing out now. Haxey bowed and made his escape with as much dignity as he could muster.

The January 1397 Parliament was the first that had been held for two years; there was much to discuss. As predicted Sir John Bushy was appointed Speaker. He presented himself before the king to make the customary declaration: "Your Majesty, if I should err in anything I say, I request that my companions, the Commons, not be held responsible for my ignorance or neglect, if I say something without their consent."

King Richard nodded. "I accept the choice of the Commons."

Moving on, under Mowbray's direction Bushy duly presented the petitions to the Lords. Other business was attended to at first. They did not want to fund the king's proposed expedition to Milan in conjunction with Charles VI of France. They were not obliged to pay for the king's personal wars, though of course they had no objection if he wanted to mount the campaign at his own cost. Even though he was displeased, Richard didn't expect any other answer and the Commons were encouraged.

It was time for Bushy to present the petitions. "We have four items the Commons would like to present to the king," he said to the Lords who sat in front of Richard. "Number one: they would draw to Your Majesty's attention the Statute made in the days of Edward III that sheriffs not remain in office for more than one year. This statute has been consistently abused."

Richard sat calmly in his throne—wisely, he hoped they were thinking. "There are times," he said evenly, inclining his head, "common sense must take precedence over rulings made in haste. Surely it would take a year for the sheriff to properly learn his duties. It would be more to my profit if a man of experience continues in the office, subject to his good conduct."

"Yes. Ahem." Bushy shuffled his papers. "Number two: the Commons are concerned about the great oppressions and outrages perpetrated on the Scottish borders in breach of the truces made between our countries. They beg that a remedy be ordered at the good discretion of the king and his lords."

Richard nodded again. "I am in accord that the lords should discuss any remedy that is practical, as long as it is possible to bear the costs."

This was reasonable enough. The Speaker went on to point three: "The Commons are concerned about the statute made for Livery and Maintenance. It restricts the wearing of livery to household servants and those directly retained by the lords. However, there are too many instances where this is being abused. Casual yeoman are wearing the badges of the lords, and their reckless and murderous behavior has been a threat to both liberty and royal justice."

"We shall see that the laws are more scrupulously obeyed," was the kingly answer.

So far, everything went better than expected. Bushy hesitated before presenting the fourth petition, but there was no remedy. "Your Majesty, the Commons complain that the great and excessive cost of the king's household should be reduced, namely regarding the multitude of bishops who hold lordships, and their attendants, and also the great number of ladies and their attendants who stay in the king's household at his expense." He cleared his throat, looking at the king.

Many of the members of Parliament had been present during the bad old days of the king's minority. The parallels between ten years ago and today—especially when Richard lost all of his rights—were apparent to one and all. And humiliation was only part of it; as the king had been forced to watch helplessly, his closest friends and advisors were declared traitors. The lucky ones—like Robert De Vere—escaped into permanent exile. The unlucky ones—like Richard's beloved tutor Simon Burley—were mercilessly executed. What most of today's members did *not* know was that these same Lords Appellant were behind the present petitions.

But things had changed and the members of Parliament wouldn't appreciate being manipulated again by the Lords. After the Merciless Parliament—once their objective had been accomplished—the Appellants had lost interest in governing and drifted away to attend to their own concerns. The rare accord between the Lords and the Commons disintegrated. The Commons slipped back into their traditional opposition.

Many of them cringed when Richard jumped to his feet. "I am grieved that my liege Commons should take it upon themselves to regulate *my* household or *my* person—infringing on my prerogative," the king started slowly. By the end of the sentence his voice had risen in volume. "That my own subjects should presume to object to anyone I choose to keep in my company!" His fists clenched, Richard roared at the assembly, "You have offended against my majesty and the liberty I inherited from my ancestors!"

He whirled around to the seated Lords. "Duke John of Lancaster, I insist you discover who has presented this petition and bring him to me so he may answer in person!"

Gaunt was not lax in obeying. As Richard reseated himself, the duke pulled the Speaker aside and interrogated him while others protested in dismay, looking furtively at their irate sovereign. Richard spoke to no one.

Finally, Sir John Bushy agreed to name the offending party and Haxey was hustled forward amid many apologies to the king—and denials, for Haxey was not even a member of the Commons. Richard did not relax his temper; like an avenging angel, he raised his arm and pointed at the unfortunate scapegoat.

"Anyone who stirs up the Commons to attack the royal prerogative should be tried for treason." His voice rolled over the assembly like a tolling bell. "This man is guilty and should be condemned to death." No one dared object as Richard scrutinized the assembly, looking for more offenders. After he had given them enough time to consider their position, he lowered his arm. "However, since he is a man of the cloth, he is remanded to the custody of the Church. Take him away and place him into the keeping of the Archbishop of Canterbury."

Haxey did not dare look at the king, though at this moment he was beginning to doubt Richard's promise. As he was led away, Sir John Bushy turned to watch.

Richard stood for a moment, observing the turmoil in the hall. Yes, things had certainly changed in his favor. During the Merciless Parliament, while the Appellants directed the persecution of his adherents, the Commons acted determined, harsh, and uncompromising. But look at them now! They didn't know whether to throw themselves on his mercy, blame each other for angering him, or give him anything he demanded. Enjoying the disorder, Richard sat down and watched the members argue with each other, while Bushy pushed his way through clusters of disputants. After a while the king tired of his amusement and gestured for the chancellor to command order.

Sir Bushy stepped up to the bar. "Your Majesty," he began as the more influential members crowded behind him, their heads bent in humility. "It was never our intention to say anything that would cause offense or displeasure to your royal majesty— especially of that business concerning the management of your own household." As he paused, the others murmured their agreement. "We understand such things are none of our business, and we humbly beg your forgiveness. We were only concerned about your honorable estate, and it weighs heavily upon us that we have offended you. We humbly submit ourselves to your grace and royal will." Bowing, he stepped back.

Richard could barely contain his glee. Mowbray was right! He was finally in control of the Commons and all at once he saw he was free to pursue the next step in his agenda. This was only the opening cloudburst; the tempest would come later.

He beckoned the chancellor over and whispered in his ear. As the members waited breathlessly, the chancellor stood and banged his staff on the floor. "The king, of his royal goodness and graciousness, has decided to excuse the Commons their misapplied petition. He has declared he wishes to be a good lord to you as it was always his desire."

The declaration could not have been better received. Cheering, the members bowed and threw out their arms as though to embrace the king. The Commons were truly his.

Haxey was quietly given a full pardon three months later, and over the next several years he served Parliament over and over, accruing much prosperity in the process. At the same time, Richard took the opportunity to recall the exiled judges from Ireland, though he assured everyone he had no intention of reversing the judgments of 1388.

Not yet, anyway, he said to himself. *Time will tell.*

CHAPTER 5

"See? It's finished. Do you like it?" Princess Isabella lifted up her skirt and twirled around while Richard clapped in appreciation.

"You look beautiful," he said, kneeling and holding out his arms. His nine year-old wife dashed up to him and threw her arms around his neck as he gave her a hug. Kissing Isabella on the cheek, Richard stood, grasping her hand. "Come, sit with me," he said, leading her over to a wide bench near the fireplace. "It's chilly today."

Although Windsor castle was still the king's largest and most elaborate residence, the high-ceilinged rooms were draughty and the spring sun did not shed much warmth through the windows. Richard sat on the bench and draped his cloak around Isabella's shoulders as she snuggled under his arm.

"Tell me about your lessons," he said, adjusting the circlet on her hair.

"Oh, Bishop Robert tells me I am most proficient in Latin. He has already started teaching me letters."

"And Greek?"

"Well, I'm not quite as good at Greek. Yet." She smiled slyly. "Did you remember my marchpane?"

Acting surprised, Richard patted his gown. "Ah," he exclaimed, tugging on a pouch tied to his belt. Giving her a sideways glance, he pulled the strings and drew out a bundle wrapped in a handkerchief. "Don't eat it all at once," he warned. "It's very difficult to get more. It comes all the way from Venice, just like the paper you so love to write on."

"All right, just a bite." She gingerly unwrapped the almond paste bar and took a taste. As Richard smiled at her, the door opened and John Holland entered, along with the Bishop of Lichfield.

"Ah, there you are," Richard said, removing his arm from Isabella's shoulder. "Come, sit with us by the fire."

The others bowed before the king then turned to the queen. Clutching her marchpane in her left hand, she extended her right for them to kiss.

Richard gestured for them to sit. "As you know, I have been investigating evidence of my great-grandfather's miracles, especially around his grave in Gloucester Cathedral. I've personally visited the sites and have consulted with prelates and lawyers to determine whether the miracles were genuine." He pointed to a table that was piled with manuscripts. "There is the dossier of King Edward II's miracles. I put it in your care, the both of you, to present to Pope Boniface IX."

The bishop went over to the table and glanced through the parchments as John sat down.

"I'm hoping the pope will determine that this is enough," Richard went on. "I'm hoping the two of you will provide any additional, um, incentive to get the process of canonization started."

Lady de Coucy appeared in the doorway and the princess wriggled off the bench. Richard gave her a little pat on the shoulder. "I will see you for dinner, my dear." She jumped back and kissed him before trotting off to her governess. Richard smiled after her indulgently. "She is sweet, isn't she?"

Holland nodded. "I hope you don't mind my asking why this is so important to you?"

Richard's face clouded. "The canonization? I'll tell you. Edward II's usurpation put such a stigma on the English crown it has never recovered. Remember how they used it against me!" His brother nodded again. Gloucester had threatened the king at least twice that he knew of—once in the Tower and again when Richard tried to save the life of Simon Burley. He could only imagine how much damage that threat did to the king's spirit.

"Well, John," Richard went on. "There's nothing I can do about my great-grandfather's usurpation or his murder. But if he was made a saint, that would rehabilitate his memory and restore the tarnished reputation of the crown." Musing on this, Richard stroked his beard. "There is such a cult around Thomas of

Lancaster, my great-grandfather's enemy. They wish to declare him a saint! How dare they! He was a traitor. He died a traitor's death." He looked at Holland, almost as if for confirmation. "What's more, if I were to validate the judgments against Lancaster—which never should have been reversed—the Lancastrian inheritance would revert back to the crown."

John couldn't help himself; his mouth fell open in shock. "How can that be possible?"

Richard waved a hand in dismissal. "What was reversed can be reversed again. They all go together, you know. My great-grandfather's reputation restored, and Lancaster's standing back to where it belongs."

His brother let out his breath. "Daring, sire, but impractical, I think. It would never hold."

"You don't think so?" Richard adjusted his sleeve, a sure sign he was displeased; everyone had recognized this gesture from long ago. "I tell you, John. I don't want Lancaster to succeed me."

"Well then, we'll have to promote Mortimer. Many think he's heir apparent, anyway."

"That's no better. I don't favor Mortimer."

"Then, who?"

"Why not York?"

Holland choked back a laugh. "I doubt the duke would be interested in such responsibility."

"Not the father. Rather the son."

"Edward?" John sat back in his chair. "Rutland? I dare say he wouldn't object!"

Richard watched his brother closely, then he looked across the room at the bishop, who was pretending not to listen.

"Hmm. Ignore the whimsy of an idle mind. Let's get back to your mission."

In June, Richard was hosting a feast at Westminster Palace when the real trouble began. All the great lords were there with their wives, and the dukes sat with the king, facing perpendicular tables giving easy access to servants. Among the guests were many

46

soldiers from the recently surrendered fortress at Brest, who were quietly enjoying the king's bounty.

The meal over, Richard was enjoying his hypocras—spiced wine—when the butler came forward with an elaborately decorated silver box and opened it before the king.

"Ah," Richard breathed, leaning forward. "The comfits. Just what I've been waiting for." He turned to his uncle Gaunt. "I especially love the anise seeds." He carefully gathered a few, thoroughly coated in sugar. "Oh, and the pine nuts. Here. Do try the ginger."

Gaunt obliged, passing a few delicacies to his wife. Gracious as always, she offered some to the Duchess of Gloucester, who pointedly turned away. The king gave Katherine a sympathetic grimace, eliciting a smile in return. It didn't matter to Richard that the others objected. The Duchess of Lancaster was elegant and beautiful and he liked her. Just to empathize his support, a few months ago Richard had scandalized his nobles again by legitimizing their four children, now called the Beauforts. All had been born out of wedlock, since Katherine had been Gaunt's mistress for twenty-five years. But for their bastards to climb into the line of succession? Unheard of! That outrage gave Richard a gratuitous satisfaction. Even more to the point, he had bound Gaunt closer to his own interests, while tweaking the noses of the Lords Appellant—especially his cousin Henry, half-brother to the Beauforts. Let them sort it out.

"My Lord," came a harsh voice from his other side, interrupting his thoughts. Sullenly, Richard turned to his uncle the Duke of Gloucester. "Have you not noticed our companions who are here?" Gloucester continued.

Keeping his face blank, Richard raised his eyebrows. "Good uncle, what companions do you mean?"

"My Lord, they are your people who have come from Brest who have faithfully served you, yet have been badly paid. They don't know what to do next."

The king made a gesture with his hand. "That is easily repaired. I will make sure they are paid in full." He turned around in his chair. "Sir Thomas Percy," he called. "Where is Sir Thomas Percy?" Calmly, he reached for his hypocras while he waited.

As steward, Percy was always nearby. He came forward and knelt before the king. "What are your wishes, sire?"

"Our men of Brest, there," the king said, pointing to the soldiers. "My uncle of Gloucester complains they have nowhere to go. Make arrangements for four good villages near London to take them in at my expense until they receive their due." Thomas nodded and took his leave while Richard turned to his uncle. "Does that satisfy you?"

Gloucester straightened, throwing back his shoulders. "That's not really the point, is it? Sire, you ought first to hazard your own life in capturing a city from your enemies, before you think of giving up or selling any city which your ancestors have gained at such great cost to themselves."

The hall fell silent. Richard gripped his chalice. "What are you saying?"

"I said, you should hazard your own life before giving away cities your ancestors worked so hard to obtain!"

John of Gaunt tried to intercede, putting a hand on Richard's arm. The king shook him off. "Do you think I am a merchant, that I wish to sell my land? By St. John the Baptist, no. No. You know it is a fact that our cousin of Brittany has paid back the loan which *our ancestors* have lent him against the city of Brest. And, since he has honestly met his debt, isn't it only fair he should have his pledge back again?"

Trying to calm himself, Richard took a deep breath. "Or is it better for you if I were to renounce our obligation? You would prefer I disgrace myself?"

"Nay, sire." Gloucester knocked over his wine, causing a distraction. By the time the servants sopped it up, he had regained his composure. "It is a pity we have spent so much on improving its defenses."

"It served its purpose," Richard answered before leaning toward Gaunt. "My uncle goes too far," he whispered, reaching for more confits. "If he had his way we would never be at peace."

Gaunt sighed. "I will speak with him."

"His constant harassment is unendurable." They watched Gloucester leave the table and beckon Arundel to join him. "Look at them," Richard frowned. "Plotting again."

48

"Surely not, sire." Gaunt smiled wryly. "They would not do so in front of you."

"Oh yes, they would." Richard didn't appreciate the irony. "The more they provoke me, the happier they are." Glumly, he rested his cheek against his hand and glared at the men who made his life so miserable.

Gaunt didn't realize it, but this was the beginning of the end for Richard's antagonists. Gloucester had attacked the king publicly one time too many. The man's arrogance knew no bounds. It was time to put an end to it. In the eight years since he took control of his government, Richard had kept a tight rein on his temper and suppressed his true feelings. Even his worst enemies had received grants and estates so they would drop their guard. Just to show he had no hard feelings, he had given official pardons to the Appellants. A lot of good it did him!

The Haxey incident back in January had been mostly forgotten, except by Richard. He saw it as the first move in a new campaign launched by his enemies. *No, they weren't going to get away with it this time.* He would be the one to strike first. Richard had been only waiting until he could gather his supporters about him, and then he could finally put his plans into action. Just this month, the pope promised to give Richard's petition his careful consideration and Holland was back from Rome. Now was the time.

The Wardrobe was a good place for a meeting. Located near Baynard's Castle with easy access to the Thames, this elegant mansion had also been used as a London home for Richard's mother, Princess Joan—and before that, for his grandmother, Queen Philippa.

A quick supper was served, and as the servants poured wine Richard looked over his friends and advisors with satisfaction bordering on pride. These men were his choices, not left-overs from his father's generation—with a couple of exceptions. The Earl of Salisbury had distinguished himself fighting for the Black Prince. Sir William LeScrope served with Gaunt in Aquitaine. Both were good soldiers, and very reliable. The rest of them were closer to Richard's age—ambitious, dashing, and above all, loyal. As family, his half-brother John Holland was beyond reproach; so was his nephew Thomas Holland. John Beaufort, who was recently legitimized, owed Richard his gratitude. Thomas de Mowbray the Earl of Nottingham, although tainted by his association with the Appellants, had come back to him and proven his usefulness. Richard's cousin Edward, Earl of Rutland was a boon companion. Thomas Despenser was married to Rutland's sister, though more importantly, he was the great-grandson of Hugh Despenser, Edward II's favorite; this made him dear to Richard. These eight men would more than suffice for the king's plans.

"My friends," Richard started, nodding to the room in general, "there is much I wish to discuss. As you know, my uncle Gloucester has been stirring things up again—especially concerning my peace policy. But there's more than that. It's no secret that he and the other Appellants set Haxey up against me in the January Parliament." He glanced sideways at Mowbray, whose timely warning had served him well. "Then, when their plot failed, they refused to attend my Great Council in February. And just last month, Gloucester insulted me in public. I will tolerate no more of his insolence!" His voice rose at these last words.

The others sat very still, even though Richard tried to smile disarmingly. They all knew his temper. Ever since Queen Anne had died, he had become distant and irritable. Rarely did he express happiness, or pleasure, or even contentment—except when he was with his child princess. Even in unguarded moments, the king seemed unreachable these days—and today was certainly not an unguarded moment.

"I will never, ever, let them get the upper hand again," he said, more to himself than his witnesses. "It is time they answered for their treason."

Not a few of the council caught their breath. Only Rutland dared to object. "Sire, you have extended pardons to all of them."

Richard stared at him so long Edward wondered if he would be next. But no, it had to be said and Rutland was sure of himself.

"What's done can be undone," the king said finally. "Though their treason cannot be erased so easily, especially as

50

they continue to defy me." He got up and started walking around the table. The others had to twist around to watch him. "When I was young and powerless, they saw fit to manipulate Parliament to achieve their selfish ends. Those days are over. It's my turn, now. I mean to bring the Crown back to the splendor and magnificence it possessed in the days of Edward I—when the Crown ruled Parliament, not the other way around. But first, I intend to show the Appellants how well I learned from their stratagems. You, my friends, will appeal—accuse—these men of treason. Counter-Appellants, we will call you. It's only fitting justice."

Everyone stared at the king. This was totally unexpected. Poor Thomas de Mowbray nearly fell out of his chair. After all, he was one of the five original Appellants, though he had been late to join them and his participation had been minimal. The same went for Bolingbroke. From across the room, Richard stopped and regarded him.

"It is the three of them I mean to punish," he said. "Gloucester, Arundel, and Warwick. I remember well that you and my cousin Henry tried to save Simon Burley."

Somewhat reassured, Mowbray swallowed. His mouth was suddenly dry. "We will appeal them...for the Merciless Parliament?"

"Oh, yes. Although I suspect they are trying again, they have yet to answer for their former treasonable activities. And bear this in mind: once the traitors are gone and their estates forfeited, I will redistribute their lands so you—my adherents—will govern, not my enemies. My supporters will bolster the throne—supporters I can count on, and who will grow strong under my patronage."

No one dared speak, though all were cognizant of great possibilities. Richard seated himself again. "Now that you understand my intentions, I welcome any suggestions as to how we should achieve our ends."

The so-called Counter Appellants looked at each other. There could be no doubt; they were to be conspirators—all of them. There was no room for hesitation—no time for scruples. Even if they wanted to, it was already too late to back out.

Richard waited patiently for them to get used to his proposals. After all, he had waited eight years—eight years of prudence, restraint, caution—and planning. He could stand a few more minutes. So many times he had wanted to move against the Appellants, yet he never felt safe enough, or strong enough to withstand the inevitable backlash. Things were different now; he had his father in-law, the King of France behind him. He no longer had to worry about hostility from across the Channel and, by extension, from Scotland, France's allies. The Pope needed his support. The Commons were amenable. He had already ensured the favor of his uncle, John of Gaunt by supporting his marriage and legitimizing his bastards. There was nothing to stand in his way.

He could count on John Holland to lead. His brother could teach him a few things about unprincipled behavior, even though he had come a long way since those reckless early days. It was true Richard had never entirely forgiven him for slaughtering his friend Ralph Stafford over a quarrel between their squires. But Holland had made good on his oath to support three priests who prayed for the soul of the deceased, and he had served John of Gaunt very well during his continental campaigns. Now he was Richard's man.

Leaning forward, the king caught John's eye. "What do you think?"

The other shrugged. "They are very popular with the people. At least, Gloucester and Arundel are."

"Hmm. Yes. We should send out proclamations declaring that the Appellants are arrested for new offenses."

"Perhaps," said Mowbray, "although we may have to resort to more severe measures if their retainers stir up trouble."

"All right. I will send writs to the sheriffs to arrest troublemakers. Then I will raise an additional two thousand Cheshire archers for royal service." He ignored the signs of discomfort in the room. Already his bodyguard was causing problems. "This is all very good. But how do we accomplish this?"

"The Appellants' arrests?" Holland said. "You will have to detain all three of them at the same time. Otherwise, one might get away."

"I think you are right..."

"Sire, I have an idea. I will open up my Thames-side mansion at Coldharbour for a grand feast held in your honor, where everyone will be invited to attend. We can arrest them after the feast when they are well fed and watered."

For a moment, Richard actually smiled. "The simplest ideas are the best. Let's send out the invitations."

Not a lot of time was wasted. On the sixth day after the Ides of July, the great lords gathered for the feast, along with all eight of Richard's confidants, plus bishops and high-ranking London dignitaries. John of Gaunt and Bolingbroke were there, as well as the Duke of York.

Before the guests showed up, a messenger from the Duke of Gloucester was received. Kneeling before the king, the man could barely keep himself from trembling. "Sire, my lord the duke sends his apologies. He is gravely ill at Pleshey and begs to be excused."

Richard bit his lower lip in anger; this was not the time to show his displeasure. He dismissed the messenger without any outward display of temper and gestured to Mowbray, who approached from across the room. "Gloucester is not coming. This makes things more difficult for us. Put out orders to collect all the people you can find and hold them ready for me. After supper, we ride to Pleshey."

Hiding his annoyance, Richard offered the Earl of Warwick the place of honor. The king was at his most charismatic this day, and even pretended he didn't mind that Arundel had not shown up, either. After some small talk with Warwick, the king gestured to Thomas Percy, his steward, who leaned forward, listening. "Have the Archbishop of Canterbury attend me after dinner," Richard whispered, "in the solar. I would have a word with him in private." Percy nodded, stepping away while Richard turned back to the earl.

"I sympathize with you concerning the Gower estates," he said as he personally poured some wine into Warwick's chalice. "It was a very difficult situation, I understand, with good arguments on both sides." He risked a glance at Mowbray, who had profited from this particular case. "Do not grieve for the loss of this lordship. I will compensate you with land of equal value."

Warwick's guarded expression softened. "I am most obliged," he said. "How fares it with the queen?"

Richard's smile reached his eyes. "She is adapting well to England. Truly, she blossoms like a flower. Every time I visit her at Windsor, she seems to have grown another inch."

"I hope we get to see her again soon."

"Ah, that is a thought. For now, we are concentrating on her schooling." Richard turned the discussion to husbandry, which he knew was one of Warwick's favorite topics.

By the end of the meal, the Earl of Warwick was thoroughly enjoying himself when Richard suddenly stood up, his smile gone and his face like stone. Warwick slowly placed his goblet on the table and held his breath, suddenly overcome with dread.

"Arrest this man for treason," Richard declared, pointing but refusing to look at Warwick. A score of the king's Cheshire archers marched into the room and approached the earl. Stunned, Warwick looked around the table. Nobody would meet his eye. Two of the burliest archers grabbed the earl and pulled him from his chair. "Take him to the Tower," Richard ordered. He sat, adjusting his sleeve before nodding at Holland, who got up and left the room.

Sobered, the guests slowly emptied the feast hall, anxious to get away. Holland came back and whispered in the king's ear. Those who were left at the table watched as John opened a door and the king disappeared into a room.

Bolingbroke leaned toward his father. "What do you think he is doing now?"

Gaunt picked at his teeth with the point of his dagger. "You noticed who was missing, did you not? I fear the king has a parlous reckoning in mind toward the Appellants." He placed his other hand on Bolingbroke's wrist. "I regret you were among their number."

"And the Earl of Nottingham," Henry said, jerking his head toward Mowbray, who was hovering near the door. "He is back in the king's good graces, as I trust I am."

"Just like Warwick was earlier this afternoon. You are walking a knife's edge." He ran a thumb across his own blade before sheathing it.

"Father, I joined them to protect your interests. Gloucester might have claimed the throne, else." He sighed. "I never thought he would go so far."

"That may be true, but the king will never believe it. We can only do our best to appease him."

Bolingbroke pursed his lips. "Does that mean ruling against them in Parliament?"

"If it comes to that? God forbid. But I fear we must."

"Even my uncle?"

Gaunt shook his head. "I can't imagine. Let's pray to God it doesn't come to that."

Thomas Arundel, the Archbishop of Canterbury stood while Richard pulled the door firmly shut. Though taller than the king, he tried to make himself appear shorter by rolling his shoulders and bowing his head. The king gestured to his chair and the archbishop nearly collapsed into it.

"There is something you have to do for me," Richard said.

Arundel nodded, not trusting himself to speak.

"I need you to persuade your brother to surrender."

The archbishop blinked, stunned. "Why in the world would I do that?"

"Take heed—it's only for appearance sake. You know the delegates from Germany are considering electing me as Holy Roman Emperor. What you don't know is that the only thing stopping them is their belief I can't control my own magnates." Despite himself, Richard was getting agitated. He walked across to the sideboard and poured himself a cup of wine, downing it in one gulp. "This is only temporary. Once the Germans are aware of the Appellants' detention, they will go home and I can release your brother from custody."

Thomas rubbed his sweaty palms against his leg. Could Richard be trusted? He just saw what happened to Warwick.

"I swear by St. John the Baptist that no bodily harm will come to your brother if he hands himself over peacefully."

The other sighed deeply. "All right. I will go to my brother at Reigate."

"Very good. I will send Edward of Rutland and Thomas of Kent and a small retinue of men with you, who will be instructed to wait outside while you speak to the earl. You are very persuasive, my lord. I'm sure you can convince him." Turning, Richard left the room.

Arundel stared at the closing door. How could he serve such a king? It was unchristian to hate someone, but there were times when Richard inspired nothing else in his breast. How could he ask his brother to surrender? On the other hand, what choice did he have?

Richard, Earl of Arundel was not to be so easily convinced. As Thomas shed his outer garments and moved to the fireplace, he paced the room. Stopping, Richard put his hands on his hips; his normally florid face was scarlet, making his bulging eyes even more pale than usual.

"The king sent you? Is this to do with my absence today?"

Thomas sat as a servant brought him some ale. "Partly. The king arrested the Earl of Warwick as soon as the meal was finished. It all happened very quickly."

"I dare say. And what of Gloucester?"

"He didn't show up."

"Ha. The king must be very disappointed."

Thomas nodded. "He is very good at hiding his feelings."

Arundel paced some more. "So what does he want from me?"

The archbishop felt a wave of sadness wash over him. How could all this have been avoided? "Brace yourself. The king wants you to surrender."

"Surrender! For what? You must be jesting!"

"I wish I was."

"That's absurd. You can't possibly expect me to voluntarily resign myself to the king's deceitful plans. He cannot be trusted." Stopping, Arundel glared at his brother. "How could you be party to this?"

Thomas sighed. "Do you think I had any choice? Better this comes from me than one of his henchmen."

"I'll grant you that." Briefly putting a hand on his brother's shoulder, he resumed his pacing. "Why is he doing this?"

"The electors have told him his bid for Holy Roman Emperor is in jeopardy because he can't control his own magnates."

Arundel snorted.

"He wants to temporarily imprison his old enemies to demonstrate his authority," Thomas went on. "Only until they are convinced and return to Germany."

"Why didn't he tell me this himself?"

The archbishop gave a brief laugh. "Have you ever known him to be straightforward?"

His brother gestured in acceptance.

Taking courage, Thomas spoke in earnest. "The king swears on the bones of John the Baptist that no harm will come to you."

"His oaths mean nothing! I'll tell you this: King Richard will do anything to lay his hands on me so he can put me to death."

Thomas drew in his breath. "Surely not."

They were interrupted by servants bringing in some bread, cheese, and fruit for a light supper. In silence, the two brothers ate a couple of bites.

"You know he wants his revenge for the Merciless Parliament," Arundel said finally. "He holds a grudge to this day."

The archbishop frowned. "That may be. But you have your pardon." He pushed a half-eaten piece of bread aside; he could barely eat it, his throat was so dry. "Consider this..." He paused as Arundel raised his brows. "The king did not give you a request. If you don't obey his order, there's every chance you and your heirs will be attainted."

"Brother, I'll be condemned anyway." Arundel looked around his room as if to memorize every feature. "Still, I know if you fail to convince me, you will be in jeopardy also."

He stood, reaching for his sword-belt. "I will go. Take me now, before I change my mind."

"Bring your pardon." Thomas felt like there was lead in his limbs. He shrugged into his cloak, hoping he was doing the right thing. Surely his brother was mistaken. And if not, he would be burdened with terrible guilt for the rest of his life.

After supper, King Richard called for his traveling cloak and strode into the courtyard where a great commotion could be heard. Dogs were barking, grooms led horses across the cobblestones, knights shouted at their squires, captains prodded their soldiers into formation. Mowbray had gathered quite a large escort. The Counter-Appellants were ready, as well as a score of royal retainers, two score Cheshire archers, and many soldiers. Mowbray sat holding the reins to Richard's palfrey.

Mounting, the king turned to his Earl Marshal. "You have done well, Thomas. Take us to Pleshey Castle. I want to arrest the Duke of Gloucester for breakfast."

If Mowbray felt any surprise, he knew to hide his feelings. Turning, he gestured to their followers. "Forward!" he bellowed and urged his horse to a trot.

Richard pushed his party hard; they rode all night, for Pleshey was more than forty miles away, northeast of London. He feared his uncle would be prepared for him and ready for a siege. But no, all was quiet. Pleshey was a grand motte and bailey castle—one of the largest mottes in England. Below the stone keep, an inner and an outer bailey surrounded the hill, accommodating a substantial garrison and all the trades needed to support the establishment.

Rosy pink clouds hugged the horizon as the royal retinue stopped before the moat. The drawbridge was down and a pair of guards stood before the gate. "Lord Holland," Richard called, and his brother pushed his mount forward. "While I wait here, take ten

58

of your men and inquire whether the Duke of Gloucester is home. Say the king has come to speak with him."

Holland gestured to his followers and the group crossed the drawbridge. It was so quiet the footfalls of their horses echoed as they clattered across the wooden platform. Seeing the king's banners, the guards opened the gates and Holland passed into the courtyard. Gloucester's steward, awkwardly fastening his belt, hurried forward to meet them.

"Is the duke at home?" Holland asked, still astride his horse.

"Yes. The duke has been ill. He and his lady are still abed."

Holland nodded. "I beg you, please be so good as to tell the duke that my lord the king has come to speak with him."

"I shall do so. Please, come inside."

Holland sent one of his men to summon the king before following the steward into the bailey, where they dismounted. Shortly thereafter, a blast of trumpets announced that the king was moving across the drawbridge. Though his men were tired, they soon revived, having finally reached their destination. Servants brought forth pitchers of ale, bread and cheese. Relieved that there was to be no fighting, there was a general air of cheerfulness— between Richard's men, of course.

Finally, the Duke of Gloucester could be seen walking down the steps from the keep. He was dressed only in a linen tunic with a mantle thrown over his shoulders. His hair had not been brushed and he was coughing. Duchess Eleanor followed with her ladies. Reaching the king, Gloucester knelt, saying "My lord, you are very welcome. How is it, Your Majesty, that you come so early without warning me of your visit?"

Still on horseback, Richard looked down at him. "Good uncle, go and dress. We need you urgently at the Council. Please, you must come with us."

Nodding to his wife, Gloucester turned back, though for a moment he started coughing so hard he had to stoop over. Finally, straightening, he mounted the stairs, followed by Holland and his men.

Still astride his horse, Richard pretended not to notice. "How are the children?" he asked the duchess.

"Very well." She paused, unable to hide her distress. "Sire, my husband is terribly ill. He cannot travel."

"He knows his duty, my lady. He will come."

"The ride will do him great mischief. I fear for his life."

"Madam, my uncle is a vigorous man. He will be well."

Richard turned aside to speak with his captains; he tried his best to ignore the duchess while they waited. Finally, the duke came back down with Holland's men.

"We must go," Richard announced.

Eleanor grabbed her husband's arm. "Stay," she begged. "This can wait."

Gloucester shook his head sadly as a groom came up with his horse. "I cannot." He kissed her on the cheek and mounted.

"My Lord, I am ready." Gesturing farewell to his wife, he followed the king into the outer bailey and over the drawbridge. The duchess had climbed the stairs in the gatehouse and watched them from the battlements. He turned in the saddle, taking one last look as she waved dismally. Once out of earshot, he couldn't maintain his composure any longer. "Sire, what is this all about?"

Freed from dissimulation, Richard allowed his face to show his anger. "You would not come to me despite all the messages I sent. So I have come to you. And now I arrest you."

Gloucester contemplated the large entourage. He could see it was useless to resist. "I hope you will show me enough mercy to spare my life."

Richard's eyes narrowed. "You shall have as much mercy as you showed to Simon Burley, when the queen went down on her knees before you." He reached into his sleeve and brought out a rolled parchment. "Read this. Here are the charges against you."

Coughing, Gloucester reached for the paper with a shaking hand. Blinking several times before he could focus, he read the charges, his mouth moving as he deciphered the words. "I can reply to this," he said finally.

"And so you shall. Thomas de Mowbray," Richard barked, "here is your duty as Captain of Calais. The Duke of Gloucester is in your charge. Take him there at once and lodge him in the castle. Keep him under good guard."

At that, Richard put spurs to his horse and galloped away with a small following. The rest stayed with Mowbray, who escorted the duke to a waiting ship on the Thames.

CHAPTER 6

A week after Gloucester's arrest, summons went out for the upcoming September Parliament. Richard was in high spirits. The Earl of Warwick was securely installed in the Tower. Rutland had taken the Earl of Arundel to Carisbrooke Castle on the Isle of Wight. Gloucester was safely ensconced in Calais Castle. All that remained was to decide the best procedure in accusing the former Appellants of treason. The king was determined to follow the original devastating process as closely as possible. Oh, the irony would not be lost on his magnates, or anyone else for that matter. But for now, the paperwork was enormous and royal clerks were in and out of his solar in great numbers.

Someone offered Richard a parchment and the king was struck by the long fingers and slender hand which reminded him of his own. He glanced up, about to say something when the words died on his lips. For just a moment, he had the impression he was facing himself in a looking glass. It was uncanny; the brown eyes were his, the long nose, the arched brows, even the lips. Amused, the clerk gave him a smile and even the expression looked familiar. Richard noticed his own mouth had dropped open. He closed it before sitting back in his chair.

"Have I seen you before?" the king asked.

"Sire, I have served you for years, though only in the chancery. This is my first day at the palace."

"Ah." Richard squinted up at him. "What is your name?"

"Richard." The other paused. "Richard Maudeleyn."

"Richard. That can't be an accident." He looked around the room. "Leave us. I will call you when I am ready." He stared at Maudeleyn while the others departed. "Sit, Richard."

Looking around, the clerk found a chair. He sat across the table from the king. For a few moments they stared at each other.

"It's uncanny," Richard said. "I can't believe I'm looking at myself." He had a thought. "Wait here."

Striding to the door, he opened it, gesturing to one of the guards. "Bring me a looking glass. Yes, you heard me."

He closed the door, leaning against it. "Are my eyes playing a trick on me? Come, stand up." As Maudeleyn stood, Richard faced him. Their eyes were on the same level. Standing sideways, touching shoulders, he noticed there was no difference in their height.

At a knock on the door, Richard accepted the hand mirror. He looked at his face then held it up for Maudeleyn to observe himself. Then he did it again. And a third time.

Maudeleyn took a shaky breath. "I'm a little surprised, too. People have told me I looked like you, but I never realized how much."

"Hmm. Perhaps my father had more mistresses than I thought. I know I have two bastard brothers; it looks like I may have a third."

Trying not to look insulted, Maudeleyn pursed his lips. "I never thought of myself as a bastard." He paused. "Then again, I always wondered if I was an orphan. I had no resemblance to my father..." He caught himself. "Oh, I see. He wasn't my real father."

"I can't think of another explanation. We can't ask my father and I wouldn't want to embarrass your mother, so we won't talk about it at all. How does that sound?"

The other shrugged.

"However, now that I've found another brother, stay close to me. I need a new confessor and you shall live in the palace, Richard Maudeleyn." A smile spread across the king's face. "I foresee we shall be great companions."

Watching his new collaborator leave the room with a small pouch of coins, Richard leaned back in his chair, chewing on the end of a quill. He was glad for a moment alone. The formal Appeal of Treason had been presented to his Great Council. He was truly committed. And now it was time to confront his worst dilemma. What to do with the Duke of Gloucester? The man was fractious and disagreeable in the extreme, but for some reason, he was popular with the Londoners. For now, his uncle was safely across the Channel. What would happen when Richard accused him of treason before Parliament? Would his carefully constructed plans fall apart in the face of popular dissent? And what of his other uncles? As Steward of England, John of Gaunt would preside over the Lords. How far could he be pushed?

There was no question Gaunt would agree with Richard's assessment of Arundel; there had been bad blood between them farther back than the recent Northern rebellion. Really, how could Arundel have launched such an insipid attack against Lancaster? Of course, his harangue failed miserably; too bad for him, the damage was done. Richard almost rubbed his hands together in glee whenever he thought about it.

However, Gloucester was another matter. Could Richard truly expect his uncles to denounce their brother? Many times Gloucester had caused problems over the years; often Gaunt didn't agree with his behavior. But to expect his uncle to declare Gloucester a traitor? Richard shook his head. That would probably be asking too much.

No, something else had to be done. But what?

Pulling over a fresh piece of paper, Richard dipped his quill, hesitating before writing. He had to talk this out. Even for him, this was a major decision. He walked to the door and pulled it ajar. The guard outside came to attention.

"Summon Sir Edward of Rutland," he said briefly. Closing the door, Richard nodded to himself. Yes, Edward had a clear head. He would see all the dark corners in Richard's plan—and probably approve.

Tapping his fingers on the table, the king waited, deep in thought. As one of the Counter-Appellants, Edward was already deep in his confidence. He liked his cousin's mettle; Edward had proven himself resourceful again and again. Still, Richard had never mentioned he would prefer to see York as his heir—not to Edward, anyway. That would be giving him too much power. There's no telling what he would do with such knowledge.

A short knock and Edward came in, smiling when Richard offered him some wine. "How did you know I was thirsty?" he said. He poured a cup for himself then sat in a chair, leaning back and crossing his legs. He knew the king allowed him this informality.

"I need your help," Richard said.

Edward raised one eyebrow. "Is anything the matter?"

"No. Not yet." Richard frowned. "It's about my uncle."

"Gloucester? He hasn't escaped, has he?"

"No, no, nothing like that. I just can't see how we can try him before Parliament."

"Hmm." Edward put the cup down. "I was afraid of that."

"You saw it too? There's so much at stake. I'm not sure I can risk a confrontation. The Commons might feel too much sympathy for him. And what if Gaunt refuses to condemn his brother? The strain might alienate him from me. I can't have that."

Rutland was silent for a moment. "You said he was sick when you arrested him."

"Yes." Putting a hand to his chin, Richard got the point. "Who is to say he didn't die in prison...from his illness?"

"It's conceivable. As long as it happens soon. It's already been a couple of weeks since his arrest."

Richard sighed. He had finally achieved what he had wanted, after so many years. And now the moment had come... Why was he squeamish? Gloucester deserved everything that was coming to him. "I must get his confession first," he grumbled, "or this whole undertaking would be pointless." He glanced at Edward, who had already started writing. *Good Lord, that man never lets his conscience slow him down!* For a moment Richard contemplated his cousin, torn between admiration and dismay. There was no doubt; Rutland knew how to get things done.

"I agree," Edward said, sitting up. "It must be achieved judiciously, before witnesses. There must be no question the confession is authentic." He dipped the quill in ink and started scratching again.

Letting out a deep breath, Richard made his decision. "All right. Let me see. Today is August 16. I will summon Thomas de Mowbray and command him to interview the Duke of Gloucester, then do what is necessary. It has to be now, while he is ill, to convince everyone he died of natural causes. I will have the writ properly enrolled with tomorrow's date so everything is in order."

Edward stopped writing for a moment. "We must make it general knowledge that Gloucester has perished. When I send dispatches to sheriffs I'll instruct the messengers to let them know by word of mouth that the duke has died. We'll send out squires to local pubs; they can start rumors. Our lads won't complain about that errand! Then we can send others to the market and make sure they have loose tongues. The gossip will be all over London in a day or two."

"We'll give it a week. When Mowbray has done his duty, the report will be true—"

"And Gloucester will be finished by August 25."

Rutland filled two cups and picked up his own, handing the other to Richard. "To our dear uncle, may he rest in peace," he said in mock sincerity.

Richard grimaced, but a sense of vindication smothered any lingering doubt about the righteousness of his plans. All he had to do was think about Simon Burley and Robert de Vere—and the promises he made to them. They did not deserve their fates. The Appellants did. All of them.

Thomas de Mowbray raised a shaking hand to tap on the king's solar door. He knew this day would come; Richard was putting him to the test. It must be pretty bad since the king wouldn't send him a message in writing. And Thomas also knew, if he wanted to keep his head, he would have to do the king's bidding or follow the fate of the senior Appellants.

There was no turning back. Sighing, Thomas knocked on the door.

"Come." The voice sounded tired.

Richard was all alone in his little room. No witnesses. He looked out the window without turning and waved Thomas forward. Mowbray noted that even now, Richard was dressed in the finest robes, as if cloaking himself in regality. This was not a good sign. A voluminous dark green satin houppelande brocaded with gold peacocks was belted above his waist, and a high stiff collar hugged his chin, looking like it held up his head.

66

There was a table between them. Platters with meat pies, savory quiche tarts, fruits and cheeses were laid out to tempt his appetite, though Thomas wasn't sure he could swallow anything down. At least he knew the wine would be of the best quality, and a goblet had already been poured for him.

Richard sat and gestured for Thomas to follow before helping himself to a tart. Taking a bite, he studied his visitor as though trying to discern his trustworthiness. Mowbray smiled thinly; he felt the same way about the king.

"I thank you for coming. We rarely get to talk privately these days."

So, that's how it was going to be! The king would pretend friendship before striking the fatal blow. Oh, Thomas knew him so well. Those innocent eyes crinkling at the edges, the corners of his mouth just barely turned up, the confidential voice—before you knew it you trusted his familiarity. He had always been so with the queen—and with certain intimates, like Robert de Vere. With them, his warmth was genuine. But never with Thomas. Like the rest of Richard's courtiers, Mowbray hoped the king's kindness would last, but he could change in an instant and you didn't know where you stood with him. Long ago, Thomas had his confidence—before his marriage to Arundel's daughter. Ever since, he had learned to be on his guard.

"Sire," he said, nodding.

"We've been through so much together," the king went on wistfully. "Once we've gotten this treason trial behind us, things will be so much better." He gestured as though throwing something away. "Back to the current business. I've had enough of the criticism, the antagonism, the blustering. Always passing judgment on me because I wouldn't commit this country to war. It had to be done, Thomas." His eyes narrowed. "They were planning something against me. The last time, they caught me unawares. I will never let that happen again."

Mowbray knew who *they* were. He wondered if Richard was still justifying his arrests—to himself.

"I need to surround myself with magnates I can trust," Richard went on, "like you."

Trying not to squirm, Mowbray reached for a cheese. "Sire, I am at your command."

"Good. It is time we finished what we started."

"Oh? We have been hard at work building our case for the treason trials."

"Yes, yes. That is all very good. I'm talking about my uncle Gloucester."

Thomas held his breath.

"When his time comes, we will announce to Parliament that he died in prison," Richard said reasonably, adjusting his sleeve so that the white velvet lining lay against his arm. "Of his illness."

His illness. From his daily reports, Thomas knew Gloucester was recovering. He was about to say something when Richard held up his hand.

"His death will be announced next week. Not officially, but through reliable sources."

Richard could see Thomas was shocked. "Surely you understand why," he said, trying unsuccessfully to keep the annoyance from his voice. "He can't be allowed to defend himself before Parliament. It's too dangerous."

"Um..." Thomas did not know what to say.

"Look, I can't be seen condemning my own uncle. Nor will I put my other uncles in the position of condemning their brother. Surely you can see that!"

Miserably, Thomas nodded.

"As Captain of Calais and Earl Marshal of England, it is your responsibility," Richard said reasonably. "It is well known he was seriously ill when I arrested him. No one will be surprised if he dies."

Thomas wasn't so sure, but he didn't dare argue. He stood, wanting to get as far away from the king as possible.

"One more thing. You need to get his confession of treason first. That is most important."

"His confession." Mowbray shuddered. "What if he refuses?"

"You must use your most powerful gifts of persuasion to convince my uncle that a confession is his best way to avoid an act of attainder. He must think of his wife and children."

Ha, Mowbray thought to himself, *who does he think I am? The Archbishop Arundel? I have no gifts of persuasion.* To Richard, he said, "I will do my best."

"Make sure you do. I am relying on you."

Thomas bowed, not trusting himself further. It didn't seem to matter; Richard was already deep in thought and barely saw him leave.

The king hadn't given Mowbray much time. Maybe it was just as well; best to get it over with. Bound for Calais on the first merchant ship he could engage, Mowbray leaned on the gunwale, looking ahead. Even for him this was asking a lot. He wasn't a cruel man by nature. Admittedly, he didn't like Gloucester and he disagreed with the Appellants when it came time to pass judgment on Simon Burley. Nonetheless, there was something deeply disturbing about this whole Counter-Appellant movement. Nobody cared anymore about the Appellants—nobody except the king. Their time had passed. Gloucester was an irritating firebrand, but his influence with Parliament had waned. Arundel had withdrawn to his estates years ago and seldom involved himself in politics. Warwick had been almost a nonentity from the first.

The only thing left was the king's need for vindication. It was true that Richard suffered outrageous humiliation ten years ago—much more than he deserved—not to mention his distress at the great number of friends murdered and ruined. It was all done to satisfy the malice of these three Appellants. Was the king's extravagant retribution proportionate to their sins? Does the passage of time mitigate the evil of their actions? It would take a wiser head than his to answer those questions.

On the other hand, if their estates reverted back to the crown, what a windfall for Richard's favorites! The king was incredibly generous to his followers.

Mowbray looked over his shoulder as the sailors called to each other. There were times he wished for a simpler life. The worst thing those fellows had to worry about was where their next mug of ale was coming from. *How had he allowed himself to get mixed up with Richard's pack of self-serving favorites?* The wind gusted in his face and he brushed his hair back. Oh, who was he fooling? He was no better than them. He couldn't deny he was an acquisitive man—what courtier wasn't? He could see a dukedom ahead if he only did what Richard wanted. And why not? If it wasn't him, somebody else would do the deed. And benefit from it.

Armed with his self-justification, Mowbray readied himself for his first visit to Gloucester since he was imprisoned in Calais Castle. The ship slipped past Lancaster Tower, built by Edward III during the siege of 1346. From the dock, Mowbray could see the castle which stood at the corner of the walled city overlooking the harbor. He wondered if Gloucester was watching them from the high tower; the man had little else to do.

Facing the harbor across a strip of sandy beach, a large fortified gate opened to a wide street leading to the cathedral. Calais was a handsome city, and its importance could not be exaggerated. It was known as the gateway to the continent, both militarily and for commerce. Mowbray was proud of his captainship and reminded himself, once again, that he needed to discharge the king's new command to hold onto it.

Once inside the castle, he ordered two of his most trusted knights to accompany him to the duke's chamber. He needed witnesses. Gloucester was housed in a comfortable set of rooms appropriate to his rank. Two men guarded the door.

"Announce me," Mowbray said. He waited a minute while the guard said, "The Earl of Nottingham," and then entered, followed by his knights. Gloucester was sitting at a table writing; he did not stop to acknowledge his visitor. Aside from an unshaven chin and unbrushed hair, he looked his normal self.

Finally, after he judged enough time had passed to demonstrate his supremacy, the Duke of Gloucester put his quill down and sat back in his chair. "So, the Earl of Nottingham finally graces me with an interview," he said, sneering. "To what do I attribute this honor?"

Mowbray sat across from him. His men stood by the door. "I am at the king's service."

"I am sure you are. What new titles has he bestowed on you this month?"

Gloucester was making his task easier all the time. "None yet, but he did make the Earl of Rutland constable of England."

The Duke's face fell. "My title. The office hasn't even fallen vacant. Yet."

"Apparently the king wanted to make sure it wasn't vacant."

"And what does he plan to do with me?"

Mowbray hesitated. "I suppose it depends on how cooperative you are."

"Is that so? There's not much I can do in this god-forsaken castle. Just what does he want?"

"My Lord, he wants your confession. About the wrongs you did him in the Merciless Parliament."

"Oh, is that all? A confession? A death warrant, rather! Does he think I am a fool?"

Mowbray feared this would happen. "It might improve your chances."

"Of what?"

"Your defense at the treason trial in Parliament."

"A treason trial?" Gloucester rose to his feet and walked across to the empty fireplace. He leaned against the mantle, staring at the floor. "That little bastard. He really means to go through with it?"

Thomas said nothing. Calling the king a *little bastard* was enough to get anyone in trouble, though he guessed it didn't matter anymore.

"How many of us are on trial? Obviously, you aren't."

Despite himself, Mowbray reddened. Not for the first time, he wondered if he was next. "Yourself, the Earl of Arundel, and the Earl of Warwick."

"Of course. Are the others in custody?"

Mowbray nodded.

"And they are to appear in Parliament?"

The other nodded again.

"And I am permitted to make a written confession." Gloucester whirled around. "Let me tell you something, Thomas

71

de Mowbray. Unless I get my day in court, like the others, the king will get nothing from me! You tell him that."

This was not going well. Mowbray stood. "You are obviously upset, my lord. Take your time. Give it some thought. I will return tomorrow."

"Do what you will. It matters not."

Little did Gloucester know how much it mattered—at least to Mowbray. He only had a few days to accomplish his assignment. With a heavy heart, he went to his quarters in town and told the servants to bring a meal and wine to his private chamber. Lots of wine. He wanted to eat alone and drink himself into a stupor. Let tomorrow take care of itself.

Of course, tomorrow came and things looked no better. Gloucester was adamant, and Mowbray was sure he could do nothing without a confession. The next day was the same, and the day after that. He even brought up the threat of attainder, but to no avail. Finally, he gave up and returned to England.

How was he going to approach the king? He knew he needed help. For once, Mowbray decided to push aside his natural antipathy toward John Holland and approach him. If anyone knew how to manage Richard, it was his half-brother. He found him at Westminster, getting ready for a council meeting with the king.

Holland gestured for him to enter. "Ah, our Captain of Calais, back from his mission. I trust you were successful?" He watched as Mowbray came slowly into the room and sat heavily. Frowning, he poured the newcomer a mug of wine. "Maybe not."

Mowbray took a deep draught and poured himself another. "You know the duke. He is the most stubborn man I know."

"That he is." Holland studied the other. "He is still alive."

"Very much so. I couldn't get a confession out of him. He insisted on pleading his case in person."

The other grunted. "I'm not surprised." He started gathering his papers, stalling for time. Finally, he looked at Mowbray. "Rumors are rampant. Everyone thinks the duke is dead from his illness."

"I'm sure." Mowbray took another drink. "John, I've never been so afraid for my life. I don't know how to tell the king I failed. I can't think straight."

Holland paused. "Without a confession, the king would never get a declaration of treason from Parliament." He sat, rubbing his forehead. "He knows that."

"With your help, maybe we can break the news in a way that won't destroy me."

Holland thought some more, then jumped to his feet. "Stay here. Let me get Rutland."

Nodding, Thomas laid his arms on the table and sank his head in despair. He was still in the same position when Holland came back, accompanied by Edward.

"Killing the Duke of Gloucester is not an easy task," Mowbray spoke into his arms.

Rutland walked up to him, placing a hand on his shoulder. "Sit up, man. We are all in this together."

Sighing, Thomas obliged. He wiped spittle from his mouth. "I couldn't do it."

Edward looked at him with something like sympathy, though Mowbray knew he actually felt scorn. To Rutland, compassion was weakness; Thomas knew that.

"It's not the end of the world," Holland said. "We can fix this."

A glimmer of hope. "How?"

"As long as the deed is done before Parliament, no one need know when."

"Oh." Mowbray slumped again. One way or the other, he was still compromised.

"Once the king gets over his initial surprise, he will think of a way around this. He always does." John turned to Rutland. "Let's find him before the council meeting starts."

Holland led the way; he knew where the king was. When they opened the door, Mowbray was surprised at the apparition of two Richards in front of him. The king glanced up; this was his new amusement.

"Ah, Thomas. This is my new secretary, Richard Maudeleyn."

Edward smiled at Mowbray. "I was taken aback the first time, too. Astonishing, the resemblance, isn't it?"

"Uncanny." Mowbray bowed before the king.

Richard looked at him expectantly. "What news?"

The other lowered his head. "All goes well in Calais?"

"And the duke?"

Mowbray glanced sideways at Holland, who nodded encouragingly. "Sire, the duke is well."

"He lives?" Richard's voice went up in volume.

Taking a deep breath, Mowbray looked directly at the king. "Sire, he refused to write a confession. I thought it prudent to delay."

"Prudent! I told you next week." The king gripped the arms of his chair.

"Sire, he wanted to present his defense in person."

"I said *No*!" Richard was standing now, visibly shaking.

Rutland decided to step forward. "Nothing is lost," he said smoothly. "I have an idea."

Richard turned on him, ready to strike. All three of them were against him.

"Please, sire. We need to think clearly. We need your wisdom."

Glowering, Richard sat. Mowbray was so relieved his legs nearly gave out.

"What is your idea," the king asked icily.

"It's still a couple of weeks to Parliament," Rutland went on, ignoring the king's tone. "Gloucester thinks he has a chance to speak out. Though as time goes on, he will come to understand his opportunity is gone and the only way he can save himself is by pleading for mercy. You will get your confession."

Richard turned his head, staring at the window. Clouds were scurrying past as though to get away from his anger. Oh, how he wanted to break something. But Rutland was right; he needed to keep his wits about him. He waited for his breathing to slow before he turned back to Mowbray.

"I will give you another chance to redeem yourself. Do not fail me again."

Bereft of speech, Thomas bowed a second time.

"My uncle needs to understand he has no choice in this matter. I will send an official to him." He paused, thinking. "Yes, I know just the man. Sir William Rickhill, justice of the common

74

pleas. He lives in Kent, not far from Dover. He owes his position to me."

"If I am not mistaken," Rutland said to Mowbray, "you already have a writ, dated August 17. Is that correct?"

"Yes, I have it here." Thomas pulled it out of a bag hanging from his shoulder.

Rutland took the writ, looking it over. "It is a commission to gain an interview with the Duke of Gloucester and report what is said."

"Which wasn't done," interjected the king.

"But all is not lost." Edward turned to Maudeleyn. "You will draw up another commission with the same date and a different message. The new one will be addressed to Rickhill instructing him to accompany Thomas Mowbray, the Earl Marshal, to Calais. Under pain of forfeiture. Nothing more." He paused, thinking. "Rickhill doesn't need to know the reason he is being sent. Once he gets to Calais, Mowbray will give him this first commission." Edward held it up. "Naturally he will be sworn to secrecy."

Holland nodded vigorously. "With the dates of Aug. 17 on both commissions, it will still seem to validate our original timing."

"As long as Gloucester is taken care of directly after the confession," Richard muttered. He glared at Mowbray. "You will see it done correctly."

Thomas nodded, though it was plain Richard wasn't satisfied. "Edward, send some of your best men to ensure my orders are carried out."

"Consider it done, sire."

"And take care of the details," the king said, leaning back. "Now, what have you drawn up for Parliament?"

Mowbray can be forgiven for not paying a lot of attention to the rest of the meeting. The enormity of his task ahead was overwhelmed by the relief he felt at escaping Richard's wrath. Once was enough. By hook or by crook, he would see it done this time around.

CHAPTER 7

William Rickhill was not used to a lot of travel, nor was he the kind of man who engaged in intrigue. He was a proper administrator turned justiciary, who loved to keep his books in order and gave serious attention to cases under his authority. Imagine his surprise and alarm when he was dragged out of bed in the middle of the night by a persistent banging below. Wrapping a cloak around his shoulders, he went to the top of his stairs while a servant opened the door and put his eye to the gap.

"I have a message for Sir William Rickhill," said a gruff voice. "A message from the king." The servant turned around and looked worriedly up the stairs; Rickhill nodded. Pushing open the door and handing over the message, the lightly-armed soldier stepped inside and leaned against the wall. Rickhill could see he wasn't about to leave. Shrugging, the justice opened the letter.

The commission was dated about three weeks earlier. It read, *"Sir William Rickhill, you are commanded, under pain of forfeiture, to immediately accompany the Earl of Nottingham to Calais, and do what he should tell you."* Rickhill looked at the man. "What is your name?"

"John Mannering, my lord."

"Are you to accompany me to Calais?"

"To Dover, my lord. I am instructed to wait while you prepare yourself."

Sighing, Rickhill resigned himself to this unpleasant task. One could never understand the whims of a king, and it was not up to him to question the unusual circumstances. In a short time he was ready to go and followed Mannering out the door; a saddled horse was waiting for him.

They rode all night and reached Dover after the sun was well above the horizon. If he wasn't so tired, Rickhill would have appreciated the beautiful sunrise and the emerald green tinge to

76

the Channel. As it was, he obediently boarded the merchant ship waiting for him; Mowbray, the Earl Marshall, had already gone ahead. The captain graciously allowed him to use his cabin, and Rickhill slept most of the way to Calais. On arrival, he was taken to the house of a Lombard woolen merchant and given lodgings. It was all very organized.

In the early evening, at the hour of vespers, a servant of Mowbray came for Rickhill and took him to the earl's hostel. Mowbray stood and greeted him, offering food and drink and a seat of honor. The justice gratefully accepted, though naturally he was suspicious of all this secrecy. Still, he knew the answers would be revealed in time. Mowbray was a good and gracious host and waited until Rickhill was finished before coming to the point of his visit. He reached into his satchel and pulled out a sealed commission.

"The king has an assignment for you," he said quietly, tapping it against his palm. "I must have your oath that none of this will be revealed to any person whatsoever."

Rickhill gulped. "I swear, on God's honor."

From the king's justice, this was sufficient. Satisfied, Mowbray held out the scroll and watched as Rickhill unrolled it and read the contents. He blinked, then read it again before looking up in astonishment.

"I don't understand. It was reported that the Duke of Gloucester is dead. It's been publicly announced in both Calais and England."

Mowbray grimaced. "As you see, this is not the case."

"And I am to interview him. For what purpose?"

"The duke and the other two Appellants have been appealed of *Lèse-majesté* concerning events from 1386-88. They will be tried for treason. You are commanded to get his statement which will be presented to Parliament on his behest."

Rickhill shifted in his chair. He was under no illusions about the seriousness of this commission. He remembered the Judges from the Merciless Parliament, who had all been exiled to Ireland—after they were condemned for treason and nearly hanged. In fact, his own appointment to the bench was to fill one of their vacancies. "This bears the same date as my instructions to come to Calais."

Mowbray brushed away the objection. "It is no matter. You know letters patent can take two or three weeks to deliver."

Rickhill considered this, but he was still not convinced. "I must have witnesses," he said.

The earl looked up, considering, and nodded. "Very well. I will have my two esquires, John Lovetot and John Surrey call on you at dawn. They will accompany you to the duke."

This would have to do. Rickhill went back to his lodgings, prepared for a restless night. By morning, he had considered all his options and determined how he would approach this dangerous meeting.

The Duke of Gloucester was attended by a number of his followers; Rickhill recognized five of them. The prisoner didn't look like he'd been mistreated. He was well fed, there was furniture in the room and plenty of writing materials and books. That was somewhat encouraging. Gloucester straightened when the justice entered his room, and his companions retreated to the far wall. Mowbray's esquires stood near the door.

Rickhill bowed slightly. "Your Grace, I have been sent by the king with certain instructions I must read to you. But before I do this, I must make two requests. First, I beg you not to be displeased with me, for I am only acting by the king's command under pain of forfeiture." He paused, and Gloucester nodded. "Secondly, that you write down what you wish to say to me and keep a copy for yourself."

The Duke nodded again. "What is your commission?"

Rickhill unrolled the scroll. "The king says, *You are to hold an interview with the Duke of Gloucester in which he explains, in his own words, matters and points as relates to the 1386 Parliament, the establishment of the derogatory Continual Council, the unlawful acts of the 1388 Parliament and the dishonor shown to my person. Carefully report under your seal what he shall say to you.*"

All the while, Gloucester stared at his hands. When Rickhill finished reading, the duke looked stunned. Finally, he shook himself as if to bring his thoughts under control.

78

"Please sit, Justice Rickhill." One of the squires brought over a chair. As Rickhill gratefully lowered himself, Gloucester scowled. "So, I am finally brought to account. When is Parliament scheduled to meet?"

"It opens on September 17."

"Hmm. Just over a week." Gloucester tapped his fingers on the table. "Instead of calling me, they send you for a confession. This is the end, isn't it?"

Not knowing what to say, Rickhill bowed his head. Apparently, the duke didn't know his death had already been widely reported.

"Can I discover a last bit of mercy in my nephew's heart?" The duke rubbed the back of his neck. "I suppose that is my only hope." He stared hard at Rickhill. "Has the king spoken to you about this?"

"I knew nothing about this commission until I was brought to Calais. The Earl of Nottingham gave me the writ."

"I expected as much."

Sighing, Rickhill got up. "As I requested, please put everything in writing and make a copy for your records. I will return this evening."

Rickhill didn't have much hope for the duke's cooperation. To his surprise, Gloucester took the king's command very seriously. It was early in the evening when the justice returned with Lovetot and Lancaster; by then, Gloucester was alone with his clerk. The finished confession and his copy were on the table. The duke looked strained, while at the same time he had a sense of stoicism about him. He gestured to the table.

"Take it."

Rickhill obliged then seated himself. "Please, read it to me. I would hear it in your own words."

"All right." Gloucester picked up the document and held it close to his face. "Please," he said to his clerk, "light some candles. The Earl Marshal can afford it." He cleared his throat. "I, Thomas of Woodstock, on the eighth of September in the twenty-first year of my lord the king, by virtue of a commission directed to William Rickhill, justice, I acknowledge that I was one of those, along with other men, who instigated and assented to the

79

making of a Commission. In this Commission we restrained my lord's freedom, and along with others, took upon myself royal powers—though truly I did not know or realize at the time I was acting contrary to his regality, though I know now." He looked up for confirmation and Rickhill nodded. "Also, at the time I came armed into my lord's presence, and into his palace, albeit I did it out of fear for my life. I acknowledge for certain that I did evil and acted against his regality and estate. Also that I slandered my lord in the presence of other persons. But I swear, upon pain of my soul, I meant no evil thereby."

He paused, wiping his forehead. "Please, a drink," he said to the clerk. Rickhill watched as he raised the cup with a trembling hand. This was a Gloucester nobody ever saw.

"All right. Inasmuch as I, along with others, discussed, out of fear for my life, the question of surrendering my homage to my lord—I fully admit we discussed this. Whether we agreed to do it or not, I truly cannot remember but I believe we did. Also, I was present when the question of the deposition of my lord was discussed. I acknowledge in truth that we did, for two or three days, agree to do this. But then we performed our homage and our oaths to him and restored him to as high estate as he had been in previously. Nevertheless, I acknowledge that I acted disloyally and unkindly to him who is my liege lord, who has been such a good and kind lord to me. As for anything else, I swear that ever since, I have not been aware of any gathering directed against either him or any others about his person.

"Concerning all these points I have confessed to William Rickhill, justice, through which I readily acknowledge that I have, by my disloyalty and unkindness, offended my lord and acted against him. Yes, truly it was my intention and my wish to do the best I could for his royal person and estate. Nevertheless, I am well aware now that my actions and deeds did not fulfill my intentions. I declare, it never was my desire to do anything that might have been distressful or harmful. I beseech my sovereign lord the king that he will grant to me his mercy and grace, for I put my life, my body, and my goods wholly at his will, as humbly and as meekly as any creature can do. I beseech his high lordship that he vouchsafe me his compassion and pity, even though I am unworthy."

Rickhill would have doubted the sincerity of this confession but for the obvious distress the duke exhibited. His voice shook at the end and he repeatedly wiped his brow. Gently, the justice placed the document on the table. "Place your seal on it, if you would." He stood, waiting. "Is there anything else you wish to add, concerning this business? I will communicate it personally to the king."

After sealing the confession, Gloucester walked with Rickhill to the door and put a hand on his arm. "Yes, there is one matter I remembered only after writing the confession. I admit I said to the king, that if he wished to be a king, he should stop begging to save the life of Simon Burley. Please, tell the king for me, by word of mouth."

Mowbray's esquires followed Rickhill out, leaving Gloucester alone with his clerk. For a long time, the duke stared at the door. He couldn't get Richard and Anne out of his mind, begging for Burley's life. He hadn't forgotten to mention it in the confession; it was just too painful to confront. All the events of ten years ago had been brought back into focus, and this was the first time he actually saw them from Richard's point of view. The boy had struggled to be heard, and their only answer was to force him to submit to their control. At the time, he had been convinced that his way was best for the country. Was it really so? Or had his selfish desires clouded his judgment? He shook his head, but could not make the doubt go away. Perhaps the trauma had damaged the king. Perhaps they had gone too far.

Gloucester sighed. Well, he had done the best he could. As he knew too well, the wheel of fortune turned for everyone. Ten years ago, he was at the top and the king was at the bottom. Now, it was the total opposite. If ever he got out of this situation, he vowed he would never criticize the king again. Richard was a man now. Like a man, he could make his own mistakes and live with them.

The room was chilly and gloomy; light from the candles didn't reach into the corners. The duke wrapped a long scarf around his neck and sat once again, picking up a book, though he neglected to open it. Time moved slowly in this awful place. Letting the book fall into his lap, his eyes closed.

He was suddenly shocked awake by five men who entered the room, then three more. His clerk scurried away with his copy of the confession. One man blocked the door—as if he could get past these assassins! Standing, Gloucester reached for his dagger then remembered it had been taken from him.

"Ha! Is that you, Fraunceys? So even Rutland is conspiring against me! And you, Colfox! And William Serle, Mowbray's dog. Where are my attendants?"

"Forget about that. You know why we are here," said Serle. "Make it easy on yourself."

"And spare you the pleasure of killing me?" Gloucester lunged at him, wrapping his hands around Serle's throat. His grip was strong the man staggered under his ferocity. But only for a moment. Two of the others grasped the ends of Gloucester's scarf, pulling with all their might. He let go of Serle and clawed at his neck, to no avail. Throwing out his arms, he struck one of the attackers, but his strength was failing and he was gasping for breath. Dropping to his knees, Gloucester kept struggling until he fell forward. One of the others caught his body before the face smashed onto the floor; they were told not to leave any marks.

"Is he dead?" asked Serle.

"Let's put him on the bed and hold a pillow over his face, just to be sure. Help me pick him up," said Colfox. Three others came to his aid and together they wrestled the duke over to his bed. It was evident that he was gone, but they applied the pillow just to be sure. After a long wait, Serle gestured for them to leave. The Earl Marshal was waiting for their report.

The following morning, Rickhill decided to ask the Duke of Gloucester a few more questions. When he got to the castle, a surly guard blocked his way.

"I've come to see the duke."

The guard shook his head. "No. Permission has been denied."

"Do you know who I am? I am here on the king's orders."

"And I am here on the Earl Marshal's orders. He has instructed me that you are no longer to enter the castle. Under any circumstances."

"This is outrageous! Where is the Earl Marshal?"

"He cannot be disturbed. His instructions were clear."

Harboring the deepest suspicions, Rickhill sent messages to Mowbray. The responses were the same. He was to return to England and personally deliver the duke's confession to the king. Seeing no other recourse, the justice obliged and took the next ship to Dover.

It took Rickhill five days to reach London, and he learned that King Richard was at Westminster Palace. When he was announced into the lesser hall, the king was having an animated chat with the Bishop of London, and numerous other ecclesiastics and courtiers were amusing themselves. A group of musicians played a lively chorus and pairs of dancers strutted around in a circle, bowing and twirling to the music. In one corner, gaudily dressed men were sitting around a table betting on a game of cards. A valet approached Rickhill and leaned an ear while the justice asked for an interview with the king.

Richard looked up and nodded, excusing himself and beckoning Rickhill to follow him into a private room. The king was accompanied by a clerk who bore an amazing resemblance to him. Richard seated himself, adjusting his scalloped sleeves which hung all the way to the floor, scrunched up by a string of pearls from elbow to shoulder. Rickhill tried not to stare; he had never seen such magnificence.

"You have come from Calais?" Richard asked.

"Yes, sire. I came directly here."

"Did you successfully accomplish your mission?" This was only a formality. Rutland's henchman had passed Rickhill on the way to Westminster and had already reported Gloucester's death. Over the years, Richard had gotten into the habit of testing his public servants; one never knew where disloyalty might be lurking.

Still uncomfortable that he had been refused a second interview with Gloucester, Rickhill nodded, pulling out the duke's confession. He hesitated before handing it to the clerk. "Sire, I respectfully request an exemplification—an officially registered copy—of this document."

The king suppressed his annoyance; Rickhill had done him a good deed, and, after all, he was chosen for his efficiency. "Very well. We shall do so at once. Richard Maudeleyn, my clerk, is in my confidence." He gestured to a chair. "You may sit. Fortunately, the chancellor is here at Westminster getting ready for Parliament, so he can seal your exemplification while you wait. Let me offer you some wine while Maudeleyn copies the report."

Rickhill sat, looking around the room. It was paneled with fine oak wainscoting, and the stained-glass windows bore royal coats of arms. While he waited, the Earl of Rutland came into the room and bent over Maudeleyn, reading the document out loud.

"Upon pain of my soul, in relation both to these points and to any other foolish or negligent deeds which I have committed, I declare it never was my intention, or my desire, or in my thoughts, to do anything that might have been distressful, or harmful to the salvation of my liege lord's person—and so I will answer before God at the day of judgment." Edward glanced at Richard. "By God, he will."

This seemed as good a time as any for Rickhill to deliver his oral message. "Sire," he said, "the Duke of Gloucester bade me tell you something else, which he forgot to include in this document. He acknowledged that he said if you wished to be a king, you should stop begging to save the life of Simon Burley."

Richard grabbed the arms of his chair and his eyes grew wide. He looked at Rutland, who took a seat at his side and put a hand on his wrist. Rickhill reminded himself they were first cousins. Even so, this familiarity was striking.

"That is the most damning statement of all," Edward said in a low voice. "He wouldn't commit it to paper."

Not knowing the reference, Rickhill hadn't fully appreciated the import of Gloucester's statement. He looked in confusion from the king to Rutland.

"That was one of many threats to my regality," Richard admitted. "More will come out in the days to come."

The quill kept scratching as Maudeleyn copied the words of the confession. Regaining his composure, the king leaned toward Edward. "Have my uncles of York and Lancaster arrived with their men-at-arms?"

"Yes, as you instructed they brought 1000 men each for your protection. Lancaster's force has been settled at Smithfield. My father's men have found lodging in the city."

"And our cousin Bolingbroke?"

"He just showed up this morning. We are settling them into quarters near the Manor of Hyde, thanks to the Abbot of Westminster."

"Then all is ready for tomorrow." He glanced at the window. "Come, let us inspect the building works. Join us, Justice Rickhill. Attend us while you wait."

The Westminster great hall had been badly in need of a new roof for many years, and Richard had embarked on the largest, most expensive project of his reign. Rickhill followed the king and earl into the vast space, which echoed with hammering and sawing and shouting from the dozens of workmen. Piles of timbers lay on the floor, waiting to be raised by huge cranes to the height of over twenty-eight meters.

"Amazing, is it not?" Richard said to Rickhill. "They frame these timbers near Farnham, in Surrey, take them apart and ship them by barge and wagon to Westminster before reassembling them." Overwhelmed, the justice kept turning around, gaping at the immense hammer beams. Richard pointed to the massive arches. "These span eighteen meters," he said proudly. "Not a single supporting column in the whole space."

They had to walk halfway down the hall to exit. Men bowed to the king as he passed. "The construction is too important to be interrupted by Parliament," Richard said. "So I ordered a temporary building to be erected just outside. They'll reuse the timbers after Parliament is over." As they went out they encountered a group of Cheshire archers, all wearing Richard's livery.

"Ah, here's our Dycun," one of them exclaimed. "We were just inspecting the raised walkways."

Rickhill looked around, astounded. He had heard the king used his Cheshire guards to watch over him at night—and to follow him everywhere—but he was surprised to see such informality! So the rumors were true; the king did give them special treatment.

"Hello John," Richard said, patting the guard on the back. "Has the rest of your company made it to London?"

"Aye, sire. We have four hundred archers now." He pointed to the platforms erected along the outer wall. Since the timber-roofed structure was open on all sides, the Cheshiremen would have a full view of Parliament. "I just wanted to be sure this framework will hold us."

"Watch closely tomorrow." Richard squeezed his arm before continuing on his way. "I don't want anyone causing me trouble."

"That we will, Dycun. That we will."

They walked into the open structure and approached the raised platform for the officials. The king's throne had already been erected, sitting high above the other benches, surmounted by a red canopy and a gold crown. "This meeting space will be awkward for everyone," Richard said, "and more than a little crowded. At least they won't waste time arguing. We have much to do. Come, let's see if Maudeleyn has finished."

Everything was in order, and Richard sent Rickhill to the chancery so his copy of Gloucester's statement could be fixed with the Great Seal. Meanwhile, the king and Edward scrutinized the original.

"I'm surprised he was so remorseful," Richard mused.

Rutland grunted. "He was looking for mercy. He had no other opportunity."

Running a finger along some of the last statements, Richard shook his head. "It's too much. Before we're done reading it to the Commons, there won't be a dry eye amongst them. Their sympathy will overturn everything I'm trying to accomplish. No, this won't do."

Anticipating Richard's next command, Maudeleyn pulled another piece of paper closer and dipped his quill.

"Yes, let's rewrite this thing," Richard said. "We don't need to add anything; that would be unjust. We merely need to make a few deletions. The first thing we will do is eliminate the date. Nobody needs to know when this was written." Richard glanced at Edward for confirmation.

Rutland nodded. "As far as we are concerned, this was written before August 25."

Reading aloud, Richard recited the professions of guilt. He couldn't deny it; he felt gratified—almost appeased. "This is all very good. Except for the nonsense about his intentions. Of course he knew what he was doing; he knew exactly how to hurt me. He showed no mercy to my advisors." He paused, remembering. "My friends."

The others kept silent; after all this time, they could see the pain was still raw. The king recovered himself, shaking his head. "Let's remove most of the drivel. The last two paragraphs where he is begging for mercy—remove them altogether. We don't need that. We only need to convict him of treason. I don't think anyone will object, once they hear his last confession."

While Maudeleyn was writing, Rutland moved his chair closer to Richard. "What of Rickhill? Surely he'll know the difference."

"Edward, you must pay him a visit. Reward him well. When he reads our copy before Parliament, make sure he understands he is not to make any objections, under pain of forfeiture."

"As you wish. He is a wise man. I'm sure he will comply."

Richard surrounded himself with his closest associates at supper that night—the eve of his greatest, most critical Parliament. Because this was a special occasion, he had a large table set up in his Painted Chamber, originally built by Henry III as part of the royal apartments. Long and narrow, the chamber had a canopied bed at one end, with a large wall painting of Edward the Confessor above it. Tall arched windows graced one side, while the opposite wall was painted with biblical scenes.

The king invited all his Counter-Appellants, as well as Bushy, Bagot, and Green, his closest councilors. These last three, all no higher than knightly rank, had served him more efficiently than the rest of his barons put together. After this Parliament, when he was truly free of all restraint, he would know how to reward his loyal retainers. Mowbray failed to show up, but the king affected not to notice.

Richard was at his most charming. Now that all their preparations were over, he allowed himself to relax and called in his minstrels, who sang verses to the accompaniment of lute, recorders, violin, hand-bells, and a four-stringed mandolin.

"Tell us the story of the miser who pretended his own death," Richard called when they had finished a particularly lively song. Stepping forward, a long-faced bard dressed in a short parti-colored tunic and hose bowed and removed his floppy hat.

There once was a rich ferryman from London who was so miserly that he would not give the light from his candles to his neighbors. Yes, I heard that mice and rats would not even go near his house because there was never a bit of food left over for them. Well, one day he came up with the idea that if he feigned his own death his servants would fast for the day and he would not have to feed them. So he wrapped himself in a shroud, intending, later on, to suddenly come back to life. But lo and behold! When his servants thought he was dead, they were overjoyed! They broke into his cupboard and took all the breads and cheeses and had a great feast in celebration. Our miser was so outraged that he struggled to get out of his shroud so he could chastise them. But one of the servants, thinking he was a ghost, grabbed an oar and beat his master to death!

Richard roared with laughter, slapping Holland on the shoulder. Wine flowed freely around the table, and when the bard finished, he and his little band were showered with coins. Holland broke into an old troubadour's song and the others followed, weaving back and forth and trying to outshout each other. The king's chamber knights joined the party and the merriment continued unabated.

Much later that same evening, after the others had gone their way, Mowbray had himself announced to the king. Richard was playing chess with Edward when Thomas entered the room; the king had his back to the door and didn't bother turning around.

"So you finally decided to come," he said, his voice flat.

Mowbray moved forward and dropped on one knee. "Sire, the autumn winds held my ship back at Calais."

Richard narrowed his eyes. "That's not the reason."

Damn the king and his suspicions! There was no point in denying his lie. Mowbray started pacing around the room. "It's like this, sire. I'm one of us and one of them at the same time. I can't accuse them of treason. Where does that put me?"

Richard frowned. "Have you not demonstrated your loyalty?"

"I was loyal then as I am now. I am many things, but not a hypocrite. I could barely look Gloucester in the face."

"But you did. He admitted his wrongdoing."

"Isn't that enough? Must you impose the ultimate penalty?"

Eyes wide, Richard stared at the earl. *Was he wrong about Mowbray's fidelity?* "Do you question my judgment?"

Thomas knew he was in trouble. He glanced at Edward whose expression was carefully guarded while he moved a piece on the board.

"No, no, no. It's not that," Mowbray said hurriedly. "This is just awkward for me. I am your devoted servant."

Richard picked up a chess piece. "Then see that you heed my wishes. I need all eight of you present when it comes time to make the appeal."

"Don't worry, I will be your spokesman," Rutland interjected. "That should take the attention away from Thomas."

Bowing, Mowbray left the room. Once again, he was glad to escape relatively unscathed. He knew how close he was to disaster. How to stay in the king's good graces? Somewhere along the way, his skills as a courtier had failed him. Would he ever recover Richard's goodwill?

CHAPTER 8

"There shall be one king over them all. Never again shall we have a divided kingdom." The new chancellor, Bishop Stafford of Exeter, raised a finger in emphasis. "Ezekiel 37:22."

Standing before Richard, the chancellor looked over the Parliament assembly. Behind him, on a raised platform, sat John of Gaunt to the king's right, presiding as Lord High Steward of England. Next to him sat the Duke of York and Henry Bolingbroke; there was no doubt they would follow Lancaster's lead in every way. To the king's other side sat Archbishop Thomas Arundel and the other bishops. In front of the chancellor, the members were all standing, crowded together under the temporary roof in the hopes that the rain would hold off.

Stafford's voice rang out clearly. "For the realm to be well-governed, three things are needed: first, the king should be powerful enough to govern. This means he must be in full possession of his regalities. Secondly, his laws should be properly enforced. For this to happen, they need to be backed by appropriate punishment. Thirdly, the king's subjects should be duly obedient. Parliament is obligated to punish those who restrained the king's natural authority in the past, and precautions need to be made so these offenses are not repeated in the future."

This was a stronger stance than had ever been taken before, and the Commons shifted uncomfortably while the chancellor proceeded to the usual opening business. Then it was the turn of Speaker Bushy to step up to the bar. As agreed from the night before, Bushy started with his first petition. "Your Majesty, I would remind you how in the tenth year of your reign, the Duke of Gloucester, the earls of Arundel and Warwick, and Thomas Arundel, then chancellor, compelled you to accept a Council that governed this realm without your input. This was prejudicial to your regality and did you great injury. I petition this

Parliament to revoke the act of 1386 and annul the Continual Council and all that flowed from it."

Richard affected a neutral pose, though he couldn't help but hold his breath. Attacks on his prerogative started during the 1386 Parliament when Michael de la Pole was impeached and they forced the Council down his throat. And that was only the beginning. By the time the Merciless Parliament was over two years later, his very crown had been threatened and his loyal friends murdered.

This was the first step toward his full retribution. Everything depended on how the Commons received this petition. Were they with the king, or against him? Richard waited, afraid to move. The crowd murmured, squirming under the gaze of the Cheshire archers—lined up along those specially built platforms around the perimeter of the open courtyard. Finally, someone shouted *hear him, hear him* and all of a sudden men were clapping their hands and waving their approval. Richard let out his breath; they were truly his partisans now, the exact opposite of the situation ten years ago.

Encouraged by the response, Bushy went on. "I further petition this Parliament to revoke the pardons given to the Lords Appellant in 1388. The pardons were traitorously obtained with the illicit collusion of Archbishop Arundel!" While the Commons expressed their approval, Bushy elaborately raised his arm and pointed at Arundel, who stood up to defend himself.

"Not now," Richard interjected, holding up his palm. "You may reply on the morrow. Please, Lord Archbishop, withdraw now."

Frowning, the archbishop obliged. No one paid attention to him as he quietly slipped from the hall.

Ignoring him, Richard stood. "I give my assent to each of your petitions. Nonetheless," he added, glancing over at his uncle York. "I will respect the pardon of all the other members from the Commission, for I recognize they have proven their loyalty to me."

There was a stir as the Duke of York and the old Bishop of Wykeham fell to their knees, weeping tears of gratitude. Despite himself, the king felt a tinge of guilt. In his eagerness to prosecute his enemies, he had inadvertently attacked others. On the other hand, they weren't entirely innocent. "Get up, uncle," he said in a low voice, and Gaunt helped his brother off the floor.

Anxious to get on to the next order of business, Richard nodded to the chancellor. "Taking into consideration my opening statement," Stafford said, "I must emphasize that the perpetrators of the Merciless Parliament are to be put on trial for their traitorous deeds. They were abetted by many co-conspirators. However, King Richard wants to strengthen the goodwill of his subjects, and to this end he offers a demonstration of his affection. He is prepared to offer a general pardon to all guilty persons, provided they sue for their pardons before the feast of St. Hillary, Jan. 13, of next year—" He had to pause until the grumbling in the crowd died down. "With the exception of those who will be impeached in this Parliament, and fifty persons whose names the king reserves to himself."

The grumbling swelled in volume, and Bushy spoke to a few knights before stepping back to the bar and waving for the crowd to settle down. "Your Majesty, at the Commons' behest, I beg you to disclose the fifty names."

"In due time," said the king. He gestured for the chancellor to continue.

Stafford consulted his papers. "The king has ordained a new statutory definition of treason. Anyone in the future, who incites the people against the king, usurps or undermines the king's regality, that person shall be adjudged a false traitor and should suffer the appropriate penalty. Anyone who proposes the king's death or deposition shall be adjudged a traitor."

A little less enthusiastically, the Commons gave their assent. Richard exhaled, vindicated. Finally, after eleven years, the questions to the Judges had been enacted into law.

But there was more. "The king has also determined that, since this Parliament will be addressing capital crimes, the consent of the clergy will not be required." Because of their vows, the prelates could not impose the death sentence; therefore they had to be removed—just as in the Merciless Parliament. The Commons grew restless again, and some of the braver knights voiced their disapproval.

92

Bushy needed to shout. "The king has commanded that the prelates appoint a proxy to represent them." Many of the bishops were on their feet now, and there was a lot of movement in the throng. Fists were raised, people were getting shoved. Many were clamoring at the king and his advisors.

Suddenly the Cheshire archers, who up until now had stood quietly on their platform, decided to impose order. One after the other, they came to attention and bent their bows, drawing their arrows and holding, ready to release. Someone in the crowd noticed and shouted, pointing. Others turned and cried out, spreading panic. People ducked their heads; others threw up their hands; the lucky ones on the edges tried to escape.

Richard leapt to his feet, stretching out his arms. "Hold! Hold!" he shouted. "Stay your bows."

That was enough. The archers relaxed their stance and the frenzy passed. But the Commons were suddenly a much more malleable force.

"I suggest the clergy appoint Sir Thomas Percy as their representative," the king said. As he expected, nobody objected. The motion was passed without another comment.

This was enough for one session. Richard gave notice that the Lords and Commons could go back to their lodgings. Subdued, they filed out, afraid to look up at their threatening sentinels. The king watched, a half-smile on his face. All in all, he had had a fine opening day. Everything had gone as planned.

The next morning, Richard sent a messenger to the archbishop telling him to stay in his lodgings. In his absence, and in the absence of the prelates, Bushy laid charges of treason against Thomas Arundel. In 1386, as chancellor it was his duty to act in the king's favor. Rather, he voted against the king. Again, in 1388 he called Parliament and acted to the prejudice of the king's regality. Because he was a man of the cloth, he was impeached rather than condemned to death and was sentenced to forfeiture and exile.

This went off smoothly, but Bushy's next charge was undertaken with less confidence. "Your Majesty," he said, bowing twice for good measure, "the good Commons have asked me to clarify the identity of fifty unnamed persons excluded from the general pardon."

Richard stood, his eyes shooting fire. "I will not give you their names," he said in a low voice, "and those asking me to do so deserve death themselves." Even Bushy took a step back, and, seeing he had gone too far, Richard controlled his temper. "See here," he said, "if I named the guilty ones, they would escape, while others associated with them, who have nothing to fear, would take needless fright. Can't you see?"

Indeed, they could not see at all. It was time to move on.

The fifth day of Parliament all eight Counter-Appellants made their entrance, dressed in crimson robes trimmed with white silk and powdered with knots of gold. Arms joined at the elbows, just like the Lords Appellant of 1388, they approached and knelt before the king. Then they stood and stepped back one pace—all but Edward, Earl of Rutland; he was to be their spokesman.

"Your Majesty, we appeal Thomas of Woodstock, Duke of Gloucester, Richard Fitzalan, Earl of Arundel, Thomas Beauchamp, Earl of Warwick and Sir Thomas Mortimer of high treason." Mortimer had recently been added, as the king never forgot that he treacherously murdered Thomas Molineux at Radcot Bridge. It mattered not that Mortimer was in Ireland at the moment. "These men had conspired to depose the king, to withdraw homage, and to rise in armored insurrection against his Majesty."

"Your appeal is duly noted," Richard said, still seated. "We will proceed to the trial of Richard Fitzalan, Earl of Arundel."

John of Gaunt, Lord High Steward, presided. Tall, proud, and stern, Gaunt looked down his nose at Arundel as the earl was led in, dressed in his peer's robe and a red hood.

"Lord Nevill, remove the prisoner's belt and his hood."

Arundel glared at Gaunt while he was divested of the distinguished tokens of his rank. While Rutland read the articles of the appeal to him, he continued to glower at the duke.

"What is your response?" said Gaunt.

Setting his mouth, Arundel refused to answer.

"I repeat, how do you respond to these accusations?"

"There is no point in replying! I know you have ordered me to be put to death in order to seize my possessions."

Some of the Commons grumbled at that, but Gaunt was losing patience. "Sir Richard, you are fortunate that we give you the opportunity to reply. If we followed *your own* law, from the Parliament of 1388, you would only be permitted to respond Guilty or Not Guilty. As you did with Nicholas Brembre."

"What was done ten years ago was in response to the circumstances of the time. If errors were made then, I have been pardoned by the king!" He held up the scroll. "I had no desire ever to remove myself from the king's grace—"

"That pardon is revoked, traitor!"

"Truly you lie!" cried Arundel. "Never was I a traitor!"

"Then why do you seek a pardon?"

"To silence the tongues of my enemies, of whom you are one!" He wiped his mouth. "And to be sure, when it comes to treason, you are in greater need of a pardon than I am. In truth, John, if you were to be interrogated closely, it would be found that your actions have been far more prejudicial to the king's interests than mine."

"That is enough," interrupted Richard. "Answer the appeal."

Turning to the king, Arundel said, "I see it clearly now: all those who accuse me of treason, you are all liars. Never was I a traitor. I still claim the benefit of my pardon which you gave me of your own free will."

"I granted it, provided it was not to my prejudice," retorted Richard.

"Therefore the grant is worthless," said Gaunt.

At this point, Bushy saw fit to step in. "That pardon has already been revoked by the king, the Lords, and us, the faithful Commons."

Arundel rounded on the Speaker. "Where are those faithful Commons?" He affected to look around the hall. "I know all about you and your crew, and how you have got here—not to act faithfully, but to shed my blood. The faithful Commons of the

95

kingdom are not here; if they were, they would without doubt be on my side, trying to keep me from falling into your clutches. They, I know, are grieving greatly for me; while you, I know, have always been false."

Incensed, the members railed at the earl. "Look, Lord King," shouted Bushy, "at how this traitor is trying to stir up dissension between us and the commons who have stayed home."

More shouting ensued, and the king permitted it to go on. Let Arundel suffer the humiliation he had borne all alone, ten years ago.

Then Bolingbroke rose to his feet. "Did you not say to me at Huntingdon, where we first gathered in revolt, that before doing anything else it would be better to seize the king?"

Turning red, Arundel pointed at him. "You, Henry Earl of Derby, you lie in your teeth! I never said anything to you or anyone else about my lord king, except what was to his welfare and honor."

Then the king interjected, "Did you not say to me at the time of your Parliament, in the bath behind the White Hall, that Simon Burley was worthy of death? And I replied that I neither knew nor could discover any reason for his execution. And even though my wife, the queen and I interceded tirelessly on his behalf, yet you and your accomplices, ignoring our pleas, traitorously put him to death." He looked down at his hands, which had drawn themselves into fists. Turning to his uncle, he said, "Pass sentence on him."

Arundel knew he had met his doom. As Gaunt passed judgment, he barely listened.

"I, John of Lancaster, Steward of England, adjudge you a traitor and sentence you to be drawn, hanged, beheaded and quartered on Tower Hill, where Simon Burley was beheaded. Your children shall be disinherited, and their children shall be excluded from Parliament and from the king's council forever." If Gaunt was expecting some kind of response from Arundel, he was destined to be disappointed. "I advise you to acknowledge your guilt and throw yourself on the king's mercy," he prompted.

Arundel answered with a sneer. "I submit myself to the mercy of the Supreme King. I am quite ready to die." Taking that for his last answer, Gaunt turned to King Richard.

The king stood. "Out of recognition of your birth, and because of the consideration you showed Simon Burley, I lift the penalties of drawing and hanging. You may proceed."

Even his worst enemies couldn't deny the earl's boldness, though it availed him little. He looked straight ahead while his hands were bound behind his back and he was led out of the palace precincts, destined to walk on foot to Tower Hill. The Cheshire guards were already lined up; they were to accompany the prisoner to deter any possible rescue attempts. Many of the nobles mounted fine steeds and preceded Arundel through London; among their number were Thomas de Mowbray, his son-in-law, and Thomas Holland, his nephew. At Arundel's request, they loosened his bonds so he could give alms to beggars along the roadside. When they reached Charing Cross, an Augustinian friar heard his confession. They continued through Cheapside, and the crowd kept growing while Londoners called his name, lamenting and sending blessings as much as they dared. The king would have been surprised—and displeased—to have witnessed such a display of affection. He never understood the fickle behavior of his Londoners.

As they reached Tower Hill, an official asked Arundel once again to admit his treason. Up to that point, the prisoner had maintained a proud silence, but this was too much.

"Why do you afflict me at my final hour? I tell you, I know not the cause of my ruin, except I could not please the king in the manner he desired." Resting his eye on Mowbray, he said, "And you, and Holland, shame on you both for your lack of gratitude. The time will come when men will marvel at your misfortune, just as they now wonder at my fate." Giving them one last scornful look, he turned and mounted the scaffold.

The executioner, holding a sword, was waiting and untied Arundel's hands. For a moment, the earl looked over the crowd and nodded, comforted that his popularity, at least, would survive him. As Mowbray climbed the ladder behind him, Arundel turned to the swordsman. "I forgive you," he said, handing him a coin, "on the condition you strike my head off with one blow." He reached up and ran a thumb across the blade's edge. "It seems sharp enough," he added, attempting—and failing—to make light of it. He glanced at Mowbray and turned so his son-in-law could tie the blindfold. Then he knelt, his body upright. Mowbray stepped back.

The executioner raised his sword and struck cleanly. The head flew into the crowd, but the body didn't move. It held its position, some remembered, for as long as it took to say the Lord's Prayer before falling forward with a thud onto the platform.

Crossing himself, the Augustinian friar collected the head and his fellow monks helped remove the body to their church on Broad Street. He was laid to rest in the choir near the high altar.

It was Mowbray's task to inform the archbishop of his brother's fate. Thomas Arundel was still under house arrest at his lodgings, and few men were brave enough to visit him. It was not good policy to be seen with a man in such disfavor. Mowbray was different; the king had sent him.

The archbishop received him in his garden, wearing long robes and a hood that nearly covered his eyes. He was clutching at his upper arms, and Mowbray wondered if he was chilled by the crisp air—or was it the impending news? When Arundel looked up, his hopeful expression faded. "They've done it, haven't they?"

Mowbray sat heavily. The earl had proved a troublesome father-in-law and an ungrateful ally, but that didn't make it any easier to break his fate to his brother. "He was declared a traitor."

The archbishop turned away, hiding his tears. "Is he to be given no mercy?"

"Your Grace, it is over. They took him to Tower Hill."

Arundel whirled around in disbelief. "Already?" He crossed himself, twice. "My poor brother. And his heirs?"

"Disinherited."

"I would expect nothing less. Our king is an unforgiving man." His lips moved and Mowbray suspected he was silently cursing Richard. The archbishop sighed, his face drawn with sorrow. "It's my fault," he started, his voice strangled. "I let Richard trick me into persuading my brother to give himself up."

The other closed his eyes. That was so like the king.

"He could have escaped," Arundel added. "He didn't need to go like a sheep to the slaughter."

Sadly, Mowbray shook his head. "You know he never would have fled. That was not his way. It might have gone even worse for him if he hadn't given himself up."

"No, Thomas. It couldn't have been worse, even if they laid siege to his castle. He could have gone down fighting."

"Oh, your grace. He did. He did. Never did a man show more courage."

Arundel's eyes got big and he crossed himself. "What kind of world do we live in? I'll tell you, Nottingham. This won't be the end of it. Look to your own devices. You and other lords might be next."

CHAPTER 9

On the sixth day of Parliament, Sir Thomas de Mowbray was instructed to produce his prisoner, the Duke of Gloucester. In a hush, Mowbray stood and advanced to the bar, alone. Addressing the king, he said, "Sire, I cannot obey your command because the Duke of Gloucester is dead. By order of my most excellent lord the king, I held the duke in my custody at the king's castle in the town of Calais, and in this same prison he died." He waited, holding his breath. To his surprise, the Commons accepted his statement with remarkable calm.

Since rumors of Gloucester's death had been circulating for a month, no one was surprised, though there were a few in attendance who wondered at the posturing. However, since the king had already taken possession of the duke's estates, formalities needed to be followed. Mowbray held aloft a document. "Here I have his signed confession," he declared. "The Duke of Gloucester has given his statement to Justice Rickhill under his seal. My lord, please come forward and read the confession in the duke's own words."

Standing, Rickhill accepted the document from Mowbray and turned to the assembly. Looking down at the copy, he immediately noticed that the date had been removed. He cleared his throat, remembering the veiled threat coming from the Earl of Rutland. If he valued his position—his very life, most probably—he would not make a pother about any changes made to the original.

The king and the Lords and the Commons waited patiently for him to begin. "I arrived at Calais Castle about eight in the morning and was brought to the Duke of Gloucester. His memory was good, and it was apparent to me he was well treated. In the presence of John Lancaster and John Lovetot, I showed him my commission from the king and said if there was anything he wanted to say, he should put it all in writing. This, then, is the document he handed over to me later that same evening."

He held it up before his face. "I, Thomas Duke of Gloucester, by the name Thomas of Woodstock," he began, "in the twenty-first year of King Richard, in the castle of Calais..." Gaining confidence, Rickhill proceeded to read the confession Richard had so carefully revised. Not that much had been changed, after all—only a few deletions. Gloucester admitted his guilt in the many deeds opposed to the king's majesty, though he claimed he did not appreciate the seriousness of his assaults on the king's regality. It was all there in the confession.

Once he had finished, Rickhill raised his eyes to Richard, hoping his performance was acceptable. The king nodded briefly, then gestured to Thomas Percy. The royal steward took over while Rickhill gratefully withdrew. The next step had all been prepared, and in short order the lords judged Gloucester a traitor to the realm and pronounced the same sentence as Arundel's. The duke's guilt was manifest; not a word was raised in his defense. Even John of Gaunt forbore to object.

While they were at it, because of his traitorous behavior as chancellor during the Merciless Parliament, Archbishop Arundel was officially stripped of his temporalities and sentenced to perpetual banishment from the realm. He was allowed six weeks from Michaelmas to take passage from Dover to France. It was quite a day for Richard. He decided to crown his achievements by delivering the message to Arundel himself. A score of Cheshire archers accompanied him, just for protection.

The archbishop did not look well. He greeted the king with a long face, bags under his eyes and a pale complexion. It looked like he hadn't slept for days. Ignoring his appearance, Richard swept into the room, calling for wine and taking a seat on the archbishop's chair.

"I have come to tell you myself," Richard started, trying to look solemn. "You have been impeached for your role as chancellor in the illegal activities of the Merciless Parliament—all of which were injurious to my regality."

He clasped his hands, trying to look contrite. "I'll see what I could do to countermand it," he said hurriedly.

Struck speechless, Arundel slowly lowered himself onto a bench.

"Nonetheless," the king continued, "I would recommend you prepare yourself to leave the country, for they have pronounced your banishment."

Despite himself, Arundel drew a ragged breath. "I don't want to leave the country. I was born here; I intend to die here."

Richard angled his head, hoping he looked sympathetic. "Try not to be too dejected, and don't refuse to go into exile. I assure you, it won't last for long. You shall return without fail before Easter. And as long as we two are both alive, no one but you shall be Archbishop of Canterbury." He waited for Arundel to take heart from his promise, but he waited in vain. Then, struck with a sudden impulse, Richard reached for the hem of his robe and turned it over, exposing a gold brooch. "Look. See this jewel? When I send it to you as a token, do not tarry and come straight to England. I'll keep it safe for you along with the jewels and ornaments of your chapel."

Arundel wanted to believe. He knelt, kissing Richard's hand.

"Rest assured," the king went on, "you will not be deprived of your See. Come, bring to me the Cross of St. Thomas of Canterbury and I will swear an oath upon it."

While Arundel went to his chapel, Richard adjusted his sleeve and took a sip of his wine. By the time the exile reached France, he would learn that this was all pretense; Richard had already chosen his successor. The soon-to-be ex-archbishop should be grateful he was protected by the Church, else he would have followed in the footsteps of his traitorous brother—all the way to the scaffold. Oh, what a slippery bastard he was, pretending to support the king, all the while plotting with his enemies. Did he really think Richard didn't know he was among those stirring up trouble before January's Parliament? And he did such a good job shielding Haxey from the king's wrath. Ha!

As the archbishop returned with the Cross, Richard gave him a bland smile. He would swear this oath and confess his sins later. For now, he had to ensure Arundel left the country. One more antagonist out of the way.

There was much more to be done. First, the heirs of Gloucester and Arundel needed to be debarred from their inheritance. Then the lords and bishops needed to swear that they would observe all deeds, censures, and sentences decreed at this Parliament. Once the king was satisfied, they moved on to the next item: Thomas Beauchamp, Earl of Warwick was put on trial.

The eldest of the Appellants, Warwick had weakened under the rigors of his confinement, relaxed though they were. As he was led into the chamber, his shoulders hunched over and he shuffled forward, looking at his feet.

Bolingbroke leaned toward his father. "He looks like a wretched old woman," he muttered. "He must have heard about Arundel's fate."

Gaunt frowned, silently agreeing with Henry. "Remove his hood," he declared.

While court clerks performed their duty Warwick attempted to help, though his fumbling impeded their efforts. Some of the members whispered amongst themselves.

Gaunt waited until the earl turned around to face the king. "You are accused of raising an armed force to oppose the king's men at Radcot Bridge and participating in the Appeal against King Richard's advisors in 1387-88. How do you plead?"

Warwick looked around the room for support, seeing none. He was not the stuff of martyrs. "My Lords," he answered, his voice breaking, "I admit my guilt." Sobbing, he fell to his knees. "Your Majesty, I trusted in the wisdom of the Duke of Gloucester and the Earl of Arundel and the spiritual integrity of the Archbishop of Canterbury." Tears ran down his face as his shoulders shook. "I curse the day I ever met them," he coughed, barely able to speak. "They unduly influenced me with their treacherous behavior. Nevertheless, if you truly adjudge that I have done wrong, then I throw myself upon the king's mercy!" Sobbing, he could say no more.

Richard gestured for his uncle to get on with the sentencing. Gaunt stood, adjusting his robes. "I, John of Lancaster, Steward of England, adjudge you a traitor and sentence you to be drawn, hanged, beheaded and quartered on Tower Hill—"

Warwick interrupted him, raising his hands. "Lord King, I truly deserve death for what I have done, but I implore you. Have mercy on me! I am a loathsome, remorseful penitent. Take pity on my soul and spare me. I beg of you!" He sobbed even louder.

Gaunt paused, watching this pitiful display with disdain. All around him, men raised their voices, adding their own pleas of leniency. Salisbury stood and exclaimed, "Sire, none of the Beauchamps had ever done treason against the crown. Sir Thomas is an old man and easily influenced." Others added their opinions, calling for mercy.

Richard sat back in his throne, trying not to gloat. It would have been better to see Gloucester thus. Still, at least one of the Appellants acknowledged the depth of their depravity. He stood, as the Commons quieted down; all one could hear was the sobbing of the terrified earl.

"By St. John the Baptist," the king exclaimed, "Thomas of Warwick, your confession is more pleasing to me than the value of all the lands of the Duke of Gloucester and the Earl of Arundel put together!"

Nonplussed, Gaunt turned to the king for instructions.

"I grant you your life," Richard said to Warwick, "and commute your sentence to life imprisonment and forfeiture of your goods. I am sending you to the Isle of Man under the guardianship of Sir William LeScrope."

Warwick was overcome with relief. Salisbury hurriedly stepped down and helped him out of the way before the king changed his mind.

Richard remained standing, for there remained one last piece of business before this session was adjourned. He hoped everyone realized that his purge was so much less extensive than during the Merciless Parliament, where the Appellants indulged in a blood bath. They took the lives of many whose only sin was allegiance to the king. Richard congratulated himself on using great restraint. And now, it was time to hand out honors and titles to those who helped him.

"Henry Bolingbroke, Earl of Derby, come forward," he announced.

Glancing at his father, Henry advanced and knelt before the king.

"Sir Henry, you have served me well and defended my rights against the Lords Appellant. I pardon you for your participation in said events. I hereby create the title of Duke of Hereford and bestow it upon you along with the lands of Herefordshire belonging to your late wife's father."

There. That should keep him loyal, Richard thought. He was most pleased by Bolingbroke's expression of surprise mixed with gratification. Then he called Thomas de Mowbray.

"Sir Thomas, you have served me well and defended my rights against the Lords Appellant. I pardon you for your participation in said events. I hereby create the title Duke of Norfolk and bestow it upon you along with the Earl of Arundel's castles and Lordship of Lewes in Sussex."

Mowbray's face was even more incredulous than Bolingbroke's. He was not expecting to get away so easily.

And this wasn't all. Sir Edward of Rutland was created Duke of Albemarle. Richard's half-brother John Holland was created Duke of Exeter. His nephew Thomas Holland was made Duke of Surrey. Richard also created four new earldoms including one for his steward Thomas Percy, who became Earl of Worcester. All of them were given parcels carved out of the massive estates confiscated from the disgraced Appellants.

This was enough for the moment. The chancellor declared this session at an end, to be reconvened at Shrewsbury on January 28. All that remained was for the Lords and Commons to gather at Westminster Abbey and participate in the same oath-giving ceremony held at the end of the Merciless Parliament. As the king sat crowned and enthroned, prelates and nobles individually swore before the shrine of Edward the Confessor to maintain all the acts of Parliament forever. The knights swore as a group.

Richard thought he would feel triumphant, or at least satisfied. But no, it wasn't enough. He still didn't feel safe.

He couldn't help it; as Richard received their oaths, he felt something was missing. He kept glancing over at his uncle

105

Lancaster, who stood by his side, arrogant and commanding. How much power he had accrued over the decades! The Duchy of Lancaster was a Palatinate, giving Gaunt sovereign rights in its jurisdiction. The king couldn't touch it. The law courts, the sheriffs, judges, senior officials all belonged to his uncle. It was a kingdom within the kingdom. Back in 1390, in his eagerness to bind Gaunt to his cause, Richard had granted inheritance rights for the County Palatine, and the title of Duke would descend to his male heirs. Before that, Gaunt had held the title during his lifetime only. Now, Henry Bolingbroke stood to become the next Duke of Lancaster.

Despite himself, Richard broke into a cold sweat. *What had he been thinking? How could have he been so short-sighted?* Back then, when he had just taken the reins of power into his own hands, he had been so afraid of the Appellants he would do anything to protect himself. And now, only seven years later, he was in control and still faced a challenge to his throne. Potentially, that is. When old Gaunt died and Bolingbroke inherited everything, he would be powerful enough to challenge the king. *This just can't be allowed!*

If Richard thought all his troubles were over, he forgot to take public opinion into consideration. For the last few years the Earl of Arundel had retired to his estates, but the people had not forgotten his generosity from the old days. They remembered when he was admiral and had shared his great booty of wine from the hundred captured Flemish ships back in '87. Already there was disorder. Not even a week had passed since Arundel was laid to rest at the church of Austin Friars, when reports reached the king that miracles were seen at his gravesite. Hundreds of Londoners gathered around his tomb. The church was so crowded people had to stand outside, waiting their turn to pay their respects to their hero. Someone swore that his head had been miraculously reattached to his body, and others took up the irrepressible claim that Arundel should be a saint.

Then Richard's nightmares began. The first one was merely the earl's unwelcome appearance in an otherwise bland dream. But soon, Arundel's bloody corpse came to life, rushing at the king, howling in spectral wails, chasing him, appearing and disappearing, until Richard woke up in a cold sweat, gasping for breath. He was afraid to go to sleep and became irritable, unapproachable, until finally he summoned his uncle John to investigate the source of his torments.

Though exasperated at having to drop everything and attend the king, John soon forgot all of his annoyance at the sight of his nephew. Richard was sitting in his solar, all alone, staring out the window when Gaunt approached him, slowly lowering himself onto the bench.

"You look ill. Are you all right?"

Richard turned bloodshot eyes at him, barely focused. He rubbed them, hard. "I need your help, uncle. His ghost. He is haunting me."

Is he talking about my brother? thought John. *I would expect no less.*

To tell the truth, Richard wasn't the only one bedeviled by the fate of the Appellants. For the hundredth time, John chastised himself for not doing anything about his brother—not objecting to Gloucester's sentence, nor raising the alarm about his suspicious death. He kept telling himself there was nothing he could do about it—that he was better off protecting his son's inheritance rather than defending his brother's lost cause. But those arguments would fall to pieces when it came time to face God's judgment, and he knew it.

He raised his eyes to Richard's. "Who is haunting you?"

"Arundel, curse his black soul. Did you know, uncle, that his grave has become a shrine?"

Gaunt shrugged. "It will pass."

The king shivered. "Why are the people of London so disrespectful? Why must they always defy me?"

John could relate. The ashes of his Savoy Palace still remained untouched, as a hideous reminder of the Peasants' Revolt.

"My nightmares grow worse," Richard groaned. "It is said that his head has reattached itself to his body."

John crossed himself. The vision was too terrible to contemplate.

"There's something I need you to do," Richard went on. "But not alone. Take with you Rutland, Holland, Mowbray, and Percy. All of you, go to the church of Austin Friars and exhume his body. Do it in secret, I exhort you!" He took a ragged breath. "I want you to tell me whether this miracle is true. And then move the corpse to some secluded spot, pave over the grave, and leave it unmarked. I will have no shrines to Richard Fitzalan!"

John grimaced at this unwelcome order. But he knew better than to object. The others were in London, as the king knew, so he arranged for them to meet him the following night on Throgmorton Street.

It was well past midnight when a very unhappy group of nobles gathered before the high stone wall beside the church. The friary was a huge complex of buildings and gardens with the church in the center. A full moon reflected against the white walls with stark clarity, giving the courtyard an eerie blue glow. An owl, roosting in the church tower, hooted three times.

John gestured toward the Prior's house, adjoining the cloister. "Go wake them up," he commanded his squire, who obligingly banged on the portal. Nothing happened and he drew his dagger, striking with the pommel again and again until the door cracked open and a timid friar looked out. Impatiently, Gaunt pushed his way in. The sleepy monks backed away, bowing.

The Prior stepped forward, his hair askew. "My Lord Duke, we apologize for not welcoming you. We were abed."

That was obvious. No matter. "Show us the grave of Earl Arundel," John growled. "Fetch us a torch."

The friars rushed to do his bidding. Four torches were gathered and lit. John handed one to Percy and kept one for himself, while the Prior led the group through an adjoining passage. Their weak flames flickered against the low vaulted ceiling. Entering the church through a side door, they walked down the left aisle and into the nave. Arundel's grave was in its own chapel to the left, the stone coffin carved with angels on each corner. Clearly, the earl had thought ahead and prepared his own sarcophagus.

"Remove the lid," Gaunt ordered. The friars hesitated, unwilling to desecrate the tomb. "The king's orders," he added in a threatening voice. Even in such circumstances, he insisted on obedience.

The lords waited while two friars went for tools. "This is immoderate," Holland grumbled, shifting from one foot to the other. The air was cold like a cave, and the shadows pressed down on their little assembly. "What possesses the king?"

"Guilt," Mowbray answered, though he paused when Gaunt glared at him. "We all feel it to some extent."

Scowling, the duke turned away. In good conscience, he couldn't argue with Mowbray. What he really wanted to do was take him aside and interrogate him about what happened in Calais with his brother. Though he knew such a step would be useless; he wouldn't get the truth, not from those lips. And there was a good chance Mowbray would go right to the king, tattling about his prying. That's the last thing he needed.

The friars went to work, prizing off the stone lid. They tried to stop it from dropping to the floor, but at the last minute it slipped from their hands and hit the pavement with a boom, cracking in half. The reverberations rushed back and forth through the nave, unnerving the witnesses until the echoes finally ceased.

Approaching the tomb, Gaunt gasped. The head had been sewn back onto the torso.

"Who did this?" he bellowed.

The Prior stepped forward. "He was our patron."

"That is no matter. He is lucky his skull doesn't grace London Bridge. If the king wanted his head attached, he wouldn't have removed it in the first place. Take those stitches out!"

More time was wasted while they fetched a pair of scissors and a small knife and pincers to pull out the ligatures. While he waited, Gaunt bent his steely eyes on the Prior. "The king orders that he be buried in secret, to avoid the senseless spectacle that has been going on all week." He could see the man's head sink into his shoulders. Everyone knew what a financial boon the pilgrims generated for the church. "Surely you can bury him in your crypt."

109

The Prior's eyes slid over to the monk next to him, who pulled back his hood. "We have another who will be laid to rest on the morrow. The hole is already dug."

"Good. Then put the earl's body under his. They can be interred together. You shall move him tonight, before we leave."

Resigned, the friars did as Gaunt commanded. Surrounding the body of the earl, eight monks reverently lifted him from the stone coffin and carried the corpse down the stairs, while the Prior wrapped Arundel's head in a linen cloth and followed. They were flanked by others bearing torches which threw an uncertain light before them. Of course, the monks knew their way. Gaunt and his companions followed, carefully testing the steps.

They stood back and observed while the friars lowered the earl into the hole, said a prayer over the body and threw down a thin layer of dirt. Once they had finished, Gaunt gave them a sack of coins for their trouble. "The king does not want to hear about any further demonstrations near the gravesite of Earl Arundel. You will tell them his body has been translated elsewhere and they are to disperse. If the king's orders are violated, this friary will be disbanded."

The king may not have had the power to disband the friary, but no one doubted John of Gaunt's threats. There were no further gatherings of pilgrims, and the king's nightmares came to an end.

How did Richard know that Arundel's head was reattached? No one could guess the answer—least of all the king.

CHAPTER 10

Even though it was early afternoon, the December sky was so overcast it felt closer to evening. Having visited the king in Windsor, Bolingbroke was returning to London and had just passed Brentwood when he turned at the sound of hoofbeats. Alarmed, his guards surrounded his horse and they all drew their swords. But as soon as the newcomer was close enough to recognize, Henry sheathed his blade.

"What ho," he said as Thomas de Mowbray pulled rein. "You are in a hurry."

"To speak with you," the other answered, looking askance at the guards. Nodding, the riders fell back, leaving the two of them alone.

"I heard you had just passed through town and I hastened to catch up with you."

Bolingbroke blinked in surprise. For the most part, he and Mowbray had little to do with each other. He couldn't imagine what could be so important as to compel the other to follow him at such a frantic pace.

"What is it? What has happened?"

"Henry, we are about to be undone!"

"What! Why?"

"Because of Radcot Bridge."

Letting out a grunt, Henry gestured his dismissal. "Nonsense. We've just been granted dukedoms—not to mention our pardons. From the king himself."

"Come now, Henry. We don't have to look far to see just what the king's pardons are worth. Now that he has dealt with the other Appellants, he will turn his attention to us." As if to downplay his sense of guilt, he held out a hand, catching a few snowflakes. "It's a funny old world, but treacherous."

Henry shook his head, narrowing his eyes at Thomas. You never knew about this one; he had always been a lone wolf, looking out for nobody's interests but his own. Henry hadn't trusted him, even when they were temporarily joined in opposition to the senior Appellants, back in '88. What was he up to now?

Best to take a neutral stance.

"I shall continue to place my trust in the king's words," Henry said, "for I know of nothing I have done to offend him in any way. As long as he wishes it, therefore, I have no intention of withdrawing my support or my fealty from him."

Mowbray jerked his shoulders in impatience. His horse fidgeted and he yanked the reins. "You don't understand," he said angrily. "Had it not been for certain people, you and your father would have been seized and put to death when you came to Windsor after Parliament."

"What are you talking about? What certain people?"

Mowbray looked around to ensure nobody was in earshot. "Myself, Edward of Rutland, John Holland, and Thomas Percy, who was secretly told about the plot. We swore amongst ourselves we would never assent to the ruin of any lord without just and reasonable cause."

Henry frowned. This all sounded too contrived. "And this so-called plot?"

"Oh, aside from yourself I was among the intended victims. Along with Rutland, John Beaufort, and John Holland."

"We were all to be killed? Who are the plotters?"

"There were four of them: Thomas Holland, William LeScrope, the Earl of Salisbury, and Thomas Despenser."

Shaking his head again, Bolingbroke was unconvinced. "This makes no sense. Why would they kill us?"

"With the king's countenance, they would get us out of the way and earn more patronage for themselves. We were told they are also trying to convince the king to reverse the judgment concerning Earl Thomas of Lancaster from back in Edward II's day."

"God forbid!" declared Henry. He knew that Thomas of Lancaster's rebellion against Edward II endured as one of Richard's obsessions. First judged a traitor by Edward II and

112

executed, Lancaster's conviction was reversed by Edward III. The inheritance went back to Thomas's younger brother Henry. Two generations later, John of Gaunt inherited the dukedom by right of his first wife. If those old judgments were reversed again, Earl Thomas's inheritance would be forfeited to the crown. Gaunt would be ruined, and so would Henry.

"Don't you see?" Mowbray pursued. "They seek to destroy the Lancastrian power. King Richard is behind this."

Pursing his lips, Henry considered. "If this is true," he mused, "we can never trust them."

This wasn't as outlandish as it sounded. There were rumors that Thomas Despenser was agitating for recovery of his ancestor's estates—forfeited in 1326 under Edward II. Salisbury still claimed the lordship of Denbigh, taken from his uncle. Even Thomas Holland had an ancestor who lost his earldom and his life during that rebellion. Only LeScrope didn't fit the pattern, though he was known to be an acquisitive man.

But the king... could he be complicit? Or, knowing Mowbray's character, could they be conspiring together to entrap Henry?

"Certainly not," Mowbray said, interrupting his thoughts. "Even if they don't succeed with their present plans, they will still be plotting to destroy us in our homes ten years from now."

Considering the last Parliament, Henry couldn't deny the possibility. "What do you propose we do?"

Mowbray shrugged. "I was hoping you could make a suggestion. We are in this together."

Are we? Henry wasn't so sure. "I need to consider this. We don't want to make any false moves."

"Agreed. Send me word." At that, Mowbray spurred his horse into a canter, leaving a bemused Henry behind. He turned to his retinue.

"John, ride back toward Windsor. My father must have left by now and is following the same route we are. I must speak with him. Tell him to meet me at Chiswick." Gaunt's favorite stopping place between Windsor and London was a comfortable palace known as Sutton Court, surrounded by a moat. It would be safe enough.

113

Gaunt showed up late that night. As he pulled rein in the courtyard, his son approached. "What has happened?" John said worriedly. "Are you all right?"

Henry held the reins as his father dismounted. "There is trouble. I must consult with you."

"Of course." John looked around. "I don't see any disturbances."

"No, no. Not here. Come, they are preparing a light supper for us."

Between the two dukes and their retinues, this was a much larger party than the steward was expecting. Nonetheless, a lively fire was crackling in the hearth and a table was laid out with bowls of stew and bread. Not an extravagant feast; still, it was enough for this time of day. Henry had little appetite, anyway. Not so, his father. Satisfied, Gaunt ate heartily and let out a belch. "All right. What do you need to tell me?"

Pushing his half-eaten stew aside, Henry put his elbows on the table and told about his encounter with Mowbray. John listened intently.

"I'll tell you, father. I don't know whether to believe him or not. He had a wild look about him that bespoke alarm."

"Hmm. I think he's more afraid for himself than for you, after that terrible business with my brother. If there has been foul play, Mowbray is implicated regardless of his guilt." He let out a deep sigh. "My poor brother. He was always too reckless with the king."

Henry studied his father's face. They had not spoken about Gloucester's death; he didn't know how to approach the subject and Gaunt had kept his feelings to himself. "You do suspect foul play, then?"

John took another spoonful of stew and chewed it in silence. "We may never know," he said finally. "He was ill..." His face betrayed simmering discontent. "Just when did he die? It is too dangerous to speculate. My brother was doomed either way." A log fell in the fireplace, sending up sparks. There was no other sound in the room. "And his blood is on the king's hands," Gaunt added, almost in a whisper. "Here, have a piece of bread." He tore off an end, holding it out.

114

Automatically, Henry accepted it. "I don't understand why Mowbray would search me out. What could we possibly do to protect ourselves?"

"Let's think about this. He said there was a plot against our lives?"

Henry nodded. "And Rutland, and John Holland, and John Beaufort. And Mowbray himself. Or so he says."

"My heir, my son in-law, my recently legitimized son, my nephew. The only one not related to me is Mowbray. Could he be one of the plotters?"

"That doesn't make much sense either, does it? Then why would he turn around and warn me?"

"Unless he was trying to ensnare you. If the king is involved, and if you say nothing about Mowbray's suspicions, you could be later charged with conspiracy. If you were to absent yourself, you would be seen as guilty. If you were to involve yourself in a counter-plot with Mowbray, the results could be disastrous, and again you would be guilty. He could be goading you into making some imprudent move that would ruin you in the king's eyes and raise him in Richard's favor."

"I'm beset from all sides!"

"Not exactly." A servant knocked and entered, removing some bowls and pouring more ale. While they waited, John pulled out a small case from a pouch and opened it, extracting a gold toothpick. As the door closed, he leaned back, concentrating on a molar. Henry got up and paced back and forth before the fire.

"Let's assume for a moment the king is involved," Gaunt said quietly. "If we bring this plot to him..." He looked up, inspired. "If *I* bring it to him, he will have no choice but to deny his complicity. If he is not involved, which I doubt, he will be more aware of the insidious conspiracies among his precious inner circle."

Henry continued his pacing. "Mowbray told this to me in confidence. If he is sincere, it will be a great betrayal."

"Could he be sincere?" Gaunt stared at his son, his eyes piercing.

Henry shrugged. "He warned me that our lives are in danger."

115

"Our lives are always in danger."

"I am not comfortable with this course of action."

"Son, there is no easy way. No matter what you do, there are bound to be repercussions. It remains for us to choose what is best for our house."

"Yes. I understand." Henry sat down again and took a deep draught of ale. "Would to God he had never found me."

"Perhaps it's for the best," John said, staring at the fire. "The incessant plotting has to end."

"Then you think we should tell the king."

"Let me do it. Alone. You can stay out of it for now."

"Very well. But father, bring extra guards. To Shrewsbury, as well."

John grunted. "I'll put my informers to work. They will have much to do the next couple of weeks."

"And the old Lancaster judgment? Do you think the king could reverse it?"

"He is capable of trying. I think we will request that he confirm a full quitclaim for any of Thomas's possessions. Just in case. If he denies this request, he will be exposing a deeper malevolence that can't be missed. I don't think he can risk that." Nonetheless, Gaunt looked troubled. "One thing at a time. We will let this rest for a week. If nothing further happens, I will go to the king."

Having held his Christmas court at Lichfield—between Nottingham and Shrewsbury—Richard welcomed John of Gaunt on the Epiphany. It also happened to be the king's thirty-first birthday. Richard adored the religious ceremonies in this cathedral, and naturally a second mass was held in his honor. On the way to services, he never failed to stop before entering through the arched double doors, when he was sure to point out to anyone who was listening that this was the first cathedral built in England with three spires. He would exclaim over the row of kings and saints in the frieze which ran all the way across the front of the building, hoping that one day, he would sit amongst their number. After the services, an elaborate feast was held where the new Archbishop of Canterbury, Roger Walden, presented the king with a gilded crucifix. Not to be outdone, Gaunt had his servants carry a gold salt cellar to the head table. It was a meticulously crafted ship mounted atop a mermaid. Richard clapped his hands in delight.

Reluctant to disturb the king's celebrations, Gaunt left off his discussion until the following day. So far, his informants hadn't uncovered any suspicious activities, which didn't necessarily mean that Mowbray's story was a lie. Many times he had been the target of assassination attempts; he knew how cautious men could be when they had so much to lose.

When Richard stood to meet him in his private closet, the king's face was open and friendly. Try as he might, Gaunt couldn't detect any covert expressions.

"Why, uncle," he said, holding out his arms, "I missed both you and Henry at our Christmas celebrations."

"We regret not being able to come," John said. "We had much business to attend before the upcoming Parliament session."

"Well, you are here now and welcome." He hugged his uncle and sat, smoothing his robe. "What is it you needed to speak with me about?"

John looked at the chamber knights and Richard dismissed them.

"Sire, something has come to my attention that is very disturbing. I am distraught by the implications."

Richard raised his eyebrows. "Do tell."

The other hesitated. *Was the king this good as dissimulation?* "Thomas de Mowbray spoke with my son on the road to London. He said there was a plot against Henry and myself, Rutland, John Beaufort, and John Holland. And himself."

Telling the rest of the story, John watched the king closely. He left out the part about the Lancastrian inheritance—at least for the moment. At first, Richard grimaced, then he blinked repeatedly. At the end, he shook his head. "It makes no sense," the king said. "What possible benefit would they achieve in doing this? Why would Thomas Holland kill his own uncle?"

John wanted to believe Richard with all his heart. He thought they had attained a semblance of peace between them—

even amity. If Richard was plotting against his life, all these years of hard work and tolerance would be ruined. "Perhaps they seek to dismantle the Lancastrian inheritance?" he ventured, hoping for a forceful denial.

Instead, Richard looked deep in thought. He glanced quickly at John. "Your patrimony?" A covetous look crossed his face, quickly squelched. "That would be foolish, indeed. It would disrupt the whole aristocracy."

Especially if half of us were killed, John thought. He was not comforted.

"We must bring this out into the open," the king declared. "This cannot be allowed to fester. I must hear this from Henry's lips."

There was little more to say, and claiming fatigue, John took his leave. Richard slipped over to the window and watched his uncle cross the courtyard to the bishop's guest quarters. How could things have gotten so out of hand? *Damn that Bolingbroke! Why did he have to go running to his father?* There was no stopping it now. Once Gaunt was told about the conspiracy, there was no suppressing it—or the details. Richard could have handled his cousin, but not his uncle. Never his uncle.

Mowbray's actions were confusing. What game was he playing? He was never one of the supposed victims. Was he trying to cover up his guilt? Ever since the Gloucester matter, he had been acting strangely. Still, Richard hadn't expected him to lose his nerve and go crying to Henry. On the other hand...

He watched a pair of clerics rush across the courtyard. A gust of wind blew off one of their hats, sending the frantic man rushing to catch it. The hat bounced off the ground and out of his reach. Suddenly a smile spread across Richard's face. The answer was within *his* reach. Maybe things could work out better than he anticipated. Once Mowbray learns he has been betrayed—once Richard tells him—he's bound to react with ferocious anger. This could turn into a righteous feud. What delicious irony to watch the two remaining Appellants face off in deadly earnest. Perhaps they could destroy each other in the process and relieve Richard of the trouble?

He had to find some way to turn this argument to his advantage. It shouldn't be too difficult.

It was just a few days before the Shrewsbury Parliament when Mowbray answered the king's summons. Once again he was faced with an uncomfortable meeting, because Sir William Bagot had just whispered that his regrettable outburst had reached the king's ear. He didn't even have time to compose himself!

Bagot tapped on the king's door and opened it quickly, entering the room first and taking a seat at the secretary's table. So even this indignity was to be public. Bagot had served Mowbray in the past—and before that, he had fought with Bolingbroke at Radcot Bridge. And now, he had squirmed his way into the king's confidence. How did that happen? Here, too, was another man Thomas couldn't trust.

Mowbray went down on one knee, trying to control his apprehension. A quick glance at Richard told him nothing; the king was impassible. He looked at the floor.

"Thomas, something has come to my attention and I need to ask you about it. Is it true you met Henry Bolingbroke on the road to London and accused me of conspiring against him?"

"Sire!" Mowbray was shocked. "How could you ask me such a thing?"

"How could you accuse me of such a thing?"

"I never did! Bolingbroke lies!"

"Then what did you tell him?"

For a moment, Thomas was at a loss. He knew he was compromised. "I was concerned about the plots surrounding this court."

Richard stared at him. "There are always plots."

"Sire." Thomas paused. "Your Majesty. I don't know what Bolingbroke told you, but he only cares about his own house. He would say anything to gain power at my expense."

"Hmm. That is possible," Richard said quietly. "They think too much of themselves."

Mowbray jerked his head up. Did he hear the king correctly?

"They are too powerful," Richard said, looking directly at Thomas. "That's why my great-grandfather ruled against Thomas of Lancaster." After watching his victim squirm, Richard glanced away, adjusting the embroidery on his sleeve. "Henry gave me his statement in writing yesterday. I am very displeased." His voice was controlled, dispassionate.

Mowbray almost choked. On both knees now, he shuffled forward. "Your Majesty. Forgive me, I beg you. I meant no harm. That man twisted what I said to make me look guilty."

The king studied him. He could see that under the man's chagrin, the anger was building. "Perhaps they suspect you are part of the conspiracy, yourself," Richard suggested.

Mowbray's eyes narrowed. He was practically grinding his teeth.

"John of Gaunt was most ardent about Lancastrian loyalties," the king added before standing up. "Come, William. We have more work to do with the chancellor before the start of Parliament."

The king left the room with Bagot, neglecting to dismiss Mowbray, who remained on his knees, letting out a ragged breath. How could Bolingbroke betray him like that? His actions went against every code of chivalry—nay, simple human decency demanded he respect such a dangerous confidence. That Henry might tell his father was a chance Thomas had been willing to take. That they would tell the king—that was beyond his wildest imagination. This must have been Gaunt's doing; Thomas did not doubt it for a second.

He stood, brushing his knees. There was only one way he could see to regain Richard's favor—and his self-respect. He had to kill John of Gaunt.

Soldiers restlessly milled around the bailey of Stafford castle while the Duke of Lancaster perused a letter sent to him in haste by his son, who was already with the king. He had been on the verge of starting out when the messenger rode in, his horse practically spent. Tearing open the letter, John shook his head, annoyed at yet another complication to an already tangled situation.

I have been warned by Sir William Bagot, Henry wrote, *that Thomas de Mowbray may attempt to ambush you on the way to Parliament. He has been incited by the king, who confronted him with accusations. Take extra precautions.*

Never one to shrink from a challenge, Gaunt shouted for his captain. "Double the guard," he ordered. "I expect trouble on the way to Shrewsbury." He paused, a hand on the man's arm. "No, wait. Maybe we can beat the Duke of Norfolk at his own game. I will ride ahead with a small contingent. You will follow right behind, close enough to hear if I am attacked, and just out of sight."

"With extra men," the other added. "I shall send a small troop ahead of you as well."

"Yes. Good plan."

Though their party was delayed a couple of hours, Gaunt was well satisfied. When they finally rode forth, ten soldiers preceded the duke, well-armed but displaying no banners. After giving them a small head start, John followed with another twenty men—flaunting his standard so there would be no mistake. A hundred men-at-arms rode behind him, prepared to jump into action.

As they approached the ford over the Severn, Gaunt held up a hand, stopping his men. They were surrounded by forest on two sides; it was the perfect place for an ambush. They listened, hearing nothing.

"It's almost too quiet," John said. Suddenly, an arrow whizzed past him, smacking into the knight at his side. Luckily the man was armored.

"Go!" John shouted, spurring his mount. Followed by a handful of guards while the others turned to face the hidden enemy, Gaunt dashed into the shallow river, spewing great sprays of water. They could hear a clash of weapons from behind. But John wasn't safe; before he reached the other side, a knot of mounted armored men stepped from the forest and blocked his way. Undaunted, the duke drew his sword and charged them. His own men struggled to keep up.

Not expecting such a forceful response, the antagonists hesitated a moment, when from behind they heard the shouts from Gaunt's forward guards. They thought the small party was of no account and realized belatedly they shouldn't have let them pass. Now the assassins were caught in a pincer. This was more than they bargained for; turning their mounts, they preferred to take their chances with the ten soldiers than face Lancaster. They spurred forward, swords raised, and engaged with the leading knights. Soon the road was filled with twisting, rearing horses, men falling to the ground, shouting and clashing blades. Badly outnumbered, the assassins expected no mercy and received none. Two of them dashed into the forest, followed by determined avengers.

Dismounting, John looked at the chaos on the other side of the river. His large contingent had arrived and had mostly plunged into the forest, looking for fugitives. The rest of the assailants were either on the ground or in custody.

He turned as his captain dragged forward a wounded man who fell to his knees. "Who hired you?"

John's captain slammed a gauntleted hand against the prisoner's helmet. "Answer the duke."

Unbuckling his helm, the man pulled it off, exposing a shock of red hair. He glared at his captor before answering. "I don't know."

The other shoved a foot into his back and the prisoner fell forward, dropping the helm. "God's blood, man. You don't expect us to believe that," the captain growled.

On hands and knees, the man shook his head. "Believe what you want."

Stepping forward, Gaunt grabbed a handful of hair and slid a dagger from his belt. Pulling his captive upright, the duke held the point under the man's chin. "Don't throw your life away. Just tell me who."

Holding his breath, the prisoner shook his head as best as he could.

John nicked him in the neck, drawing a bead of blood. "I'm running out of patience."

Coughing, the prisoner raised his right hand in surrender. "Stay. I'll tell you. It was the Duke of Norfolk."

Gaunt thrust him forward, releasing his hair. "Mowbray," he grunted, "As was foretold. How could he be so foolish?"

"Or desperate," the captain said.

John dismissed the offender. "Let him go. Let them all go. It's not worth the trouble killing them."

Shrugging, the other gave his orders. John remounted and crossed back over the river, relieved to see that his man who took the arrow was on his feet. Holding up the shaft, the knight grimaced. "This got caught in my surcoat. Look at this." He raised the fabric, exposing a dent in his breastplate. "Luckily for me, it came at an angle and only had a broadhead tip."

John put a hand on his shoulder. "That arrow was meant for me. I won't forget it."

The duke's retinue put itself back in order and escorted him to Shrewsbury without further incident. Just nine miles from the Welsh border and surrounded by stone walls, Shrewsbury was built inside a loop of the River Severn. The old Norman castle, rebuilt by Henry III, guarded the opening where the two sides of the river almost touched. On the other end of town, the great Abbey was accessible by the stone English Bridge, which was lined with shops and houses. Limited in size by its geographic situation, the town was crowded and ill-equipped to host such a large gathering for long.

Since he was so late, John was obliged to locate his troops in a field nearby. Once his men were settled, John searched out his son who was staying at the mayor's house and told him the news.

"I can imagine the king encouraged him," Henry said as a servant handed him a goblet of wine. "Why else would he have done it?"

"I don't know. Why would Richard encourage him?"

Henry shrugged, walking over to the window. "He is suspicious of everyone."

"Hmm. I will not create a disturbance over this. For now. Let us see what develops."

"It doesn't look promising. You know, they are already calling this the Revenge Parliament."

Gaunt ran a hand over his forehead. "It's not over yet. We must find a way to disarm the king—put *him* on the defensive. I don't like what you said about reversing the old Lancastrian judgments."

Nodding absently, Henry sat beside him. "Your reasoning is sound. But first, we must get past this Mowbray issue."

"That's what I'm thinking of. If you accuse Norfolk of murdering the Duke of Gloucester, the king will have to be implicated. In front of God and the world."

Panic spread over Henry's face. "It's bad enough as it is. That would be too much."

John covered his son's hand with his own. "It doesn't have to be now. We'll find a way to make a proper accusation that should expose Mowbray for the malefactor he is. Don't worry. Mowbray won't dare show his face today. Or tomorrow. You will have free rein to read aloud your statement. Uninterrupted."

CHAPTER 11

The Duke of Lancaster and Henry Bolingbroke pushed through the throng attending the Parliament at Shrewsbury Abbey. Richard's Cheshire archers could be seen scattered throughout, casually leaning against walls and making themselves generally unobtrusive—though everyone was mindful of their presence. Seven Counter-Appellants, clad in their crimson robes, stood before the king and chamberlain. They respectfully waited to recite their pre-arranged petitions. Sir Thomas de Mowbray, the eighth Counter-Appellant, was conspicuous by his absence.

They picked up where they left off just a few months ago. "Your Majesty," started the spokesman, the Earl of Rutland, "we feel the procedure and verdicts of the 1388 Parliament usurped your royal prerogative. We also feel they were outside the sphere of parliamentary competence. Hence, we petition this house to repeal all the acts and judgments of said Parliament."

After a short discussion, the Lords and Commons assented; the Parliament of 1388 was declared invalid. All judgments against Richard's friends and adherents were revoked. It was that simple. Even the Judges were exonerated, for on further consideration, the current judges asserted that if questioned, they would have come to the same conclusions.

For Richard, the rulings were bittersweet. His task was accomplished. On the other hand, things were not as before. Never as before. The new decrees would not bring back Simon Burley, Robert de Vere, Nicholas Brembre, and all the others who were executed or died in exile. Chewing on his lower lip, he stared at Bolingbroke, who was doing his best to appear inconspicuous. Sitting quietly next to Gaunt, Henry lowered his head, not speaking to anyone or even looking at his neighbors. *There is a slippery eel,* Richard thought. As long as his father was alive, Henry was untouchable. He would have to wait; Richard needed

Gaunt's support more than he needed Henry's condemnation. But John of Gaunt would not live forever.

Tomorrow Henry Bolingbroke would expose himself for the Judas he truly was. That, at least, was some compensation.

First, in the morning, there were a couple of things that needed to be done. The king made sure that anyone who tried to repeal the judgments of this Parliament, would be declared traitor and punished to the full extent of the law. Once the Lords and Commons voted their agreement, Richard beckoned his Speaker forward and whispered in his ear. Straightening, Bushy addressed the Lords. "The king would extend this condition to all future monarchs, so they should be bound never to annul proceedings of this Parliament."

As the king waited, the prelates spoke amongst themselves. Finally, the Bishop of Winchester stood. "Your Majesty, I regret to say there is no precedent for holding future kings to your will. We do not believe this is possible."

The bishop sat, while Richard scowled, gripping the arms of the throne. It felt like hours before he conceded. "Very well," the king said finally. "I will write to the pope and ask him to excommunicate anyone who seeks to repeal any Acts of this Parliament, now and forever. And now, Sir Henry Bolingbroke, Duke of Hereford, you will come forward and present your statement against Sir Thomas de Mowbray."

Henry suppressed a chill. Richard chose this moment of uneasiness to thrust him into everyone's face. But there was no helping it; he was committed now. Glancing at his father, he rose and approached the throne. Most of the people in the room knew nothing about his complaint and watched curiously.

"Repeat to this assembly the report you submitted to me in writing," Richard said.

Bolingbroke turned. "As his Majesty commands, I will describe the events of last December, when the Duke of Norfolk spoke treasonous words to me." He proceeded to read the document, relating his whole conversation with Thomas de Mowbray, omitting nothing—even the tacit accusation that the king was involved in a plot to destroy the House of Lancaster.

Bolstered by his father's support, he spoke evenly, not betraying the least uneasiness.

Though nettled by Henry's composure, Richard forced himself to sit quietly, staring at the ceiling as the damning evidence was exposed to the world. Since Mowbray was not available to present a rebuttal, Bolingbroke's words fell on the listeners like a death knell.

Mowbray's death knell. He had brought it upon himself.

When Henry had finished, the king stood. "Sir Thomas de Mowbray, having already attempted to murder the Duke of Lancaster on his way to this very Parliament, has proven himself a scoundrel and a felon. From the Duke of Hereford's words, he has also demonstrated his maliciousness. I hereby strip Sir Thomas de Mowbray of his office of Earl Marshal."

Looking at the faces surrounding him, Richard was not encouraged. Most of them looked troubled; some were frowning, others were whispering to their neighbor. The king told the chancellor to suspend the session until the morrow, then marched past the bewildered Bolingbroke who hadn't been dismissed. Richard left the silent chamber, knowing full well it would soon burst into debate once he was out of earshot. He didn't care. There was much to think about. Summoning the Earl of Rutland, he took refuge in the bishop's palace.

When Edward let himself in, Richard was pacing the room. "There you are," he said grumpily. "Sit down."

Rutland knew when to stay silent. He had learned how to read Richard's face, though this time he wasn't entirely sure why the king was so upset.

"I can't do it now," Richard said, stopping and gesturing for a servant to bring some wine.

Edward cleared his throat. "What is it you can't do?"

"I was planning to reinstate the verdict against Thomas of Lancaster from 1322. He was a traitor to Edward II and deserved his fate. But now, with Bolingbroke connecting me with this alleged plot, the timing would be all wrong. I can't do it now."

Edward nodded. Things were complicated enough as it was.

The king stopped and a sly smile crossed his face. "On the other hand, nothing would stop me from reversing the judgments passed against the Despensers. They were Lancaster's enemies then, and they still are today. That should send a message to Parliament."

"And that will please Thomas Despenser, who could reclaim his grandfather and great-grandfather's lands."

"And bind him even closer to me. I need all of your support. All of my Counter-Appellants."

The other nodded graciously. "Especially as you have just lost Mowbray's support, if you ever had it."

"Mowbray." Richard practically spit the word. "He can't be allowed to prevail."

"Against Bolingbroke? Or yourself?"

"Huh. Both. He can't be relied upon."

"Can Henry?"

Looking sideways at Rutland, Richard shrugged. "Not really. But he'll listen to his father."

"Perhaps..." Edward looked down at his nails, "perhaps you can use this quarrel to your advantage."

The king sat, leaning forward. He was always open to suggestions. "How so?"

"Let them destroy each other."

"Ahh. That would be magnificent." For a moment, Richard allowed himself to contemplate the notion.

"Don't let the argument drop," Edward continued. "Mowbray must account for himself. Let him be the guilty one, at least for a while."

"That shouldn't be difficult." The king leaned back, pondering his options. "I think I had better shut this Parliament down before this turns into a worse scandal. I don't need anything new to disrupt my achievements."

"You have done well, this Parliament."

"I have, haven't I? I reversed all those wretched judgments from 1388. I put the Judges' rulings back where they should be; we've redefined treason on my terms. I've brought the Commons over to my side and elevated a new nobility who will support the crown. I've destroyed my worst enemies—" A look of

128

uncertainly crossed his face and he stopped. *Had he?* Two of the Appellants were still walking around.

"You have proven yourself a wise and capable leader."

"Yes, yes. We shall see how it goes."

The following day, Richard opened Parliament with his announcement that the 1322 judgments against the Despensers would be annulled. Right away, this caused consternation amongst the Lords, for many had laid claim to some of the forfeited lands. Richard assured them they could petition to be excluded from the upcoming resettlements, but that didn't calm anyone down very much.

Undeterred, he launched into an announcement that he would issue a general pardon for the crimes of the Merciless Parliament, in return for a grant of the wool subsidy for life. This was unprecedented. The wool subsidy was the king's most reliable source of funds; with a life grant, he would hardly ever need to call Parliament again. By this point, everyone was so grateful for the pardon, they voted the subsidy. Things had gone just the way he planned.

Richard was pleased. "I remind you," he added, "that persons seeking their pardon would still have to sue for it individually."

Yet another threat. Nothing had changed.

Richard may not have intended to use the pardons as a means to identify his potential enemies, but it certainly worked out that way. After all, the pardon was extended to guilty persons; if they were innocent, they need not apply—in theory. Of course, who wanted to take a chance? Over the next three months, more than 500 people applied for a pardon, just to be sure they weren't one of the unnamed fifty. It is not recorded how much money they paid to acquire the king's clemency but assuredly their contributions swelled the exchequer's coffers admirably.

The Shrewsbury Parliament lasted only four days. When Speaker Bushy suggested that a committee of eighteen be assigned to deal with outstanding petitions, the members of Commons agreed willingly, as did the king. After some discussion, Richard declared, "this Parliamentary Committee is given full authority to settle the debate between Henry Bolingbroke and Thomas de Mowbray."

Four days later, the king issued a command to all the sheriffs of England that Mowbray must appear before him. Then he took his court west toward Wales, accompanied by a large band of Cheshire archers. The king's bodyguard went with him everywhere, for he never felt safe—although the unfortunate locals were more threatened than the king. Complaints of rape, theft, and violence followed the royal progress. It was said the Cheshire archers acted like conquerors in hostile territory. But since disturbances were a part of everyday life, the protests fell on deaf ears.

In late February, Richard stayed over at Oswestry, an old Norman motte and bailey castle. It was surrounded by a bustling market town near the Welsh border, formerly belonging to the Earl of Arundel. Now it was the king's castle. He had summoned a meeting of the Parliamentary Committee to deal with some unfinished business—mainly the dispute between Bolingbroke and Mowbray.

However, there was something he had to do first. Before the Committee was to assemble, he had agreed to John of Gaunt's request for a private meeting.

Richard sat enthroned as father and son approached. They were a formidable pair. In his 58th year, Gaunt had achieved a level of grandeur setting him above everyone else of his rank. Tall, stately, and aristocratic, he radiated authority. Richard shook off a wave of envy, wishing he could impress others in the same way. Even Henry, looking fit and handsome, was overshadowed by the old patriarch.

After bowing, John stood, his hands clasped in front of his stomach. "Your Majesty," he began with a sonorous voice, "we have come forward to request a quitclaim for all castles and lands formerly owned by Thomas Duke of Lancaster and regranted to his brother Henry by Edward III."

Richard pursed his lips. *Damn that Mowbray! He started all this.* Try how he would, he couldn't think of a good excuse to deny Lancaster's request. If he did, he would be exposing his duplicity in the whole stinking plot. *On the other hand,* he thought, adjusting his sleeve, *there are different ways around this quandary.*

Catching himself, the king nodded. "After due deliberation, I have decided to release all rights and claims for the lands and possessions formerly belonging to Thomas of Lancaster. My dear uncle, this is because of the love I feel toward you." He gestured to Bushy. "Prepare the writs." He averted his face so Gaunt couldn't observe his expression of bitterness. *So much for his grand scheme to reverse the 1322 judgment against Lancaster.* Gaunt had won this time, the wily old fox.

No more needed to be said. John and Henry backed from the room, bowing. They had gotten the assurance they needed; it was best to remove themselves as quickly as possible.

Henry's biggest challenge was yet to come. He still had to face Thomas de Mowbray. Worse yet, his father had decided that now was the time to accuse Mowbray of murder. Only, *he* was the one who had to deliver the blow.

The Parliamentary Committee crowded into a hall of the old stone keep whose major function was for defense. Small, high windows let in scant sunlight, and torches added plenty of sooty smoke to the already suffocating atmosphere. Richard sat on a raised platform flanked by his Committee, of which John of Gaunt was a member.

This time Mowbray was present, though he was forced to stand in silence while Bolingbroke read the statement just as he had done before. Only now did he recognize the damage he had done to himself by not showing up in Shrewsbury—not that he had much choice, after the failed assassination attempt.

When Henry finished, the two antagonists glared at each other while Richard leaned to the side and conversed quietly with Bushy. Looking over at the pair, Richard decided he had given them enough time to stew.

"Well, cousin of Lancaster, now that you have read the petition, have you anything further to say before all present?"

131

Henry pulled off his black hood. "My lord, as the petition states, I say, in truth, that Thomas de Mowbray, Duke of Norfolk, is a traitor, false and recreant toward you and your royal majesty, to your crown, to the nobles, and to the people of all your realm."

Nodding toward Thomas, Richard said, "And what do you have to say?"

Red in the face, Mowbray took a deep breath. "My dear sire, by your leave in answer to your cousin, I say that Henry of Lancaster, Duke of Hereford, has lied like the false traitor and disloyal subject that he is!"

"Your Majesty," interjected Bolingbroke. "I have further charges to lay against the Duke of Norfolk. I accuse him of withholding funds to pay the men-at-arms who guard your city of Calais. He has received from you 800,000 nobles and has kept much of it for himself. Secondly, I state that he is the cause of all the treason committed in your realm these last eighteen years." He paused while members grumbled in dismay. "Furthermore," Henry continued, "while he was Captain of Calais, I accuse him of murdering my beloved uncle, the Duke of Gloucester."

Richard threw back his head, blinking in shock. *This wasn't what he expected!* How dare Bolingbroke raise the subject of Gloucester's murder! That episode was over and done with; the last thing Richard needed was another scandal. The unpredictable Mowbray might claim he was acting on the king's command, just to save himself.

"Ho," said the king, standing up. "We have heard enough of that." He turned to the chancellor. "Have Thomas Holland, Duke of Surrey, arrest these two lords upon my pleasure." This was standard procedure. Both accusers needed to be detained. All was very orderly and Holland led the adversaries from the room. The Committee discussed the next step.

"Your Majesty," said the chancellor. "I believe we must refer this matter to the Court of Chivalry, while we determine whether any proof can be found to these assertions." Panel members nodded quietly. "I suggest we reconvene in two months' time," he added.

The king agreed to the proposition. There was a bit more business to attend to, and then the Committee retired. That

132

evening, Richard tried to enjoy himself by listening to the Earl of Salisbury, who read his new poetry to an intimate group. Salisbury was one of the most educated of all Richard's favorites, and his poetry readings were well attended. Tonight was no exception. But when John of Gaunt entered the chamber with a small following, the evening was ruined.

John was no fool; he knew he was intruding, but this couldn't wait. He stood patiently in the rear of the room until the earl had finished; then he joined in the polite applause. The king would have to acknowledge him sooner or later.

Richard stood. "My dear friend, you have given us great pleasure. Please join me later for a drink of wine before retiring."

Salisbury bowed and left the room, accompanied by many of Richard's courtiers. Sighing, the king turned as Gaunt, York, Rutland, and Holland approached.

"This must be about Henry," Richard said.

Gaunt nodded. "Your Majesty, we are willing to stand as surety for my son."

The king cocked his head, considering. "Your son's appeal against Thomas de Mowbray is most disturbing," he said. "I don't understand the reasoning behind his accusations."

Gaunt and York looked at each other, though the former felt a twinge of conscience. His younger brother didn't know that this was his planning. How else could they air the suspicious death of Gloucester? As planned, Henry stopped short of holding the king responsible; without proof, it was suicidal. Would his accusations bring out the truth? Probably not.

John cleared his throat. "Sire, with my son at liberty, perhaps he will be able to substantiate his claims. If he is detained, nothing can be done."

Richard paced a couple of steps, then turned. "All right. I agree." He beckoned the captain of his Cheshire guard forward, who was standing at the door. "Summon my treasurer. He will settle the indemnity with these Lords for the Duke of Hereford."

No one offered to stand bail for Thomas de Mowbray, so he was kept in honorable confinement, first at Windsor and then at the Great Wardrobe in London.

CHAPTER 12

On April 28 the Court of Chivalry was held at Windsor Castle. Thanks to Edward III and his ransom payments from the French war, the old buildings had been beautifully renovated, and the enormous great hall accommodated the huge crowd. At a nod, the herald stepped forward. "Oyez, Oyez." His voice reverberated against the vaulted ceiling. "The king commands that Henry of Lancaster, Duke of Hereford and Thomas de Mowbray, Duke of Norfolk be brought forward."

The crowd hushed as the two dukes—resplendent in their respective heraldic tunics—came forward and bowed before the king. Upon standing, they glared at each other before turning their attention to the king and his retinue.

"My Lords," said Richard, "it is my pleasure that you make peace together. It would be much better for the tranquility of our kingdom if you agree to end this unfortunate dispute. Make matters up, I implore you." He looked at both of them in turn.

Mowbray was the first to speak. "Saving your favor, my dear sovereign, it cannot be. My honor is too deeply concerned."

Frowning, Richard turned to Bolingbroke. "Henry, will you be reconciled? If not, tell the Duke of Norfolk and myself why this is not possible."

Henry gestured to a knight at his side. "Your Majesty, with your permission I would have Sir Thomas Erpingham speak on my behalf."

Everyone knew Erpingham was Henry's most trusted companion, knighted by Gaunt and serving with Henry all the way back to his Lithuania crusade when he was a young man. The king nodded and Erpingham stepped forward. "Dear and sovereign Lord," the knight began, and then reiterated all the accusations Henry had made before the Parliamentary Committee.

His eyes resting on Henry, Richard's mind wandered until Erpingham said, "...and he has, by malice, caused the death of the Duke of Gloucester, whom God assoil. The Duke of Hereford says, and I on his part, that he will prove the truth of this statement by his body between any sunrise and sunset."

Richard bit back words of reproach. This whole thing had gotten out of control and it was not going to go away. No matter what happened, he was still implicated in Gloucester's murder; no one would believe Mowbray would do such a foul act without orders. "Cousin, do you acknowledge these words as your own?"

Ignoring the king's tone, Henry nodded. "My dear lord, I do; and I also demand of you the right of wager of battle against him."

Now it was the turn of Mowbray's knight. In bad humor, Richard gestured for him to speak. "Most dread sovereign," the man said, "behold here Sir Thomas de Mowbray, Duke of Norfolk who answers, and I for him, that with respect to all which Henry of Lancaster has said, it is all falsehood, and he has lied wickedly like a false and disloyal knight against you, your crown, and your royal majesty. This he will prove, and defend himself as a loyal knight ought to do in encounter against him."

Frowning at Mowbray, Richard said, "Is this your speech? Do you wish to add anything more?"

Norfolk was ready with his response. "My dear Lord, it is true I have received so much gold from you to pay your good people of Calais, which I have done. The city of Calais is as well guarded as it ever was, and no person has lodged a complaint against me. My dear and sovereign Lord, I have made many journeys in France and in Germany in your service where I expended much of my own treasure, and I did not receive payment at the time. Some of the funds you gave me for Calais were used to reimburse me. Also, I acknowledge that I once laid an ambush to kill my lord of Lancaster, but we have since made peace between us and for which I thank him. This is what I wish to say, and to support it I will defend myself against the Duke of Hereford. I beseech you to grant me justice, and trial of battle in tournament."

Richard looked questioningly at Gaunt. How in the world could Mowbray have found the opportunity to beg the duke's forgiveness? He saw no answer in those steely eyes.

The king stood. "I order both of you to withdraw while I consult with the council." As the Parliamentary Committee gathered in the judges' chamber, Richard beckoned to Gaunt. "What was Mowbray referring to? Did you forgive him?"

The duke scratched his chin. "No, sire." But recollecting something, he raised his eyebrows. "Wait. I remember that ridiculous assassination attempt before we went to Scotland. He did ask my forgiveness afterwards, stating it was Robert de Vere's doing."

"That was thirteen years ago!" Richard smirked. "How clever of him not to make a distinction." The smirk turned into a grimace. "He will pay for that deception."

The council sat, waiting for the king to speak.

"What say you, my lords?" Richard looked at Bushy.

"Sire, we have not learned any definitive proof of the challengers' accusations. If they do not withdraw their complaints, we will have no choice. We must refer it to trial by combat."

The king looked at Gaunt, who was staring at his hands. The duke glanced up, his eyes full of tears. He knew he was partially responsible for this. Slowly, he nodded.

"Very well. Let us get this over with."

Once reassembled on the platform before the crowd, the herald summoned the two rivals. Both men faced each other, the breach between them as impassible as a raging river.

Richard stood. "Sir Henry Bolingbroke and Sir Thomas de Mowbray, I ask you once again: will you not be reconciled?"

Both men shook their heads. Hereford pulled off his glove and threw it on the ground. Stooping, Mowbray picked up the pledge.

"All right," said the king, stamping his foot. "By Saint John the Baptist, I will never more attempt to reconcile the two of you. You shall have your trial by battle at Coventry in September. Prepare yourselves."

A little over four months were to pass before the great tournament. This was no everyday event; there were a lot of preparations to be made. The tournament field had to be leveled and fenced off. Benches needed to be constructed to support a large crowd. Letters needed to be sent to foreign countries, inviting barons and knights to attend. The combating parties each made special arrangements for a custom set of armor to be built for this occasion. Henry wrote to the Duke of Milan and arranged for his best armorers to design and build his harness. Mowbray sent to Germany.

In the meantime, Richard decided to take his queen and his household on a royal progress to the midlands. He found himself able to relax for the first time since Henry started his quarrel, and he was looking forward to hunting in the chases north of Lichfield. Stowe Pool, under the ownership of the bishop, was an important fishery and a favorite stopping place for ducks. Richard loved duck. So did his falcons.

For once, the sky was perfectly blue and the air was still. The king spoke lovingly to his gyrfalcon and turned to Rutland, who rode beside him with his own white goshawk.

"Let us fly them together," the king said. They waited until the beaters were in place near the water's edge before removing the birds' hoods and casting the falcons into the wind. The birds quickly rose almost into the clouds when one of the beaters started his rat-a-tat on a little drum. Four ducks were flushed from the reeds and the falcons turned immediately. Each shot toward its chosen prey, slamming into it so expertly the ducks dropped from the sky like a stone. Two under-falconers swam into the lake to retrieve the game.

"Just feed my bird the heart of the duck," Richard said to the master falconer as he swung his lure to recover the raptor. "We'll want to fly it later, at heron."

The falcon returned to the king's outstretched arm. He replaced the hood, making kissing noises. "I love that bird," he said. "He puts all the others to shame."

John Holland and Salisbury joined them and conversation fell into the familiar pattern of past hunts. The afternoon promised lots of activities and the four of them took turns with their birds until Richard started to show restlessness. They knew his moods; the king had something on his mind. His companions sat in silence for a few minutes while Richard turned his falcon over to its keeper. He held out a hand for a swig of wine. John pulled a leather bottle from his belt.

"I heard the Count of St. Pol is coming over from France to see the tournament," he said, handing over the wine. Richard nodded in thanks before taking a drink. "I'm sure he will bring a large entourage," John added.

Salisbury cleared his throat. "Sire, do you think they will go through with it?"

"I have no doubt," the king said. "Both men think their honor is at stake."

Rutland let out a laugh. "The last two Appellants turning on each other. How very suitable."

"You mean convenient?" Richard took another drink before handing it back. "I wish it was. If one of them is killed on the field, the other will be even stronger."

"Hmm." Rutland nudged his mount closer to the king. "Do you believe Mowbray's story?"

"About the plot to kill Lancaster?"

"And myself," Edward muttered, "and Holland. And Beaufort."

"See how absurd that sounds? No, I don't believe it."

"I don't either," said Holland. "That my nephew would plot to kill me? What purpose would that serve?"

"None that I can see," Richard said, waving his dismissal. "Perhaps Mowbray was attempting to make himself a hero. I don't appreciate being dragged into it."

"Absolutely not. Bolingbroke was right in telling you." Falling into his usual habit, Rutland tried to gratify the king.

"No, he told his father. My uncle told me. There's a difference." For once he glowered at his cousin, but Rutland was not unduly concerned.

"Is it possible," Edward mused, changing the subject, "that it was Bolingbroke who spoke treason to Mowbray? Then, to stay out trouble, could Henry have turned the story around?"

"Hmm." Richard nodded. "That could be possible. Thomas isn't as clever as Henry and wouldn't have known how to answer that, save to accuse him of lying."

"Well, wouldn't it be expedient if they managed to kill each other?" Rutland pursued.

Richard shrugged. "It would suit me to be rid of them both. It would suit me very well."

Salisbury turned on his horse. "Perhaps there is another way to be rid of them."

"Oh?"

"Stop the tourney. You have the right."

The king chewed his lip, thinking. "How would that help me?"

"Send them into exile. Tell them they are too close to the throne to risk their extinction."

"Ha!" Still, Salisbury had Richard's attention. "Could I get away with that?"

"Mowbray has few friends these days. As for Bolingbroke, he always wants to travel. He could spend as much time as he pleases fighting in tournaments, going on crusade, playing at being a great knight like he always does."

"Give him an annuity," Holland suggested, "and he should be perfectly content."

Richard smiled at the thought. "This requires some consideration. I can't afford to antagonize my uncle."

"I doubt if you could find cause to exile Henry forever," Salisbury said. "On the other hand, a lot could happen in five or ten years."

"And by then, he would have lost his influence here," Rutland mused. "It could be just as useful to you as his death."

"Except for his inheritance," Richard laughed. But his humor faded quickly. "After Gaunt's death, his wealth and power would exceed the crown." He frowned at Edward. "That's not a comforting thought. Perhaps it would be better to see him beaten on the tournament field."

139

"If he loses but is not killed—"

"He would be executed anyway, as a condemned traitor." They all fell silent at that.

"He is a formidable jouster," said Holland, finally.

"So is Mowbray. I would say they are about equal."

"Then there is no surety on that score," said Edward.

"No. It would be in God's hands." Richard tried, and failed, to look virtuous.

"If he comes out successful—" John hesitated.

"He would be incorrigible. The people's champion. At my expense." Richard grumbled. "The more popular he makes himself, the harder he will be to control. What's more," he muttered, "I can't have him making an issue out of Gloucester's death."

That was the crux of the matter and everyone knew it. Nobody dared answer. Bolingbroke was an untested force. For now, he was content to live in his father's shadow. But that wouldn't last forever.

Ever since Parliament, discontent in the country was never far below the surface. Unrest had been reported in Kent and Essex, and local sheriffs had their hands full keeping order. The king spent as little time as possible in London. He was having trouble sleeping at night and had increased his guard of Cheshire archers to watch his bedchamber. His standing bodyguard was several hundred strong, and their presence was everywhere. This just served to make matters worse.

At Nottingham, Richard was preparing for another council meeting when he summoned Rutland, John Holland, and Thomas Percy.

"I just learned there was another altercation in Croydon, this time against the lord mayor. Two men were killed! I tell you, I can no longer ride through the South in safety, thanks to the troublemakers in London and the neighboring counties." His voice was pitched higher than usual. "They showed themselves my enemies ten years ago, and they persist in their hostile behavior. If this continues, I will take measures against them." By now, his

140

closest adherents were concerned about his growing paranoia. But there was only so much they could do. The king was restless and impatient and didn't take well to having his opinions questioned.

Even Rutland was at a loss. But not for long.

"Perhaps if the counties appoint a proctor to act on their behalf, they can offer securities to Your Majesty." He looked over at Percy for confirmation.

Thomas cleared his throat. "Something in the way of a charter," he suggested.

Richard whirled around. "That's it! A blank charter, offering me *carte blanche* over their lives and possessions. They must admit their guilt for all their treasons and evil doings against my person, and swear it won't happen again. Only then will I accept their submission." He thought for a moment. "As long as they comply, the blank charters will not be enacted and they will retain their liberties."

"Protection," muttered Thomas.

Richard stared at him, his eyes narrowing. "Yes, protection."

Who needed protection more? The king, or his subjects? Thomas wondered. Rutland and Holland had business elsewhere but he stayed behind. He could see that Richard could use some company.

"More wine?" he offered, and the king nodded.

Pouring for both of them, Thomas sat on a window seat, leaning back. "I was with Gaunt those days during the Merciless Parliament and missed all that terrible business. Just what happened between you and London?"

"Faithless, self-serving jackals," the king muttered. "One minute they cheer you and the next they stab you in the back. They offered help and provisions to the Lords Appellant even while they promised to close the city against them. They joined the army that marched against Robert de Vere, who was only trying to protect me. My poor, valiant friend." He looked into his chalice. "All those seventeen counties joined the Appellants. And they wonder why I am so unforgiving? The only people who stood with me were killed. Or at best, driven into exile. One doesn't

141

easily recover from that kind of betrayal." He couldn't chase the bitterness from his voice.

Thomas nodded, deep in thought. "And you wonder if they are capable of doing it again?"

"People don't change, do they? I must do what I can to protect myself."

Protection. There it was again.

"It's a risky decision, sire. With these blank charters you might drive them to desperation." Thomas knew he was taking a risk in saying so. He trusted to his intimate relationship with the king. Luckily, Richard chose to consider his words.

"I see the danger. London and I had an even worse altercation five years ago. I remember; you were in France then, too. They refused me a loan and then, when I got the money from a Lombard merchant, they were so irate they attacked him and beat the poor man almost to death. As you can imagine, I was infuriated. I deposed the mayor and removed my government to York. That put some sense into them. After many months I agreed to come back, but only after imposing a fine of £10,000. The welcome they gave me was quite gratifying, even if they didn't mean any of it."

Thomas knew the story, though he could see Richard felt better after talking about it.

"So you see," the king went on, "we've been through worse. Once my subjects understand that they need only respect me, we will get along just fine. I'll put you in charge of keeping the charters under lock and key. Now, do we have everything in order for the council meeting?"

After Nottingham, the king took his young queen with him to finish the royal progress. In Worcester he supervised the work done on cathedrals. In Gloucester he checked on the progress of Edward II's canonization. In Bath he expanded his own retinue with knights and squires pilfered from Lancaster. He even attended a judicial duel in Bristol between an English squire and a Scots knight.

The king was happiest when visiting his own principality of Chester. The proximity to Wales gave added security. He traveled to Holt Castle, just south of Chester city and across the river Dee. Having absorbed Holt into the principality after the death of Richard Arundel, the king favored this splendid fortress and ordered the removal of vast sums of the royal wealth from London to his new treasure house.

Holt Castle was significant by its shape: a pentagon with five round towers. A five-sided interior courtyard followed the shape of its outer walls. Riding side-by-side with his queen, Richard led his retinue through the detached barbican tower and across two drawbridges. Once inside, he pointed up. "See, my dear? Wait until we climb to the top of the tower. We'll be able to look almost all the way to Chester."

Isabella smiled, exposing a missing tooth. "Oh please. I would love to see that with you."

Richard dismounted and helped her down. "Come, I'll show you." He beckoned to the constable of the castle as they climbed the kitchen tower, which was on the river side. When they reached the battlements, Isabella crossed her arms on top of the embrasure, standing on her toes to look out.

"See over there, in the distance?" Richard pointed north. "That's where we're going tomorrow. Tonight, we will have a wonderful meal of fresh trout, taken from the river." He brushed aside a lock of hair that blew over her face. "You're not cold, are you?"

"Oh no. I like the wind."

Richard turned to his constable. "In a week's time, the first of my treasury should be delivered to this stronghold." He pointed to the river. "It is my wish that you replace the postern gate with a dedicated watergate."

The constable scratched his head. "That would require cutting a deep channel from the gate to the Dee."

Richard nodded. "Between that and the moat, the castle will be much more secure. Spare no expense; this must be a priority."

The other bowed. "As you wish, sire. Consider it done."

Later in the evening, as the household enjoyed a small banquet, they were entertained by a Welsh bard who accompanied himself on a large harp. Although his poetry was recited in English, his songs were in Welsh and Isabella sat quietly, enthralled by the strange lilting tongue. Richard smiled at her. She was still a child, and as precious as a daughter. Anne would have loved her.

He turned to speak with the Bishop of St. Asaph when a messenger came into the hall and whispered into Percy's ear. Showing surprise, the steward led him to the king.

"What is it?" Richard was mildly annoyed at the interruption but leaned back, ready to listen.

"Sire, the Earl of March is dead."

"Dead!"

The bard stopped in the middle of his song. Everyone stared at the king.

"Roger Mortimer dead? How did it happen?"

"He was killed leading a raid against MacMurrough in Ireland."

Richard let out his breath in frustration. "Blast it, I told him to wait for me. He has undone almost everything I achieved over there." Catching himself, Richard looked at his dinner guests. Roger Mortimer owned many estates in Wales, and not a few from his affinity were sitting in this very room. Luckily only the men closest to him heard his comment.

The king gestured at Percy to call for silence. "I have just learned the Earl of March was killed in Ireland during a skirmish." He waited while his guests talked amongst themselves. "This will not deter my plans to take an expedition to Ireland," he added in a louder voice. "Rather, it is imperative we avenge his death. By next summer we will retrace our steps from four years ago."

Rutland approached and leaned over Richard's shoulder. "His oldest son is five," he said quietly.

Richard nodded. "That takes the Mortimers out of the succession, at least for now."

"Making Lancaster the next in line."

Richard looked sideways at Edward. Both of them knew how he despised Bolingbroke. "We shall see," the king said, "after Coventry."

CHAPTER 13

People traveled from all over England to see the great tournament; some came from Scotland and many from France. Coventry was ready for the massive numbers who would witness the greatest event since the tournament at St. Inglevert eight years before. A huge set of seats was prepared for the spectators, as well as a platform for the king and his nobles. The lists were sixty paces long and forty wide, with a seven foot-high barrier to separate the jousters. The knights' pavilions stood at either end, roped off with fluttering pennons bearing each man's device.

At eight o'clock in the morning on the 16th of September, the Constable Edward of Rutland and the Marshal Thomas Holland arrived to organize the lists. They and their twenty followers were dressed in red doublets with silver girdles on which was written *Honi soit qui mal y pense* (shame on whoever thinks evil of it) the Order of the Garter motto. Meanwhile, the attendees started to arrive—the foreign nobles taking places of honor—and there was much jostling for position, while the sergeants-at-arms kept busy maintaining the four-foot gap around the lists.

At nine o'clock Henry Bolingbroke entered the field on a white courser gorgeously barbed with blue and green velvet, sewn with swans and antelopes in gold thread. His shield bore the red cross of St. George, with a silver background instead of white. He was wearing his full armor under a doublet encrusted with his embroidered coat of arms. Followed by six knights on white horses, similarly decked out, Henry moved majestically forward and stopped next to the barrier. The constable and marshal came out to meet him. Rutland stepped forward and raised the visor of Henry's bascinet.

"As per the Gages of Battle, it is my duty to demand that you tell us who you are, what you want, and for what purpose you have come hither."

Looking straight ahead, the knight answered, "I am Henry of Lancaster, Duke of Hereford, and am come here to prosecute my appeal in combating Thomas de Mowbray, Duke of Norfolk, who is a traitor, false and recreant to God, the King, his realm, and me."

Nodding his head, Rutland beckoned a priest forward who carried a crucifix and open missal of Gospels.

The marshal took over. "The Holy Father is here to administer three oaths. First, you must swear that your petition is true from beginning to end and that you will maintain it, God willing."

Henry nodded and said, "I swear."

"The second oath is that you have no other arms than those we assign to you: no other knife, large or small, nor any other pointed instrument, nor any charm, enchantment, or experiment with which to conquer your adversary." Again Henry nodded. "The third oath, that you will make your adversary surrender, or you will kill him, and depart out of the lists before sunset. Will you enter the lists on these points?"

"I will," said Henry, closing his visor. He crossed himself, then called for his lance. His squire ran forward and handed up the weapon and shield. Followed by his six knights, Bolingbroke rode slowly to his pavilion, which was covered with red roses. Alighting, he entered the tent to await the coming of his enemy.

After Bolingbroke had made his exit, a quartet of blaring trumpets announced the king. Accompanied by the queen, all the nobles of England, the Archbishop of Canterbury, the Count of St. Pol—who was the constable of France—Richard made a show of standing before his throne and acknowledging the cheering of the spectators. His Cheshire archers pushed their way through the crowd, trampling over feet and generally making a nuisance of themselves, though the atmosphere was so festive even their presence didn't dampen the enthusiasm.

Richard sat on his throne and gestured for his herald to proceed. Standing with a scroll, the herald cried, "Oyez, Oyez,

147

Oyez! It is commanded by the king, by the constable, and by the marshal, that no person, poor or rich, be so daring as to put his hand upon the lists, on pain of having his hand chopped off. None may enter the lists save those who have leave from the king, upon pain of being drawn and hung."

Facing Henry's pavilion, the herald continued, "Oyez. Behold here Henry of Lancaster, Duke of Hereford, appellant, who is come to the lists to do his duty against Thomas de Mowbray, Duke of Norfolk, defendant. Let him come to the lists to do his duty, upon pain of being declared false."

This was the signal for Mowbray to come forward, riding a black horse barbed with red velvet embroidered with lions of silver and mulberry trees. Opening his visor, the constable, accompanied by the marshal, gave him the same oath as Bolingbroke. Once accomplished, Mowbray rode into the lists, shouting "God speed the right!" and went up to his own pavilion, dismounting and hanging his shield on the saddle-bow.

The marshal and constable called for the lances to be brought forward. Both were measured, to determine they were exactly the same length. Once satisfied, the lances were returned and the herald declared that the knights should do their duty.

Facing each other on opposite sides of the list, the two dukes sat upon their chargers while the air was filled with murmurings from the crowd. They couched their lances and lowered their visors. The trumpets blared once again and the spectators held their breath. No one wanted to cause the least distraction, though a flock of geese flew over their heads, honking as though to encourage the hesitating rivals. Henry was first to spur his stallion forward, quickly gaining speed.

Suddenly a baton flew into the air and hit the ground before him and a voice called "Ho! Ho!" Pulling back on his reins, Henry brought his horse to a savage halt, practically forcing him onto his haunches. Mowbray hadn't moved as yet.

Richard was standing, for it was he who had thrown the baton. This wasn't unprecedented; as their liege lord, he was entitled to take their quarrel into his own hands. Breathing heavily, Henry pulled off his helmet. He had been prepared to strike with all his skill or die in the process. To be suddenly yanked away from such total concentration was almost more than he could bear.

"Squire, take the Duke of Hereford's lance away," Richard ordered. "Both of you, return to your pavilions while I discuss the matter with my council."

Henry glanced up at his father who stood behind the king. The shocked look on Gaunt's face brought him back to reality. His father had been prepared for the worst; what was he thinking now?

Richard and his parliamentary council retired to a long pavilion erected behind the raised platform. "Sit, uncle," said the king, pointing to a chair beside his throne. Gaunt practically collapsed onto his seat. The others ranged along two benches with a table between them.

"My lords," said the king, "I cannot stand by and witness the destruction of my contentious dukes. Either one of their deaths would cause great harm to this kingdom." The others muttered to each other, but no one was certain what to say out loud.

"Is there another way we can resolve this crisis?" Richard continued, raising his hands in supplication.

No one was fooled. The king knew his own mind; it only remained for them to discover what he wanted and take the burden off his shoulders.

Gaunt cleared his throat. "If there is to be no combat, how are we to determine whether honor has been served?"

"Ah, good uncle. As far as I am concerned, both are culpable and undeserving of pity. Let us consider this logically. The two former Appellants—" Richard glanced at his uncle— "met and discussed their vulnerability in the eyes of the law. They must have had a disagreement; it's only natural when a man has a guilty conscience. The less scrupulous of the two betrayed the other's confidence and denounced him; he even accused him of treason. Come, my lords, do you honestly suspect he didn't have the same thoughts himself?" Richard looked at his councilors who didn't meet his eyes. "As I see it, both are guilty in varying degrees."

149

Rutland—the only one present who had discussed this with Richard—knew when to speak out. "Sire," he said, "perhaps outlawry would serve your purpose."

"What was that? Outlawry, did you say?" The king appeared sufficiently surprised.

"If the combatants were out of the country for a period of time, all this would blow over like a bad storm. They would be chastised but not blooded."

Gaunt let out a heavy sigh and Richard turned to him. "It is you I am thinking of, as well. Would you not prefer your son to live in comfort overseas, so he could return to his patrimony?"

"If it must be so."

"Henry is young," said the Earl of Northumberland. "Let him go to Prussia, or to the Holy Sepulcher. He can visit his sisters in Spain and Portugal, or voyage wherever it suits him. All the knights and nobles overseas will welcome him."

"It is so," Gaunt nodded sadly.

"And I would grant him an annuity so he would want for nothing," Richard mused.

"But sire," interjected Thomas Percy, "as the duke said, how to determine the truth of this matter?"

"There are times when other considerations take precedence," Richard answered somewhat testily.

"The king's gesture is not against the laws of chivalry," York reminded the council.

And so the argument went back and forth for two hours while the dukes waited impatiently inside their pavilions and the restive crowd attempted to amuse themselves. Finally, the king and his council returned to their seats.

The herald stepped forward. "Oyez, Oyez. The Duke of Hereford and the Duke of Norfolk are commanded before the tribune of the lists."

Still wearing their breastplates, the two dukes presented themselves before the king. Bushy moved next to the herald, a long scroll in his hand. "Oyez. My lord king has acknowledged that Henry of Lancaster, Duke of Hereford, appellant, and Thomas de Mowbray, Duke of Norfolk, defendant, have both appeared here valiantly, and that each was, and is, ready to do his duty like

150

a brave knight. My lord king has also declared that, even though the issue at stake involves treason, the two dukes are so close to the throne in both blood and arms that the realm would be greatly imperiled by either man's dishonor. Our gracious lord, grieving in his heart, even though they did not merit it—for each of them was more to blame than any other—decided to take the issue into his own hands. Therefore, by the full advice, authority, and assent of parliament, he has declared, for the peace and tranquility of the realm, and in order to avoid quarrels, particularly between the said dukes and their supporters, that Henry of Lancaster shall quit the realm for ten years, and, if he returns to the country before the ten years have passed, he shall be hung and beheaded."

Even before Bushy finished, a rumbling from the gathering grew into a great roar, as every throat shouted its objection. The uproar grew so loud no one could hear each other speak. The king's unjust declaration was felt by all—no less by the unhappy duke, who fought back tears of rage. As the spectators expressed their dismay, the king sat unperturbed in his throne, knowing his Cheshire archers would maintain order if need be.

Richard was satisfied with this solution. At last, Bolingbroke endured a taste of his own humiliation, ten long years ago.

When the noise died down, the king gestured for the herald to continue.

"Oyez, Oyez," he shouted. "Hear the judgment of the king and council."

Bushy held up his scroll. "That Thomas de Mowbray, Duke of Norfolk shall quit the realm for the rest of his life, and shall choose whether he would dwell in Prussia, in Bohemia, or in Hungary, or would go beyond the sea to the land of the Saracens and unbelievers. That he shall never return to set foot again on Christian land. All his lands shall remain in the king's hands, to reimburse the money he had received for the payment of the Calais garrison and misapplied. Meanwhile, he shall be allowed 10,000 nobles a year for his use."

The crowd grumbled again, though not nearly so much as at Bolingbroke's fate. Mowbray had not ingratiated himself with the common people and few were willing to risk supporting his cause.

"The king orders that both of you shall have left the realm by the 20th of October, under pain of treason."

Richard stood. "I would see both of you in my pavilion, the Duke of Hereford first. Herald, declare this tournament at an end."

The entertainment was over and the disgruntled spectators began to disperse. Taking John of Gaunt with him, the king entered his pavilion, followed by Bolingbroke. Once the tent flap had closed, Henry fell to one knee.

"Sire, you have dishonored me!"

"Nonsense. I have spared you."

"But sire, I do not deserve this. I only wished to expose the treachery of your disloyal knight. I will be perceived everywhere as a traitor."

"Shh. Do not take it so. I will send you with letters patent explaining your innocence so you will be received favorably wherever you go."

Gaunt made to kneel beside his son. "Your Majesty, take pity on an old man."

Distraught, Richard took him by the arms, raising him up. "Please, stop. This is not necessary."

"Nevertheless, I beg you to mitigate your sentence on my son."

"Uncle, uncle. You distress me. Get up, I say." Richard brushed the dust off of Gaunt's robe. "Take heart. Because of the love I bear you, I will reduce Henry's banishment to six years."

Ten years or six, it didn't matter to the Duke of Lancaster. He knew he would be dead before his son came back from exile. But, afraid to exasperate his nephew, Gaunt lowered his head in acquiescence.

"Listen to me, Henry Bolingbroke," the king went on, "it has been decreed, under the authority of parliament, that you will not, under any circumstances, travel in the company of the Duke of Norfolk, nor of Thomas Arundel former chancellor of England. You shall not communicate in any way with either of them. No letters, no messages, no intercourse of any kind. Is this understood?"

"Yes, sire." Henry allowed himself to look at Richard. For a moment their eyes locked. Henry couldn't repress the loathing he felt, and the king was the first to look away.

"Be of good cheer," the king said, gathering up his cloak and sitting on his throne. "If all goes well, I shall recall you within the year. And if, God forbid, your father dies in the meantime, I will keep your paternal inheritance for you. But you must abide by the terms of this ordinance."

"Sire, we shall do so, in all loyalty," Gaunt remarked before Henry had a chance to answer. Grasping his son by the arm, he bowed and practically dragged him from the tent.

Richard didn't care. He had gotten what he wanted. It only remained for him to dispose of Mowbray.

He didn't have long to wait. Exchanging angry glances with Bolingbroke as he entered the tent, Thomas quickly knelt before the king. "Sire," he said, "I don't deserve this sentence of outlawry."

This was all so much simpler in the planning stage! It was easy getting rid of Bolingbroke; Richard had disliked him since they were boys. But now that he faced Mowbray, fonder memories came flooding in. There were so many days in their youth they escaped the watchful eyes of his guardians, riding spirited horses deep into the country. They searched out hiding places where they could climb high on a cliff, or cool streams where they would strip down and swim, just like ordinary boys. They sparred together while Richard learned to fight, though Mowbray, a natural swordsman, always treated him gently. Thomas usually traveled with Richard as his grandfather's household moved from place to place, and often found a way to provide the king with entertainment.

But no, that was a long time ago. Before he became one of the Lords Appellant. Before he turned traitor. And now, it was too late to look backward. For his own self-protection, Richard knew that Thomas had to go. His eyes stinging with the reminder of his old friend's disloyalty, the king found strength in anger.

"You say your exile is undeserved. How could you side with Arundel? You married his daughter without my permission. You tried to kill my uncle Gaunt—not once, but twice!"

Flustered, Mowbray couldn't formulate an answer.

"As for the funds you misappropriated at Calais—"

"Sire, that is unfair. You sent me overseas on many embassies and did not pay for any of my expenses. In Calais, I took care of the garrison. You had no cause for complaint—"

"It was not up to you to decide how to apportion my money!"

"Surely this isn't treason!"

"Then you were absent at Shrewsbury, when I needed you."

Sire, you know I felt conflicted about the judgment."

Richard slammed his fist on his chair arm. "I know very well! You bruited your dissent both privately and publicly! Much to my mortification! You undermined my authority!"

Mowbray hung his head.

"And no wonder you didn't show up! You dared not face me after ordering the ambush of my uncle! After I had made you Duke of Norfolk and given you lands belonging to the traitors! This was how you repaid me?"

Mowbray opened his mouth to reply, then thought better of it. In his current mood, the king wouldn't accept any argument.

"You are fortunate I chose exile for you," Richard said, standing and turning away. "Take your knights and go. And remember that you are forbidden to make contact with Bolingbroke, or Archbishop Arundel, upon pain of death. I will give you an annuity of 1000 pounds per year."

Frowning at the king's back, Mowbray stood. "Then I am never to see England again."

"It's in God's hands."

First Thomas de Mowbray then Henry Bolingbroke took leave of King Richard at Windsor, where they were given letters of protection and safe conduct. They also received letters of patent granting the right, through their attorneys, to receive livery for any inheritance that might fall to them during their exile. "You must understand," Richard said, "you are forbidden, under pain of treason, to request the reversal of my decision or sue for permission to return before your allotted time."

Mowbray did not linger and departed without a word, accompanied by six of his knights. On Richard's signal, Gaunt and Bolingbroke remained, waiting for his pleasure.

Pushing back his sleeve, Richard reached for a scroll. "I have letters of protection for seventeen of your knights to accompany you into exile. And I license you to travel with up to two hundred servants. Take whatever plate, jewels, horses and baggage you need." Richard hoped that would soften the blow somewhat. If not, well, he'd done the best he could. "I will keep your son, young Henry, by my side. It will be good for him to accompany me to Ireland."

Henry stood. "As you wish, sire. In any case, I leave you with a heavy heart."

"I will write to you, cousin. You have my permission to stay for one month in Calais before leaving our sovereign territory."

What more was there to say? Accompanied by his father, Bolingbroke proceeded to London, where he settled his affairs, appointed attorneys, borrowed money, gave presents and made arrangements for transportation from Dover.

For the next week they stayed at Henry's London residence, and as the days ran out Henry could no longer keep up the pretense of equanimity. On the evening before their departure, as Henry and his father were sipping their wine after dinner he put a hand to his eyes and tried to suppress a sob.

"Oh, my son." Gaunt leaned across the table, reaching out a hand. "Take cheer. If I were your age, I would gladly jump at this opportunity. You can visit your sisters in Portugal and Castile. You can go on crusade."

Sighing, Henry grasped his father's hand, a tear running down his face. "I am under no illusions," he said. "Everyone will regard me as a traitor, for what innocent man would be treated as such? How am I going to show my face?"

"Richard has sent letters of recommendation."

Shaking his head, Henry stood, walking to the fireplace. "Can you imagine me holding out his letters like a supplicant? It would be the worst of humiliations."

"It won't be necessary. Your reputation has already preceded you."

"I fear it is in tatters!" Catching himself, Henry lowered his voice. "But that's not the worst of it. I won't be able to watch my children growing up. They won't even know me when I come back."

"At least Thomas is coming with you."

"That is a blessing. I do love the boy."

Crossing back to his father, Henry knelt beside him. "Worst of all, I fear I may never see you again." He took John's hands, raising them to his forehead. "I will never forgive the king if that happens."

Blinking rapidly, John pulled his right hand away, placing it on Henry's head. "It will be as God wills," he said quietly. "The best I can do is make sure your inheritance is intact."

"Better yet, take care of your health. What would my life be without you?"

A sad smile crossed John's face. "You will be your own master. I think you'll surprise yourself; once I am gone, your deeds may very well eclipse my own."

The next day, Henry and his father left his London palace with a large entourage, headed for Dover. As they opened the gates and stepped into the road, they were greeted by a crowd of Londoners. The well-wishers threw flowers in front of Henry's horse, swinging their arms and calling his name. People leaned from their windows, flapping colored cloths. Waving appreciatively, Henry wondered what Richard would do when he found out about this enthusiastic send-off—though, he admitted to himself, Londoners were notoriously fickle. He hadn't done anything of particular note to deserve all this adulation. It could be just that they didn't like the way he was treated by the king.

Every street was the same, lined on both sides by adoring supporters. "England won't be safe until you return!" someone shouted. Others cried, "There goes our only hope!" All the way to Dover, through every town they passed, people from all walks of life emerged to give their support and cheer him on his way. *Maybe he really was the people's hero.* Henry soaked it all in, knowing this was going to have to last him a long time.

Too soon, father and son stood on the dock, looking east across the Channel. Henry's pennons—tied to the rigging of his waiting ship—flapped in the wind, breaking the silence between them. The surf, usually so calm, buffeted the shore, sending spurts of cold spray across their faces. Blinking from the gusts, pulling his hair out of his eyes, Henry extended his other hand. Gaunt grasped it with both his own.

"Godspeed," John said. "I have received letters from the King of France who welcomes you with open arms. He is reserving his Hotel de Clisson in Paris for you and your household."

Seagulls squawked overhead and Henry looked up at them while gathering his thoughts. "I am most grateful, I assure you. I don't know how long I can stay before they start treating me like a supplicant."

"Fear not. Stay as long as you need to. Your presence enhances his court." He smiled, letting go and stepping back as his son moved away to board the ship.

As he watched Henry's fleet navigate its way out of the harbor, John of Gaunt relaxed his cheerful expression. He was under no delusions; even standing still while the wind buffeted his back, he felt the overwhelming need to sit down. He was always tired, and the pain in his left arm would not go away. Opening and clenching his hand, he thought about all the things he should have said to Henry—all the advice he meant to give while his mind was fresh. Now it was too late.

He turned, accepting his horse's reins from his squire. "It's time we went back to Leicester Castle," he said. "My Katherine is waiting there for me. I need a rest." Looking once again at the ships, he sighed and mounted, followed by his retinue.

The sun had already set when Richard relaxed in his receiving chamber with the queen and a few of his guests. They were at Eltham Palace and the king had spent a long day working out details for his upcoming Irish expedition. A trio of minstrels sat in the corner, quietly playing their lute, harp, and recorder; no singing was required this evening. A knock on the door was followed by a chamber knight leading a young lad into the room. Well behaved, the boy immediately knelt before the king.

"Ah, there you are," Richard said. "Come, sit beside me." Gesturing to his left, the king smiled at the youth while a servant brought a chair. The boy sat on the edge of the seat, his back straight.

"Isabella, this is my cousin Henry's son, another Henry. Henry of Monmouth." The queen smiled as young Henry quickly knelt before her, kissing her hand.

"They call me Hal," he said. "I have heard so much about you."

The queen blushed while Richard patted the chair again. "How old are you, Hal?" he said.

"I just turned thirteen last month."

"Ah, then you are three years older than the queen. That's good. She needs companions her own age when I am not around."

Hal turned a questioning look at the king.

"You will be staying with us, Hal, now that your father is in France."

"Yes," the lad answered, looking into the king's eyes. "I am to be your hostage."

"Oh no, don't refer to yourself that way. Many older sons of nobles are brought up in their overlord's household. You are to receive training as befits your station." Richard glanced over at Rutland. "I think he shows great promise, don't you?"

"For certes," said Edward. "Hal, I am another cousin, son of the Duke of York. You can always come to me if you need anything."

Richard leaned forward. "Do you know how to dance?"

Hal nodded proudly. "You may not know this, but my father is a talented musician. I can dance, sing, and play the clavichord and lute."

"Splendid!" Richard turned to his minstrels. "Young Hal will dance with the queen."

Changing their instruments, the musicians struck up a lively tune while Hal stood, offering his hand to Isabella. Smiling broadly, she adjusted her headdress and joined him. The servants quickly pulled the furniture to the side and after a few experimental steps, the two young people started twirling around the room. Richard turned, gesturing to the few lords and ladies who were watching.

"Join them, please."

Not needing a second invitation, the gaily dressed courtiers fell in, while those without a partner clapped in time to the music. Richard leaned toward Holland. "He's reserved like his father, but I think we can overcome that."

John nodded. "I see you have something in mind."

"Oh, yes. Bolingbroke is a lost cause. But if I can win over his heir, then Lancaster won't be as much of a threat to me." He glanced playfully at John. "Besides, I think I like him." The dance was ending and Richard stood. "I think I'll dance with my wife."

Hal graciously relinquished his partner and strode about the room as the next song began. He paused when he saw the king standing with Rutland, then turned in some surprise, wondering how Richard could have moved so quickly. No, there was the king dancing with Isabella. Who was that fellow?

Since everyone was watching Hal, Richard's look-alike came forward, an amused smile on his face. "Don't worry, everyone does that," he said. "I am Richard Maudeleyn, the king's secretary."

Hal let out a grunt. "You startled me. I assume you must be a relation?"

"His half-brother. Richard finds me most useful when he doesn't want to be bothered with a foreign dignitary." He grinned. "Don't tell anyone."

"Ha!" Hal laughed out loud. "I'll bear that in mind." They watched the dancing for a moment. "Can I ask you a question?"

"Of course."

"If I wanted to give a present to the king, what would you suggest?"

159

"Hmm. Since he has the best of everything, that is a good question." Maudeleyn put a finger to his lips. "You know, the king has a weakness for sweets. A box of comfits would please him immensely."

"Ah, I am in your debt." Hal bowed before slipping away. Perhaps his new home wouldn't be so bad after all.

CHAPTER 14

Christmas festivities were held at Lichfield in the West Midlands. This year, for the very first time, Richard felt in full control of his kingship, and he was determined to celebrate accordingly. Heralds were sent out far and wide to announce the celebrations and jousts to be held, culminating in a grand tournament on Twelfth Night, the king's 33rd birthday. It was reported that every day, over twenty cattle, three hundred sheep and countless poultry were ordered to feed the immense entourage. Ambassadors came from as far away as the Byzantine Empire, adding luster to the royal court. The papal legate attended as well, hoping to prop up the king's uncertain support after all that noise about France and England trying to end the schism.

Alas, the festivities were dulled when messengers from Leicester arrived with the sad news that John of Gaunt was seriously ill and expected to die. Richard waited until after Twelfth Night before saddling up and leaving with a small entourage to travel the forty miles to Gaunt's castle. It was a cold ride and the king silently agreed with his companions, who complained about the icy roads in January. They were grateful to find a small monastery along the way to spend the night, though accommodations were sparse. No matter; the hall was warm. The next day, crossing the River Soar, they approached the fortress which dominated the countryside atop a tall motte. A somber Duchess Katharine greeted them, bending down to kiss young Hal on the cheek.

"I'm glad you brought him," she said to Richard. "He will bring a smile to his grandfather's face."

Leaving his retainers in the great hall, Richard put his hand on Hal's shoulder. Together they followed Katharine to Gaunt's sleeping chamber. The king was shocked at the alteration in the great duke's appearance. The last time he had seen him,

161

John was tall and strong, his black eyes flashing, his mouth set in determination, ready to react to the least provocation. Now, as though taken down by a predator, he was flat on his back with big bare feet sticking out from under the covers. His complexion was pale, his chest sunken in, and he was practically drooling from a slack mouth.

Katharine leaned over the bed and whispered in John's ear. His eyes fluttered open and he had trouble focusing on Richard's face. Then he saw Hal and he stretched out a hand.

"There you are, boy," he whispered as Hal approached, "the very image of your father at your age." John gazed up at Richard, who stood a few feet from the bed as though afraid the sick man was contagious. "Don't worry. It's my heart, nothing else." He took Hal's hand. "You have a large legacy to uphold. You must prove yourself worthy."

"Fear not, grandfather. I will be ready."

"I'm sure you will. Now leave me alone with the king." He looked at Katharine, who gave Hal a nudge on the back, going out with him.

Richard pulled up a chair, sitting next to the bed. "I didn't expect this. I thought you had many good years in front of you."

"It seems that the life went out of me the day Henry left."

"Nonsense, uncle. He's been away before."

"But not under a cloud of disfavor. My son is bereft, and so am I."

Richard ran a hand across his forehead. "For now it is out of my hands. Is there anything I can do for you?"

John closed his eyes, taking a few deep breaths. "I am concerned about Henry's inheritance," he said, his voice a whisper. Tears ran down his face.

"He has his attorneys," Richard said, trying to keep the annoyance out of his voice.

"You have the power. Promise me you will treat him fairly."

"I will, uncle. Henry will not want for anything."

"Then I may rest." John lifted a hand briefly and let it fall.

His duty discharged, Richard left the room as quickly as possible. Seeing his uncle in this state was unsettling.

162

John never left his sickbed again. On February 3 he breathed his last, leaving instructions that he was not to be embalmed or buried for forty days. After three weeks his body was taken by easy stages to London. He wished to be buried next to his beloved first wife Blanche of Lancaster at St. Paul's Cathedral, surrounded by candles: ten for the broken commandments, seven for neglected works of charity and the deadly sins, five for the wounds of Christ, and three for the Trinity. The king attended the funeral along with all the dukes, earls, and dignitaries. Conspicuous by his absence, Henry Bolingbroke was obliged to pray for his father's soul in Paris alongside the entire French royal family, knowing full well their loyalty lay with King Richard. He never felt so alone in his life.

The week before Gaunt's funeral, Richard met with his advisors at Kings Langley—not far from St. Albans. Most of his counter-appellants were present as well as his loyal councilors Russel, Bushy, Bagot, and Green. Thomas Percy was absent, but it was just as well. Since he was one of the executors of Gaunt's will, his position was too delicate for him to be trusted.

Richard tried to hide his trepidation. This was the moment he had been dreading for years. John of Gaunt was the king's staunchest supporter; not so his eldest son, who was assuredly beyond reconciliation. When Gaunt died, Bolingbroke was the heir to wealth and resources that could easily challenge the crown. As Duke of Lancaster, Henry would own hundreds of manors and more than thirty castles, not to mention the vast Bohun inheritance he received through his dead wife. Countless ecclesiastic patrons owed him their loyalty, as well as innumerable retainers of all social ranks.

But this was a trifle compared to the County Palatine of Lancaster, which functioned as a kingdom within a kingdom. The County Palatine had its own Chancery and its own justices; it collected its own taxes and made its own rules. Once again Richard cursed his foolishness for granting inheritance rights for the County Palatine after he took possession of his crown. Back then, he was so grateful to Gaunt for propping up his throne he would have done almost anything to guarantee his loyalty. But now, only a few years later, he was paying the price. This was an impossible situation. No monarchy would tolerate it. He needed to find a way out of this mess.

"Let me describe the situation as I see it," Richard said to his council. "In six years, when Henry comes back from exile, I will be faced with an enemy more powerful than any of my uncles had been." Despite himself, he grimaced. "It would be a disaster for this country. Law and order will collapse. Completely. Lancaster and his affinity will operate without restraint. I cannot allow that to happen!"

No one in the room paid much attention to a threatened breakdown of law and order. That had already happened years ago, when anyone wearing a magnate's livery could kill and rob with impunity. But all were cognizant of the very real threat to Richard.

After a moment's silence, Holland spoke up. "It seems the only way to control Bolingbroke is to control his inheritance."

Richard held his breath. *Such a bold statement!* Of course, he had been thinking the same thing himself, but he had hesitated to bring it out into the open. Now it was done.

"I promised him he could sue for his inheritance through an attorney," the king said slowly.

"Promises can be broken."

"Hmm. I don't dare confiscate his lands. That would turn every baron against me."

John leaned forward, warming to the subject. "You don't have to go that far. You would merely take *seisin* of his lands, as is your right. The crown would hold his lands until he comes back and does homage to you...after his exile. Then he can sue for his domains through the judicial system."

"Which could take years," muttered Rutland.

"And in the meantime, the income would go to the exchequer," Richard mused, "which I need for Ireland."

"And by then," John said with satisfaction, "your agents would have lessened Henry's influence over his estates. You will have diminished his power."

Richard looked over at Edward. "What are you thinking?"

164

His cousin frowned. "Henry will not take this quietly. He has a lot of supporters who will see their patrimony under threat."

The king pursed his lips. "Yet he has no supporters overseas—none that will oppose me. The King of France will honor our treaty. The pope seeks my favor. Nonetheless—" he glanced at Russel, "I will send orders to every sheriff in the kingdom, proclaiming that no letters from foreign parts be opened until shown to myself or my council. That should deter him from causing trouble."

Rutland shrugged. "I doubt whether you can enforce that."

"As long as Henry receives his annuities, he should be content. He was never interested in politics. I think we have more important things to worry about."

Russel nodded, deep in thought. "There's more you can do," he speculated. "Honor all the existing Lancastrian pensions, and insist that the retainers serve the crown only. As long as their annuities continue uninterrupted, they won't care. Their loyalties will be transferred to you."

A smile spread over Richard's face. "And Lancaster will pay for it. Very good." The king looked around the table. His eyes stopped at Bushy. "What is it, Sir John?"

Looking sideways at Holland, Bushy cleared his throat. "It must be made legal. Otherwise it won't stand."

Scowling, the king pushed his chalice forward. A servant scurried up with a pitcher of wine. "Go on."

"The Parliamentary Committee?" Turning, Bushy directed this question at Bagot and Green.

Bagot busied himself searching through a pile of parchments. "The Committee has been dismissed."

"Then let's recall it," said Richard.

"Sire, it's not as simple as that," Bagot said. "The Parliament Roll explicitly states that the Committee was created to address left-over petitions and make a decision concerning Bolingbroke and Mowbray."

"Well, we are still dealing with Bolingbroke and Mowbray," Richard retorted.

165

Bushy raised his index finger. "We can manage this. I will have my clerk revise the Parliament Roll so that the Committee is established to terminate petitions—" he hesitated, thinking—"*and all other matters moved in the presence of the king in accordance with what seems best to them.* That should cover everything."

"Well done. Let us arrange for the Committee to meet at Westminster after Gaunt's funeral. We shall also summon a council to announce the Committee's decision, immediately afterwards. Richard stood, waiting for everyone to agree. "Thank you, my lords. You have been very helpful."

After the king left, the others were quick to follow—all except William Bagot who slouched over the table, rubbing his temples. Although by now he had dedicated himself to the king's service, he never forgot the years he served with John of Gaunt and Bolingbroke. Gaunt, always a strict taskmaster, nevertheless treated him fairly, even showing him favor on occasion when he needed legal protection. He saw how the wind was blowing; someone needed to warn Henry.

Pulling a blank paper toward him, he opened his inkwell and sharpened a quill. In these dangerous times, he had to be careful what he said; one never knew if a message would get waylaid. Pausing for a moment, staring at the door, he came to a sudden decision and started writing. "He is your sworn enemy and you should help yourself with manhood."

Calling for his favorite servant, Bagot folded the paper and sealed it with his ring. When the man hastened forward, Bagot pressed the note into his hand. "I entrust this to you. Take it to Henry Bolingbroke in Paris and tell him to prepare for the worst."

The Parliamentary Committee required a quorum of at least ten out of its eighteen members; Richard made sure to supply more than the minimum. In addition to his Counter-Appellants he summoned Edmund, Duke of York and Henry Percy, Earl of Northumberland, as well as three bishops. They debated all morning.

Much to Richard's surprise, the Duke of York took the lead in the opposition. Normally quiet to the point of lackadaisical, up until now Richard's uncle had been always present when needed, always reliable, always acquiescent. The only time Richard ever saw him assert himself was during the Merciless Parliament, when he stood up against his brother, the Duke of Gloucester, as Simon Burley's life hung in the balance. For that, Richard was ever grateful.

Leaning forward over the table, York pointed at his nephew. "I must object. This is not right." When Edmund was upset his thin white beard started shaking. Richard couldn't help but stare in fascination.

"What do you object to, uncle?" Richard said sweetly.

"It, it, it is wrong to deprive Henry of his inheritance. Wasn't Gaunt a pillar of support? Don't his wishes deserve to be respected? What has Bolingbroke done to deserve this treatment at your hands?"

"Why, uncle. He has been declared traitor by this very council. Even his father acquiesced."

"That may be, but mark my words. If you wrongfully seize Henry's rights, deny his heritage, you, you will bring down a multitude of curses upon your head."

At a loss for words, Richard turned to Holland for support.

"Duke Edmund," John said, "this is not for all time. King Richard seeks to take Lancaster under royal protection during the period Henry is in exile. Surely you can see that an outlaw cannot accept any benefit from an inheritance."

Grunting, the Duke of York sat back heavily.

"There you have it," Richard asserted after a brief hesitation. He had regained his composure. "Chancellor Stafford, you will announce our decision to my council so all may swear to uphold the acts of the Shrewsbury Parliament."

The council waited for Stafford's announcement. It was such a large assembly it could almost have qualified as a Great Council. All waited while the Parliamentary Commission entered the hall and took their places.

Stafford stood. "We have received a petition from Henry, Duke of Hereford that his attorneys be permitted to seek livery of his inheritance, as per the letters patent granted to him." The chancellor paused as the members murmured between themselves. "After careful deliberation, it has been determined that the letters were granted inadvertently and without due consideration. These letters are blatantly contrary to the judgments given at Coventry." Grumbling grew louder and Stafford was forced to raise his voice. "A man convicted of treason is not in a position to claim any benefit from such letters. Hence, the Parliamentary Committee has resolved to repeal them."

Most of the members were shocked into silence. What exactly did this mean? Thomas Percy, permitted to attend the council as an executor of Gaunt's will, stood uncertainly. "Surely this is out of order," he suggested. "Bolingbroke is clearly the heir to the Lancastrian estates."

"In this act," the chancellor continued, ignoring the interruption, "all petitioning to the contrary by Henry or his associates is forbidden, under penalty of treason. The king will hold all lands in trust belonging to Henry of Lancaster, Duke of Hereford, until he or his heir shall have sued the same out of the king's hands according to the law of the land. Also, the Committee has resolved that the letters of patent granted to Thomas de Mowbray, Duke of Norfolk shall be likewise revoked and annulled."

This last was almost a given; the resolution was accepted without comment. Percy sat down, intimidated by the penalties. The last thing he needed was to find himself imprisoned for a lost cause.

Richard glanced at him for a moment before moving on to the next order of business. "We must establish an unbreakable precedent for these new laws," he said. "All the acts of the last Parliament and all the judgments of Coventry as well as this session need to be upheld. I would have eighteen prelates, sixteen peers, and four commoners swear an oath on the cross of Canterbury, brought forth for this purpose. This oath is to be proclaimed in all the counties, cities, and boroughs."

Another oath. *Protection,* thought Percy. *The more oaths that are sworn, the less effect they will have. Why can't Richard see this?*

Later that evening, Richard dined informally with his new nobility, as he liked to call them. He raised his cup.

"I could not have done it without you," he said. "You are my great lords, my lieutenants, my deputies. I will place the Lancastrian estates in your charge until Henry or his heir can claim them back in a judicial court." The others raised their own cups, unsure how to react. Richard saw their hesitation. "Much can happen in six years," he said. "Henry could go on pilgrimage to the Holy Land; he could die—" Richard's eyes flashed as he considered the possibility. "Meanwhile, to you, Edward of Rutland, as Duke of Aumale I give you custody of Leicester, the honors of Pontefract and Bolingbroke. Thomas Holland, as Duke of Surrey I grant to you the honours of Lancaster, Tutbury and the lordship of Kenilworth. To you, John Holland, as Duke of Exeter I give the Lancastrian lordships in Wales. You, Thomas Despenser, I create the first Earl of Gloucester, with the Beauchamp lands in the Severn valley. And you, William LeScrope, as Earl of Wiltshire you will have custody of the lordship of Pickering."

"What of Bolingbroke?" said Thomas Percy, still resistant to the whole idea. "You know this cannot go unanswered. He will consider himself disinherited."

"He still has all of his Bohun inheritance, as well as Derby and Hereford which he holds in his own right. I am not a tyrant!" The king glared at Percy; Thomas had been steward of the royal household for four years and yet he still thought of himself as Lancastrian. "Listen to me. As long as he receives his annuity, his needs will be well taken care of. When he returns from exile, he may receive his Lancastrian inheritance—after he renews his homage to me. Meanwhile," he gestured to the group as a whole, "you are free to replace his officials with your own."

When the dinner was over, Edward Rutland quietly took his leave. "My father awaits me," he said to Richard. "I am to travel back with him to King's Langley." Deep in conversation

169

with Holland, Richard absently held out his hand and Edward kissed his signet ring, bowing and slipping from the room. Thomas Percy followed, making his obeisance, though the king ignored him.

"You know I don't want Bolingbroke back," Richard was saying in an undertone to Holland. "Maybe I can find a way to extend his exile for life." He shook his head as if to perish the thought. Even for him this was too much. At least for now.

Had Richard bothered to pay attention to the two men who left so quietly, he might have been even more disconcerted. Thomas had slipped an arm through Edward's, bending to whisper into his ear. Rutland listened closely, though his head shook ever so slightly in disagreement. From a distance, anyone would have thought they were old friends, discussing some private concern. But from close up, the expressions on their faces would have been enough to set tongues wagging.

"This is going to cause us a lot of trouble," Thomas said. "Lancaster's affinity will not be diverted so easily. Especially under these circumstances."

"I know. I know. There's no time." Edward gave Thomas a black look. "What are your intentions?"

Just in time, Thomas caught himself. He didn't know whether he could trust Rutland or not. "Nothing. Not now. I owe my service to the king."

"Yes. We both do. Forgive me, my lord. I must go." Pulling away, Edward increased his pace. The only one he wanted to confide in was his father. Edmund would know what to do.

Edmund Langley, Duke of York, sat astride his horse, watching patiently as his son gave last minute instructions to his squire. He shifted in the saddle, trying to ease the pain in his back. His fifty-eighth birthday was coming up in June, and he felt every bit the elderly statesman. And no wonder: advanced arthritis—*arthetica*—centering in his spine made it nearly impossible to get out of bed for up to a week. On his best days, it took great fortitude to ride and function like a normal person. Lack of exercise was taking its toll. It would be polite to call him portly, and he had recently commissioned a new suit of armor to accommodate his expanding girth.

This morning he was fading fast, but Edward was anxious to speak with him and he had a good idea what was bothering his son. Together they took the high road out of London, northwest to Edmund's manor. Trying to ignore his pain, the duke glanced toward his son who was still struggling with some inner conflict. His heart went out to Edward; although in his mid-twenties now, his son still seemed too young to carry all the responsibilities thrust upon him by the king. Earl of Rutland at seventeen, admiral of the northern fleet at eighteen, constable of Dover castle, Lord Warden of the Cinque Ports, constable of the Tower, Lord of the Isle of Wight—and these were only some of his greatest honors. After Gloucester's death he was made constable of England, and soon afterwards Duke of Aumale. Just last year he was appointed Warden of the West March toward Scotland. This last duty required him to secure the border before joining the king in Ireland. No wonder he looked so unsettled.

"What is it, son?"

Edward tried to put on an unconcerned face, but failed. "I'm troubled, father. This business about Bolingbroke..."

Edmund waited. He shared his son's distress.

"I don't feel right about it. If Richard could do that to him, the most powerful noble in the country, what about the rest of us?"

"Is this the only reason you are troubled?"

Edward grunted. "He's every bit as much my cousin as King Richard is. You were right. What Richard is doing is wrong. In so many ways."

"And yet you are benefitting from it. We may all benefit from it."

"That makes it so much worse!" Catching himself, Edward lowered his voice. "I know the king is thinking of you— and me—as his successors."

They rode for a minute in silence.

"I doubt it will come to that," York mused. "I, for one, do not want to be king."

"Nor I, I assure you."

Edmund raised an eyebrow. He had thought otherwise.

"No father. I see what kingship has done to Richard. Even his friends can't trust him. Look what he did to Mowbray."

Nodding, Edmund took a drink from his wine flask. "And we all agreed to it. We have to live with that now. The next question is what shall we do about it?"

"That's what's bothering me."

Edmund sighed. "He's making me regent in his absence, you know."

"Yes. I know."

"Anything could happen. I must do my duty." He looked forward, the worry etched on his face. "As long as I am able."

"Do you think Henry will come back to claim his inheritance?"

"I hope to God he doesn't!" It was Edmund's turn to catch himself. "There are many who sympathize with him. Very many."

"Including yourself, I think."

Edmund grimaced in pain, shifting again in his saddle. "My personal feelings don't enter into it. I must do my duty."

Edward knew when to end this discussion; he had his answer. He admired his father's judgment, though at times he wished Edmund would assert himself more strongly. What would he do in his father's place if he were regent? What would he do if York changed sides?

CHAPTER 15

There was still much preparation ahead before going to Ireland. Mortimer's killing emboldened the enemy, and this time Richard intended to finish the job he had started four years ago. Decades of mismanagement and corruption had alienated the few loyal Irish that remained, and the achievements of his first expedition already showed signs of unraveling. If the king didn't intervene in person, the English colony was in danger of disappearing altogether, overrun by local Irish chieftains encouraged by their success.

The king summoned his great magnates to Windsor; the only one missing was Rutland, now in Scotland. Most of the royal household officers were in attendance as well.

Richard was under no illusions; he expected to stay in Ireland for at least a year. He was bringing his regalia, jewels, relics, confessors, clerks of the signet office, purveyors, chamber knights and officials, and of course minstrels. "I am stockpiling arms at Holt Castle in Cheshire with £40,000 for use as my treasury," Richard told his council. "Last month Thomas Holland preceded us with 150 men-at-arms and 800 archers. I have deposited over £14,000 at Trim in Ireland for the troops' wages. We will require upwards of 200 ships, and at least 50 will remain in action to blockade the ports."

He pushed a stack of papers over to Holland. "John, we have surveyed all the available merchant ships from the Thames all the way around the coast to north Wales," the king said. "I am issuing warrants for the impressment of vessels, crews, horses, and equipment. Engage the ship masters under penalty of forfeiture, and offer them the standard wages from the time they leave port. Sailors are to be impressed into service as usual. John," he said, turning to Salisbury, "I intend to wage war from the ships as well as from land. The larger vessels will need to be altered. I suggest you build platforms with wooden crenellated towers at the bow and stern to protect the archers. We'll need stalls and ramps for the horses."

Holland made some notes for himself, then looked up. "How much time do we have?"

"I intend to depart from Milford Haven by the end of May." That gave them about two months. Holland looked over at Salisbury. There was no time to waste.

Planning went on while Richard took a break, walking in the courtyard with Hal. The king liked the boy's company, pleased with his grasp of all things military. "Listen and learn," he said, putting an arm around Hal's shoulders. "The way I see it, there are three types of Irishmen. We have the wild Irish, our enemies. They live in the mountains and bogs and the forests. They abide by their own rules and are outside the protection of the English. Then there are the rebellious Irish who are descended from the original conquerors and have intermarried with the natives. Their territory is called the English pale; they might be brought back under control. The rest are the obedient English, our settlers. They are the merchants, the soldiers, the townsmen. They live mostly in Leinster and the port cities. Those are the ones deserving our protection."

As they walked past an archway, the Earl of Salisbury emerged with a short, cheerful man whose clothing indicated that he was from France. Bowing, the man gesticulated broadly, pulling off his hat. A long feather trailed on the ground.

"Sire," said Salisbury, "I am pleased to introduce Jean Creton, valet de chambre to King Charles."

Creton bowed again. "Your Majesty," he said, "my lord king has sent me over to observe and better understand this great country of England. It is my hope to travel in your retinue to Ireland."

Richard smiled, exchanging glances with the earl. "You are welcome in my train, Jean Creton. When you write to your king, please send my salutations." He gestured a dismissal and continued his walk.

"Sire," Hal said as soon as the others were out of hearing, "I understand the Irish are a very hardy race and difficult to bring to battle. What do you plan?"

Richard squeezed his shoulder. "You heard right. They ride small and fast horses, unarmored. In fact, they don't even use saddles. No stirrups. They ride on cushions and control their horses with spurs strapped to their bare feet." Hal's mouth dropped open in surprise. "It's true," Richard assured him. "And they are so fast our cavalry could not get away from them. I saw with my own eyes an Irishman catch up with one of my squires. He leapt from his horse onto the back of my squire's mount and pulled him onto the ground from behind." He shook his head. "That was the end of the poor man. But one of my archers took care of the attacker."

He bent over, picking a daisy from the garden. "This was one of Queen Anne's favorites," he said, taking a sniff and shrugging his shoulders. "Can't smell anything. So let's see, our last campaign to Ireland was in 1395. You were...nine years old, weren't you? I'm sure you didn't pay attention!"

Henry nodded, grinning.

"Well, no matter. I learned a lot during that campaign. That's why our proportion of archers to cavalry is so high. The heavy cavalry couldn't chase the Irish in the forests. So instead, we used them to surround the rebels with a ring of iron—that's what we called it. We threw up many fortified garrisons around Leinster so that MacMurrough was trapped."

"Just like Edward I did in Wales," interrupted Hal excitedly.

"Exactly. We split our mounted archers into small raiding parties and they carried out most of the fighting. Our ships blocked their ports while we burned villages and crops and raided their cattle. Finally they were forced to surrender and present themselves to me personally. From there it became a matter of diplomacy."

"Then what happened?"

"MacMurrough paid homage to me and the lesser chieftains followed. If I had been able to stay longer, things would have worked out better. But there was trouble with the Lollards back here in England and I was forced to return prematurely.

Unfortunately, the Earl of March, who was Lord Lieutenant of Ireland, didn't follow my policy. He was too aggressive and he alienated many of my allied kings. As you see, he paid for his foolishness with his life. And now I have to start all over again."

"Are you planning the same kind of campaign?"

"I have fewer resources this time, and fewer troops. Still, it should be pretty much the same. But there is a chance MacMurrough has learned from his mistakes, in which case it might not be as easy this time."

Richard was soon to learn how prophetic his words would be.

On the 25th of April, though preparations continued, it was time for Richard to move his growing forces to the west coast of Wales. His 500 Cheshire Archers had assembled, and he wanted to remove them from the neighborhood of Windsor. That morning, as he walked hand-in-hand with Queen Isabella toward St. George's Chapel, he noticed she was unusually quiet. Taking a quick glance back at their courtiers, who were following at a respectful distance, he bent toward her.

"Can you spare a smile for me?" he asked.

She looked up, tears in her eyes. "You are leaving today, aren't you?"

Richard sighed. "Yes, my dear. I must go.

"Alas, my lord, will you leave me here?" She began to weep, not caring that they had witnesses.

His eyes tearing, he went down on one knee, taking her in his arms. "By no means, my sweet. But I will go first. And you, Madame, shall come there afterwards."

"Oh, please take me with you!"

"Ah, I cannot." He kissed her, then kissed her again. "There will be trouble on our arrival, and I cannot expose you to danger. Once I am settled in Dublin, then you can come and grace my royal court. Now dry your eyes." He pulled a handkerchief from his sleeve and dabbed her face. "Come, let us take mass and afterwards enjoy some wine and comfits."

He led her to the chapel and smiled at her as the canons brought up St. George's mantle and laid it across his shoulders. Soft chants rang through the church and the service droned on, while Isabella held onto the king's hand as long as she could. Although they had been married three years, Richard still treated her like his daughter. But she adored him, impatiently awaiting the time she would grow up and call herself his wife in truth. Time moved very slowly in his absence, and she dreaded his leave-taking.

After mass, they took refreshments in the Deanery while he spoke softly into her ear. But the time for dawdling was at an end. While the courtiers watched, Richard lifted the queen from the ground and held her in his arms a long time, kissing her again and again—at least forty times, someone said.

"Adieu, Madame, until we meet again." He put her down and kissed her three more times. Then he embraced all the ladies in the court and mounted his horse, blowing a kiss to his queen. Trumpets sounded and his knights kissed the hands of their mistresses before they followed. They rode through the bailey and out the barbican to the cheering of the crowd.

Hal rode behind the king as well as young Humphrey of Buckingham, eldest son of the late Duke of Gloucester. Hal was under no illusion; no matter what King Richard said, he knew he was a hostage along with Humphrey. Nonetheless, the king continued to treat him with favor—as opposed to Humphrey, who was ignored most of the time.

They took a leisurely route through England and Wales toward their destination of Milford Haven in Pembrokeshire. Milford had grown up around a natural harbor in the estuary, which boasted a fine port, large enough for a substantial fleet. As a result, there was a lively market from which the ships loaded their fill of bread, wine, cows, salt meat, and plenty of water. Nonetheless, they had to spend eleven days waiting for the wind to change. But no one minded. The atmosphere was festive and minstrels played day and night. While they waited, Richard's household servants loaded pavilions and other provisions onto the waiting ships.

When the weather changed they were all ready, and the king boarded his flagship with great pomp. It was an easy crossing and they landed at Waterford in less than two days. Used as a port since Viking times, Waterford easily accommodated the king's fleet. It was not particularly wealthy, though. Its inhabitants were mostly poor—even wretched if you can believe Jean Creton's account. The harbor had silted up; the ships couldn't come in close enough to unload onto a pier. So the locals were obliged to girt their tunics about their midsections and wade into waist-high water. One by one they accepted bundles onto their backs and unloaded the ships by hand, until all the supplies were piled high onto the wharf. The king's men were forced to lead their horses down ramps into the water, followed by the nobles themselves, grumbling about the inconvenience.

It took a few days to reorganize, but soon the English were on their way north toward Dublin, through enemy territory on the west side of the mountains. Richard wasn't concerned. Already Thomas Holland had achieved some successes even before they landed and the Irish were retreating. They traveled eighty miles to Kilkenny without incident.

But the king was uneasy about Rutland's continued absence. "Where is my cousin?" he muttered. "I expected him to meet us here." Edward was supposed to have wrapped things up on the Scottish west marches and brought his army across with him.

"Perhaps he was held back by storms?" ventured Salisbury.

"Perhaps. We must wait for him."

And wait they did. One week turned into two before Richard decided to move on. Packing as much food and wine as they could carry, his army traveled deeper into Leinster. The gentle hills gave way to dense forests, and the king put his whole army in battle array facing the deep woods—for his scouts told him MacMurrough was nearby, ready to attack.

Richard sat astride his horse in full caparison, gold leopards embroidered upon red fabric. The army waited, watching the sun move across the sky. They heard nothing except the shrieks of hawks flying in circles overhead. Already it was getting

178

uncomfortably hot and the knights raised their bascinet visors. Losing patience, Richard summoned his captains.

"MacMurrough has grown wary," he said to them. "I suspect he no longer desires to face us in battle. Then we must bring the battle to him!" He smiled grimly as his captains voiced their agreement. "Let us establish a base camp here and gather the local people to cut a road into this impenetrable forest. We shall fire the settlements and capture their cattle. Let us see how tough he is when his people are starving!" The response was lukewarm; they all knew their task would be fraught with irregular fighting, just like in Wales. But the king ignored their lack of enthusiasm. They had a job to do and there was no turning back.

"I have every confidence that we shall bring MacMurrough under our wing once again," Richard insisted. "Come. This day is not wasted. I intend to recognize those who have excelled through their valor and resolution. First of all, I summon thee, Henry of Monmouth."

Surprised, Hal nudged his horse forward, facing the king. Like the others, he was mounted and in full armor. As Richard unsheathed his sword, Hal's eyes grew wide.

"I have often heard from my ancestors," Richard said, "that one named Henry would be born among his kindred who shall be renowned all over the world for his praiseworthy and glorious deeds. I believe that Henry is yourself." Richard tapped his sword on both of Hal's shoulders. "I knight thee, fair cousin. Henceforth, be proud and valiant."

Leaning forward, Hal was glad Richard couldn't see his face. He was taken unawares and was overwhelmed by the king's favor. In so many ways, Richard gave him more approval than his own father ever had. He blinked back tears, torn by conflicting loyalties. As Richard summoned eight more squires and knighted them, Hal took his place among the other knights, glancing gratefully at them as they patted him on the shoulders.

Meanwhile, the servants and attendants were busy setting up pavilions and raising standards. If it weren't so dangerous, the setting might have seemed festive. The camp rung with the hammering of stakes and the chopping of trees. Cooks set up tents and started fires for meals. Squires roped off enclosures for the

179

horses. By nightfall, wine was distributed and men sat around fires, singing war ballads and telling stories.

In the course of the next two days, surly locals were put to work chopping down trees and clearing the way for the royal army to progress through the forest in battle array. The king and his heavily-armored knights rode first, though the bulk of the force was light cavalry armed with bows. Only the archers would keep the Irish at bay.

Hal rode farther back alongside his fellow hostage Humphrey who was quiet and obviously annoyed that he wasn't chosen for knighthood. Apparently Richard's hatred of Humphrey's father extended to the son. Hal tried some desultory conversation with his cousin, though he was soon discouraged by lack of response. He was about to nudge his mount forward when the most chilling, ear-splitting yowls burst from somewhere to the side. Startled, he turned in his saddle and peered into the forest. The trees were so densely packed together the sun couldn't pierce all the way to the ground. All he could see were boggy, thick patches of mud under moss-covered logs and sticky branches.

Suddenly the man next to him fell from his horse with a cry and the soldiers scrambled to nock their arrows, though they couldn't immediately spot an enemy. The shouting came from here and there, close then far away. A long, thin dart whistled past Hal's head and buried itself in the chest of another soldier. Hal's horse reared and he struggled to bring it under control. Swords were useless here and he didn't know what to do.

"Get down, man!" someone shouted. "Lower your head."

Hal threw his arms around his mount's neck and pushed forward, but already the attack faded away. Sobered, he slipped from his saddle and bent over the first man who was felled. The poor soldier lay staring at the sky, an arrow protruding from his neck. Blood was still spurting from the wound. Is this what they had to look forward to?

King Richard rode back to see what was happening. "Are you hurt, Hal?" he gasped.

Embarrassed to be singled out, the youth shook his head. "Others were not so fortunate. Their darts are strong enough to pierce armor."

"We must bring our archers up and post them everywhere. These devils will attack from any direction." The first lesson of the expedition had been fast and furious. It was not to be the last. Shouting, screaming bedlam erupted at all hours of the day and night. The English archers were proficient at taking down unwary attackers, but the army lost as many as they killed. Foragers and stragglers were easy prey. No one felt safe. When they did stumble across a settlement, they were quick to take revenge, setting fire to everything that would burn. The populace fled before them, taking whatever livestock they could drive away. However, the deeper they ventured into Leinster, the more they realized their supplies were not holding out. This cat-and-mouse game served no purpose. There were very few hamlets in the first place and they could not bring MacMurrough into the open. Richard decided to change course and take the route below the Wicklow Mountains; they would head east toward the coast. By now they only had a couple of days' rations left.

As they came to a clearing before the pass, a horn sounded and a bedraggled chieftain stepped from the trees, a drawn sword in his hand and a rope around his neck. He was followed by a dozen men, "naked and barefoot like criminals ready to be put to death," said Creton in his memoirs.

Richard narrowed his eyes. "I remember you. Aren't you Conall, MacMurrough's uncle?"

"Aye," the man said, falling to his knees. "We have come to beg for mercy."

"Mercy, Mercy," said the others, holding up their hands in supplication.

Richard leaned toward Salisbury. "This could be a sign," he murmured, staring at the wretches. "These are the first. There are bound to be more." He cocked his head, noting how their ribs poked through the flesh. "They are a sorry bunch," he added, more to himself. He thought for a moment, then came to a decision. "Friends, as to the evils and wrong you have committed against me, I pardon you on the condition that each of you will swear to be faithful to me for all time to come." He watched quietly as they all agreed to his terms, then gestured to one of his knights who would serve as a negotiator. "Conall, will you take my envoy to your nephew?"

Dropping his head in shame, Conall demurred. "I dare not face him," he said.

"Then show my knight the way. You don't have to speak with MacMurrough."

Reluctantly, the chieftain nodded. Richard turned to his envoy. "Go to that self-proclaimed King of Ireland," he said bitterly, "and tell him if he comes to me like his uncle, with a rope around his neck, I will admit him to my mercy and grant him castles and lands in abundance. Meanwhile, we will continue to Arklow on the coast. I ordered supply ships to dock there."

No one expected MacMurrough to accept the king's terms, and the army continued their trek, knowing that tomorrow, they would be eating their last meal. As expected, an arrogant refusal came back.

"He said that for all the treasures of the sea he would do no such thing. He would rather fight until all his strength is gone." A roll of thunder greeted the messenger's answer, and a frowning Richard looked up as the first raindrops hit his head. It soon turned into a downpour.

"Let's go on," he said, though in a thrice his horse's hooves sunk into the muck.

"We have no choice but to continue," Salisbury muttered. "We dare not venture into the forest."

The rain persisted for hours, and by the time it stopped the exhausted travelers dropped where they stood, pulling their cloaks around them for warmth. The air turned clammy even in this summer night, and there was not a stick dry enough to make a spark.

Four days passed thus, with no more food to be had and daily downpours to hasten them on their way. Even the horses were drooping, for there was little grain left and no grass. When they finally reached Arklow, three ships full of provisions were waiting for them.

"Sire, look!" Salisbury was the first to exclaim, while those around him seemed to wake up from a stupor. "Your supply ships! You were right!"

Kicking his horse, he dashed forward, only steps ahead of his followers. As they reached the shore, the men threw themselves out of their saddles and waded into the water, not even bothering to remove their armor. Seeing their approach, the sailors lowered baskets of bread. Starving soldiers grasped and devoured what they could before passing the remains to those behind them. Soon the water was full of splashing, shoving, shouting brawlers. Fortunately, there was enough bread and wine for everyone and, once satiated, the men spread out into the town, drinking and stuffing themselves, passing out in the streets and generally having a good time.

By the next morning, they were on their way. Richard was anxious to get to Dublin, directly north along the coast. Many of his soldiers were still recovering from the night before. At least they were fed, and from then on they could be supplied from the sea. The worst was over for the English army.

Alas for Richard, the worst was about to begin. Unbeknownst to him, Henry Bolingbroke was on his way to England, intending to claim back his inheritance. And there was nobody to stop him.

CHAPTER 16

Edmund of Langley, Duke of York, sighed while he flipped through a stack of parchments on the table. If he had thought his term as Richard's regent would be quiet and undemanding, he was soon persuaded otherwise. Richard required yet another series of forced loans from individuals throughout the country; he still hadn't collected all the pledges from before. Edmund knew that only about half of these loans would be honored—as usual—but if he didn't send out deputies then none would be collected.

As of necessity he was housed at Westminster, much though he disliked the place. Nonetheless, London served as a gathering spot for all the royal yeomen the king had summoned to await the regent's orders. Even though Richard had taken with him the vast majority of experienced captains and the best trained soldiers in the country, at least he gave some thought to security for those left behind. Edmund shrugged. Not that it mattered much. Richard also took his privy wardrobe consisting of replacement bows, arrows, arms and armor, as well as hundreds of horses and the wagons needed to convey them all to Milford Haven. It was to be hoped Edmund and his council wouldn't need a strong military force because there was very little left to draw upon.

He looked up in surprise when William LeScrope, the Lord High Treasurer, strode into the chamber. "I thought you'd be in France by now," he started, but paused at the expression on LeScrope's face.

"My Lord, he's here."

"Bolingbroke?"

"Yes. When I reached Dover, the shipping had been seized by Lancaster. I came right back to report."

184

Edmund covered his eyes with his hand. "I was afraid something like this would happen." He shook his head. "I assume the constable of Dover Castle was nowhere to be found?"

"Not before I left."

"Do you think we can trust him?"

LeScrope hesitated. "John Beaufort? Henry's half-brother? It appears we have no choice. But I do have some tidings. On my way here I was told that the Lancastrians have occupied Pevensey Castle."

Turning, Edmund gestured to a yeoman guard. "Summon the council. We must see to our defense."

The rest of the day, orders went out to secure the South. The sheriff of Kent was ordered to raise shire levies to guard Rochester castle. The sheriff of Surrey was commanded to raise troops to keep the Lancastrian garrison shut up inside Pevensey Castle. John Beaufort was instructed to review the fortifications of the Cinque Ports under his control. The Archbishop of Canterbury was ordered to raise men for the defense of his city. Edmund wrote a letter to his son Rutland, who he thought was still in the North securing the border of Scotland.

Then he wrote to the king in Ireland. "I do not know where Bolingbroke intends to land," he said. "We have not been able to locate him, though he has commandeered shipping from Dover. I suspect he will look for support in Yorkshire. We do not know how much aid he has found in France."

This was just the beginning. Over the next week, Edmund received reports that many of the Lancastrian strongholds were already holding out for Bolingbroke—even before his landing. From York to Wales, every day he learned about estates rising for Lancaster. Some threw out their new steward, hastily appointed before their royalist lord sailed to Ireland. Warwick castle was seized by former Beauchamp retainers for Henry. Former Arundel estates prepared to defend themselves against King Richard's return. The more orders Edmund sent out, the more news he heard about Lancastrian risings.

Finally, on the 6th of July, the council meeting was interrupted by a messenger, who had not even taken the time to freshen himself. Handing a scroll to Edmund, he stood breathing heavily as the duke gave it a cursory look.

"Tell us what has happened," Edmund said.

"Henry Bolingbroke landed at Bridlington the 29th of June." As they knew, Bridlington was due east of York—near Lancaster's territory. "The under-sheriff of Yorkshire sent me with this message."

"How many men did he land with?"

"I'm not sure. At least two ships' worth. There's one more thing," he added. "Bolingbroke also met Hotspur there."

"Hotspur!" Edmund straightened abruptly. "What was he doing in Bridlington?"

"He was collecting payment from the exchequer for his services as Warden of the East March," said LeScrope. "I issued the funds myself."

Groaning in pain, Edmund sat back, rubbing his neck. "Now I have to worry about the Percies, on top of everything else. I know they have grievances against the king." Hotspur and his father, Henry Percy, ruled Northumberland like a separate kingdom. *If they joined Bolingbroke...*

Shaking his head, Edmund dismissed the messenger before turning to the council. "Any suggestions?" His question was mainly directed at Bushy, Bagot, Green, and Russel—Richard's most loyal henchmen. Of all the council members, they had the best knowledge of the king's intentions.

"We should send messengers to York ordering them to hold against Bolingbroke," Bagot volunteered.

"Noted. We will need to send them money to shore up their defenses."

"And Nottingham," Bagot added, "and Holt. Especially Holt, where the king has stockpiled arms and treasure."

"Let us request assistance from the earls of Westmorland and Northumberland," Green suggested.

Edmund nodded. "We need to determine whose side they are on at the soonest. That should flush them out."

Bushy raised a finger for attention. "We need to order all the ships on the western coast pressed into service at once, to aid the return of King Richard. We'll send them to Waterford."

186

"Noted. I will write to the king this day and tell him we are advising Sir Peter Courtenay to prepare Bristol for his arrival. He will need provisioning for the troops. After we gather our forces, it is my intention to meet the king there."

"Let me take your message to Chester," Bagot declared, "then on to the king in Ireland. Meanwhile, Chester can begin raising loyalist support."

York nodded his agreement.

"How will we protect London?" asked Bushy.

After a moment's thought, Edmund turned to LeScrope. "I think it will be necessary to move the chancery to the fortress of Wallingford, where the queen now resides. The government can operate safely there and communicate down the Thames to the exchequer in London."

So far, everyone was in agreement. For a moment, silence filled the room. Bushy cleared his throat. "What are we to do about Bolingbroke?"

Edmund let out a deep sigh. "I'm still concerned about a possible attack from France. We can't leave the south coast defenseless. For now, we need to see what Bolingbroke's intentions are. If he has returned to reclaim his inheritance, I have no desire to hinder him. The son of Lancaster has every right to his patrimony." His back stiff, he moved his whole torso, looking around the table with unusual firmness.

"We can't just let him invade!" Ever the king's man, Bushy was appalled.

"No, we cannot. We must do our duty. But I will not act rashly." Bushy was about to object and Edmund held up a hand to stop him. "I know my nephew well. He is a wise man and not prone to foolish gestures. We shall raise a loyal force and confront him. For now, we will move north to St. Albans, which will bring us closer to Henry and our troops coming from East Anglia."

Two days later, the council left Westminster and gathered strength at St. Albans before taking a circuitous route to Oxford—dragging along the chancellor, treasurer, and enough clerks to compose proper writs and documents. After Edmund reached Oxford, the officers continued on to Wallingford. And safety.

It was just as well, because already the regent's army of 3000 was disintegrating. At best, many of his soldiers were ambivalent; at worst, some of them didn't want to fight Bolingbroke at all. Edmund wasn't surprised when a new messenger arrived from York, his face betraying bad news.

"What is it this time?" the duke asked wearily.

The messenger removed his hat. "My Lord, I have come to tell you that the Earl of Northumberland and his son, Henry Percy have joined forces with Henry Bolingbroke. The Earl of Westmorland is with them."

The duke sighed heavily, closing his eyes. Bushy and Greene leapt to their feet in dismay. "How long ago?" cried Bushy as he leaned on the table.

"They declared their intentions five days ago."

"God's blood. They could be halfway here by now!"

Edmund dropped his fists to the table. "Don't be foolish. He can't move that fast."

"What are we to do?"

"For one thing, find your courage!" Langley's beard shook in his annoyance. "This is no time to take fright."

"All is lost," grumbled LeScrope.

"You lose the battle before it has even been fought. Are you so terrified of Bolingbroke?"

"If he brings the North with him, yes!" LeScrope answered.

York glowered at them. "Then you are no use to me here. Perhaps you should go to Bristol and prepare for the king's arrival."

"Yes," Bushy agreed, much too quickly. "We shall leave this very night. Right?" He turned to Greene, who nodded.

"I will come, too," LeScrope said. "It will be easier for me to administer the treasury from there."

They were as good as their word. Edmund watched from the tower of Oxford's dilapidated castle as the core of Richard's closest advisors galloped westward with a small group of retainers. The setting sun turned the sky a deep pink as the silhouettes of his fellow council-members faded from sight. Edmund rubbed his eyes, knowing that his vision was failing

188

along with the rest of his body. Oh, how he wished he could go with them! He felt it in his bones: this was the beginning of the end. More than ever, the regency weighed heavily on his shoulders. This task was for a younger, more ardent supporter of the king—not someone who sympathized more with the wrongdoer than the one who was wronged against. No matter which way he turned, the consequences would be dire. And he had to bear the burden all alone.

CHAPTER 17

The two earls faced each other across the table, a platter of untasted breads and cheese between them. The older of the two took a sip of ale and slowly put down his mug, his face reflecting uneasiness. Henry Percy, first Earl of Northumberland, was a proud man. His ancestry went back to the Norman Conquest and his family considered themselves uncrowned rulers of the North, even though sometimes they conflicted with the king in the South. Grey of hair and beard, at age 57 he still felt hale and hardy, ready to take on any enemy that challenged his authority. Left eye squinting, he regarded his cousin Ralph Neville, Earl of Westmorland with misgiving. After all, their two families had been rivals for years; on occasion the Nevilles were given lands and offices taken from the Percies, just to satisfy a whim of the king. Just two years ago Ralph received his earldom, putting him on a par with Percy. Having been rewarded for his support of the nefarious Revenge Parliament, surely Westmorland was the king's man. On the other hand, his second marriage to Joan Beaufort made him brother-in-law to Bolingbroke. Percy wasn't sure which claim on his loyalty was stronger. Nonetheless, at the moment, Percy and Westmorland needed each other if the North was to remain strong in the face of the upcoming chaos.

"All right," Ralph said wearily, reaching for the pitcher and refilling his own cup, "what is this all about?" He looked around the great hall, noting all the Percy banners hanging on the walls. "You are mighty far south from your usual haunts." The castle of Wressle was just north of the River Ouse, not far from York.

"Aye. I could say the same for you."

Westmorland shrugged. "One can never be too sure these days." He hesitated. "What have you heard about Bolingbroke?"

"We understand he landed at Ravenspur on the Humber then continued north to Bridlington, sometime the end of June. My son Harry was at his manor of Seamer, just a few miles from there. He sent me a message to come south, while he went to see what Bolingbroke was up to. I'm expecting him today."

The other nodded. "Bolingbroke is taking a big risk."

"Is he?" Percy scratched his neck. "I'm not so sure. I've heard that many of Lancaster's strongholds have been girding themselves for a siege. Or for action, more like."

"Like Pontefract?"

"Especially Pontefract. Between Gaunt's retainers and dependents, Bolingbroke has so many supporters he need only snap his fingers and they will come running."

"And now that the king has gone—"

"That was no accident! Bolingbroke has many friends who have kept him informed of Richard's movements. Ah, there is Harry now!"

The door flew open and Harry Hotspur blew in, accompanied by a rowdy group of followers, laughing and shouting and calling for ale as they gathered around the table. In high spirits, Hotspur sat next to his father, his brown eyes crinkling. Tall, bearded, brown-haired, handsome, and intense, Percy's son was one of those men who could never sit still and who always drew a crowd. And his men would follow him to the ends of the earth.

"What ho?" said Percy, thumping him on the back.

"Great tidings, father."

"Aha! You saw Bolingbroke, then."

Hotspur reached for the platter, pulling it forward. "Not only did I see him, I agreed to support him."

"So—" Percy grimaced. He could never convince his son to bide his time. God forbid he should wait until conferring with wiser heads.

"He swore an oath to me," Hotspur said simply. "He has come to claim his own."

"Nothing more?"

"Nothing."

Percy grunted. "You know better. He's risking his neck for that? No matter what promise he extracts from the king, first chance Richard gets, he'll do to him what he did to Gloucester. And anyone who supports him, including us." He shifted in his seat, facing his son. "Who else came with him?"

"Two ships' worth of knights—about sixty or so. Oh, and Archbishop Arundel was with him, as well as young Thomas, earl of Arundel, who escaped from Holland's custody."

"Is that so? Well then, I'm not surprised the lad went over to his uncle. But I *am* surprised to see the archbishop and Bolingbroke working together. Remember, it was Gaunt that condemned Arundel's brother to death. He and Bolingbroke are unlikely allies."

"On the other hand, that helps explain why Henry dared to return," Westmorland muttered. "Arundel would make a bargain with the devil if it meant getting his power back. He's the brains behind this plot—you can be certain of that."

"Well, that settles it." Percy slapped his knee. "The archbishop wouldn't risk coming back unless something greater was promised. It would take a king to give him back his archbishopric."

"But—" Hotspur tried to interrupt.

"Think on it, son! You're talking treason here. Return from outlawry? For the sake of Lancaster?" He grunted again. "But of course Arundel could overlook everything if Henry restores him to Canterbury."

Hotspur wasn't entirely convinced. "Bolingbroke said he had no designs on the crown."

"He has to say that, son. It's too soon to declare a rebellion."

Westmorland leaned forward. "Make no mistake, Harry. If Bolingbroke forces Richard to restore the Duchy of Lancaster and nothing more, his life will be forfeit. Eventually the king will want his revenge. He *must* go all the way. He has no choice. No matter what he says."

Percy nodded in agreement. "He's right. And what's more, if we join Bolingbroke, we will be guilty of treason, too." Absently, he pulled the bread tray toward him, taking a piece. "On the other hand, here is an opportunity that will never come again. If we support Bolingbroke, he will be beholden to us in a way Richard never was." He paused, thinking. "That bastard! He has insulted us one time too many. Do you know, Ralph, that Rutland recently petitioned the king to appoint me Warden of the Middle March? It was more than he could manage and he knew it. And the king turned me down! For no good reason!"

Westmorland shook his head. "I'm not surprised. He's afraid of our power in the North."

"As well he should be. No one else can command the loyalty needed to control the border. Gaunt knew it and he was worth a dozen Rutlands. Well, son," he said to Hotspur, "perhaps you did the right thing. We will support Henry Bolingbroke, once he is willing to pay our price. We can bring 30,000 men to his cause, but it won't come cheaply."

Hotspur looked uncertain. "But the heir to the throne—"

"Is Mortimer," Percy assured him. "I know you feel protective of the boy. He's the nephew of Harry's wife," he said aside to Westmorland before placing a reassuring hand on Harry's arm. "Yes, well son, we're putting the cart before the horse. Let us see what Bolingbroke intends to do. He's always followed his father's lead; perhaps we can take old Gaunt's place and play the patriarch."

As Henry Bolingbroke made his cautious way through Yorkshire, connecting with his allies and gathering eager supporters, the Percies and Westmorland set about recruiting forces of their own. Once Bolingbroke reached Pontefract, Lancaster's great stronghold, it was clear to everyone his venture was a success. Men came from all over the North: Lancashire, Staffordshire, Derbyshire, and Lincolnshire as well as Yorkshire. And this was just the beginning. A date was set for July 15 for all the other magnates supporting Bolingbroke to gather at Doncaster, just south of Pontefract. It was there that Henry was expected to declare his intentions.

The two Percies and Westmorland rode before their huge army, gaily dressed in heraldic colors, pennons flying.

Northumberland had not been disappointed. Men flocked to his banner as soon as he put out a summons. He could be proud that no matter what the king thought about limiting his influence, he could count on the loyalty of his countrymen. As their captains arranged for the men to camp in the fields surrounding the city, the lords rode down High Street toward the Carmelite friary where Bolingbroke was staying. When they entered the great hall at Whitefriars, Percy saw Henry patiently listening to a trio of barons all speaking at the same time. He knew them all intimately: William, Lord Willoughby, Ralph, Lord Greystoke, and William, Lord Roos. All were important men and their presence demonstrated Lancaster's influence.

Bolingbroke had grown a beard since the last time Percy saw him; his dark hair was longer and brushed back—but his eyes! There was a new determination there, a confidence and boldness he had never shown while under his father's shadow. Here was a man to be reckoned with, and for a brief moment Percy was taken aback before his natural belligerence asserted itself.

At that moment Henry saw them and raised his arm. "Well come, Earl Percy! I've been waiting for you."

Exchanging glances with Westmorland, Percy moved forward, gesturing for Hotspur to follow. "My Lord," he bellowed. "We have brought a vast host to represent the North in your worthy cause."

"Henry, Harry, Ralph," Bolingbroke said, clasping each of their hands in turn. "There is much for us to discuss. Please, dine with me." He returned to those he had just been speaking with. "The friars have prepared a repast for you, my lords," he added, gesturing to a small group of monks waiting by the door to the refectory. "Please, take advantage of their generosity. By honoring you they honor my father." All knew that Gaunt was one of the founders of this friary; his son naturally commanded the allegiance of the brethren. As Archbishop Arundel, dressed in his episcopal robes, encouraged the lords and knights to follow him into the hall, Bolingbroke ushered the Percies and Westmorland into a private chamber.

The choicest dishes had been reserved for Henry and his guests, and they fell to with enthusiasm. After their initial hunger was sated, the earls wasted no time attempting to maneuver Bolingbroke into revealing his plans. He picked at his food, eyes darting around the room while he put them off with simple answers. Finally, Percy put down his knife.

"Come now, Henry. This is not the time for prevarication. If we are to risk our lives supporting you, we must know what your intentions are."

Pursing his lips, Henry finally faced Percy. "All right. I appreciate you are my major support. You know this. What I am to say is between the four of us." He glanced at Harry and Ralph then back to Percy. "What I am going to tell the world is that I have come to reclaim my duchy as rightful heir. I have no designs on the crown. Between *us*, if I get the support I need, I intend to put the king under our control and reform his household. This is no more than we did ten years ago."

Percy took a slice of apple tart, putting it on his trencher. "This is all you intend to do. To make the king a figurehead, answerable to a council."

"And why not? He has demonstrated poor judgment in running the country."

"I'll grant you that. But what happens in ten years, when he regains power?"

Henry looked fixedly at him. "We'll have to ensure he never regains power, won't we?"

Hotspur was already fidgeting. "You have no intention of usurping him, then?"

"None."

Harry frowned. "Will you swear an oath to that?"

Considering for a moment, Bolingbroke nodded. "You are right, Harry. I need to come out into the open. I will swear an oath publicly—right here—before everyone who has gathered at Doncaster. Will that satisfy you?"

The other nodded. "Yes. Very well."

Percy cleared his throat. "Where will you go from here?"

"South. Toward Bristol. Unless I learn otherwise, I assume Richard will return the way he came. Through Wales. Much depends on when and where we encounter my uncle York."

"As regent, he is bound to summon a large army." Percy glanced at Westmorland. "Ours needs to be larger."

"And so, much of my itinerary will be through my Lancastrian estates," Henry said in agreement. "My retainers have every reason to ensure I don't lose control of my patrimony—" he glanced back and forth at his companions—"as I already have, at least on paper. If I am correct, the reality is much different." He stood, pushing back his chair. "And now, my friends, I have much to do before tomorrow."

Finding themselves dismissed, the Percies and Westmorland made their way back to their troops. Hotspur was still not satisfied with the way their meeting went.

"I don't trust that man," he muttered.

"Trust?" Percy said sarcastically. "Trust does not enter into it. Bolingbroke is never going to tell us what he truly plans to do. It's up to us to make sure he acts in our best interests."

"Ours and his had better be the same, then. Is that what you're saying? If this fails, our heads will roll." Hotspur shook himself, trying to purge the thought.

"We'll earn a traitor's death. Make no mistake." Percy grimaced. "But listen, son. We will not fail. Richard has taken all his supporters to Ireland with him. York will..." He gestured a dismissal. "He has no army. He has no stamina for this. Nor, from what I heard, does he have the heart to fight his own nephew. From the beginning he objected to Henry's disinheritance."

Reaching his camp, Westmorland broke off, waving goodbye. Waiting until he was out of earshot, Percy stepped closer to his son. "This is our best chance to regain everything we have lost these last twenty years." He glanced at Westmorland who was giving instructions to his guard. "And keep Neville in his place. We'll never get anywhere with Richard. But once we put Bolingbroke in our debt will we will rule in the North as we once did."

Considering, Harry nodded. "I see. Yes, it's worth the risk."

"Good. Tomorrow Bolingbroke will commit himself and we'll be there to do whatever he needs. He's never commanded an army in the field, remember. Who else will lead tens of thousands of men? We will." He put a hand on Hotspur's shoulder. "You know he'll have no time to worry about Scotland, either. Now that Rutland is leaving to join the king in Ireland, I will make sure Henry appoints me Warden of the West March in his place. You'll see."

The following day, the Percies joined Bolingbroke and a large host of newcomers gathered at the Carmelite friary to witness Henry's declaration. Flanked by Arundel, Archbishop of Canterbury, and Thomas Arundel, the exiled heir, Bolingbroke stood calm and determined, relieved that the insecurity was over. Lancaster had stood firm for Lancaster. There was no more question of turning back.

As the talking diminished in the hall, Henry held up a jeweled box. "Here are the relics of Bridlington, lent to us by the good friars so that I may swear a holy oath before all of you. My intentions are clear. I seek only the inheritance of my father, John of Gaunt, Duke of Lancaster. But that is not enough!" His voice boomed through the room. "I am your champion of justice and liberties! I am here to ensure good government." Henry paused, encouraged by the applause. "All Cheshiremen will be removed from King Richard's household." The cheering increased; the Cheshire guard had gotten away with terrorizing the public too long. "And in the future, taxes will only be imposed with the assent of parliament, and then only if judged necessary."

As the noise continued, Henry nodded benevolently. He was riding high on the approval of his peers. Holding up his hands, Bolingbroke was about to say more when a sharp voice cut through the din.

"Will you take the crown?"

Henry frowned, recognizing the voice of Harry Hotspur. "That is not my intention. I intend to bring the king under control with good and strong leadership. I swear to this on the relics of Bridlington!" He turned to the archbishop who took the box and held it firmly while Bolingbroke placed a gloved hand on the lid. "I swear before God I seek only to reclaim my inheritance. I do not seek the crown. But I will ensure that you are governed well, as is your right. And if anyone more worthy of the crown could be found, I will willingly withdraw."

There was jostling among the crowd and Henry saw that Hotspur was forcing his way outside. Well, let him go. He would deal with Harry later.

CHAPTER 18

No sooner had Richard and his exhausted army reached Dublin than Edward of Rutland landed with his men-at-arms and archers. Despite his annoyance, Richard was glad to see his cousin and embraced him in front of everyone.

"What happened to you? What took you so long to get here?"

Rutland held out a hand for a water-skin. "I negotiated a treaty with the Scots so they would refrain from raiding the West Marches. Then we were held back by the weather."

Richard accepted his explanation. "Come. We have much to discuss."

And discuss they did. For the next few days, the king sat with his best and wisest advisors and tried to piece together a new strategy. Meanwhile, Richard sent out parties to track down the errant Irish chieftains who had learned so much since the last expedition. So far, his Irish venture had been a debacle.

"I wasn't expecting immediate success anyway," Richard assured Rutland. "That's why I brought my household officers with me—"

His throat tightened around his last words as William Bagot was ushered into the council chamber. Something had gone wrong. Bagot wasn't supposed to be here.

As the knight knelt before him, Richard put a hand on his head. "What news?"

The room was silent as two dozen pairs of eyes locked onto the self-appointed messenger. Still on his knee, William looked at the king. "The Duke of York sent a messenger to you the week before I left. Did you not receive him?"

Puzzled, the king shook his head.

"Oh, sire, I am disconsolate to deliver such unwelcome tidings. Henry Bolingbroke has landed on your shore with a band of traitors."

Richard turned pale with anger. For a moment he was speechless. "Good Lord, this man plans to deprive me of my country!" he finally gasped.

The others stared at him in amazement. How could this possibly be a surprise?

"I have letters from the Duke of York," Bagot said, pulling a small packet from his wallet.

Richard reached for them with a shaky hand. "Where did he land?"

"He touched down near Pevensey, then continued north along the coast. The Duke of York was raising troops to contain him as I left..." His voice trailed off.

"How long have you been traveling?"

"Seven days."

Richard clenched his fists, closing his eyes. "Your tidings are already seven days old. So much can happen in a week." He turned toward Rutland. "Surely he would go to his own lands—to Lancaster." He looked at the men attending his council. Most of the people he put in charge of the Lancastrian estates were sitting in this very room. *And it was his own fault!* "Who is guarding the henhouse?" He tried to smile, but his mouth trembled.

No one knew what to say. They hadn't had the time to establish their authority—or even visit their new acquisitions.

"We must return at once," the king insisted, standing up.

The room burst into immediate arguments. No one was in agreement. Richard turned from one to the other of them.

"The Duke of York plans to move his forces to Bristol," Bagot said. "He expects to meet you there. He has already sent orders for ships to gather at Waterford for your return."

"That will take too much time," Richard protested.

"Sire," Thomas Holland interjected, "our troops are scattered right now. We need that time to bring them back together."

"How many ships do you have at Dublin?" asked Rutland.

"No use," grumbled Thomas. "The port is too small. Waterford is the only harbor large enough to accommodate the fleet we will need for the army."

John Holland leaned forward. "Our fleet is busy harassing the coast. How are we going to find them all? You don't want to return with an insufficient force."

Salisbury stood. "It is important the king resists the rebellion in person!"

"Lancaster—a threat?" Rutland practically spat the word. "He may be good at tournament fighting, but what kind of soldier is he? He has never commanded an army. He has no political influence."

Taking a deep breath, Richard tried to calm himself. "You are right, Edward."

"Don't underestimate the man," Salisbury urged. "His father's affinity will follow him."

"I have retained many of them," Richard objected. "It has cost me a tremendous amount of money."

"They may not be steadfast."

"Don't forget," insisted John, "that if you leave hastily, all our work here will be for naught."

Sitting heavily, Richard put his head in his hand. "I can't believe this is happening."

Again, no one dared remonstrate with him. Ever since Gaunt's death, the king had been so intent on his own stratagems, he couldn't conceive that Bolingbroke would take matters into his own hands. And not one of them had tried to slow him down; it was not in their interest, after all. They had benefitted from Richard's liberality.

"Sire," Salisbury ventured, "surely your Cheshire subjects will stay loyal."

Richard looked up at him, a glimmer of hope on his face. "Of that, I have no doubt."

"Well then," Rutland exclaimed, "let the Earl of Salisbury precede you. He can go to Cheshire and raise an army while you gather your forces at Waterford. Then you can return to

Milford Haven. Since York plans to meet you at Bristol, it only makes sense to join forces with him in the south. From there, once you learn the whereabouts of Bolingbroke you will know how to proceed."

"Why not have the king sail to Chester?" the Earl of Salisbury pursued.

Rutland turned on him. "You must know the harbor has silted up. There is no way Chester can accommodate the fleet. Conwy is the only port where you can disembark. But then what would York do if the king landed in the north?"

"He is right," Richard said, coming to a decision, "I can join my uncle and march north from Bristol, and you can march south from Chester. We should be able to catch Bolingbroke between the two of us."

"Meanwhile," Rutland said, "let us not act in haste. John is right. We must make sure we leave ample funds and soldiers behind to continue what we started here. It will take a few days to summon our scattered forces, and perhaps better tidings will come forth."

Satisfied for the moment, the king beckoned Maudeleyn forward. "Richard, bring a quill and parchment. We have no time to waste."

Richard's council did all it could to rein in the confusion over the next few days. The king could barely control his panic while his advisors bickered among themselves. But Rutland's suggestions emerged as the most rational plan, considering how little they knew about events in England. The Duke of York sent as many messages as he could, but by the time Richard was ready to leave for Waterford, there was still no definitive answer as to where Bolingbroke was headed. But at least York confirmed he would wait for Richard at Bristol.

There was no more time for delay. Richard gave a commission to the Earl of Salisbury, appointing him governor of the principality of Chester and North Wales. Thomas Holland, Duke of Surrey was put in charge of the government in Ireland. But there was one more thing Richard had to do before he left. He summoned Hal, Bolingbroke's son, for a private conversation— just the two of them.

Hal had not been involved in the recent discussions. In fact, he had heard nothing but gossip, which was bad enough. When he entered the king's private chamber, he was shocked at the change which had come over Richard. The king seemed to have aged ten years since the last time he saw him. In response to Richard's gesture, Hal sat on the edge of his seat, leaning forward.

"How much do you know?" Richard asked.

Hal looked at the floor. "I heard my father has returned to claim his inheritance."

The king grunted. "I doubt he will stop at that. From what we heard, he has already killed some of my liegemen." He leaned back, studying the youth. "You know, Hal, it is you I fear for. Because of your father's unfortunate behavior, you are the one who is likely to be deprived of his patrimony."

Undaunted, Hal looked Richard in the eye. "My gracious king and lord, I too am much grieved by what I hear. But surely, it must be apparent to you—as it is to me—that I am innocent of my father's deeds."

"Indeed," nodded Richard. "I am well aware that no guilt attaches to you for what your father has done, and I regard you as blameless on that account. Nonetheless, for your own safety, I am resolved to send you and Humphrey to Trim castle until all this is over."

Hal knew better than to argue. Richard stood and walked him to the door, putting an arm around his shoulders. "There are times I think of you as the son I never had," the king said softly. "I know well there is one Henry shall do me much harm," he added, almost to himself, "and I know it is not thou." Kissing Hal on the cheek, Richard opened the door and gave him a nudge. *Some hostage.* He could never harm the boy.

There were too few ships at Dublin. The three royal vessels that had delivered supplies were standing by; two more had arrived the previous day. The rest were presumably on their way to Waterford. No one knew for sure.

"What has been loaded on board?" Richard asked the shipmaster.

"Your treasury and jewels, sire, except what was delivered to Trim castle. Five tons of wine. We have packed cases of plate, some clothing, household furnishings—"

"Forget about unnecessary supplies," Richard interrupted. "Make room for as many horses as you can—" He looked around, considering. "But not our warhorses, at least not this trip. What else is ready, waiting for transport?"

The shipmaster looked at his list. "Sire, we still have 141 hauberks of mail, 500 bows, 3000 sheaves of arrows, 200 pounds of gunpowder, tents and royal pavilions—"

"So much." The king closed his eyes for a moment. "All right. These ships must sail for Milford Haven as soon as possible, then return for more supplies to be loaded." Walking away, he pulled Rutland by the arm. "We leave for Waterford in the morning. All of my council comes with me. Edward—" he stopped short. "Am I doing the right thing?"

The other straightened his shoulders, knowing the king had acted on his advice. "Sire, you are doing what you must."

A week later, after two days of sailing Richard reached Milford Haven. Most of the fleet disembarked there, while Richard's ship continued through the estuary and made for Haverfordwest, six miles north. The castle there was strong and well-built, in the care of Thomas Percy for the last six years so it was in good repair. Richard knew this was a strong base from which to operate; he had many loyal chieftains in that portion of the country.

There was no time to lose. "Edward," he said to Rutland, "the best place to start raising troops is Carmarthenshire. I will stay here a couple of days and gather as much information as I can. More of our fleet should arrive with our men from Ireland. Then I will move east, stopping at Whitland Abbey to collect funds, then on to Carmarthen Castle. I'm told that's a total of 30 miles." The king mopped his head, though the sweat was from anxiety rather than heat. "Thomas Despenser," he went on, "go and muster your tenantry in Glamorganshire. We will recruit locally while you are away, then march east alongside the Bristol

Channel to join you. Then together we can cross the Severn to Bristol."

The situation was far from satisfactory. Until they learned more about Bolingbroke's movements, they could do little more than send out messengers and wait. Richard was all for attacking Henry at the first opportunity, but even he knew a wrong move could be fatal. Little did he know that events were soon to overtake him at a pace he could never have imagined.

CHAPTER 19

The market town of Berkeley lay halfway between Gloucester and Bristol on a hill overlooking the Little Avon River. Its castle, built on top of a Norman motte, was notorious for being the site where King Edward II was murdered, though that had nothing to do with the Duke of York's stopping here. Lord Berkeley, encouraging reconciliation, had generously offered his estate as a meeting place.

As York walked through the encampment, his subdued discussion with John Beaufort was noted by all the disenchanted troops, who stirred their pots and stretched their legs alongside campfires that had been burning for two days. Even though Edmund suspected John of collusion with Lancaster, he couldn't afford to alienate the man by accusing him of anything. Although John's fleet failed to stop Henry from landing on English soil, that was no proof of ill intent. On the other hand, they *were* half-brothers. It was more than possible that Henry even appropriated John's ships. Edmund wasn't sure he wanted to know.

"We had 3000 men when we left Oxford," Edmund was saying. "Now look at us. We are down to one third that number." He threw up his hands in frustration.

"Well," John answered, "those who were paid for fifteen days had already done their time, though I believe the men paid for twenty days are still with us."

"That may be so," growled the Duke of York, "but I think we've lost more to desertion than honest means." He looked around at the army. "Their hearts are not in this, nor is mine, if I must tell the truth. I've served the king as best I could, but if confronted with my nephew Henry, I don't see how we could fight with any conviction. I fear our men may just lay down their arms."

John kept walking, looking aside at his companion. "Is that why you are moving so slowly? We could have been at Bristol two days ago."

Edmund sighed heavily. "I am torn with indecision. Henry has not been treated fairly, and I can't in good conscience blame him for coming back. I just don't know what he plans to do." He knew Beaufort shared his feelings.

"Let me ask you this," John pursued. "If faced with Henry and his army, would you at least negotiate with him?"

"Of course I would," Edmund said. Hesitating a moment, he added, "I am hoping it comes to that."

"Then let me arrange it."

The Duke of York tried to hide his relief. "You may do so. I know he is not far from here. We will await his approach." But he stopped, putting a hand on John's arm. "I am willing to negotiate only—nothing more. I represent the crown of England. No matter how I feel, Henry Bolingbroke is an outlaw and a traitor. He has much to answer for."

It was soon arranged. Edmund waited for Bolingbroke inside the church of St. Mary's along with some of his sub-commanders, who were willing to go along with whatever he decided. The church was old and poorly lit from small windows high in the wall, but Edmund didn't mind. It was better that Henry couldn't see his face. As they paced across the flagstone floor, their footsteps echoed against the silent table tombs of the Berkeley family. Their recumbent effigies lined the nave, hands pressed together in prayer. Pigeons fluttered under the vaulted ceiling.

The church doors swung slowly open and Henry almost glowed from the afternoon sun. He stood a moment letting his eyes adjust to the gloom before stepping inside, followed by the Earls Northumberland and Westmorland, Harry Hotspur, and the Archbishop Arundel.

Standing before the altar, the Duke of York drew himself up, sticking out his chin. "You have much to answer for, Henry Bolingbroke. How dare you drag your horde of bandits across England, pillaging the good people who have done nothing to deserve this outrage?"

Henry extended his hands. "Uncle, uncle. Give me a chance to explain."

"Don't uncle me! You have been forbidden to return these six years, and here you are, just as soon as the king conveniently leaves the country. Surely you must know I speak for him."

"I do, your grace. And I trust your good judgment."

"My good judgment!" York sputtered. "My good judgment! I judge that you are outlawed."

His eyes clear and earnest, Henry took a step forward. "It was Bolingbroke who was outlawed. I speak for Lancaster."

Opening and closing his mouth, Edmund was at a loss. The trembling of his thin white beard betrayed his inner conflict. Henry took advantage of his discomfiture.

"Uncle, listen to me. My poor father, whom I was not allowed to see even at the last, would have trusted you to look after my entitlements just as he would have looked after Rutland's claims had they been challenged. I ask no less of you. You know I have been wronged..." He paused, waiting for an answer. None was forthcoming. "And what have I done to deserve this treatment? What treason have I done? I only ask to be given what I was promised: the ability to sue for my inheritance. I have come to claim my own."

Unresolved, York lowered his head. Percy stepped up next to Henry.

"This issue touches all of us," he said in his gruff voice. "We stand united behind Lancaster. If such a great inheritance can be taken away, then none of us are safe."

Beaufort leaned over to speak in York's ear. "They already number 30,000. It seems all of England supports Bolingbroke."

Edmund looked sideways at John, who nodded at Henry.

Bolingbroke had dropped to one knee. "I am prepared to swear to this, before the altar," he said.

Throwing up his hands, Edmund turned toward the altar. "Then do so, nephew." He crossed his arms, waiting.

Exchanging glances with Percy, Henry moved forward, kneeling under the great crucifix. "I swear, as God is my witness,

I have come to claim my inheritance. That is all." He crossed himself.

"Hmm." York was unconvinced. "Why do you need such a large army to merely claim your inheritance?"

Considering his oath discharged, Henry stood. "I am well aware that if I fell into the king's hands, my life would be forfeit."

"So you will confront the king as well?"

"If I must, uncle. I believe he seeks to enrich himself with Lancaster's patrimony. Many would call King Richard a tyrant. Many feel he needs the guidance of wiser heads."

"Like yours, I suppose?" York's voice sounded shriller than he intended.

"And yours, uncle. We have had councils before."

Snorting in disgust, Edmund turned his back on Henry.

"Surely you have heard the cries of the people," Bolingbroke pleaded. "The king is not satisfied with one pardon. He requires many. He demands surety from every side. No one knows whether he is safe from arrest. No one knows whether his possessions will fall prey to the king's cupidity. As Lord High Steward of England I have sworn to right these wrongs." This was the first time Henry used this title, inherited from his father. No one debated his right to it—even York.

Turning again, Edmund balanced on legs spread wide. He put his fists on his hips. "Right these wrongs? By deposing the king?"

"That is not my intent." Henry gestured to his followers. "Ask them. They would not follow a usurper."

Setting his mouth, York glared at Henry's companions. They stared back at him, not giving an inch. Finally, Edmund relaxed; there was reason in Lancaster's words. These were distinguished men, not foolish adventurers. They had a lot to lose.

Standing there, he felt a vast weight slipping from his shoulders. Let someone else carry the burden. He had done all that he could, and it was not enough to save his imprudent sovereign. Events were moving ahead—inexorably—regardless of his efforts.

"So be it. I no longer have the means to oppose you." Pausing, York raised a finger threateningly. "But do not assume I give you a free hand in this. You are bound by your word."

Allowing himself a smile, Henry put on his gloves. "I hope to convince you we mean to do the best for England's sake."

"Not the king's," Percy muttered to Westmorland. No one else heard him.

The following day, Bolingbroke's army—now augmented by the Duke of York's troops—descended on Bristol. John Beaufort joined willingly as well, though the Earl of Northumberland looked askance at him; John was considered by many to be one of Richard's minions. However, Bolingbroke's friendly behavior toward his half-brother could not be denied and so he was accepted into their ranks.

On reaching Bristol, Henry's army encamped in the fields just outside the city which had long ago outgrown its walls, tucked tidily inside the channel which flowed around the old town. The imposing square castle, with its own set of walls, dominated the region. Possession of Bristol was critical to controlling access to South Wales. It would be difficult to besiege, but Henry Bolingbroke wasn't concerned. He could see men peeking out at them from the wall ramparts. He knew that the sight of York's standard flapping alongside Northumberland and Westmorland's banners would be enough to strike fear into their hearts. Sitting astride his horse, surrounded by his supporters, Henry sent a herald forward to demand entrance. Much to his surprise, the city gates opened almost immediately. They rode forward along the main street, through a crowd of citizens who regarded them cautiously. And silently.

The castle wall reared up in front of them; its gates remained shut.

"I know who the castellan is," said York. "Peter Courtenay. He has been very loyal to King Richard."

"We'll see about that," growled the Earl of Northumberland. Taking matters into his own hands, he moved forward, gesturing for the herald to back away.

"Henry Bolingbroke, Duke of Lancaster and Lord High Steward of England, orders you to surrender this castle." Decades of command had trained his voice to carry vast distances. Henry Percy was not a man to be taken lightly.

A soldier appeared atop the barbican gate. "My master, Peter Courtenay, holds this castle for King Richard."

"Tell your master that Duke Henry commands an army of 30,000 and requires the use of this castle."

The soldier disappeared. Percy sat on his horse for five minutes before running out of patience. He pulled on the reins and walked his mount back and forth in front of the wall. "I give you fair warning," he bellowed, "anyone who wishes to surrender now will be allowed to go free. Anyone who does not will be beheaded. It is your decision!" Turning, he rode back to Henry.

It didn't take long to get a response this time. Ropes were thrown from the top of the wall and men began climbing down, hand over hand. Hitting the ground, they dashed away. Soon, others jumped from the lower window of the castle and ran to the wall, following their lead. It was too much. The castle doors blew open and men emerged, dashing across the bailey and finding escape wherever they could. The barbican gates eventually gave way and soldiers poured out, hands over their heads. Finally, Peter Courtenay came out of the castle, walking slowly as his men ran past him. He stopped before Bolingbroke and handed him the keys.

"The castle is yours," he said.

Courtenay's loyalty to the king and his timely surrender saved his life that day, but prospects were not good for William LeScrope, Sir John Bushy, and Sir Henry Green. They were too recognizable to flee, and York's defection came as a blow to their hopes. Edmund watched unhappily as they were arrested and dragged off to prison cells.

Courtenay had more to tell Bolingbroke as they sat down to a hearty meal. "I just heard tidings this morning," he said, pulling out a chair for Henry. "King Richard has landed in Wales."

Reaching for a cup of ale, Henry paused. "Where? When?"

"My messenger tells me he landed at Milford Haven four days ago with a small fleet."

"I was supposed to meet him here, at Bristol," York said, shaking his head regretfully.

"It was fortunate for us he changed his mind," mused Henry. "I wonder why he stopped there."

"Perhaps he thought to gather support from Wales." Edmund pursed his lips, still uncomfortable about changing sides. "He may still try to sail here."

"He could. Depends on how well informed he keeps himself. I think he will find he has limited choices. He can't approach Bristol by land. I have many estates near the Vale of Glamorgan and the populace has already welcomed my message-bearers. My castles, up and down the Wye valley are already in arms and will resist any loyalist approach. Now that we have LeScrope, Bushy, and Green in custody, Richard will find no support here."

"They must be executed," Northumberland growled.

Henry blinked, surprised. "I don't think these men have given sufficient cause to warrant their death by my order."

"Can't you see?" Percy pulled out a knife and thrust the point into a roasted pigeon. "Those men are evil counselors to the king. They have been behind every tyrannical action from condemning the Appellants, to enforcing fines for the king's pardons, to confiscating your estates. They are greatly hated by the people, who will acclaim you for executing them!"

Despite himself, Henry grimaced. "Execution is not my aim."

Percy exchanged glances with Westmorland before tearing off a pigeon leg. "There are times when severity is required. Those men deserve death. If you want our continued support, you must go through with this." He took a bite of the meat.

Sipping his wine, Henry observed Percy over the rim. *Is this how it was going to be? Was Percy going to threaten him every time he didn't get his way?* He didn't come this far to serve as Northumberland's puppet. On the other hand, he needed the earl; Percy had decades of experience in both warfare and

212

negotiation. He could learn much from the old man if he let him serve as his second in command. And of course, it was impossible to forget that the bulk of Henry's army came from the North.

Percy had big shoulders; let him bear much of the load. His uncle York wouldn't mind.

Henry put down his cup. "All right. Our prisoners will serve as an example."

The next morning, LeScrope, Bushy, and Green were brought before Henry Bolingbroke and his military court. Henry sat at a table with the Duke of York on one side and the Earl of Northumberland on the other. The three captives were thrust to their knees.

Henry looked hard at his prisoners, his eyes narrowed. "For decades you have served the House of Lancaster," he said accusingly, "and yet now you are accomplices to the seizure of my inheritance. You, William LeScrope. What gave you the right to take over my castle and Honour of Pickering?"

"And you," interrupted Percy, not giving LeScrope a chance to answer. He leaned forward over the table, pointing a finger at Bushy and Green. "Did you think I would just stand by and watch you steal my estates on the Scottish Marches? First you mishandled the truce which we worked so hard to establish, then you seized lands in the king's name."

Archbishop Arundel put a hand on Percy's shoulder, wanting his turn. "I haven't forgotten your vicious attacks on my brother Richard at the Parliament of 1397. Then you turned your attention to me and accused me of treason, without giving me a chance to defend myself. For that alone, Sir John Bushy, you deserve death!"

Bushy's mouth worked, but he restrained himself. The only thing he had left was his dignity; he wouldn't diminish it by useless objections. He could hear the crowd outside the window shouting his name—and they weren't begging for him to be set free.

Bolingbroke stood. "As Lord High Steward of England I condemn you to death," he said, waving his dismissal. "Take these men and remove their heads," He frowned as the prisoners were

213

dragged away. When they reached the castle bailey, the crowd's frenzy redoubled.

"See what I mean?" said Percy, well-pleased with himself. "This will only increase your popularity. I recommend you send their heads to London, where they are most hated."

Henry agreed. With the archbishop's help, he composed a letter: "I, Henry of Lancaster, Duke of Hereford and Earl of Derby, commend myself to all the people of London, high and low. My good friends, I send you my salutations and I am letting you know I have come over to take my rightful inheritance. I beg you, let me know whether you are on my side or not. I don't care which, because I have enough men to fight all the world for one day, thank God!" His eyes unfathomable, Henry looked up at Percy. Then he wrote a last sentence: "Either way, accept this gift I am sending you."

The executioner entered the room with the three heads in a white basket. Henry refused to look at them. He handed the letter to Percy. "See that it is sent, my lord."

CHAPTER 20

Richard was more tired than he should have been, and the fifteen-mile ride to Whitland Abbey felt like thirty. Perhaps it was the rough terrain; perhaps it was the heat. But Richard suspected that his spirit was weighing him down. How could things have gone so wrong?

When the royal party reached the abbey, Maudeleyn—who had preceded them—came forward with a grim face. Exhausted, Richard blinked back his tears. *Now what could have happened?*

"What is it? Come, tell me."

Maudeleyn led Richard into a small chamber and went over to a desk, picking up a wrapped package. "This is from Westminster. The exchequer sent us 1000 marks for your use."

"And that makes you sad?"

Maudeleyn sighed. "No, sire. It's the message that came with it. I have sorry tidings. It's the Duke of York."

"What happened to him?"

"Sire, he has gone over to Bolingbroke."

Richard backed into a table, putting out a hand to keep from falling. "He's deserted me?" His voice came out as a squeak.

Maudeleyn jumped forward, supporting him. "My dear Lord. From what I have learned, he was forced to capitulate. It is said his forces deserted *him*."

The king closed his eyes. "God in heaven. My uncle has abandoned me."

Holland and Rutland dashed into the room. Seeing the king, they stopped short. "Is it true?" Edward said.

Richard stared at his cousin. "How could he? How could your father abandon me?"

For once, Rutland was at a loss for words. He shook his head as others came in behind him. Soon the room was full of people.

215

Thomas Percy brought the king a cup. "Drink this, sire."

Absently accepting the wine, Richard took a deep draught. It didn't help. He looked up at his steward. "What are we to do?"

John Holland started pacing. "Let's not act too rashly. We need to know more before we can make any decisions. I say we continue on to Carmarthen in the morning. Surely we will be able to gather more information, and Thomas Despenser will meet us there."

There was no point in berating Edmund for what his father had done. But Richard couldn't help himself; he wouldn't speak to his cousin—wouldn't even look at him. *Did he know what his father was going to do? Did he persuade me to delay in Ireland so York could join forces with Lancaster?* Edward slunk around like a guilty cur. People had warned Richard that he couldn't be trusted, but the king had always ignored them. Now he wasn't so sure.

Richard spent most of the evening sequestered with Maudeleyn, writing letters to local Welsh chieftains in an attempt to garner support. The exercise did little to bolster his hopes. Without a regent, who would support his cause?

The following day, when they reached Carmarthen Despenser was waiting for them, as promised. Once again, a long face gave notice that more trouble was forthcoming. Richard had barely dismounted before Thomas blurted out his bad news. "Sire, I wasn't able to recruit my tenants. Bolingbroke's castles bordering on my shire are holding for Lancaster and the local people refuse to go against him. The way to Bristol is blocked to us."

Exhausted, Richard put an arm through his. "Come, Thomas. Bad news can wait. I need to sit down." They walked together into the great hall and Thomas waited until the king had rested before finishing his report. The others gathered around them.

"Bristol is taken," Despenser said. "Bolingbroke moved very quickly across the midlands, gathering supporters along the way. He took Bristol without a fight."

Richard put his head in his hand. "How could he have moved so fast?"

"There were none to stop him." Despenser looked at the others. He swallowed, his mouth dry. "There's more."

"More..." The king raised his head. "What more?"

"They have executed Bushy, Green, and William LeScrope."

As the others gasped, Richard looked at him in disbelief. "Why?"

Shutting his mouth, Thomas Despenser stepped back. Suddenly he realized that bearing bad news could prove deadly.

"Bolingbroke has overstepped his authority!" burst out Holland. "He had no right to execute the king's officers!"

"He sends me a message." Richard's voice was uncharacteristically harsh. It was obvious to everyone: Bolingbroke was acting like a king.

All the next day, Richard and his council discussed their options while his army began to slip away. No one had the stomach to fight the king's battle. The Welsh were a pragmatic people. Although they were loyal to the crown, as far as it went, they felt this dynastic quarrel had little to do with them.

Thomas Despenser started the discussion. "We cannot rely on our forces here to defend you. I think you should put to sea and take refuge in Bordeaux. You will be well received there, and you will be able to get aid from France, or Gascony. I say it's better to withdraw from an enemy than put yourself in his power."

"Nay," said John Holland, "by St. George! If you will be ruled by me, sire, I say go by night up the coast of Wales to Beaumaris, and thence to Conwy. There you will be secure in your own possessions."

"I would be equally secure at Bordeaux," answered Richard.

"That is true," said John, "but if you go to Bordeaux, everyone will say you have fled without being pursued. It would make you look guilty, as though you had committed some crime. Or people might think you are afraid. Whereas if you go to Beaumaris, you can put to sea if threatened, and go whithersoever you choose: Ireland, or even then, Bordeaux."

Thomas Holland, Thomas Percy and Maudeleyn agreed with Despenser; Rutland kept his opinions to himself. But Richard didn't care about his cousin's reticence. He turned to Holland. "The Earl of Salisbury awaits me at Conwy with the army he is raising from Cheshire and North Wales. How can I abandon him?" No one had an answer to that.

"I think Salisbury is our best hope." John said finally.

"If I travel along the coast of Wales," Richard pursued, "I would keep the Cambrian Mountains between myself and Bolingbroke, wouldn't I? He wouldn't be able to track me."

"Yes, I think it would be the wisest choice."

Despenser sighed. "The roads are terrible and it will be a harsh journey. But we already know you cannot go to Bristol. I have learned that the Wye valley toward Hereford is also crawling with Lancastrians, so that way is closed to us as well. If you must go along the coast, then I shall go with you."

"And I," said Maudeleyn.

"I shall go," said John Holland, "and my nephew Thomas as well."

In the end, it was decided that Richard should only take fifteen people with him. For one thing, he wanted to travel as quickly as possible, which negated bringing a large contingent. Secondly, he wanted to remain incognito so as not to draw attention to himself. His party would include three Cheshire guardsmen, seven knights and two clerks. Also Richard would be bringing three Bishops, including his close friend Thomas Merks, the Bishop of Carlisle. The king found their spiritual support comforting.

"Sire," said Rutland. "Let me stay here and take command of what forces we have left." Richard looked at him skeptically.

"I should stay also," interjected Thomas Percy. "As steward I feel I must secure the goods you leave behind, as well as those ships that haven't arrived yet from Ireland."

Gazing at his steward, the king nodded reluctantly. Perhaps Percy would have a steadying effect on Rutland. "I shall miss you both."

"Ah, Your Majesty," Edward reassured him, "we will move north when all is ready, and as you move south from Conwy we'll squeeze Bolingbroke between us."

218

Richard didn't feel very optimistic. He wished he had gone to Conwy instead of Milford Haven in the first place. *Why did he follow Rutland's advice?* Looking askance at Edward, he muttered, "We shall see. It's in God's hands."

It was too late for regrets. How could he have suspected that York would fail him?

Later that night, Richard dressed as a friar to avoid recognition and slipped away with his little retinue. Rutland and Thomas Percy watched them depart from the castle ramparts. At first they stood in silence. Finally Edward turned with a sigh.

"Our army dwindles hourly, you know."

"But we can supplement it when more ships arrive from Ireland," Thomas reminded him.

Rutland put an arm around the other's shoulders, leading him inside. "Listen. I received a message from my father." Ignoring Thomas's surprise, he unfolded the letter and pulled a rushlight forward. "Here is what he says: 'The whole country has risen in support of Lancaster. Percy and Westmorland have contributed more than half the army, and more join every day. I was helpless to stem the outpouring of support, and my own men were on the verge of mutiny. As you know, I couldn't in good conscience do battle with your cousin. His cause is righteous, for he has sworn an oath that he has only come back to reclaim his inheritance. I believe the king's cause is lost and he will have to accept Lancaster back into his fold.'" Looking up from the letter, Rutland's eyes met those of Thomas. "My father and your brother both support Bolingbroke. How can we fight them, especially in a lost cause?"

Percy stared at the letter, not even trying to hide his conflict. Richard had rewarded him generously throughout his career. He'd confided in him. How could the king see this as anything other than the worst betrayal?

In the end, what mattered most? Family or fealty? His family ties were too strong to deny, yet he had always managed to balance his obligations. There had never been a conflict before.

He looked up at his companion. Rutland had as much— nay, even more reason for gratitude toward Richard. Where was his regret?

"And yet you said we would move north and squeeze Henry between our armies," Thomas said guardedly.

Edward's eyelids quivered—the only sign of emotion he betrayed. "That was to spare the king any indignity. He knew how impossible this suggestion would be."

Did he know? Richard was no fool. On the other hand, he trusted Edward implicitly. Or did he?

"Let us get a good night's sleep," Thomas said finally. "We'll make our announcement in the morning."

Thomas was up early the next day; he had slept barely at all. Nonetheless, though he had bags under his eyes, his face showed resolve. Calling all the remaining king's household together, he looked at their trusting faces and his mouth began to tremble.

"I suppose you have learned by now that Bolingbroke has taken possession of Bristol. Every day our position here in South Wales becomes more and more indefensible. Last night, the king rode out with a small guard to join the Earl of Salisbury at Conwy." He paused, watching as they erupted with indignation. He held out his hands, trying to quiet them. "But before going, the king commended himself to you. He thanks you for your good and long service and said that he intends, when God and kinder fortune smiles on him, to reward each and every one of you according to your merits."

Tears started running down his face and he broke the rod of office across his knee. "I disband this household. I advise you to leave this place and save yourselves as best as you can."

Making sure Richard's remaining treasure was locked away inside the castle, Thomas kept the key to the chest on his person and accompanied Edward of Rutland north to find Henry Bolingbroke. Lancaster's tracks were not hard to follow; his army left a swath of desolation in its path.

It took seven days for Richard to travel the 130 miles to Conwy. On the way they spent the night at Aberystwyth, Harlech, Caernarfon and Beaumaris—all good ports which might be a point of departure in case of emergency. But the castles were not prepared for the king and Richard had to join his companions on straw beds for the night. Finally, in the first week of August, they reached their destination. The morning sun was just peeking above the horizon when the king's party came within view of the castle. The city walls were still in shadow, with its twenty-one towers and three gatehouses, connecting with the castle on two sides. The forest had been cleared and the newcomers had a long view of the formidable site.

But the fields were empty. Turning to Holland, Richard couldn't control his anxiety. "What happened to everyone? I expected an army here."

John was every bit as confused. There was no mistaking what was before their eyes. Broken-down tents littered the ground. Burnt-out fires were scattered here and there. Dogs sniffed around the pit latrines on the edges of the camp. No one could be seen anywhere.

Tired, dirty, and hungry, the little party picked up their pace and Richard threw off his hood. The towers were well manned, and once the guards recognized the king the gates swung open. Richard rode down the main street as the townspeople gathered to greet him, bowing as he passed. At the castle gate, Salisbury waited for him, surrounded by his retainers. He wasn't even trying to hide his dismay.

Dismounting, the king pulled off his gloves, handing them to his brother. Without taking his eyes off Salisbury, he approached, his face smoldering, as the others knelt.

"Where is my army?"

With tears running down his face, Salisbury rose, but he couldn't look at the king. His shoulders shook with sobs. "Sire, 40,000 men I had brought together for you. I kept them in the field for a fortnight. When so many had gathered, I tried to persuade them to attack Bolingbroke. 'Let us all make haste,' I said to them, 'and avenge King Richard in his absence. For my part,' I told them, 'I intend to neither stop nor take rest until I have done my duty.' Alas," he continued, wiping his eyes, "once they discovered you were not with us, they began to grumble amongst themselves, saying you must be dead or else you would have accompanied me here. They had heard about the cruelty of Lancaster and were full of alarm, refusing to advance any further."

The king glared at him, unappeased. "In the name of God," Salisbury cried, "I did all I could to keep them here. But they started to desert. Some went to Lancaster, others to their homes, until I am only left with a hundred good souls." He covered his face with his hands.

Richard had little pity to spare for Salisbury. He threw up his arms, turning to his followers. "I am lost!" he cried. "Dear God, have mercy on me!"

Bishop Merks put an arm around his shoulders. "Come inside, my lord," he said gently. "You are well protected here." Dropping his head, Richard allowed himself to be led into the castle.

The king and his companions sat down to a hearty meal, though Richard barely touched his food. Picking up a small flat round cake, he put his elbow on the table and stared at it. "How faithless is the wheel of fortune," he said. "One day I am the top of the world, and the next, the world weighs down on my breast." He rotated the cake in his fingers. "We know it must be so, and yet we are still amazed when it happens to us."

The others continued eating, for no one knew what to say. Richard pushed his plate aside. "Sirs, I beseech you. Give me your advice. In time of need, a man must turn to his friends."

Most of the others looked at Holland for guidance. Sighing, he put down his knife. "Sire, perhaps it would be best to send someone to Bolingbroke, to discover why he has returned from exile in such an unlawful fashion. And what does he mean to do?" When Richard didn't respond, he went on, more boldly. "We should remind him that he was banished with the consent of his father, and it would be a great disgrace to him forever if it would appear that his rightful king was undone by him. Throughout the world, it would be rumored that he is the true mirror of treason. Let him remember his father, who would never think or act disloyally against the king's majesty."

Still there was silence in the room. Holland looked around. "If anyone has a better idea, let him speak up. There are few of us here. We must all say what's on our mind."

Pulling on his beard, Richard looked around the table. Most of the men were staring at their hands, unwilling to commit themselves. He groaned, feeling let down. "Fair brother, you speak the truth and you have made a valiant suggestion. And the rest of you?" Once again, he studied his companions. "Come now, I pray you, give me your opinion, seeing that it touches upon my honor and my life—for I know Duke Henry bears a mortal hatred toward me and has certainly done me great harm."

Silence.

"All right," he conceded, "for my own part, I can't think of better counsel. Are we all in accord?"

One by one, the others mumbled their agreement. It would have to do.

"Very well. John, will you go and deliver my message? I can think of no other who would perform this office better."

Holland nodded. "I would be honored, sire. With your blessing, I would bring my nephew Thomas."

"Yes, I trust you both implicitly."

And so it was decided that the two of them would head to Chester in the afternoon, for it was a fifty mile ride. Salisbury had received word that Henry was headed north and had already passed through Shrewsbury, so they might all reach Chester about the same time.

Before he left, Holland suggested they send a messenger south and instruct Rutland to bring the army to Conwy without delay. "I shall do so," the king answered. In a rare gesture of filial affection, he put his arm through his brother's as they walked to the door. "My heart misgives me," he said in a low voice. "I am afraid to see you go."

Raising his eyebrows, John put his hand over Richard's. "Do you think Bolingbroke would dare harm me?"

"I think he would dare anything," Richard spat. But his anger turned to despair. "How shall we prevail over this duke, who behaves so ruthlessly? How he must hate me! What treachery! Look what he did to my officers in Bristol."

"I don't believe he would act so against me," said John. "I will be merely your messenger, and must return with an answer."

Somewhat reassured, Richard let go and stepped back while his brother and nephew took their leave. Bishop Merks came up beside him. "Rest, sire. You must be exhausted."

With tears in his eyes, Richard allowed the bishop to lead him to a throne, splendidly furnished with a canopy and velvet cushions edged with gold trim. Normally the king would have appreciated the opulence. Today he didn't notice it. The churchman sat below him.

"God will know how to punish the misdeeds of the sinner," Merks said, trying to reassure him. "When Judgment Day comes, the wicked shall neither have refuge nor reprieve."

"I cannot wait until Judgment Day!" The king's voice rose to a wail. "Glorious God who didst die for us, none other than you can aid my present need!" The others crossed themselves. "Alas, when the truth becomes known in France, I firmly hope my father in-law will be outraged. For truly it will be a great scandal for him, and indeed for every living mother's son among kings!" Sobbing, he buried his face in his hands. The more he thought about the implications of his position, the more he sank into hopelessness.

The king was in no mood to make any further decisions that day. His companions watched helplessly as he withdrew into a silent depression, closing his eyes and leaning his head against the throne. It wasn't until a horseman arrived that he showed any signs of life.

Salisbury met the newcomer at the door. For a few minutes they spoke in a low voice before the earl led him into the room. Richard paled when he saw their expressions.

The man fell to one knee. "Sire, I rode as fast as I could. I wish I did not have to give you such bad tidings, but there was no one else."

"More ill tidings! What could possibly be worse?"

"Sire, the day after you left Carmarthen, Edward Earl of Rutland and Thomas Percy, the Earl of Worcester disbanded the army and went to join Bolingbroke."

Richard stared at him as though he hadn't heard. His mouth fell open in disbelief, then he roared in anger, grabbing his hair on both sides of his head. "Treachery! Disloyal vipers! None have I trusted more! How could they do this to me?"

He turned to Bishop Merks. "How could they do this to me?" he said, more softly. "My cousin. My friend. I gave them everything, and this is how they repay me?"

Merks was at a loss for words. He knew Richard wouldn't hear, anyway.

"Oh, why, why did I ever go to Ireland? Was there ever a king so betrayed?"

If it was possible, Richard seemed to shrink. He leaned forward in his throne. "Tell me. Tell me exactly what happened."

Relieved that the king didn't take out his anger on the messenger, the man stood respectfully, hat in hand. "One of Sir Edward's pages saw him reading a letter that night, even before you left. Afterwards, Edward withdrew with Sir Thomas. They had a long discussion, but nothing happened until the next morning. Then they summoned the household and Sir Thomas broke his staff over his knee and told everyone to disperse. He wept, sire, while he did it. He said we should all see to our own safety."

"He wept," said Richard bitterly. "He should weep. Faithless man. He shall regret this, especially if harm comes to me because of his duplicity."

The king stared straight ahead, seeing nothing as the man backed out of the room. His last hope for rescue having faded away, Richard had two choices: flee or wait. But the consequences remained unchanged. Conwy was a port city; he could take ship back to Ireland, though he would find scant sympathy there. He would certainly find support in Brittany or France, but a successful return from exile was far from guaranteed. If he were to leave the country, it would be tantamount to abdication. Bolingbroke would be more than happy to step into his shoes.

No, he must trust to his sacred regality; the king was the Lord's anointed! Surely once they saw him face-to-face, his subjects would remember who he was and give him the deference he deserved. Richard would wait.

225

It was a gloomy little group that waited. Richard still had his three bishops to confide in, along with the Earl of Salisbury and the French visitor Jean Creton who had traveled with him, his clerk Maudeleyn, and his other retainers who insisted on serving the king's needs. In one of his quieter moments, while Richard played a forlorn game of chess with Maudeleyn, Salisbury watched them from across the room. He leaned aside to Creton. "Look at them bent over the board. Two manes of red hair, two sets of fine hands caressing the pieces. One looks like the mirror of the other, except for the circlet on the king's head."

Creton nodded his agreement. "Truly the resemblance is remarkable."

"I wonder," said Salisbury, tugging on an earlobe, "has the king ever used him for a decoy?" At that moment Richard looked over at Salisbury. Did he just hear those words?

It was difficult to fill the long hours. They knew it would take about two days for Holland to reach Chester and at least two days to return, so they passed the time walking the streets in town, inspecting the ships, staring out the window, taking long meals, resting. Richard alternated between proclaiming his misfortune, worrying about the queen, writing a long letter to her, and falling into a morose silence—which was the worst of all for the witnesses.

Four days turned into six, and Richard began to panic. "O glorious God, what has become of my brother? I fear they have come to some mischief. I no longer know what to think." Although his companions tried to reassure him, they wondered if John Holland, too, took the same route as Edward Rutland and decided to betray them.

These thoughts may have crossed Richard's mind. But the truth of the matter was far beyond his worst imaginings. The Hollands were as loyal to the king as he could possibly have wanted. What no one anticipated was that Bolingbroke would detain them after they delivered their message. There was no need for Holland to return; another, more suspicious bearer of Henry's response was already on his way.

226

CHAPTER 21

Henry Percy, Earl of Northumberland had a problem. He had promised Bolingbroke he would fulfill his mission: "By reason or by craft I will bring him." He meant every word. But if he brought too many men, King Richard would take fright and possibly flee. If he brought too few, the king might slip away while being escorted to Chester.

Ever a believer in force, Percy decided to take a large contingent with him. Once they reached Rhuddlan, he had come to a decision. The castle was perched on a ridge overlooking a marshy beach stretching down to the sea. To make his plan work, he must gain entry, so he brought up his forces, positioned himself before the castle gates, and bellowed for the castellan.

Before long, an old man appeared above the barbican. He peered down at the formidable intruders. "Who demands entrance so rudely?"

"I, Henry Percy, Earl of Northumberland commands you to instantly surrender this fortress in the name of Duke Henry of Lancaster, or you and everyone inside shall be hanged without mercy!" Without pausing for an answer, he continued, "Not for all the wealth in the realm shall you escape!"

The castellan bobbed his head in fright and withdrew to consult with his men. Then he came back. "The king has lately been here and commanded me to hold it for him."

"It matters not!" retorted Northumberland, losing patience. "Surrender this castle now, or by God I will hang every one of you from the battlements!" Even from that distance the earl could tell his words had an effect.

The castellan turned his head away, listening to advice. Then he seemed to make a decision. "My Lord of Northumberland, I will yield this castle to Duke Henry on one condition: that I continue as castellan of this place for the rest of my life."

Percy almost laughed. Another man bargaining to take care of his own needs first! Well, he could relate to that. "In the name of the duke I agree to your terms," he shouted back. "Now open your gates."

At once his command was obeyed, and Percy put a score of men in charge of the castle. As for himself, he wanted to keep moving, as Conwy castle was a good sixteen miles away. Standing with Sir Thomas Erpingham, Henry's most loyal captain, Percy gestured to the road ahead. Just inland from the sea, great boulders and sharp ridges—almost mountains—defined the coast, making his passage quite hazardous in places. On the other hand, the topography was perfect for hiding his one hundred lancers and two hundred archers.

"We will march until we find a suitable place to hide the army from Richard as best as we can. I will take just five attendants so as not to alarm the king, and the army will stay behind. The only way this will work is if he doesn't notice you until it's too late. We must find a valley to camp in. Then, when he tops a hill and sees our men below, I'll need you to make sure others move behind him to block his way back. We can't let him escape."

Erpingham, who was familiar with the area, nodded. "I know just the place, not too far from Conwy near Colwyn Bay. The hills of Penmaen-Rhôs are steep and treacherous, yet the road travels through a pass there."

"Good. The less time Richard has to think, the better."

Percy and his force crossed the new stone bridge over the Clwyd and made good time for a while, tracking the coast. Soon, they were obliged to traverse higher ground just as Erpingham remembered, and they were able to settle into a vale below the crest of a ridge.

"This will serve our purpose well," said Percy. "Rely on it: by tomorrow I will convince King Richard to come forth. On your life, do not stir from your post until you see the king or myself return."

With that unnecessary command, Percy took his five followers and disappeared over the hill. He made it to Conwy just before sunset. There was a wide estuary between the Earl of Northumberland and the castle. Percy decided to send his herald across first, and gain permission for him to deliver his message.

It was thought that any distraction would be welcome, but when Percy's herald was announced, the only thing Richard felt was displeasure. This was most unexpected.

"Where is Holland?" The king looked at Salisbury, who shrugged his shoulders. The herald came forward and dropped to one knee.

"Sire," he said, "the honorable Earl of Northumberland stands below. He has sent me to request a safe conduct so he might cross over the river and tell you how Duke Henry desires to be immediately at peace with you. May it please you, for the better knowledge of the truth, to grant him leave to come? Otherwise, he will not presume to stir."

Richard stood, clenching his fist. Percy acting for Bolingbroke? The king's first impulse was to strike the man for his imprudence. *Since when had the Earl of Northumberland become Lancaster's man?* Percy's antagonism toward Gaunt went all the way back to the Peasants' Revolt. And now he was in league with that traitor—his enemy's son?

Salisbury came up beside him, putting a restraining hand on Richard's arm. But it wasn't necessary; the king had respect for the herald's office. Nonetheless, the earl leaned toward his ear. "We need to know what has happened these last weeks. I think it would be a good thing to let him come. Alone."

Straightening to his full height, Richard looked down at the herald. "I give the Earl of Northumberland permission to pass," he said, his voice higher than usual but steady.

The herald didn't waste a minute. Bowing several times as he backed from the room, he thanked the king again and again for his goodwill.

When the door closed, Richard picked up a cup and threw it after him. "Curse that bastard Percy! Is all of the North against me?"

229

Having agreed to meet with Northumberland, Richard now found another wait intolerable—even though it was only for a short time. Pacing back and forth, the king wrung his hands while those around him drew back to give him space. Finally, the door opened and Henry Percy entered, alone. He stepped forward confidently, as though his mission was welcomed. Richard turned, observing him intently.

"So my proud Earl of Northumberland has turned against me?" said the king.

Even this did not erode Percy's self-assurance. He bowed briefly. "Not at all, sire. I come as a peacemaker between yourself and Duke Henry. It is desired by all that you should become good friends for the time to come." His normal harshness was smoothed to a gentle cadence. Years of negotiations had trained him well.

Richard grunted in answer as he sat on his throne. "I already sent John and Thomas Holland to Bolingbroke with a message. Did you not see them?"

"No. It may be I took a different route, as I stopped by Flint Castle along the way."

Richard's castle. The significance of Percy's detour did not slip past the king. He had left funds and supplies there before he went to Ireland. "And why does your good duke come in arms against me?" he asked haughtily.

"Sire, I will tell you true. Duke Henry wishes for nothing but his titles and land, and all that belongs to him. And he petitions you to restore him to the Stewardship of England. The duke his father and all his ancestors have served in this position for more than a hundred years. He asks for nothing that belongs to you, for you are his immediate and rightful king."

Richard tapped his fingers on the arm of this chair. "And if I agree to restore his titles, he will disband his murderous force of rogues and scoundrels?"

For a moment, Percy lost his composure. But he soon recovered himself. "Sire," he said, changing the subject, "if it be your pleasure, I will give you his message. Duke Henry says if you will be a fair judge and true, you will arrest all those who counselled you to put your uncle Gloucester wrongly to death. If these men deny their guilt, they can await the judgment of your parliament. Duke Henry shall act as chief judge there, as his father had done, and those who have been declared guilty of treason shall be punished without partiality."

Biting back his anger, Richard temporized by adjusting his sleeve. "And who are these men you speak of?"

"I will tell you. The first is your brother John Holland. The second who deserves censure is your nephew Thomas Holland. Another is the Earl of Salisbury, together with Thomas Merks, the Bishop of Carlisle. And the fifth, I heard Duke Henry say, is Maudeleyn." The fact that three of those named stood in this very room had no effect on Henry Percy. "Such is the determination of Duke Henry. Certes, dear sire, he would do nothing foolish or unreasonable."

Richard doubted the truth of *that* statement. He shifted in his chair. "Is this all you have to say?" He had trouble keeping his voice even.

"Just this. Treat my lord fairly, and he will most humbly come on his knees before you, and sue for mercy. Once this is done, together you shall go to London. Or, if you choose to take a different road than Duke Henry, then you shall do so. And then shall parliament be declared throughout the land."

Percy saw that Richard was not persuaded. It was time for him to make his most convincing pledge. "Be sure of this: I will swear to it upon the body of our Lord, that Duke Henry shall most faithfully observe all I have said. He solemnly pledged it to me upon the sacrament when we last parted." He paused, hoping for an answer. "I will leave you to consider, sire, for I have tarried long."

An offer to swear an oath reassured the king a bit, and he nodded. "Northumberland, withdraw to your camp; ere long you shall have your answer." He watched, unhappily, as Percy bowed and strode from the room.

For a moment, all was quiet. Then, unable to contain themselves, all three of the damned men spoke at once. Richard covered his ears.

"Do you truly think I would permit Henry to harm you?" He removed his hands. "No, my friends. I love you all and I will not suffer you to go to parliament. So that they would put you to death, just for their pleasure?" He sat deep in thought, stroking his beard. "Though you can see just as well as I that all is lost, for the moment. I see no other way than pretend to grant him what he wishes." He looked sideways at his doubtful companions. "Not that I intend to go through with it. Henry cannot call parliament without my say. And you know he has never been firm of purpose," he reasoned. "I'm sure the coalition he has patched together will fall apart for lack of leadership. Henry is no politician, he has always done what his father commanded."

His friends refused to look at him; they were perfectly miserable. Once Richard admitted they were lost, they were as good as gone. How would he ever get the upper hand with Henry? But for some reason, adversity put the spirit back into the king's heart, at least for the moment. He turned to them, leaning forward.

"Listen to me. I will summon our loyal Welsh subjects to be ready for us. After all, they went away because they thought I was dead, and I'm sure they will want to redress this mistake. Isn't that so, John?"

Swallowing his bitterness, Salisbury nodded.

"So," Richard went on, "when we have spoken with Duke Henry and agree to return to London, we will take another route through Wales. If he asks us why we would do so, we shall tell him that his army has used up all the victuals and wasted everything, and we will go another way lest provisions fail us. I believe he will agree to it, and the earl has already told us so." His friends were too dejected to respond. Undaunted, he went on. "And when we find our army assembled, we will display our banners to the wind, and suddenly march with vigor against my traitorous duke."

He stood, walking back and forth. "I am sure of it, as I am sure of my life, that when they see my coat of arms, they will regret the wrongs they have done to me. I will wager that fully half of those who have gone to Bolingbroke will desert him and come back to me. For good and faithful hearts can never prove false. They will remember I am their anointed king and their rightful lord. How could they not?" He crossed himself. "God, if we trust Him, will aid us."

Pausing, Richard put a hand on Maudeleyn's shoulder. "I've been in difficult straights before, have I not? Did I not stop the Peasants' Revolt when no one else dared move against them? Did I not turn the tables against the Lords Appellant and remove them one by one?"

He caught himself, remembering Bolingbroke, his last act of revenge. "Although Duke Henry won't stay down, the bastard." He raised his chin, eyes flashing. "Rest assured, my friends: once I get him into my power, I will cause him to be foully put to death, just as he deserves. And he's not the only one. There are some of them I will flay alive. Please God, keep me strong to see my purpose through."

The others rallied. Richard was very clever and persuasive. They had no choice but to follow him, so they put their faith in his words, relying on his resourcefulness.

"That's better," he said, holding out his hand for some wine. Maudeleyn hastened to accommodate him. "Let our good Earl of Northumberland wait for our answer while we send messages to my loyal Welsh subjects. Let them gather in readiness for my signal." He turned to Thomas Despenser. "Since most of your estates are in Wales," he said, "You would serve me best if you would personally raise a force to defend me. Will you do so?"

"Gladly," said Thomas.

"Gramercy for that," the king said. "You put my mind at rest. While you are at it, will you arrange to send my letter to the Queen at Wallingford?" Thomas bowed his assent. Smiling briefly at him, Richard turned to Bishop Merks. "Your grace, I would have you consecrate the host so I can bind Henry Percy with a holy oath. May God be with us."

CHAPTER 22

Northumberland was forced to wait a day and a night before Richard recalled him. The earl's humor was not helped by the pouring rain, which forced him to move back from the estuary. Fortunately, they had come prepared for a possible lengthy stay, and their tents proved adequate to the task. When the summons came, Henry pushed away his half-eaten breakfast and grabbed his cloak to protect against the wind. He grumbled to himself as he was ferried across to the castle.

Richard and his little group were waiting for him. As soon as Percy entered the great hall, the king turned and led him to a chapel under the arch of the eastern window. Bishop Merks was standing by an altar draped with a white cloth and set for mass. Richard turned to Percy.

"Northumberland, Lancaster has sent you here to reconcile the two of us. You must swear on the body of our Lord, which the bishop has consecrated, that everything you have said is true, and that you have no hidden design of any kind whatsoever. If, like a worthy lord, you will indeed keep the agreement, then I will go with you and lodge at Flint, and there our good cousin of Lancaster can come and speak with us."

Without hesitation Percy crossed himself, then knelt before the altar. "I willingly agree to swear upon the consecrated host that Duke Henry of Lancaster has come to claim his patrimony and nothing more. I affirm to you he will observe the whole as you have heard me relate it here." Richard hesitated, but he could find no fault with the earl's conduct. What else could he do? He knelt beside Northumberland while Bishop Merks performed the mass. After it was over, the earl put his hand on the host and swore his oath.

Having performed his task, Percy stood. "Sire, I am glad you have agreed to a reconciliation. Let me ride ahead to

Rhuddlan and order your supper, and I will send a message to the duke to meet us at Flint."

Richard nodded and the earl turned to leave, but the king stopped him with a hand on his arm. "For God's sake, be sure you consider well what you have sworn. For I know truly that you are an honorable man. If you perjured yourself you would live forever in shame and disgrace."

Momentarily startled, Percy's eyes grew wide—as though he had just been cursed. Now he really wanted to get away. "Dear sire, make haste," he grunted, "for it's already midday."

Richard and his party of twelve were glad to get away; Conwy had begun to feel like a prison to them. As they rode from the castle his mind brought him back to his outgoing trip a mere two months ago. He had led the most auspicious, the most united, the most formidable army a king could ever desire. He had achieved the height of his regality. His enemies were either destroyed or powerless. He ruled by divine right—a distinction even the great Edward III never quite managed to attain.

But what happened? How could it all have come crashing down? Never in a thousand years would he have thought that Bolingbroke, who had merrily squandered his father's fortune on tournaments and travel, should suddenly turn political and rear his banner in revolt. From whence came this unusual behavior? Who was driving his cousin? And how had he managed to turn the whole country against their rightful king?

Richard shook his head. It just didn't make sense.

A brisk wind blew in from the coast laden with a chill drizzle and he pulled his hood over his head, clutching it underneath his chin. If he wasn't so anxious to get this over with he would have turned around for the comfort of the castle.

"Does it ever warm up in this God-forsaken country?" he asked Salisbury.

The other grunted. "I think they have a month of summer, but it's already past."

Buffeted from behind, at least the wind pushed them on their way. They passed through a dense forest that thinned after a few miles while their rough path rose onto a ridge, bordered on their right by huge boulders, and on their left by a sheer drop to

235

the sandy shore. They reached the summit of the hill and dismounted, for the descent was very steep. Grumbling, clutching their reins, the party gingerly picked their way down the hill, trying not to stumble on the rocks. The wind had not slackened and now it came from the north. They were most of the way down when Richard stopped with a gasp. Putting a hand out to Salisbury, he pointed into the distance where the road curved. A spot of red could be seen behind the rocks.

"Do you see it? I think those are banners." He couldn't control the trembling in his voice.

"Certainly, sire. I do see it. And my heart forebodes ill."

"Certes," said the Bishop of Carlisle behind them, "I strongly suspect that man has broken faith with you."

"He swore an oath," Richard groaned.

As they stood in indecision, Henry Percy stepped from behind a clump of trees dressed in full armor. He was accompanied by eleven men. Richard's heart sank. "I am betrayed," he muttered. "Lord of heaven help me." It would be impossible to flee, for the hill was too steep, so he stood his ground. But the rest of his party were despondent.

"O true God, what trouble have I brought down on us?"

"You know I am a dead man," lamented Salisbury. "Duke Henry has hated me ever since you sent me to Paris during his outlawry. Alas! Why did we trust his oath? It will be our total ruin."

Richard was too full of his own concerns to spare any comfort for Salisbury. Northumberland came up and knelt before the king.

"My lord, I am glad you are here, and I have come to meet you."

The king was not fooled. "Who are those people below in the valley?"

"What people? I have seen none."

"Come now," retorted the Earl of Salisbury, "we can see. There they are, right before us!"

"By St. John," interjected Bishop Merks, "Those are your men. I can distinguish your banner." At this point, the soldiers were coming out into the open. Percy's colors flapped in the wind.

Dropping the pretense, Henry Percy stood. "Be not displeased, my rightful lord, that I am concerned about your security. The country, as you know, is disturbed by war."

Richard certainly knew who brought about the disturbances. "This huge host is way more than necessary. This is not what you promised me! You told me that you had been sent with only five others." He puffed out a mouthful of air in disgust. "This is very ill done, considering the oath you made. I do not trust your loyalty."

The earl restrained his impatience with difficulty. But the king wasn't finished.

"Northumberland, this will not do. We are returning to Conwy."

"By St. George, you will not!" Percy seized the reins of Richard's horse, much to the king's alarm. "You may accuse me of dishonor, but I solemnly declare that since I have you here, I will bring you directly to Duke Henry, which I have promised him."

Richard shifted in his saddle, preparing to snatch back the reins when Salisbury interjected. "Sire!" He pointed back the way they had come. Turning, the king groaned as Sir Thomas Erpingham and ten soldiers stepped onto the road behind them, blocking their retreat.

"The God upon whom you have sworn will damn you on the day of judgment!" Richard cried. By now, his followers had broken down in tears; all feared for their lives. Trying to retain a shred of dignity, the king turned to them. "Ah, my good and faithful friends, we are all betrayed, and given without cause into the hands of our enemies. For God's sake, have patience and remember our Savior, who suffered a similar fate."

"Come," said Percy, out of patience, "your supper awaits you at Rhuddlan Castle." Their mission accomplished, he and all his soldiers mounted and rode with the captive king the last ten miles to Rhuddlan. A sumptuous meal was laid out for Richard and his companions. Unfortunately, they were too miserable to enjoy it. And they knew they had another eighteen-mile ride ahead of them, so they didn't dawdle.

Standing on high ground surrounded by a marsh, Flint was the first of Edward I's great ring of castles to conquer Wales; in fact, only the tidal estuary of the river Dee separated it from England. Unique in its construction, Flint's fourth massive corner tower was detached from the inner bailey and served as a keep—a fortified residence and last refuge in case of attack. It was to this keep that Richard and his party were directed. They crossed a drawbridge over a tidal moat and into a huge hall. They were taken to sleeping chambers on the second floor, many of which were built into the stone walls. By now, although all were exhausted, no one could rest. Richard spent many hours bemoaning his fate. He called upon God and the Virgin and St. John the Baptist. He cried for his queen. The king's companions joined him in lamenting their own fates, until, after midnight, the Bishop of Carlisle exhorted them to accept God's will. Finally, everyone settled down, though sleep evaded them.

"Let this all be a bad dream," Richard muttered, his voice muffled. "Or let me never wake up."

Henry Percy stayed on the other side of the castle. Meanwhile, he sent Erpingham to Chester where Bolingbroke was waiting. There was no doubt Lancaster would come to Flint the following day. And so it happened that while Richard and his companions looked east from the ramparts, they saw a huge army approaching along the coastal road. Shortly thereafter, they heard such a ruckus of horns, trumpets, flutes, pipes, and even drums that there was no doubt Henry's army was celebrating the fall of a king.

"Alas, now I see plainly that my end draws near," moaned Richard. "I shall be delivered into the hands of my enemies who mortally hate me though I never deserved it. Oh, why did I ever trust that serpent Northumberland?" Richard's friends drew close around him, forgetting the distance his royalty formerly demanded. Now, he was one of them though even more to be pitied, for he had the farthest to fall.

"Look," pointed Salisbury, "a small group has broken off and comes ahead."

The others leaned over the parapet, trying to recognize their visitors. The newcomers rode briskly upstream toward a crossing place, then back to the castle on dry land. Moving around the tower, Richard was the first to recognize the archbishop.

"Ah, Arundel," he said warily. "I had forbidden him to contact Bolingbroke in exile, but he was ever an ungovernable man. Now I must answer to him!" There were two others with the archbishop, and though Richard's companions recognized them, no one dared speak a word. For a moment the king was so shocked he lost his balance and the bishop put out a hand to support him. Recovering, Richard leaned even farther forward, squinting.

"I can't believe my eyes. It can't be true." He straightened. "They are wearing Lancaster's livery. Dear God, their betrayal is complete. Edward of Rutland, who should have been my heir! Thomas Percy, my faithful steward! Why have you forsaken me?"

"Courage, sire," prompted the Bishop of Carlisle. "They are still your servants."

Richard looked at him, his lip trembling. "You are right. I must remember myself."

By now, the emissaries entered the castle and Richard went down to meet them. Thomas Arundel stood in front of the others, and when they saw the king all three went down on their knees. Richard let them stay there a bit longer than necessary before gesturing that they should rise. As soon as possible, Rutland and Percy stepped back, unable to look at the king.

But Richard ignored his former friends and moved over to a window embrasure, drawing Arundel aside. The king sat on a bench, making the archbishop stand. For a moment they stared at each other; both were thinking of the night Arundel was sent into exile. Richard thought how justified his actions were, considering the present betrayal. Arundel thought how unjustified Richard's actions were, considering his years of service.

The archbishop cleared his throat. "Sire, you have brought yourself to this pass. You have misgoverned this nation and dealt falsely with your barons. You have broken your word over and over, demanded oaths when you should have gained hearts, proven that you cannot be trusted. You forget that you rule by the sufferance of your great nobles. You have shamefully disinherited your greatest duke after undeservedly sending him into exile. Can you wonder he came back to claim his birthright?"

Richard wasn't used to being castigated. No one had dared speak to him like this. All the color fled from his face, and suddenly he felt like a child again, exposed and unprotected.

"You murdered my brother," Arundel growled, "after assuring me he would come to no harm."

There was no denying it. Richard had tricked Thomas into persuading his brother to surrender himself. For the first time he feared for his life.

With an effort, the archbishop brought his emotions under control. "Do not be alarmed," he said scornfully, "your rank protects you. No harm will come to your person. Rest assured, I am here to tell you that Duke Henry awaits your pleasure. He has come to present his grievances and he petitions you to reinstate him in his patrimony."

Regaining his composure, Richard stood. "Very well. We shall dine first before Henry Bolingbroke comes before us."

Bowing, the archbishop took his leave, bringing the shamefaced Rutland and Percy with him.

Richard and his twelve companions tarried long at the table, picking at their food and saying very little to each other. It was just as well; the army had surrounded the castle in orderly ranks, continuing to play their instruments loud enough to wake the dead. After a while, some of Bolingbroke's bolder guards sauntered in, acting like they belonged there. Their prisoners were a curiosity, like the lions in the Tower. Not knowing what to do, Richard tried to ignore them, even when they laughed and pointed at him.

"Eat heartily and make good cheer," one of the rogues sputtered, "for by St. George your heads will soon be chopped off!" Sniggering, the others pushed him out of the room. More came in behind them, laughing and pointing and slapping each other on the shoulder.

The Frenchman Creton was the most frightened of all, for he had come along merely as an observer and feared that his foreignness would make him a target. He leaned toward Salisbury. "Forgive me, my lord," he said in a low voice, "I fear these men. I

240

am nothing more than a visitor, and I might come to an accidental death if I don't beg Duke Henry for sanctuary."

Putting down his spoon, the earl turned to him sympathetically. "By all means, save yourself. But please, do us a service and write down all you remember of these events. Yours may be the only chronicle surviving King Richard's downfall."

Wiping his eye, Creton took Salisbury's hand. "You have been a good friend and I swear I will do so."

The last incident with the soldiers signaled the end of their meal. Already feeling like a supplicant, Richard put on the friar's robe he had worn while traveling, and once again they climbed the steps to the roof of the tower. They watched another group detach itself from the army, this time bearing the banner of Lancaster.

"He is well accompanied," said Richard. "Looks like eleven in all, including Lancaster's herald. Let them wait for me, below."

Giving the newcomers adequate time to enter the castle, Richard led his men down the winding staircase. When he came through the archway the king paused—while Bolingbroke, fully armed except for his helmet, bowed deeply from across the inner bailey. They walked toward each other and as he got close, Henry bowed a second time, removing his hat.

Richard looked at him for a moment before pulling off his own hood. "Fair cousin of Lancaster," he said, "you are right welcome." He almost sounded sincere.

Bowing a third time, Henry kept up pretenses. "My Lord, I have come before you sent for me and I will tell you why. The people say you have governed them badly and rigorously these last two and twenty years, and they are greatly discontented. But if it pleases our Lord, I will help you govern them better than in times past."

Knowing he was at a disadvantage, Richard bit back his bile. "Fair cousin," he answered, almost choking on his words, "since it pleases you, it pleases us well."

Henry nodded to Bishop Merks and the two knights who stood beside the king. He pointedly avoided the Earl of Salisbury, who had ruined his chances to marry the Duke of Berry's daughter the year before. Turning to his followers, Henry called, "Bring out the king's horses."

Turning aside to speak with Salisbury, Richard saw the earl's face darken as he heard the clip-clop of hooves into the bailey. The king whirled around, struck dumb when he saw that his beloved white horse had been substituted with a stunted, run-down nag. A second pathetic creature was brought up as well. It was clear that he and the earl were expected to mount these hacks like common criminals. Richard turned to glare at Bolingbroke, but the duke had already exited the bailey. Jean Creton was following with Lancaster's herald and paused to give Richard one last regretful glance. Then he was gone.

"I can harbor no further illusions," Richard said to Salisbury. "We are at the duke's mercy. God help us all." Overcome by his misfortunes, Richard allowed himself to be helped into the saddle. Lancaster's guards surrounded him and the earl as they rode past Henry's waiting army, while the minstrels persisted in playing their racket as loud as they could.

CHAPTER 23

Lancaster rode at the head of his troops as the citizens of Chester welcomed him, calling his name and raining blessings upon his head. As soon as the king was seen riding his little horse—far behind the duke—the cheers turned into shouts of mockery, followed by curses and even an occasional stone. Richard couldn't believe it. Where were his loyal subjects? Chester was his special town. Over the years he had showered favors upon the populace. He recruited his elite corps of archers from amongst their numbers. And this is how they repaid him? How could this be possible?

They processed directly to the castle. Entering into the bailey, Richard was unprepared for his next confrontation. Young Humphrey, the new Earl of Buckingham came from the keep, side-by-side with Thomas, now calling himself the Earl of Arundel. Both youths, full of hatred, glared at the king while putting a hand to their swords. The specters of their murdered fathers glowed upon their features.

Dismounting, Bolingbroke took charge of the situation. "My cousins," he said harshly, all pretense of deference gone, "take the king and convey him to the corner tower. Bring as many people as you need, and guard him closely." Turning on his heel, he strode away without another word.

Richard ignored Henry, but he regarded his new gaolers with trepidation. He had left Humphrey in Ireland with young Henry of Monmouth—yet here he was! Arundel, who had escaped from his brother Holland's care was less of a surprise. Surely he searched out Lancaster while still in France. But the king never expected to find himself in their power.

"My Lord, you must come with us," said Humphrey with a commanding voice.

Richard looked around with alarm. "For God's sake, let my companions accompany me!"

Buckingham sneered at him. "By St. George, you will have no companions except us and our men. So says the duke."

Not able to control his tears, Richard turned to the others. "Ah, my dear friends, now I see plainly that I must leave you." He spread his arms and they all embraced him, putting their heads together and murmuring words of comfort. But there was no comfort to be had. After watching this sad scene for a few minutes, both of his guardians took hold of the king's arms and directed him toward the tower. The other unfortunates were led to their own cells.

None too gently, the king was shoved down the hallway and into his new prison. As the door closed behind him, he sighed, looking around. He had just, this very spring, refurbished these same apartments. He never even had a chance to use them—until now. The irony wasn't lost on him and he laughed disparagingly. Looking up at the white hart decorating the window frame, he thought about the embroidery Queen Anne was working on the night he was nearly deposed by Gloucester. The Lords Appellant had filled the bailey of the Tower with hundreds of their troops, making him their prisoner. Henry Bolingbroke was one of them, though Richard sought to bring him over to his side. His cousin was less sure of himself back then—more malleable. *Or was he?* Perhaps he was merely biding his time, letting the Duke of Gloucester make all the mistakes. He just didn't know, anymore. How was he going to get out of this predicament?

He lay down on his bed, waiting for someone to talk to him. Nobody came for hours, until finally a page brought his supper. Lying on his side, Richard watched the youth arrange a cloth on the small table, pour wine into a cup, and leave without speaking a word. That was all. No Henry, no vindictive wardens, no servants. No change of clothing.

Listening to the silence, Richard realized that for the first time in his life, he was entirely alone. No one would be undressing him, brushing his hair, or even handing him a cloth and a washbowl while he was on his close stool. There would be no one sleeping at the foot of his bed or outside the door. Well, his guards would be there, and they were far from friendly—nor would they sleep.

At least they had left him some candles, and it was starting to get dark. Alas, the hearth was cold; this room hadn't been used lately. Richard picked up a firestriker and a flint and stared at them. He had never paid attention when the servants struck a spark, but he sort of knew what they did. He could see there was some kindling in the fireplace and he knelt, holding the iron in one hand and hitting it with the flint. Nothing. He struck it again and again, frustration building, until he broke into tears and dropped the flint on the floor. He didn't hear the door open and quiet feet approach until someone knelt beside him. It was Hal!

"Oh, my boy," he cried, throwing his arms around Hal's neck. "I've never been so glad to see anyone in my life!"

Hugging him back, Hal pulled Richard to his feet. "This will not do. Let me go fetch a servant. Sit, Your Majesty."

Your Majesty. Richard hadn't heard that title for a long time. Unable to stop the tears, Richard sat on the bed while Hal went to summon help. He was soon back with two servants in tow.

"I will make sure someone is here to attend to your needs," he growled. "It is shameful that they abandoned you so." He sat beside the king.

"How did you get to be here?" Richard asked.

"When my father reached Chester he sent for me. And Humphrey. We just got here yesterday."

"You came by a shorter route than I did," Richard said bitterly. "I was ill advised."

Hal shook his head. "So much has happened. I'm not privy to most of it. It seems my father has taken on much."

"I'm afraid he means to do me harm." Richard could see that Hal was worried, too. "What of my brother? And my nephew? Do you know what happened to them?"

"I am told your brother spoke eloquently to my father, trying to persuade him against breaking his fidelity to you. But he only succeeded in making things worse. And when John desired to return to you with his answer, my father forbid him to go and

245

detained him. He also imprisoned your nephew in this same castle, though I know not why."

Richard sighed. "I feared my brother had gone over to Lancaster, like Rutland and Percy."

"No, I assure you. He even complained to me, though there was nothing I could do."

That was some comfort. Richard forced a smile, trying to lighten his tone. "But I have you, now, to keep me company."

Hal came and went for the next couple of days, keeping his movements as discreet as he could. But it was not fated to last. He had just come in with an armful of books when the door crashed open behind him. Humphrey of Buckingham stepped into the room, his hand grasping and ungrasping his dagger. He shot a look of anger at Hal.

"I thought you were here. I forbid you to visit the king!"

Hal stood to his full height, crossing his arms over his chest. "You have no authority over me."

"I have been given full authority over King Richard, and I say he is to have no visitors!"

"I answer only to my father."

"It matters not. I shall put extra guards on this door and you shall not enter."

"I warn you, Humphrey. Do not cross me."

Richard marveled at the self-assurance shown by this thirteen year-old boy. Moving up beside him, he put a hand on Hal's arm. "I would not be the cause of dissension between you and your father," he said quietly. "We both know what his answer would be. Thanks to you, I have recovered my equanimity. Go, my friend. I'll be all right."

Hal knelt before the king, kissing his ring. Then he got up and strode from the room without looking at Humphrey. Buckingham glared at Richard before closing the door.

Alone again, the king lowered his head into his hands. Each parting seemed more painful than the last. Was he to be alone for the rest of his life?

Henry Percy watched from the back of the room while Duke Henry accepted submissions from six of King Richard's retainers who rode in from Cheshire. Kneeling, the last man put his hands into Henry's. "I promise on my soul that I will be faithful to you, my Lord, never cause you harm and observe my homage to you against all persons in good faith and without deceit." Nodding graciously, the duke thanked him and instructed his steward to bestow his new badge, a collar of linked greyhounds.

At that, Percy had had enough. Striding forward, he approached the seated duke who looked up inquiringly.

"What is it?" Bolingbroke asked.

"Can't you guess? This has gone way past where we started."

"Yes?"

Tightening his lips, Percy sat next to Henry, not waiting for an invitation. "Is that all you have to say? After swearing an oath at Doncaster that you did not seek the crown? Then you affirmed it again before I went to fetch the king from Conwy—an oath I perpetuated by swearing on the host? Now both of us are forsworn!"

Sighing, Bolingbroke leaned back in his chair. "Can't you see, Henry? The people want it. Look how they flock to my standard. You know I have to send thousands back home because I can't afford to feed them all. How can I resist the crown when it is thrust upon me?"

"How can you repudiate your oath so easily?"

"I will promise to go on Crusade. I will take it up personally with the Archbishop of Canterbury."

"Ha! That's no good. Archbishop Arundel has driven you to it."

Henry looked sadly at Percy, all pretense gone. "You know I must do this. I have no choice. You saw what happened to my uncle Gloucester. That could be me."

Percy's anger melted away. *Wasn't this the same thing he told his son the day Lancaster returned from exile?*

"It was much easier to dissemble, wasn't it?" Bolingbroke mused. "The people's champion, come from an unjust exile to right the wrongs inflicted by a vengeful king. It was so straightforward, Henry. That's all I wanted."

"Was it?" Percy scowled. "Do you expect me to believe that?"

Giving him a sideways glance, the duke shrugged. "It no longer matters, does it? We are set on our path and cannot diverge. Right or wrong, I will be king."

Using the great seal he had appropriated from the Duke of York, Henry sent out writs for a Parliament to be held at Westminster on September 30. The writs went along with this letter, supposedly written by the king and directed to the sheriffs: "*Henry, Duke of Lancaster, has come to redress the defects of my government. I, King Richard, unwilling to endure any longer the evils from which my realm suffers, have, with the advice of my magnates, ordered them to proclaim the king's peace and have you put down all disturbances.*"

Would this quiet things down? Already—despite his promises to the contrary—Lancaster's unruly army had wreaked havoc on unhappy Cheshire. Pillaging, raping, and burning, Henry's disorderly rabble treated the principality no different than conquered France. He needed to get them moving as soon as possible.

For two days after Hal went away, Richard awaited his fate; this was worse than any kind of humiliation. The only company he had was the occasional page bringing him a meal. On the third day, the door opened and his gaolers stepped in, their faces stern. "It is time to accompany Duke Henry to London," said Humphrey.

"What am I to wear?" the king asked, trying to retain his dignity.

"You are wearing it already."

If Richard needed any further proof that Henry wanted to humble him, this was it. His whole life, he prided himself on a new garment every day, made of gorgeous silk, velvet, and satins, dripping with jewels—or at least, every day before he made the fateful decision to leave Ireland. Now, he didn't recognize himself.

Sighing, he went downstairs and mounted the same old nag he rode in on. Salisbury and the others were not in sight.

But at least he was in the fresh air, notwithstanding the heavy clouds threatening rain once again. Flanked by his guards, he rode several ranks behind Duke Henry as the cavalcade headed southeast toward London. Richard rode with his head down, his attention wandering.

Later that afternoon, before they had even crossed out of Cheshire, the air was shattered by the shrieks of attack. Shocked back into awareness, the king turned around on his horse, noting the frenzied activities of Henry's army. Suddenly, out of the hills, rode a thousand Welshmen, led by his old retainer Thomas Despenser, his sword held high. Intent on confusing the ducal army, they split into two, some riding directly for Richard, others trying to outflank the rearmost riders. Initially caught off guard, Henry's knights recovered quickly and spurred to meet them— some couching spears under their arms, others drawing their swords. As they made contact with the charging Welshmen, there was a brief clash of arms, then a sudden reversal. The attackers, unused to direct warfare, sought shelter in the forest. Despenser was with them.

Henry ordered the trumpeters to summon back his knights. He wasn't ready to sacrifice his men in a senseless pursuit that would put them at a disadvantage. They were well suited for fighting on level ground, not guerilla warfare. The Welsh had exposed their plan. He knew they would repeat the attacks again and again. From now on Henry would be ready for them.

It was all over so quickly. Richard lowered his head again, silently facing forward. That was his grand rescue, pitiful though it was. Despenser didn't have enough time to raise a significant force. He had tried. And failed. There was no point in blaming the man. There was no point in anything.

That day and the next, all the way to Lichfield, the Welsh harried Henry's army, picking off stragglers and keeping everyone on edge. Despite himself, Richard smiled grimly at the discomfiture of the ducal host, doing their best to put themselves between him and rescue. By now he didn't expect the Welsh to succeed, but at least they tried to redeem themselves after shamefully abandoning him before Conwy.

On the second night they reached Lichfield, another town close to the king's heart. Just the previous Christmas, Richard celebrated his holidays at the Bishop's elegant palace, with magnificent tournaments and feasting. By contrast, today he was led past the grand palace to the adjoining stone castle, which was the oldest building in the cathedral close. At least the chamber he occupied was built for comfort. The four-poster bed was topped by an intricately carved canopy, suspended from the ceiling. Side curtains, thick and heavy, were tied at the corner posts by silk cords hanging to the floor. Young Arundel and Gloucester brought him food and taunted him with his humble fare, though by now he was used to their insults and pointedly ignored them. More interested in the duke's company than their unresponsive charge, the king's gaolers left him alone, locking the door behind them.

Richard was tired and the bed looked inviting. Resisting an impulse to lie down, he sat on the mattress and looked up at the window beside it, which was larger than usual. Finally, he got up and opened the shutter. The balmy late-summer breeze was heavy with moisture and he breathed in deeply, looking out at a brilliant dark red sunset. Pulling over a bench, Richard stepped on it, leaning out over the wide sill. Straight down, there was a level patch of untended ground between the castle and the curtain wall—which was in serious disrepair. Over to his left, the stone wall had eroded away to half its height. With determination, anyone could climb over it. Richard knew there was a ditch running outside the wall, but it wasn't overly deep and it, too had been neglected.

Still standing on his bench, he looked at his bed again, putting a hand to his dagger. Thankfully they hadn't taken that from him; he needed something to cut his food with! Why not just tear the sheets into strips and make a rope? The blade should easily slice through the fabric, and he could tie it to the bedpost. It would be awkward, but...why not? He leaned over the window sill again. The ground wasn't too far away—maybe the height of three men standing on each other's shoulders.

250

Trying to control his rising excitement, Richard jumped down, moving the bench back to its original position. They would bring him supper in a couple of hours, then leave him alone like they always did. He'd have to wait until everyone was asleep. Still, it was worth a try. The castle was on the southern edge of town, so once he had climbed out of the ditch he could head toward the forest. Perhaps some of his Welsh rescuers were nearby. They hadn't given up yet, it seemed. Their last attack was just two days ago.

Alone and friendless, the king still clung to the hope that all was not lost. What else could he do? Resolving to get some sleep before his long night ahead, Richard lay back on the bed and contemplated freedom.

His cold supper lay untouched as evening deepened into nightfall. Finally, as the castle noises diminished, Richard thought he would be safe preparing his makeshift rope. First, he unwrapped the silk cords from the bed curtains. No, they didn't look strong enough to hold him. He threw them aside reached under the coverlet, dragging out the sheet. Drawing his dagger, he cut a notch in the edge so he could tear it. But the fabric was too tight! It wouldn't give. Grunting in frustration, Richard concentrated on holding the sheet and dragging his dagger straight down, forcing a ragged cut and reducing the fabric to wide strips he could tie together. It took a long time—but time was one thing he had plenty of. He was sure it was after midnight when he had tied his fabric rope to the bedpost and threw it out the window. Nobody bothered patrolling this side of the castle, so he felt relatively safe.

Taking off his friar's robe, Richard climbed onto the window sill, sitting with his legs dangling outside. He still wore his short houppelande, doublet and hose, though they were dirty now and not very well suited for clambering out of windows! Not that he had any choice. He held the fabric rope in his hand, wondering how he was going to get down to the ground. It seemed like such a good idea before, but now that he was sitting in the dark, everything beneath him was black. He didn't even know if his cord was long enough. How would he even get started? He never climbed anything his whole life. Fighting a surge of fear,

251

Richard gritted his teeth and clutched the fabric, rolling over onto his stomach and scrabbling for a toehold in the stone wall. Gasping for breath, he stayed still, listening. He heard a distant owl hooting. Nothing else. It was time.

First one hand, then the next, he slowly let himself down, almost gasping in relief when he encountered one of the knots. It was easier bracing his feet against the wall and he felt a bit more confident until his arms started shaking. It was agony, but he couldn't turn back now. He must continue; surely the ground wasn't too far away. A little more and his hands started cramping. He just couldn't hold onto the sheet any longer. By this point he no longer cared. Saying a quick prayer, he let go, hoping to land on his feet.

In a second he slammed into the ground and lurched forward, trying to break his fall with his hands. His knees hit a thick clump of weeds, overgrown with bracken which softened the blow. But his hands scraped on the wall and he couldn't suppress a groan. He rolled on his side, breathing heavily. This was terrible. Once the pain slackened, he concluded that nothing was broken and perhaps he hadn't fallen that far after all. Sitting up, he leaned against the wall and listened. Two owls were hooting now and a dog barked.

But before he even finished catching his breath he heard the shouting of pursuers, and he closed his eyes, waiting for someone to drag him to his feet. They were none too gentle. The guards came up with torches while two of the largest men grabbed him by each arm, hauling the poor king up while he tried to get his feet under him. Grumbling, they put each of his arms over their shoulders and lifted him, carrying their burden back to his room. By then, his keepers had discovered his handiwork and it took six men to drag the bed across the floor and away from the window—not that he was likely to attempt a second escape.

"I want ten armed men watching him at all times," growled Humphrey of Buckingham as the guards lay Richard on the bed. "Inside the room and out. Go," the earl pointed, "get someone to tend his wounds. He's bleeding." He looked angrily at the king. "Why in the world did you do that? What a foolish thing to do."

Richard kept his eyes closed, ignoring his tormentor. But he couldn't stop the tears that forced their way from under his lids. He knew better than anyone he had just ruined his last chance at freedom. He would never see the sun as a free man again.

CHAPTER 24

Even though Richard was stiff and sore, he was shoved onto his horse the next morning and the party proceeded on their way to London. They went by slow stages, spending the night in Coventry, Daventry, Northampton, Dunstable, then St. Albans. King Richard wasn't permitted to change his clothes the whole time. When Henry Bolingbroke and his army were two leagues distant from London, they saw a great delegation approaching. The clanging of drums and the bursts of trumpets announced the Londoners' elation. It would difficult to say which side's racket carried the day, for the duke's followers were equally demonstrative, their music carrying a totally different tune, clashing with the newcomers. Rank upon rank the Londoners marched, with each trade wearing its own liveries and carrying arms, while the mayor walked in front, a sword held up before him—*as if he were a duke* it was later said by witnesses.

Stopping before Henry, the Londoners briefly saluted King Richard who still rode his little horse in the second rank. Then they all shouted as one, "Long Live Henry, the noble Duke of Lancaster, who has conquered all England in less than a month! Such a lord deserves to be king!" and similar cries. They compared him to Alexander the Great and thanked the Lord for sending such a miracle. Letting the duke and his cortege pass through their ranks, they all turned and approached the city, singing and playing their horns and sending up such a chorus of celebration that Richard wanted to put his hands over his ears.

Finally, when they were within two miles of London, Henry called the procession to a stop and the citizens finally quieted their music. Once he knew he could be heard, Bolingbroke called out, "Earl Thomas of Arundel and Earl Humphrey of Buckingham, bring forth King Richard!"

Summoned like a criminal, the king was led before the citizens of London on his broken-down nag. Duke Henry dismounted and, with a grand gesture, doffed his chaperon toward Richard. "My lord, alight," he said. "Here are your good friends of London who are come to see you!"

His face covered with tears, the king climbed down from his mount. Placing himself to Richard's left side, Henry said, "My lords and friends, here is King Richard. I deliver him into your custody and beg you to do with him what you wish. And here, my good cousins of Buckingham and Arundel will go with you."

Richard turned to Henry in astonishment. Surely his cousin wouldn't expose him to the ill will of the London rabble! But alas, the duke's intentions were unmistakable. Like Pontius Pilate, Richard saw, the Duke of Lancaster was washing his hands of his sovereign. If he came to an accidental death, Henry could say he was innocent of the deed.

Luckily, once he was in their charge, the Londoners took the king's safety more seriously than expected. They placed him on a more suitable horse and led him through back ways to Westminster. When they ushered Richard to the royal apartments, he was presented with another shock. Just the week before, the mob had forced its way through the palace gates and into his own suite, destroying his precious tapestries, smashing his beds and furnishings, leaving his rooms a shameful wreck. No one had yet made any attempt to clean up the mess. Richard whirled around, blinking back tears.

"We've had our disagreements in the past," he said sadly. "But did my countrymen have reason to hate me so?"

Mayor Knolles stared for a moment in disgust. *He can't be serious*, he thought. *Then again, why would he have cared? We're nothing to him. Well, as the old proverb said, you reap what you sow.* He couldn't think of a better example than right in front of him.

Remembering his dignity, the mayor waved his arm for attention. "Bring something for the king to sleep on," he instructed some pages. "We must keep him here for the night."

While Richard sat, dejected, there was a bustle around him while servants cleared a space and set up a pallet for him to sleep on. "I would see the Dean of the King's Chapel," he said to the mayor.

Knolles lowered his head. "I am sorry to say he has been seized by the citizens of London."

"What! They dare assault my clergy?"

"They have been taken to Newgate."

"Newgate! They were arrested because they serve me?"

"Sire, I will take up the matter with Duke Henry. This is why you need our protection. Tomorrow we will take you to the Tower, where you will be safe."

Left alone, Richard sat on the edge of his pallet, looking at the walls of his Painted Chamber and remembering the last time he used this room. It was the night before his Westminster parliament, when he amused himself and feasted with his closest friends. It seemed like a hundred years ago. The wheel of fortune had brought him to the top at that moment. *What would he have done differently, had he known the future?* He didn't dare dwell on it.

After a long night at Westminster, the mayor and citizens of London brought the king's horse once again. After he mounted they surrounded him with a protective barrier of concerned aldermen. Walking through the city all the way to the Tower, Richard's guardians left plenty of space around the king so everyone could see him. Many were the hateful taunts that sped the king on his way. "Now are we avenged of this little bastard, who has governed us so ill!" he heard one cry. That was early on, before he ceased to listen. Occasionally, a kind voice was raised in his support, such as the boy who followed them for a while, saying, "Behold King Richard, who has done so much good to the kingdom of England!" Or was the youth being sarcastic? The king neither knew nor cared. He was more concerned by the ruffians who were trying to shove their way past the men who swore to protect him. Occasionally a rotten vegetable flew through the air, and more than once he was struck by a lucky aim, but for the most part the Londoners contented themselves with shouting and cursing. His gaolers, Arundel and Buckingham, didn't lift a finger to help; they rode in front, clearing the road.

Finally, once they passed over the drawbridge and through the barbican at the Tower, Richard felt safe. He had rarely come here in his adult life; the bad memory of past experiences never left him. And here he was, prisoner a third time. He looked up at the buildings, thinking they were exactly the same, and yet he had changed so very much. But his reverie was interrupted by a jab to the shoulder, as Arundel pushed him forward. At least they housed him in the state apartments in the White Tower, even though his ever-present sentinels were not removed from his sight. He was pretty certain that their purpose was to annoy rather than guard him.

Finally, he could remove his torn and dirty clothes and even luxuriate in a bath. For the moment, there was no need for his captors to humiliate him. Leaning back in the hot water, he was grateful the first time in his life for the ministrations of servants. Bathing was no longer taken for granted, nor was sleeping in a soft bed.

For three days Richard was alone in the Tower. This time he didn't mind. He needed the opportunity to rest, to bring himself back to a semblance of clarity. He was under no illusions about his imprisonment; he knew he was at the mercy of his merciless cousin. But at least he regained his composure, for he needed it to face the difficult times ahead.

The king's first visitor was young Arundel, who presented himself with a message from Duke Henry. "Where is Humphrey?" Richard asked, not really caring. He was intrigued by the expression on Thomas's face.

"He is...dead."

"Dead? Buckingham, dead?"

"He died of the plague. Just yesterday."

Richard crossed himself. "God struck him down," he said quietly but his voice was full of menace. "You should take that as a warning to yourself."

For a moment Arundel visibly trembled. Then he straightened. "Sire, Duke Henry desires you to come down to see him below."

257

Richard drew himself up. "I will do no such thing! Arundel, go tell Henry of Lancaster if he wishes to speak with me, he must come here."

Hesitating, the other bowed slightly and left the room. Finally, Richard felt less like a victim and more like a king. If he could only sustain the illusion!

Apparently Henry decided to oblige him, and a few minutes later the duke came back accompanied by the Duke of York and Edward Rutland. At first, Richard was shocked to see them even though he knew about their defection. But for them to join forces with that traitor as if nothing was wrong! How could they face him?

Showing respect he didn't feel, Bolingbroke nevertheless removed his hat and bowed. The other two hung back uncomfortably. "My Lord," said Henry, "here is our cousin the Duke of Aumale and his father our uncle, who wish to speak with you."

Paling in anger, Richard could barely keep his voice civil. "Cousin, they are not worthy to speak to me."

"But have the goodness to hear them," Henry insisted, gesturing to his side.

The look of hate Richard turned on York would have made a greater man quail. Edmund stepped back a pace.

"Thou villain! What could you possibly say to me? And you, traitor of Rutland! You are not worthy to bear the name of duke, earl, or even knight. You, and the villain your father, you have both foully betrayed me! I pray to God, and to St. John the Baptist, that cursed be the hour you were born. Alas that I should ever have been so fond of so false a traitor!" He stamped his foot. "For by thee the kingdom of England will be destroyed, I am convinced!"

Rather than show any remorse, the Earl of Rutland curled his lip. "You lie," he declared, and threw his hat on the floor.

Furious, Richard kicked the hat away. "Traitor! I am king and thy lord, and will still continue king and will reach greater heights than ever before, in spite of all my enemies. And you are not fit to speak to me!"

Henry stepped in and put out a restraining hand. "Enough," he said to Rutland, "or I will order the Constable to put a stop to this."

Richard whirled around, turning his anger on Henry. "Why do you keep me so closely guarded by your men-at-arms? I wish to know if you acknowledge me as your lord and king, or what you mean to do with me?"

Henry was surprised at his fervor. How many times could this man bounce back? He said carefully, "It is true you are my king and lord, but the council of the realm has ordered that you should be kept in confinement until the day of the meeting of Parliament."

Seething, Richard railed at his helplessness. "Then at least bring the queen my wife to me so I may speak with her!"

Again, Henry pretended to be concerned. "Excuse me, my lord. It is forbidden by the council."

Richard couldn't contain himself. He strode back and forth. "You have acknowledged me as your king these twenty-two years! How dare you use me so cruelly?"

"My lord, we cannot do otherwise until Parliament meets."

"Pretense! What nonsense! Such drivel!" As the others watched quietly, he continued his pacing. "Oh God of Paradise! How can You suffer the wrongs these people commit against me? I declare that you are false traitors to God as well as me. And this I will prove against any four of the best of you with my body, like the loyal knight that I am." He glared at them. "I never forfeited my knighthood! And here is my pledge!"

This time it was Richard who threw his hat on the floor. Regretfully, Henry dropped to his knees.

"Please, my lord, restrain yourself until Parliament meets. And then everyone can present his arguments."

Having spent his anger, Richard stood breathing heavily. "At least, for God's sake, let me be brought to trial so I can defend myself, and give answer to their complaints."

Standing, Henry bowed his head. "My Lord, be not afraid. Nothing unreasonable shall be done to you." Without waiting for an answer, he left the room. York and Rutland followed him.

Richard stared at the door as the key turned in the lock. "I am lost," he said to himself. "They will never let me speak to Parliament, for they have no rejoinder. I can see it; they fear me and must destroy me."

CHAPTER 25

Although Richard was destined not to know any of this, the following four weeks were fraught with anxiety for Henry. He needed to discover a procedure that would secure Richard's abdication, or his deposition, or both. It had to be regular and proper by law. Of course, the only precedent was the messy deposition of Edward II, and Henry hoped to find a more acceptable alternative. Edward was deposed first, then the weeping king abdicated afterwards—only when they threatened to disinherit his son if he refused. In this case, most of Henry's councilors favored Richard's abdication first, then his deposition. But how? Under what pretenses? The Duke of Lancaster sent out people far and wide, to search the archives and scriptoria in all the important monasteries. They were under instructions to find precedents. At this point, anything would do. He couldn't claim direct descent from a king, though he tried to resurrect that old rumor about Edmund Crouchback. It was said by some that Edmund, Henry's maternal ancestor, was actually the firstborn of Henry III, passed over because he was deformed in mind and body. But too many legal experts, including the archbishop, refused to countenance such nonsense. Henry was desperate. They had called Parliament for September 30 and time was running out.

Archbishop Arundel was impatient with all this manipulation. He wanted to keep it clean: persuade Richard to abdicate in favor of Henry. After that, the rest would be easy. There must be a way.

So Richard was visited by a succession of well-wishers who he soon recognized as spies. After all, his servants had been taken away and he was surrounded by strangers who hoped to pick up a glimmer of evidence to use against him. At first, the callers' talk was innocuous. Soon the conversations turned disturbing. One afternoon, Henry's new treasurer invited himself

261

to dine with the king. Not bothering to object, Richard continued eating.

"What is your name?" the king asked.

"John Norbury, sire." He gestured for a servant to cut him a piece of mincemeat pie.

"Norbury." Richard dabbed a napkin against his lips. "You are an old retainer of Lancaster." It was more of a statement than a question. "And you are replacing poor LeScrope, who was traitorously beheaded at Bristol."

Taking a bite, Norbury ignored the rebuff. "We must keep the government moving."

"I dare say," Richard grunted. "Without a leader, the country will quickly fall into chaos. That is, if it hasn't already."

"Duke Henry does what he can. The council—"

"Surely you are not removing my councilors!"

The other looked pained. "If you recall, sire, you agreed that Duke Henry would help you govern your people better."

"Is this how he helps me? By locking me away and denying me access to my advisors?"

"Sire, Duke Henry instructs me to tell you he is doing his best to organize his council with loyal and trusted men."

"*His* council?" Richard put down the knife. "Am I not still the king?"

Norbury bowed his head, saying nothing.

"Am I to understand I will be obliged to submit to a continual council—the same that was declared after they impeached my chancellor, Michael de la Pole?" Richard threw down his napkin, disgusted.

"I am sorry to say I am not privy to the decisions of Duke Henry."

"Well, you can tell your duke I am very displeased."

That was weak and both of them knew it. Richard was disconcerted and left the room without another word. Norbury quickly finished his dinner and disappeared. He had dropped the first hint. The king would surely mull it over.

Richard did more than that. He paced back and forth in his bedchamber, shouting at his servants to leave him alone, throwing whatever he could get his hands on at the closing door. He was no fool. He was not even king in name. His name was scorned, spurned even by his lowest countryman. But surely, his regality must have some meaning.

"They can't take that away from me," he told the empty room. "They can take away my power, but they can't take my crown."

The following day, another of Henry's retainers visited the king. Richard could see this was to be a regular exercise. "What is it you want?" he growled at the newcomer. "Make it quick."

The man bowed. "Sire, Duke Henry is preparing for Parliament. He wishes you to know that Roger Walden has stepped aside and Thomas Arundel has agreed to assume the Archbishopric of Canterbury once again."

Richard looked sideways at him and started pacing.

"The Bishop of Exeter has agreed to step down as chancellor and Archbishop Arundel will temporarily serve in his stead—"

"Until they figure out what to do with me!" Richard interrupted. "Get out!"

Daunted, the man scurried from the room. The king slapped his hands against his forehead. "My worst enemy as chancellor and archbishop! I swear, he is more dangerous than Henry."

In dribs and drabs, information was fed to Richard— whatever Henry thought was necessary for the king to know. *What was he leaving out?* That bothered Richard worse than the bad news he was given. By the time he was visited by Adam of Usk, he had fallen deeper into one of his depressions which threatened never to go away. A visitor meant little or nothing to him.

The king was sitting at his meal, once again, when Adam was announced. Looking up, Richard observed him for a moment, then went back to his supper. The newcomer sat across the table from him.

After a long pause, Richard said, "What is your name?"

"Adam of Usk, sire."

"Usk. From Monmouthshire?"

"Why, yes. That's right."

"I think I knew your father. Another Adam, I believe."

"Yes. He told me he had the honor to serve you on occasion. Some financial matter."

Richard sat back, almost grateful for a semblance of recognition from anybody. "Was he not in the service of the Earl of March?"

The other nodded, helping himself to a slice of lamb. "Both the third earl and the fourth."

"Poor man," Richard said. "Sir Roger and I had our differences, but he didn't deserve to die in such an undignified manner—at the hands of those savage Irishmen, no less. If it weren't for his slaying, I might not have made my disastrous expedition this year. Much would have been different." His eyes took on a far-away look and he pushed the food around on his plate. "My God, what a wonderful land is this, and a fickle, which has exiled, slain, destroyed, or ruined so many rulers and great men. It is forever tainted with strife and envy. Think back on the famous Boudica, whose daughters were raped in front of her by the treacherous Romans. And even though she raised eighty thousand men to repel the invaders, in the end she was forced to take poison rather than submit. Look at Edward the Martyr, killed by his step-mother so Aethelred the Unready could rule in his place. Then there was brave Harold Godwineson, killed in battle by the usurping Norman. And poor Arthur of Brittany, true heir after Richard I, murdered in his cell by his uncle John. But worst of all, let's not forget my own great-grandfather, King Edward II, forced to abdicate then killed in prison. Is it a wonder I am so forlorn?"

By now, Richard was talking to himself and Adam looked about the room, noticing the unfriendly guards standing at every door and the stealthy servants lingering about the table. Despite himself, Adam felt a great pity for this unhappy man and departed quietly, disregarding his orders to spy on the king.

As September drew on, Duke Henry was losing patience. Richard was never going to give anything up on his own; it was time to force the issue. And so, a week before the month's end, Richard's latest visitor was the former Archbishop Roger Walden. The king was sitting in his throne with the little red canopy still intact, though it drooped to one side, in need of shoring up. He watched Walden approach, his expression saddened, and leaned forward as the newcomer knelt.

"My dear Bishop, I see that you, too, have met with misfortune."

Touched by Richard's solicitude, Walden's eyes misted. "Sire, my troubles are as nothing compared to yours."

The king's mouth trembled, for he knew his old friend's visit was outside of the normal venue. "You must have something momentous to tell me, otherwise my cousin would not have permitted your visit. Here, sit beside me."

Gratefully accepting a chair, the bishop bowed his head. "Duke Henry wanted someone friendly to speak with you, sire. To prepare you."

Richard stared at him. "Prepare me," he said dully. "For what?"

With a deep sigh, Walden took both Richard's hands. "He has accepted the council's decision requiring your resignation."

The king stopped breathing. He knew this was coming. Henry had already broken his oath many times. Why else had they imprisoned him like a common felon? But now that the words were spoken, he couldn't believe it. "It is possible," he said slowly, "that I agreed to resign the rule of the kingdom, much as I was forced to do in 1386." The bishop nodded in encouragement, hoping he would continue. But Richard sat up straight in his throne. "But what about my right to speak before Parliament? Even the lowliest criminal is given the right to defend himself."

The bishop looked pained. "As far as I can tell, this is a risk they are unwilling to take."

"So I am able to say nothing. I am less than my meanest subject." For a moment he looked likely to fall into a deep despondency. But his natural conceit reasserted itself. "Must I remind him I am an anointed king? You can't just make that go away! It is a sacred trust, conferring the seven gifts of the Holy Spirit upon my head." He proceeded to name them, while the bishop mouthed the words in unison. "Wisdom, understanding, counsel, fortitude, knowledge, piety, and fear of the Lord." Richard broke into tears, sobbing, "You can't *un*king a king."

265

Not knowing what to say, Walden hoped his presence would comfort his old friend. But it was not possible. Caught up in his own misery, Richard cursed his bad fortune, his unworthy subjects, his disloyal magnates. He had said it all before, and it was only a matter of time before even he saw the uselessness of complaining. Nonetheless, the bishop was patient. He could offer consolation once his penitent was ready to listen. After exhausting himself with lamenting, Richard accepted a cup of wine.

"Let us pray," Walden said, getting ready to kneel. But the king stopped him.

"Nay. I fear God has abandoned me."

Shocked, the bishop opened his mouth to object. Richard shook his head, silencing him. "I've prayed until my knees are red and chafed. There is nothing more I can do in that respect. If it is His will that Lancaster sit on the throne of our ancestors, then I must ponder on God's judgment." He put a hand on Walden's arm. "But I thank you for your kindness. Tonight, I must reflect on my mortification."

Walden's was the only visit that would give Richard comfort. At least he was warned.

Still, he wasn't expecting matters to deteriorate so quickly. The very next day, one of Henry's sheriffs marched in, looking very strict and uncompromising. He gave a half-bow to the king who had been standing by the window. Richard turned, putting his hands behind his back to control their shaking.

"Sire," the man said, "the Duke of Lancaster has sent me to recommend that you seriously consider resigning your crown. He instructed me to tell you the country has risen in his favor and has called for you to step down."

Richard knew *that* well enough after his humiliating entry into London. But he did not deign to give the man an answer.

"The duke has steadfastly resisted demands for your execution," the sheriff went on. "Sire, you can no longer count on the support of the commons. Or your magnates."

Richard felt his face flush under sudden pressure. *Execution!* Henry had gone too far! Or was this threat from someone else? Who controlled access to the Tower? Who sent this

266

man? "And what does Lancaster promise in exchange for my crown?" the king growled.

For a moment the other was at a loss. "He made no promises," he said finally.

"And I am supposed to just walk away, after twenty-two years as your king?"

"The people demand it."

"Go. Tell your Duke Henry his offer has been declined." He turned back to the window, wondering what he was going to do next.

The following day, another stranger came in. This man looked even meaner than the sheriff. He didn't bother to bow. "Sire, Duke Henry has sent me—"

"With a demand to resign my crown," interrupted Richard. "Has he decided to make me an offer?"

The man sneered. "If you value your life, you will strongly consider abdicating the throne."

"I refuse to believe this came from Bolingbroke!" Richard finally lost his temper. "Who sent you?"

The other shrugged. "Believe what you will. It doesn't matter. You have nothing to offer except your crown. Abdicate and Duke Henry will see you are taken care of."

"I'm sure he will," retorted the king. "Leave me. Your presence offends me."

Turning his back on the man, Richard crossed to the window. He looked out over the inner bailey, watching soldiers practice their swordplay, while others made a wide berth around them. Once again, he thought back on that other time he was imprisoned in the Tower while the Appellants debated whether he should be deposed or not. On that lonely New Year's day, he thought he could never fall lower. He grunted. He doubted whether they were debating the wisdom of his deposition now. They need only figure out how to do it.

Retiring early, Richard tossed and turned, not even bothering to get up the next morning. He lay in bed, staring at the tapestry on the far wall. He knew he was losing his bravado. There was too much time to think. Did Henry really threaten him? Was his cause completely lost? What about his regality? It certainly did not help him at Conwy, while he still had his freedom.

After noon, he finally got up, not bothering to change out of his night clothes. Hearing the door open, he whirled around, ready to throw something. But his new visitor was so unexpected that he dropped, unbelieving, onto a bench. It was Thomas Despenser—who should have been in Wales raising support.

Shamefaced, Thomas darted across the room and threw himself to one knee. "Sire," he sobbed, "I am desolate."

Richard was so glad to see a familiar face he found little rancor inside of him. "What happened?"

"After Lichfield, the Welsh started deserting; they had given up and didn't want to venture too far into England. We were planning one last attack when Henry's men found us first. The Welsh scattered after a pitiful defense, but Lancaster's knights chased them down while others surrounded me. They captured many of my men and tied them to the tails of their horses, dragging them across the ground until they were dead." He put a hand over his eyes. "It was terrible. I could do nothing to help them. After that, they brought me to the duke, who offered a pardon if I joined him." He swallowed, biting back his sobs. "What else could I do? I was alone, unarmed, and defenseless. I am so disconsolate."

By now, Richard had gone beyond recrimination. There were so many desertions, one more did not make any difference. "Sit, my friend. Why did they send you?"

Thomas coughed, still on his knee. "Something happened since Northumberland visited us at Conwy. Duke Henry has decided that nothing short of..." he slowed down.

"The crown," Richard finished. "Nothing short of the crown will please him. I know. They have threatened my life if I don't abdicate."

The shock on Thomas's face confirmed he was not complicit. Then he pursed his lips. "That's not Henry's way."

Richard nodded, deep in thought. "I thought the same thing. But who could have sent these knaves?" He moved over on his bench. "Sit, I say. Come closer to my ear."

The other obliged, whispering. "I would venture to say Thomas Arundel might be behind those threats. He has been directing Henry's every move."

"The archbishop. He hates me."

"He is very ambitious."

"He's ruthless. You might be right. It makes sense, doesn't it? Henry need not get his hands dirty, but there's no doubt he consents to anything Arundel proposes." He cocked his head toward Thomas. "I still don't know why you are here."

"They want me to persuade you. To tell you that you have no choice. They are coming tomorrow morning with a writ for you to sign. An abdication."

Richard sat silent for a long time. "This is it, then. They will kill me, you know."

Thomas was shocked. "Surely not!"

The look Richard gave him was more like you'd give an innocent child. "They killed Edward II, didn't they?"

"But—" Thomas didn't know what to say. His ancestor, too, had been caught up in that revolution. It had only been two years since Richard lifted the judgments against the Despensers. What would happen if Henry became king? Chastened, he lowered his head.

Richard was watching him. "Yes," he said, "you see how deep this goes. If I fall, my new nobles fall with me. There will be no one to protect you." He paused. "Do you still want me to abdicate?"

Tears falling, Thomas fell to his knees. "This has gone beyond anyone's wishes. But I will no longer speak for Bolingbroke. In fearing for my life, I fell into his trap."

Putting a hand on the other's head, Richard gazed up, not really seeing anything. "So did I, Thomas. So did I."

The following morning found Richard in his throne, dressed in his finest robes. He was leaning back, having slept sitting up. His face was haggard and he watched through narrowed eyes as the deputation trudged into the chamber. Richard knew enough about the law to recognize that they were carefully chosen to represent the estates, spiritual and temporal. He noted them all: two for the clergy, two for the earls, two for the barons, two for knights, plus two doctors and two notaries. The great chamber was barely large enough to contain this exalted embassy in comfort. Of course, Richard didn't care.

"Since I have no one to speak for me," the king said, looking directly at Northumberland who showed not the slightest discomfort, "I shall speak for myself. What brings you here this day?"

The Archbishop of York had been chosen as the spokesman. He stepped forward and unrolled a scroll. "On behalf of the Great Council of England, we have come to ascertain whether you are willing to resign the right you have to the crown of England with its appurtenances. That is to say, in the kingdoms of England, France, Ireland and Scotland, the duchies of Guyenne and Normandy, the county of Ponthieu, and the town of Calais, and in all the other castles, fortresses and towns. This resignation stands for yourself and your heirs into perpetuity."

Richard extended his hand, trying to retain his dignity. "Let me see this in writing." The archbishop rolled up the scroll and handed it forward. The king accepted the parchment, not looking at it. "I understood that Duke Henry has returned from exile to claim his own inheritance, and no more. This was sworn to me by oath. Since when did this inheritance include the crown?" Again he glared at Northumberland. The earl stared straight forward, not returning his gaze. Disgusted, Richard stood and walked to the door. He turned before going through. "I wish to consider your request until tomorrow morning. You may go."

Another long day and night. Richard read the Act of Resignation over and over again, then strode from room to room in his royal apartments; his guards would let him go no further. He picked at his dinner, went back to the document, and as the daylight failed, lit extra candles.

"I must practice if I am forced to read this...travesty to the assembled lords." He took a deep breath, putting his elbows on the parchment. "In the name of God, Amen!" he read out loud. "I, Richard, by the grace of God, king of England and France and Lord of Ireland, quit and absolve Archbishops, Bishops, Dukes, Earls, Barons, Lords, and all my other liegemen. I Resign all my Kingly Majesty, Dignity and Crown—" he broke into a sob but read on, still sobbing, "and with deed and word I leave off and Resign them and go from them for evermore." Putting his forehead on the table, he let out a moan. Then he sat back up, took another ragged breath, and brought the candle closer to the parchment. "For I know myself to be, and have been in the past, insufficient, unable, and unsuited, and I deem myself not unworthy to be brought down." He threw back his head, looking at the ceiling. "How can I possibly agree to this?"

Getting up, he strode back and forth before the empty fireplace. It was chilly this evening and he wrapped a cloak around his shoulders. Then he stopped in front of the table again, reading. "And I swear on the holy gospels that I shall never take exception to this resignation, so help me God." Not believing this for a minute, he crossed himself. "I Richard, king aforesaid, with my own hand have written me underneath here."

He fell into his chair. "And I'm supposed to just tamely hand over my crown to Bolingbroke?" He spat out the *B*. He put a hand on his crown, sitting atop a pillow on a small table beside the throne. Then he looked down at the royal signet ring, turning it around his finger. "I suppose I must give you up too." Closing his eyes, he shook his head. "Oh, Great-grandfather," he moaned, "no one understands better than I what you went through when they demanded your abdication. I tried, dear king, to have you canonized. Now I fear my suit will collapse. Please forgive me." He paused, frowning. "But at least the tears you shed were in favor of your son. Look at my shame; I must give up my throne to my worst enemy. How can I allow this to happen?" His eyes glistened in the candlelight as he sat with the gloom darkening around him.

Suddenly, he was struck with a new thought. Pulling the inkwell toward him, he dipped a quill and drew a line through the sentence containing the words "insufficient, unable, and unsuited..." In its place, he wrote, "I understand that my government had not been acceptable to the people, and I relinquish the ruling to others." But there needed to be more. Pulling a blank page of paper from a cupboard, he proceeded to add three declarations to the document. First, that he did not intend to renounce his identity as God's anointed and true king.

271

Secondly, he reserved the profits from lands and tenements he had purchased for the making of his obit—a yearly anniversary for his soul at Westminster Abbey. Thirdly, he renounced the command of government so that Lord Henry, Duke of Lancaster, should succeed him next in the rule of the kingdom.

"There," he said, sitting back in satisfaction. "That should appease my cousin." Finally, he could get a good night's sleep.

The next day was Michaelmas. At nine o'clock in the morning the same lords promptly entered Richard's chamber, accompanied by six newcomers, including Richard's old friend, the Abbot of Westminster. Seated on his throne under the canopy of state, the king affected his regal pose, looking over everyone's head.

Once again, the Archbishop of York was their spokesman. "Sire," he said, bowing, "have you considered sufficiently what your reply to this bill shall be?"

"I have," Richard said. "I find the wording offensive and I will not sign it under any circumstances."

Judging by the distress of the onlookers, this was certainly not the reaction they expected. Where was their despondent prisoner? He lowered his glance, glaring at the archbishop. "I would like to have it explained to me just how I could possibly resign the crown, and to whom?" He was warming up to his objection. "I do not wish, nor was it ever my intention to renounce those characters impressed upon my soul by the sacramental unction received on my coronation day!" He stood, fists clenched. "You may force me to abdicate from governing, but you cannot expect me to abandon my kingship!"

Collectively, this room contained many of the most prominent, the best educated minds in the country. One after another, they argued—point by point—the most legitimate reasons he could resign his crown. Sitting back down, leaning to one side, Richard heard them out until they ran out of words. He waved his hand dismissively.

"Bring my dear cousin of Lancaster here, for I might find myself willing, under certain conditions—which I shall explain to him—to make my resignation to him alone."

The Lords accepted the king's demand and left once again, promising to return with Duke Henry after dinner. As agreed, the duke came, accompanied by Archbishop Arundel. When they entered the room the pair withdrew into a corner to confer with Richard while the others waited, outside of hearing.

This time, Henry eschewed his former deferential behavior and appeared more assertive; all pretense was gone. His lips pressed together, his eyes steely, he stood with his arms crossed, as though he begrudged this time away from other duties. "What's this I hear about conditions?" Henry asked.

Richard fought down his vexation. This was no time to throw a tantrum. "I will agree to sign this document under three conditions."

"No. You must sign this abdication unconditionally."

Richard turned away, about to tear up the writ.

"No, wait," argued the archbishop. He whispered in Henry's ear. "At least hear what he has to say."

Exhaling in annoyance, Henry nodded. "What is it you want?"

Richard paced in front of him. "I will agree to resign the rule of the kingdom to you. But you must understand, I cannot change my essence as God's anointed and true king." He paused, waiting for a response.

Henry stared at him, thinking. If Richard wanted to go on calling himself king, what did it matter? He would spend the rest of his life under lock and key, anyway. He gave a slight nod.

"I also request that I may retain the lands I acquired in order to endow an anniversary for my soul in Westminster Abbey." He waited for an answer but Henry did not oblige. Richard sighed. "Cousin, if you agree to this I will sign the abdication papers in your favor."

Henry exchanged glances with Arundel. "Very well," he said finally. "I agree to allow your obituary lands. Please now, sire, put your hand to this writ."

As Richard stood before the throne and read the document aloud, including the changes he had made, Henry and Arundel put their heads together. While the assembled lords and prelates listened to the king, the archbishop whispered in Henry's ear. "I have a copy of the original which we shall read before Parliament tomorrow. We have witnesses that the king has signed the writ. No one need know about his trifling alterations."

And so, as Richard proceeded to sign away his throne—clinging to the conviction he was still God's anointed—the sense of relief was palpable throughout the room. Many of the participants in this monumental proceeding had secret doubts about the legality of Henry's usurpation. But on the balance, all would agree that the promise of a new reign outweighed the illicit means employed to get there. At least for now.

Once the other witnesses had signed the document, Henry placed his own initials before stepping back in expectation. Richard knew what to do. Taking his crown off the pillow, he studied it one last time before placing it on the floor before Henry's feet. Then he pulled off his signet ring and put it in the center of the circlet.

"I surrender this crown—not to you, but to God," he said. Henry didn't particularly care. It was done. He would never need to see Richard again.

CHAPTER 26

On September 30, the men summoned to Parliament assembled at Westminster in front of an empty throne. Indeed, it was later said that this was no Parliament at all, since there was no king to preside. Richard would have agreed most vehemently, but of course, he was not permitted to attend. He was left all alone in his royal apartments in the Tower, aside from his ubiquitous guards, to contemplate and wonder just what was going on in his absence. He would have strenuously objected to the thirty-three charges—officiously named the Record and Process—read at length to justify Henry's usurpation. He tortured himself with a vision of Henry sitting on his throne, nodding benignly at the cheering crowd. All those men had once sworn their loyalty to him. Some had even given their love, or so he thought. Where were his trusted friends, so recently showered with titles and preferences? Not one of them dared show his face. No welcome ally ventured to commiserate with him. The whole day passed in quiet contemplation, just like every September day that preceded this one—except now, he was a nonentity, a dependent, a liability in his cousin's dominion.

On the next day, he was almost happy to see a new delegation—anyone, to break up the sphere of silence. Most of the members were the same as before, but this time they were led by Justice William Thirning in order to confer more gravity to the audience. The spokesman appeared uncomfortable to Richard—as well he should be, because he had not been privy to anything that occurred before.

Bowing, Thirning began, "Sire, it is well known to you that there was a Parliament summoned of all States of the Realm, and everything I shall say to you is on its behalf. Sire, remember that in this very room you resigned your Lordship of your own free will, and discharged all your lieges of their obedience. Hence,

275

we the commissioners as proctors of all these estates now retract their homage and fealty from yourself."

"I did not!" cried Richard, standing before his throne. "I did not renounce my Lordship! I am an anointed king. I am unable to renounce my sacramental unction. Ever."

"But wait. It says it right here. In your own Renunciation, you said you were insufficient, unable, and unsuited to govern."

"This is not true! I said that my government had not been acceptable to the people."

"But the words I read have been clearly stated in the confession. I have a copy right here!" He held it out for the king.

Snatching the paper out of his hand, Richard saw right away that it was a copy of the original Resignation—not the one he made changes to. Suddenly, it all became clear. What he had done to the confession of the Duke of Gloucester had just come back to haunt him. An omission here, a changed word there, and nobody would know the difference. Just like the hapless William Rickhill, Justice Thirning was the innocent dupe of an unscrupulous king. He was performing a farce for the benefit of an unsuspecting populace. Richard looked at the others in the room. Some exhibited puzzlement, others boredom. No one dared—or cared to—object.

Perhaps God was passing judgment on him, after all.

Smiling sadly, Richard passed the document back to Thirning. "I hope my cousin will be a good lord to me and not deprive me of the means to sustain myself honorably."

If Richard thought he was going to be permitted to live out his life as simply Sir Richard of Bordeaux, he was soon undeceived. For another month he languished in the Tower, and it wouldn't have surprised him to know there was much discussion in the Commons as to his future. He might have been more surprised to learn that many thought he should stand trial for his crimes. He had committed no crimes! Others pressured Henry to execute him. But the new king would hear nothing of that. Finally, on the 26th of October, two archbishops, thirteen bishops, seven abbots, six earls, twenty-seven peers, and three knights were recorded on the parliament roll as saying that Richard should "be kept in safe and secret ward". Two days later, King Henry pronounced before Parliament the sentence of perpetual banishment. Richard's fate had been sealed.

The following night Richard had been asleep for a couple of hours when he was awakened by a knock on his door, immediately followed by the entry of two guards carrying candles.

"Awake, sire," one of them said in a gruff voice.

Richard sat on his bed. "What is the meaning of this?"

"You are to come with us," the other demanded, pushing forward a young page carrying a black garment. "Put on those clothes."

Irritation was turning into alarm. "By whose orders?"

"By order of the king."

"I was not told!"

"Sire, our orders were very clear. We are to take you by boat to your next destination."

"In the middle of the night?" Richard stood, ignoring the servant who was proffering the tunic. "I shall not go."

"You shall, sire, or we are instructed to carry you." The man was neither respectful nor rude. He was just doing his job.

Richard snatched the garment from the page and pulled off his nightclothes. With the boy's help, he dressed and put on his shoes, taking as much time as he dared. His guards stood silently before the open door. The king looked around his room. He had nothing to bring with him; everything had been taken. Straightening to his full height, he declared himself ready.

The watergate at the Tower flowed directly into the Thames. Little did Richard know this was the very portal Archbishop Sudbury attempted to use that terrible day when the rebels murdered him, during the Peasants' Revolt. Seeing the boat at the bottom of the steps, Richard lost his composure.

"No, this is not the way I was supposed to be treated," he insisted, pulling back.

Unimpressed, his guards took the king by the arms and thrust him into the boat. One of them took up the oars while the other restrained their prisoner until he slumped onto his seat.

Other accomplices shut the gates behind them and they were in the river, heading downstream.

"Oh, why was I ever born?" Richard wailed. "No one is to know the fate of this unfortunate king!" His guards let him moan and groan as much as he wanted, for by now they were traveling with the current and the wind threw away his words like so much clatter. After a while the king exhausted himself and sat mutely, watching the shore glide by in the darkness. He couldn't see much, but he knew when they were passing Greenwich. By the time they got to Gravesend, he was too tired to complain anymore.

Over the next couple of weeks, Richard was dragged on a circuitous route. If it was King Henry's plan to confound any possible followers, he succeeded flawlessly. King Richard disappeared from sight. With very few exceptions, no one had any idea where he was locked away. And with very few exceptions, King Richard was never seen again by his countrymen.

Imprisoned at the top of the tallest tower of Pontefract Castle, Richard had nothing but time to dwell on his past mistakes. One wonders if he appreciated the irony that his window looked over the gravesite of Thomas of Lancaster, executed for leading a rebellion against Edward II. Or would the spirit of Lancaster have had the last laugh at the unhappy Plantagenet king who followed his ancestor into infamy?

The lonely captive may have lamented that he was forgotten by one and all. However, as events would prove, the fate of Richard Plantagenet was very much on everybody's mind—friends and enemies alike. Richard's story does not end here, but the rest of his tale is fraught with secrecy and confusion—so complicated it needs to be carried over into Book Three. How ironic that only a few years later, his countrymen would be clamoring for his return. Or seeking to avenge his death. Which was it? No one will ever know for sure.

END OF BOOK TWO

AUTHOR'S NOTE

For 600 years historians have been trying to figure out what went wrong. After Richard took the reins of kingship into his own hands, England became peaceful and prosperous. Chroniclers had little to talk about except the weather. Executioners were unemployed. Richard's court was the most opulent, the most admired in Europe.

The history of Richard's "Tyranny" is full of contradictions. For every claim that he was wicked and vengeful, another historian will insist the opposite. As with the king's later namesake Richard III, the usurper went out of his way to blacken the reputation of his displaced predecessor. None of Richard's contemporaries—at least, no Englishman—dared write to the contrary. Evidence of tampered Parliament Rolls, altered chronicles, and post-usurpation annals go a long way toward demonstrating this one-sided rewriting of history. Unfortunately, the truth—if you dare call it that—gets lost in translation. A study of foreign chroniclers—unfettered by concerns about getting killed—might bring us closer to the real story. And you never know if they are unbiased, either. With luck, a pre-usurpation record might still be hidden away until better days; occasionally they pop up.

I was surprised at how many incidents I believed to be common knowledge were actually contested along the way. It took a lot of head scratching to decide which scenario seemed most likely, based on a random comment here, or a lack of evidence there—or mere common sense. I thought it would be best to document some of the most controversial (as I see them) episodes. Any authors I reference will be in the bibliography.

- *The Death of Thomas of Woodstock, Duke of Gloucester*: Although it was, and still is, widely believed Richard was responsible for Gloucester's death, there was an outside possibility he died of natural causes while imprisoned in Calais. When Richard arrested him without notice, it was said by some that he was seriously ill at the time, and this was why he failed to attend Richard's infamous dinner.

However, the timing was awkward. No one knows exactly when Gloucester died. If he expired on the 25th of August as was commonly believed (though it is unknown whether this was an official announcement or a rumor) it's conceivable he might have died of natural causes. However, if he died on the 8th of September, this mortal illness seems highly unlikely. The detailed description of Gloucester's murder wasn't made until two years later, after Richard's deposition. Sir William Rickhill, who had made such detailed notes of his own participation in Gloucester's confession, gave his evidence in Henry IV's first Parliament and was exonerated—notwithstanding his own acquiescence when reading the tampered confession during Richard's Revenge Parliament. Also, Mowbray's servant John Hall gave the story of Gloucester's murder at the same 1399 Parliament, claiming he only guarded the door. As soon as Hall told his story, he was instantly hustled out and executed for his part in the murder—before he had any chance to be examined in detail.

Professor James Tait (*DID RICHARD II MURDER THE DUKE OF GLOUCESTER?*) gave us the most detailed description of this whole episode, tracking all the dates and highlighting the missing passages in the confession. As far as I can tell, this is still the most definitive argument on the subject, and he concluded that Richard was guilty as charged.

- *Henry IV's disinheritance*:   General histories tend to lump Richard's announcement to disinherit Henry—and extend his outlawry to life—all together in one episode. After taking a closer look, I saw that it was not so simple. First of all, from what I can gather, Henry was not entirely disinherited. Richard was only concerned with the Lancastrian Palatinate and Dukedom. Through the Bohun inheritance as well as the earldom of Derby and the dukedom of Hereford, Henry was still one of the wealthiest men in the country. Secondly, Richard granted Henry's lands to his allies in trust, "until Henry of Lancaster, duke of Hereford, or his heir, shall have sued the same out of the king's hands according to the law of the land or have another grant from the king." This implies that Lancaster would return at some point, though some historians think Richard intended for young Hal to receive the dukedom.

Historian C.D. Fletcher tells us that Richard's revocation of the letters patent do not at any point extend Henry's exile to life. "In fact," Fletcher says, "the only authority for such an extension having taken place is the St. Albans chronicler; scarcely the most reliable authority on such matters, and the major advocate, save Henry himself, of Bolingbroke's grievance of disinheritance." He is referring to Thomas Walsingham, who is most decidedly anti-Ricardian. But most telling of all, in the *Record and Process*—also known as the articles of deposition— there is no specific reference to Richard's seizing Henry's lands. Nor does it mention extending Henry's exile to life. "So why do these articles make no explicit reference to disinheritance?" asks Fletcher. "It seems that this is because, in the letter of the law, this simply did not happen." In such a critical document as the *Record and Process*, if it would have been safe for Henry to accuse Richard of these actions, he certainly would have done it. This is why I chose to go against the prevailing accounts.

- *Richard's flight from south Wales:* The several versions of this event are best described by James Sherborne in his article, "Richard II's Return to Wales, 1399". The confusion is compounded by the writings of Creton, who was taken at face value but who was not an eye-witness; he was with Salisbury at this moment. His confused chronology contributed strongly to wild rumors of the king's erratic behavior. Richard is popularly depicted as panic-stricken and cowardly upon discovering that Henry had taken Bristol and executed Bushy, Green, and LeScrope. It seems to be agreed upon that his army in south Wales faded away. The author of *Traison et Mort* said it diminished from

281

32,000 to 6000 in one night, almost as soon as he landed. Four other sources said he departed while the army was still in the field—though some said desertions continued—and that Percy dismissed the men and told them they were on their own. Almost all agree that Richard left secretly. I have read that Rutland and Percy woke in the morning to find him gone, and disbanded the army in response. I even read speculation that Richard was warned against Rutland's treachery and left in a hurry to save himself. But I am inclined to believe that those two men, who were always a part of the king's intimate circle, must have known he was planning to leave; otherwise, why would Percy go to such much trouble to secure the royal treasure before departing, himself? As for Richard's decision to go north, it seems to me this was his intention all along. That's why he sent Salisbury ahead to raise an army in north Wales. I think his need for disguise came directly from Henry's rapid progress and obvious threat.

In my last two years of research while writing this book, I have vacillated, myself. Had King Richard crossed into insanity, as Professor Steel concluded? Did he believe that because he was an anointed king he could do whatever he wanted, justified by divine right—thus setting a precedent for Henry VIII and Charles I? In the end, I think that if his thoughts tended that way—and they certainly could have—this was secondary to his fear of being threatened and restrained by his magnates. The horrors from the Merciless Parliament of 1387-88 still hung over his head. Getting rid of the Appellants wasn't enough. He needed constant reassurance that the populace wouldn't rise up against him—hence the repeated oaths, blank charters, and forced pardons, and of course the hated Cheshire Guard. Ultimately, I think Caroline Barron said it best in her article *The Tyranny of Richard II*: "all these are the acts of a man who was afraid; of a king, frightened into tyranny. When confronted by the hostility of his subjects Richard tried, not to conciliate them, but to trample them underfoot, and, while he thus intimidated, milked and insulted his subjects and gave them increasing cause to hate and misunderstand him, he was vainly trying to hide from himself the fact that he was at their mercy."

BIBLIOGRPHY

Armitage-Smith, Sydney, JOHN OF GAUNT, Endeavor Press Ltd, 2015

Barron, Caroline, THE TYRANNY OF RICHARD II, Historical Research Vol. XLI, no. 103, May 1968

Bennett, Michael, RICHARD II AND THE REVOLUTION OF 1399, Sutton Publishing, 1999

Biggs, Douglas, THREE ARMIES IN BRITAIN: THE IRISH CAMPAIGN OF RICHARD II AND THE USURPATION OF HENRY IV, 1397-99, Brill, Leiden, The Netherlands, 2006

Creton, *Metrical History*: See Society of Antiquaries

Fletcher, C.D., NARRATIVE AND POLITICAL STRATEGIES AT THE DEPOSITION OF RICHARD II, Journal of Medieval History 30 (2004) 323-341

Giancarlo, Matthew, MURDER, LIES, AND STORYTELLING: THE MANIPULATION OF JUSTICE(S) IN THE PARLIAMENTS OF 1397 AND 1399, Speculum, Vol. 77, No. 1 (Jan. 2002) pp.76-112

Given-Wilson, Chris, CHRONICLES OF THE REVOLUTION 1397-1400 (The Reign of Richard II), Manchester University Press, 1993

Given-Wilson, Chris, HENRY IV, Yale University Press, London, 2017

Given-Wilson, Chris, RICHARD II, EDWARD II, AND THE LANCASTRIAN INHERITANCE, The English Historical Review, Vol. 109, no. 432 (June 1994) PP.553-571

Given-Wilson, Chris, THE ROYAL HOUSEHOLD AND THE KING'S AFFINITY: Service, Politics and Finance in England 1360-1413, Yale University Press, 1986

Hutchison, Harold F. THE HOLLOW CROWN, A Life of Richard II, Methuen, London, 1961

Jones, Richard H. THE ROYAL POLICY OF RICHARD II: Absolutism in the Later Middle Ages, Basil Blackwell, Oxford 1968

McGettigan, Darren, RICHARD II AND THE IRISH KINGS, Four Courts Press, Dublin, 2016

McHardy, A.K., THE REIGN OF RICHARD II From Minority to Tyranny, 1377-97, Manchester University Press, 2012

Mortimer, Ian, THE FEARS OF HENRY IV; The Life of England's Self-Made King, Vintage Books, London, 2008

Saul, Nigel, RICHARD II, Yale University Press, London 1997

Sherborne, James, WAR, POLITICS AND CULTURE IN FOURTEENTH-CENTURY ENGLAND, The Hambledon Press, 1994

Society of Antiquaries of London, ARCHAEOLOGICA, OR MISCELLANEOUS TRACTS RELATING TO ANTIQUITY Vol. 20 (containing Creton's French metrical History), Reproduced by Forgotten Books, 2018

Steel, Anthony, RICHARD II, Cambridge at the University Press, 1962

Tait, James, DID RICHARD II MURDER THE DUKE OF GLOUCESTER? Historical essays first published in 1902 in commemoration of the jubilee of the Owens College, Manchester. Manchester University Press (1907), 193-216.

Tout, Thomas Frederick, CHAPTERS IN THE
ADMINISTRATIVE HISTORY OF MEDIAEVAL ENGLAND;
THE WARDROBE, THE CHAMBER, AND THE SMALL
SEALS, Vol. IV Manchester at the University Press, 1920

Tuck, Anthony, RICHARD II AND THE ENGLISH NOBILITY,
Edward Arnold Publishers, London, 1973

Usk, Adam of, CHRONICON ADAE DE USK, A.D. 1377-1421,
Reprinted by Forgotten Books, 2017

Williams, Benjamin, CHRONICQUE DE LA TRAISON ET
MORT DE RICHART DEUX ROY DENGLETERRE, S & J
Bentley, London, 1846 (Reproduced by Forgotten Books, 2018)